THE BALANCE

The Stone's Blade : Book Two

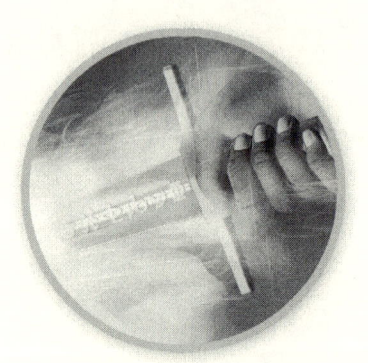

the BALANCE
the STONE'S BLADE : BOOK TWO

*Dearest Anita,
May the Stones bless your adventures with music and color. I hope you enjoy the continuation of the story.*

*Allynn Riggs
1/31/2017*

ALLYNN RIGGS

TimberDark publications

timberdark.com

The Balance (The Stone's Blade, Book Two)

Copyright © 2016 by Allynn Riggs

This is a work of fiction. All names, characters, places, and events portrayed in this book are the product of the author's imagination or are used fictitiously and any resemblance to actual persons, living or dead, business establishments, events, or locales is entirely coincidental. No part of this book may be reproduced, stored in a retrieval system, or transmitted in any form or by any means, electronic, mechanical, photocopying, recording, or otherwise, without express written permission of the publisher.

All rights reserved.

Published by
TimberDark Publications, LLC, 7683 E Costilla Blvd., Centennial, CO 80112
www.Timberdark.com

ISBN 978-0-9910002-2-7 (trade paper)
ISBN 978-0-9910002-3-4 (eBook)

Library of Congress Control Number: 2016903125

Interior and Cover Design & art by Nathan Fisher, www.ScifiBookDesigner.com
Edited by Melanie Mulhall, www.DragonheartWritingandEditing.com
Author Photo by Linda M Wilson, www.YourWorldOurLens.com

Printed in the United States of America

First Edition

16 17 18 19 20 21 SP 6 5 4 3 2 1

DEDICATION

For Kristina
Because this one is all your fault.

TABLE OF CONTENTS

Dedication 5

Acknowledgments 8

Chapter One 11

Chapter Two 21

Chapter Three 31

Chapter Four...39

Chapter Five..52

Chapter Six 65

Chapter Seven 73

Chapter Eight..83

Chapter Nine 91

Chapter Ten 107

Chapter Eleven 119

Chapter Twelve 129

Chapter Thirteen..139

Chapter Fourteen 154

Chapter Fifteen 162

Chapter Sixteen..175

Chapter Seventeen 187

Chapter Eighteen 194

Chapter Nineteen 202

Chapter Twenty 218

Chapter Twenty-One 227

Chapter Twenty-Two 238

Chapter Twenty-Three 247

Chapter Twenty-Four 254

Chapter Twenty-Five 267

Chapter Twenty-Six 279

Chapter Twenty-Seven 290

Chapter Twenty-Eight 301

Chapter Twenty-Nine 317

Chapter Thirty 330

Chapter Thirty-One 345

Chapter Thirty-Two 351

Chapter Thirty-Three 357

Chapter Thirty-Four 366

Appendix 374

About The Author 380

ACKNOWLEDGMENTS

This second book, in fact the entire series, would not be possible without my middle daughter, Kristina. Always an attentive listener, she has been and is a great sounding board for plot ideas. At times, she seems to be more in tune with the characters and their story than I am. I am indebted to her for showing me the way. More than a few years ago, when Kristina was in high school, I was struggling with the end of the then titled stand alone, *The Stone's Blade*, when Kristina said something along the lines of, "What about Ani having a twin and only they can save one of the Stones?"

Well, that question exploded the story line and my imagination quickly ran off in several directions. I managed to get those first bursts of imagination under control. Through dreams in which I asked the characters what they thought of the idea, I realized that according to Ani, she did in fact have a twin. Probably only writers understand how a character can tell you the truth about their lives and then insist that what you write is correct.

The standalone became a trilogy of titles until early in 2015 when I realized the proposed third title, *The Blades*, was destined to be well over eight hundred pages and needed to be divided so I could handle one problem at a time. Without my dear daughter, even this second installment would never have happened, and I probably would never have fully discovered this fascinating world I am delighted to share with you now.

More people who deserve thanks from me include my alpha beta reader, Nancy Koos, for putting up with multiple drafts and story changes, which she has dutifully read and commented on.

Thanks also go to my dear friend and editor, Melanie Mulhall, of Dragonheart, who has also put in countless hours of coaching, pushing, remonstrating, and encouraging me through this process of cobbling together a series truly worth reading. I could not do this without you, Melanie. You have expanded my skills and my desire to continue on this voyage. Some would say this is all my imagination, but you know this is a true story and you have helped me see the truth and given me the structure and support to tell it well.

I am in awe of the creative abilities of my cover designer, Nathan Fisher, with Ideas Ablaze. He can see inside my head and continues to make my imagination visible. And it's not just the stunning cover design, it's the whole presentation, from the interior illustrations to the star field chapter headings, that shows how much he believes in this marvelous series. Thank you, Nathan.

Thanks also to all the readers of *The Blood*. Your requests for this second book have surprised and inspired me. May you enjoy *The Balance* as much as it appears you have enjoyed *The Blood*. Let us continue to discover the worlds of *The Stone's Blade*.

CHAPTER ONE

When the door opened, Ani had no idea what to expect. She stood just inside it, surprised by the simplicity of the furnishings. The younger of the Stone Singers, Layson, having opened the door, crossed the room to stand to one side of the large desk backed by a towering bookcase. The room did not feel as alien as Ani thought it might.

So many things had happened in the last three days since she awakened on Lrakira. One moment Ani felt she understood who she was and the next she felt like she'd been stuffed into a tiny closet, unable to breathe or even think. *This is not a closet. This is not a closet.* She repeated the mantra mentally as she offered a Northern blade salute in greeting to Diani, the amber Pericha Stone's Singer and Layson, the blue Kita Stone's Singer. Diani stood, and the two singers executed sharp salutes in the Lrakiran style, a style that Ani had always assumed was from her home planet's southern continent. She couldn't stop the twinge of sadness that her mother had never explained her true family origin.

Layson walked to a small alcove with a large, many-paned window and busied herself as Diani moved from behind a desk, her gold robes rustling softly. A genuine smile lit the Singer's eyes, and Ani couldn't help smiling in response. This was not going to be an interrogation.

Diani gestured to the three chairs set around a small round table. "There should be few troubles with the differences in our languages because Singer Layson and I are equipped with bio-teachers, each containing updates from Renloret's."

As Ani nodded in understanding, she acknowledged to herself that Diani's accent did indeed resemble Renloret's. She had worried about how this conversation was going to happen without either Renloret or the man masquerading as her father in the room to translate.

"Thank you for agreeing to meet with us again, Anyala," Diani said. "We have spoken with Renloret and now have a better understanding of your upbringing. We wish to apologize for any prior insult."

Before stepping further into the room, Ani decided to clarify one of the most bothersome things. "My name may be Anyala but I have rarely been called that. Having met my namesake, the Anyala Stone, I would prefer to be called Ani. And please do not call me The Blood. That is for prophecies and fables, not real life."

The two Singers shared tight-lipped smiles at her admonishment.

Diani cleared her throat. "Ani, I welcome you to Lrakira. Singer Layson and I wish to converse with you, to answer your questions, if we can, and to verify your suitability for the position of Stone Singer." She bowed and again indicated the chairs.

Ani frowned at the last words. What more would she be required to do to convince the people of this alien world that the Stone itself had identified her as its next Singer? She had not sought the role. Pushing away the irritation at having to continually defend her identity, both here on Lrakira and on her home world of Teramar, Ani swallowed the embittered response that rose to her tongue. She took a seat.

Singer Layson approached with a tray of cups. "I hear you enjoy the occasional cup of tea?"

Ani's thoughts went immediately to Melli, her best friend's mother, and how ecstatic Melli would be to try a tea from another world. Ani smiled at the imagined conversation they would engage in—drying techniques, herb usage and combinations, water temperatures, packaging, and, of course, steeping instructions along with what ceremonies, if any, might be customary. "Yes, I do. My best friend's mother is a master tea maker. I would be pleased to participate."

Layson's shoulders dropped as she relaxed. She poured thin reddish syrup from a plain stone pot with a long, narrow sieved spout. The spout caught bits of leaves, keeping the brew free of debris. When all three cups had been filled to the brim, Ani watched as the Singers clasped hands over their cups and hummed a five-note tune.

Diani smiled at Layson. "Well done," the elder Singer praised.

Ani noticed the blush that darkened Layson's cheeks. Had she passed some sort of test?

The younger Singer turned to Ani. "It is my pleasure to welcome and serve our newest Stone Singer candidate. May the Stones be your guides and their Blades keep you safe." Taking the remaining chair, she offered her cup in a salute. Diani joined in the two-handed cup raising.

Though a bit uncomfortable, Ani grasped her cup with both hands and raised it up to touch the brims of the other two. There was a light ringing sound inside Ani's head as an approving five-note tune of the amber Pericha and blue Kita Stones echoed the tune hummed by the Singers even though the Stones were rooms away. Ani wondered if the other two women heard it, but she did not ask.

Mimicking the quick noisy slurps Diani and Layson made, Ani registered the fiery bite of the tea on her tongue before the liquid spread a light sweetness throughout her mouth. She held a portion of the syrup on her tongue and inhaled across it. The fiery spice intensified and she almost coughed, but the sweet underlay calmed the tickle when she swallowed.

Ani nodded as the sweet-fired syrup coated her throat and warmed her stomach. "That was unexpected. Melli would love to have this tea in her arsenal. Could I have some to share with her?" She would figure out how to tell Melli where it came from later.

The Singers glanced at each other. Diani shrugged. "I see no obstacle, Layson."

Again Layson blushed. "It is one of my own recipes. I will make up a package for you, along with instructions."

After several minutes of companionable chatting about tea, Ani set her cup down. "Tell me about the Stones and their blades."

Diani folded her hands. "Since the beginning, only women have been allowed to become Singers because they are more intuitive and more open to the Stones' ways of communication. The Stones communicate telepathically and visually through song, music, and color. In turn, the Singers passed on the Stones' wisdom and knowledge to the people. The Stones have been our base of intellectual and spiritual guidance since before recorded history.

"There is no record of who carved the blades, but we do know the blades are of the same crystals as their matching Stones. At first, the purpose of the blades was to protect the Stones. Each Singer received advanced training in blade skills for this purpose. Though the possibility of danger to the Stones has diminished considerably over the past several hundred years, we still maintain that training. For a thousand years, we have thrived in this symbiosis. Until now. Ani, your Anyala Stone must not die. We do not know if Lrakira will survive without all three stones."

"But I have been led to understand that my blood has saved the people of Lrakira from extinction, so even if the Stones cease to be, won't the people continue?" Ani asked.

The Singers frowned at her. Then Diani spoke. "We do not know, Ani. The Stones have not sung that verse to us."

Layson leaned forward. "We have no doubt the vaccine will be successful, but the testing is not complete as yet. Until it is proven that a woman can become pregnant and not only carry a child to full term, but deliver a child who survives, our people are still in danger. News of the vaccine was released this morn. The people are joyous, of course, but we all await the outcome of the test subjects." She nodded to Diani to continue. They seemed to have planned what information each was to divulge.

"If only your grandmother had not attacked the Anyala Stone, we could have waited the months needed. But the Stone must be saved now. I don't believe it will survive that long. We, Layson and I, are adamant that you leave for Teramar as soon as a ship can be brought in. In spite of what the medical establishment says, we are confident that the vaccine will work and more of your blood will not be needed. Our Stones have promised us that you are The Blood and your twin sister is The Balance. It is she who will save the Stone."

Ani took several swallows of tea. It grated on Ani's idea of family that it was her grandmother Selabec who had tried to kill the crystalline being called the Anyala Stone. And though Ani's mother had never mentioned anything about being from another planet, Ani had difficulty with the very idea of attempted murder—whether alien creature or not—and that was what Selabec had committed. Ani was glad her mother was not around to suffer this blow to the family's values. But it would have been nice to know exactly where her family had come from. Twenty-five years of lies were making all this more difficult to fathom.

Anger at her personal situation dissipated as curiosity welled up. "I don't understand why no one knew my mother had the Anyala Stone's blade. Don't you have them on your person at all times?"

"At first we did not know that your mother had been given permission by the Stone to take the blade with her to Teramar," Singer Diani admitted. "No Singer, Stone, or blade has been off

Lrakira before. It was not even considered. Selabec did not inform us of the blade's disappearance until a few moon-cycles before the commander, your father, arrived announcing your birth.

"There had been no reason to believe her blade was missing until the S'Roadoss Celebration. We use the blades in a ceremony of renewal that strengthens the bonds between the Singers and the Stones. The ceremony is executed simultaneously on the three continents. There is much music, dancing, and song. The blade championships are played then as well. Ships in orbit report seeing a massive light display akin to the polar auroras, but in a specific three-sided formation between the Stones' locations. In the chambers, we hear music and see those colors as well. It is an invigorating experience."

Singer Layson spoke up. "Because Selabec did not have her blade, we were unsure if we could perform the required ceremony. Kita informed me that the missing blade was where it belonged and the bonding experience for Diani and me would not be lessened. Selabec did not participate but the Anyala Stone did. This was my first S'Roadoss, so I do not know if it was different from previous ceremonies."

Diani shook her head. "It was not less for me, though I heard the aerial color show was quite different from those in the past. The people knew no difference and did not suspect that the Anyala Stone's blade was not in the Singer's possession. As far as written history relates, the blades have never left the planet before. And since we have traveled the star lanes, no Singer has left Lrakira until your mother.

"In her defense, Selabec may not have known the blade was

missing until then because we are not required to wear them constantly, as we had been in the long past, and Selabec has been known to leave her blade untouched for long periods of time. Our robes signify our identity rather than the blades. We do not need the blades to communicate with our Stones once we are bonded, though the connection is stronger if we are wearing or holding the blade when we sing with the Stones."

Diani hesitated and smiled softly as her eyes unfocused briefly. "Pericha sings that those who are not Singers must touch the Stone to hear their songs." She nodded at Ani's perplexed expression. "Yes, Anyala—oh, your pardon, Ani—I can hear my Stone even from this distance though my blade is in the wrong place. I believe it is similar to your connection to your companion, Kela."

"But I heard all three Stones when I was in the chamber three days ago, though the Anyala Stone's song was quite muted. I was not touching any of them and I did not have the blade with me."

The Singers looked surprised. "You could hear all three? We can hear only our own and then only when they wish us to hear," Diani said.

Ani nodded. "All three. Do you suppose they were in such need that they were able to forego the touch requirement? On Teramar I had frequent contact with the blade until Mother died and I buried it with her. When the casket was broken into . . ." Ani paused at the horrified expressions on the Singers' faces. "Oh, sorry. I'm guessing you didn't know about that." She waved her hands as if to erase her last words. "Listen, to shorten a too long sword, mother's body and the blade were stolen from the cemetery, though according to the imbecile who perpetrated the crime, the body turned into a green smoke and disappeared into the blade's carrying box. I didn't believe him then and I still don't, though we did find the blade—but not her body. However, in light of current circumstances I feel this is a topic to be discussed another time."

"Yes, a more complete telling of this story would be appreciated at another time," Diani said, bowing her head. "Ani, we have only recently learned of your mother's death, the desecration of her casket, and the thievery. It is most alarming. While I am personally relieved that the blade was recovered and is now in appropriate hands, please accept our sincere condolences."

Ani nodded in acceptance.

Diani sighed. "As you say, that discussion should be held later. So please do continue."

Ani closed her eyes for a breath to collect her thoughts. "When I was poisoned and injected with the coma device, Renloret and Taryn were able to use the blade to sing a Song of Healing, and then Renloret brought me here to Lrakira. You know the story of what happened after I awoke from the surgery that removed the coma device.

"If you have doubts about whether or not I am qualified to be a Singer, I think I can prove the blade accepted me because I have markings on my arms made by the blade after my championship. Renloret says it's in an ancient script that few can read, but it identifies me as The Blood." She rolled up her sleeves and presented her arms for inspection.

The Singers studied the patterned scars without a sound. Then Diani and Layson stood and honored her with blade salutes.

"As we suspected, you *are* the Anyala Stone's Singer. The blade is yours. Perhaps that is why you could hear them. You are a Singer, no matter the opinion of others, even your grandmother, unless you fail the skills test."

Alarms went off in her head. "What test?"

The Singers stood in unison, and Diani said, "A singer must be tested to be sure she can defend her Stone. Since you have had some training at blades, we assume you will be adequate. You will meet Layson in the ring after the morrow's first meal. Renloret and your father will see to arming and preparing you. Renloret is waiting to escort you."

Without another word, the Singers exited, golden robes rustling.

CHAPTER TWO

Focus, Ani.

Welcoming the telepathic contact, Ani let Kela's calm voice push away the rising anger. *Thank you. I'm ready.* She twirled the well-made borrowed blade into a Northern salute when she reached the center of the ring, acknowledging her opponent, Layson. No longer draped in the gold robes of her office, the singer answered with a Lrakiran salute. Ani scrutinized the woman in close formfitting attire while she stretched. This was not the quiet, unassuming Singer Ani had shared tea with last eve.

On Teramar, the only female bladers Ani had practiced against were her mother and on rare occasions, Melli or a girl just beginning to learn. Apart from them, all her opponents had been boys or men. Ani wondered how much Layson had been told about her skills. Renloret had mentioned that female bladers were quite common where he was from and participated equally in the blade ring, though at the time, Ani thought he was talking about the southern continent of her home world, Teramar, not this distant planet.

She turned to glare at the tall blue-eyed pilot standing near the bleachers. Exuding confidence, he waved then saluted. Only minutes before she'd stepped into the ring, his only admonishments had been that she not underestimate Layson's skills and that she should not kill the Kita Stone's Singer. Ani had no intention of doing such a thing but that did not diminish the fact that being forced to demonstrate her skills against one of Lrakira's world leaders had annoyed her enough to bring forth her best effort. Being told that she had attained continental championship status against men on Teramar had not swayed the Singers. It irked her that she would have to prove she was qualified to be a Stone Singer.

Mystified by surroundings that were nerve-rackingly similar to the blade rings on Teramar, Ani wondered how two planets so far apart could have such similar practices and settings. She shook her head to concentrate on the moment at hand. It would be inattention to the little things that would catch her, just as it had in her last fight, which had almost ended her life and put her into a coma.

Kela coached her telepathically from the sidelines. *Let the blade bend. This is not an unpredictable amateur with a poisoned blade. She is a seasoned professional, trained like yourself, and one who bears watching. Learn from her.*

Ani drew a breath and rolled her shoulders up and back to squeeze out the tension, but coiled again internally as her anger flared toward those who had set up this match. Were they hoping she would fail? They had not defined failure or success, just that she was to demonstrate her skills against an equal. If she failed would she be allowed to return to Teramar? What about finding her twin and saving the Anyala Stone? And though she wanted this farce to be over, she would not be disrespectful. If she were careful, she might be able to end the match before the end of the first round.

She hummed the opening phrase of the focus song her mother had sung before each of Ani's competitions. Layson frowned. Perhaps she recognized the tune. A smile curved Ani's lips and her adrenaline rose. It didn't matter that she was on an alien planet. She was in a blade ring, and that was home.

When the starting chime sounded, she backed away and presented the blade. They parried. Layson's methods mirrored many fighters Ani had met in the blade ring. She was intrigued that some sequences reminded her of her mother. Perhaps Layson had had the same instructor. Ani met each strike with only enough to defend herself.

Despite her own intentions and Kela's admonishments, Ani's thoughts drifted to the doctors who had drawn yet another bag of her blood the previous eve after the conversation with the Singers. They had already collected enough to create the vaccine, but when they were informed that she would be leaving Lrakira, they wanted more in case the first rounds failed to work and she did not return to Lrakira.

A quick stab by Layson startled her back to the blade ring. It was time to show them she could do more than defend herself. Charging through the Singer's defense, Ani struck Layson's chin with her free hand. She knew the rules allowed it. The Singer sucked in her gut to escape the arcing swing of Ani's blade. Layson backed off, her expression wary. Good. She was now aware of the trouble she was in. Layson's eyes flicked between Ani's hands, telegraphing a question about her ability to use the blade in either hand.

Good, she's almost ready. Ani allowed Layson to lead her to a different rhythm, and she kept a straight face as she felt the Singer's tactics change. A kick thumped her ribs. Whipping around, she answered in kind and followed up with a furious combination. This *demonstration* needed to end before she forgot she was not to seriously injure the Singer. Layson backed away, taking deep, rapid breaths. Oh yes, she knew the end was approaching. But like a champion, she would not back down. She gave a quick salute and, switching the blade to her other hand, slashed under Ani's guard.

Someone in the audience gasped in surprise at the hand change, though Ani had expected it sooner. Now she would be able to end the charade with some level of respect. She responded with her own unique moves, encouraging the Singer to press her apparent advantage. Ducking under Layson's lunge, she struck the empty wrist with the butt of her blade. Ignoring the cry of pain, Ani carried the momentum down and across to the inside of Layson's knee and on the rebound, brought the blade tip upward as her opponent's head and shoulders buckled forward. Ani watched the blade rise in slow motion, savoring the moment. It took strength and technique to ensure Layson would not die.

Shouts from the observers warned too late as the blade

skimmed past the Singer's cheek. A finger width to the right and she would have died. Ani allowed her to stumble out of range, withholding the second killing strike with great effort.

Favoring her injured leg, Layson looked at her, eyes wide with the knowledge that she had been allowed to live. Ani saluted her, Northern style, and then flung the borrowed blade toward the observers.

A startled shriek came from someone in the stands though the blade struck nothing but the blade ring's raised edging. "Now that I have your attention, I must tell you that while I appreciate the removal of the coma device, I am disappointed with my treatment otherwise. You felt it necessary to ignore knowledge of my blade championships and endangered one of your precious Stone Singers in an effort to verify my blade skills. My mother and uncle taught me well enough without disclosing my own alien roots, even to me. My mother was true to her status as Stone Singer, though none but the Stones knew she was the Anyala Stone's Singer.

"As of this moment, I am done with your demands to prove my skills and knowledge. I am through with all of you. You have taken copious amounts of my blood, and since I am assured you have enough to complete a vaccine, I am finished with being your savior, The Blood. Your people are saved. I have fully demonstrated I can protect myself, so there's no need for the constant surveillance you have provided. I promised the Anyala Stone I would find The Balance. I will honor that promise in spite of your reluctance to believe that someone raised without knowledge of your world would do so.

"Now I need time to think on these matters and about the transformation my life has undergone. I promise I will not endanger a soul. You would do better to protect your all-knowing Stones from deranged Singers. I will be allowed to walk about, free of surveillance or guards, and I will handle anyone who follows me with a complete lack of respect."

Not waiting to hear protests, she walked to the ring's edge, pulled the blade free, and motioned to Kela. They left the room. Thankfully, no one, not even Renloret, followed.

Ani sighed loudly as they hurried down the hall. She really didn't want to talk to anyone. The adrenaline of the skills test was still coursing through her body and she needed to ease out of fight mode. At her silent request, Kela led her into the second side hall to a small practice room he had apparently noticed on their tour of the blade training facility earlier that morn. Lights came on as they entered and Ani slid the door shut hoping no one would think they would stay in the building after her rant. Kela offered to guard the door and listen as Ani marched over to the practice dummy.

She began slowly, stretching through the moves, precisely placing each punch and kick. Gradually, she increased the speed and power of the strikes. Unlike the skills test, during which she'd barely broken a sweat, Ani's top was soon wringing wet and her breathing was ragged. Then the tears came, mixing with the perspiration. Why were her skills always questioned? Was it because she was female? Unlikely. Renloret had explained that female bladers were accepted on Lrakira, and the Stone Singers were trained at the highest levels. She dismissed the possibility of sexism. Did she give off some kind of aura of incompetence?

She hit the punching bag with both fists, causing it to swing, thereby making it a moving target. Had the constant questioning of her skills on her home planet, her family's allegiances, and even the alleged alien connections finally worn her out so much that she presented a less than in-charge personality? She thought she'd gotten over that. But once again, here on Lrakira, everything, including the makeup of her family, was being questioned. What were her mother's reasons for lying about having twins? There had to have been something wrong with The Balance. Otherwise, Ani could not imagine why a mother would keep such a secret.

Could it have been as simple as her mother misunderstanding The Blood and The Balance Prophecy? How was it that her mother decided Ani was the prophesied Blood of Lrakira, the child whose blood would carry the cure of the gravitus plague, which had already killed tens of thousands of women and threatened the people of Lrakira with extinction? Ani now knew that she had a twin who was the other half of the prophecy. This unacknowledged sibling was The Balance, destined to save the life of the Anyala Stone, one of the crystalline guardians who had guided the Lrakirans for over a thousand years. Ani's mother had never mentioned a twin—not to her husband, Yenne, and not to Ani—but the three guardian Stones of Lrakira were adamant that there was one alive on Teramar. This newest revelation was just one of many.

Just days from waking on this previously unimagined planet populated with two very different intelligent beings—one set that looked surprisingly similar to the bipedal people of Teramar and the other huge crystals who communicated through color and music as well as telepathically—Ani was still trying to adjust to the knowledge that her parents and uncle would be considered aliens on Teramar and not the other way round. Though not fully convinced that alien life even existed, she could not refuse to acknowledge the intelligence of those crystal stones. After hearing the music of words directly from all three of the Stones, so similar and yet so different from her own telepathic connection with Kela, Ani had promised the Anyala Stone that she would retrieve The Balance. And Ani knew she would do everything in her power to fulfill that promise. In spite of logic, Ani knew the stones were alive and intelligent, and they deserved to live.

The number of strikes had lessened on the now bedraggled dummy. She jogged around the room trying to decide what her next move should be. In the relative silence of the room, Ani heard a rumbling from Kela's stomach and became aware of an answering rumble from her own, confirming that it was most likely mid-aftermorn.

I'm hungry.

Kela's complaint brought a smile to Ani's lips. She stopped jogging and returned to the punching bag. *So?* Ani thumped the bag.

Aren't you?

Maybe. She rubbed her face. *Kela, am I going about this wrong?*

Maybe.

A knock on the door interrupted them. Kela jumped to his feet and sniffed at the bottom of the door. *It's Renloret.*

Ani opened the door. The alien pilot stood, unsmiling, but with a placid expression on his face.

She waved him in. "How'd you find us?"

"I waited for everyone else to leave and then tiptoed through the halls listening for a punching bag being tortured." Now he grinned.

She hit his shoulder then turned a guilty look at the abused bag.

Kela chuckled, and she swatted at him.

"Are they going to leave me alone?" she asked.

"You convinced them you can take care of yourself." He pulled a small bag from his pocket. "Look, here is some money. You can walk anywhere you want. I promised them you would be okay if no one bothered you. There is one thing you're asked to do before we leave."

Ani stiffened. "What now?" She recognized a guilty expression as Renloret hesitated. She was not going to like this one.

"You have a meeting scheduled with your father."

"No," she said. "I'm to meet with the man masquerading as my father? No thank you."

"Ani, I know you believe he died in the attack on the research center when you were five, but he escaped to come to Lrakira for help. If not for the time-song, he would have been back within two of your months."

"You still want me to believe those crystals can change time?"

"To be honest, we didn't know they could do that either. But they have been our guides, our leaders, for a thousand years. And this meeting is not about them, Ani. This is about you and your father. He's in just as much shock as you. Plus, he just found out his wife is dead and you are not five but twenty-five. He needs to talk to you."

She tried to push past him. "And if I don't talk to him?"

Renloret stood his ground. "You won't be allowed to go back until you do."

Kela growled at the words. *They would endanger the life of one of their guardian Stones to insist that you speak with him?*

Ani paused. What would Mother say? Ani crouched to look Kela in the eyes. *If I agree, we can leave sooner and the Anyala Stone will have a better chance of surviving.*

You're doing this for the sake of the Stone or for yourself?

Both. I owe it to Mother and I promised to save the Stone.

She stood. "All right. We'll be back at seven bells."

Renloret nodded and stepped aside, allowing them to pass.

CHAPTER THREE

Erid, Lrakira's largest moon, was three fingers above the eastern horizon and the sun had just set, coloring the western half of the sky. Ani steeled herself for the appearance of Cranite, whose rising glow was brightening the edge of near darkness in a race to catch the orbit of its skyline companion. These two would be halfway across the night sky before the third and smallest moon, Denert, would make its diagonal dash.

As Cranite added its waning crescent to her sight, Ani held her breath. Not vomiting was her first goal. The fact that none of the moons had rings brought tears to her eyes. She missed *her* moon, a moon that was singularly spectacular, a moon whose embracing rings reflected Teramar's sun at varying angles throughout the year. Drawing a sleeve across her face to catch those unwanted tears, she forced herself to watch.

On her walk to this secluded overlook, she discovered she was not as anonymous as she'd hoped. Because she had supplied the blood from which the lifesaving vaccine would be derived, she was considered to be The Blood, the prophesied savior of Lrakira. Her likeness appeared on all the news screens. Every woman and girl had saluted and some even hugged her. Fortunately, they seemed to know that she understood very little of their language and simply smiled and bowed. Those encounters had pushed Ani off the busy thoroughfares and into the quieter residential neighborhoods.

At the edge of the park, a meat roll vendor had insisted she have two of his savory rolls, refusing payment for them. Ani was embarrassed by the citywide acclaim she had garnered within her three days on Lrakira. Being treated as a celebrity had never set well with her. The fame inflicted on her after becoming Northern's first female continental blade ring champion had proven difficult enough. This was so much worse. She could barely wait to go home to Teramar.

A gentle tap on her mental shoulder reminded her that Kela was checking on her. She smiled and sent back a noncommittal reply, satisfying his concern. He would wait at the bottom of the hill until she was ready for physical company. Kela had been traumatized by the more than two weeks of zero mental contact with her on the trip from Teramar to Lrakira. Because of that, she had honored his request for an open mental link between them. Ani shivered at the memory of the silence in her mind upon waking from the coma. Her imagination was still shaken by the knowledge that Kela had suffered so for the entire trip. Their connection had been severed by the tiniest machine Ani had ever seen.

The device had been intentionally implanted by a still

unknown assailant. Now, on a hill on a planet in another galaxy, Ani struggled to remember the encounter in the cavern. He had said his name, hadn't he? If he had, wouldn't she have remembered at least that? What she *did* remember was that he had accused her mother of allowing his wife to die and there was something about her uncle. She was beginning to worry about her memory of what happened in the cavern. The details she thought should be quite clear seemed to fade before she could actually grasp what they were, leaving her with lingering feelings of uncertainty and confusion. And with each passing day, she remembered less. All she had to go on was what others had told her she'd said during the first hours after awaking from the coma. She wondered if she would ever truly remember what happened after being cut by the poisonous blade. Harrumphing at the turn of events, Ani rubbed her face, as if trying to scrub away the unimaginable.

The twists and turns of so many blades in her life over the last year were impossible to follow: the death of her mother, her uncle's flight to Southern, her rescue of Renloret from the ship crash, and everything else that had led to this moment on this alien planet. She longed to go back in time and make other choices, but as her mother would have said, "The Stones have a plan and you must follow."

Ani now knew what her mother meant by the "Stones" and she knew she must return to Teramar and find The Balance to save the life of an alien whose existence would have been beyond her imagination if she had not seen the life lights and heard the Stone's song. The Anyala Stone was barely alive, and she would make every effort to find a way to save it.

She glared at the moons, both now fully risen. They seemed to be daring her to make order out of the chaos of her thoughts. One moment she was in awe of her surroundings, wanting to soak it all up; the next moment she was devastatingly depressed at the loss of her former reality and angry that she was forced to function under new, unknown, alien rules.

What had been her first mistake? She pronounced the self-indictment aloud once she pinpointed it. "The pride of Star Valley allowed an amateur blader to draw blood first."

Kela's mental touch strengthened, reminding her that no one had expected the blade to be laced with a poison meant to immobilize her, allowing the assailant to insert the tiny device that had put her into an artificial coma. No one could have predicted the device itself. Even the star-traveling Lrakiran doctors and scientists were astounded.

Still trying to blame herself, Ani added words to the telepathic connection. *But I didn't follow my earliest lessons, Kela.* "Beware the beginner and the fanatic because they are less predictable and more dangerous than any professional you will ever face. Beginners don't know the rules and fanatics don't care." This had been her mother's training mantra.

Kela's reply was immediate. *Sheath it, Ani. That skirmish is done. You are here in my mind once again. You are well and we are going home soon.*

Home. Oh, how she wanted to be in Star Valley, drinking Melli's cinnamon tea on the cabin porch. But, she lamented, even home would be different now.

Who do you think the twin is? Ani asked.

Kela gave a mental shrug. *I have considered several options but none that fit the criteria. Perhaps your mother sent the babe to another village to keep her safe.*

Ani frowned. *I agree. I don't think she is in Star Valley.* She closed off direct communication with Kela and settled down to observe the scene spread before her. The first time she'd witnessed this she'd been totally unprepared. With a deep sigh, she opened her eyes and her mind.

Pulsing colored points of light signaled work shuttles arriving from an orbiting station. A rumbling roar announced a freighter heading for some faraway planet and other aliens she was barely able to envision. *Other* alien races. She pushed away the thought. She could handle only one trauma at a time. At least the Lrakirans looked like her.

Ani checked on the moons' progress. If she used Lrakiran time increments, she had more than a bell of time before she was to meet Renloret near the Stone Chamber to be escorted to a conference with the man claiming to be her father. Closing her jacket to the cooling mid-autumn air, she focused on the changing light show across the city of Awarna, soaking in the sight of this village on her mother's home world.

Three days ago she'd been an only child. Now, according to a trio of intelligent, singing, color-slinging crystals, she had a twin sister living somewhere on Teramar. This twin would not know she was supposed to save the life of an alien creature—one of those intelligent crystals. Ani couldn't help wondering about her twin. Was she happy? Healthy? Did she have friends? Family? Did she know that Northern's first female short blade champion was her sibling? Would she believe what she was going to be told? Would she willingly come to Lrakira to save an alien? So many questions. Too many, actually. Ani wanted to focus on just a few of them, the important ones, but which were they?

What about the horrible aliens the people of Northern were so worried about? When she thought about that, really, how horrible were the three alien Stones she'd met so far? They perched on pedestals, two singing prophetic songs and glowing in shades of amber and blue. The third was in a sorry state, barely flickering in faded green, with an amber blade embedded near its soul. Ani examined her feelings about the rock. It was another telepathic voice in her mind, similar to Kela's, and her heart ached for the injured Anyala Stone.

She rubbed at the blisters on her palms, acquired from her efforts to remove that offending blade three days ago. Then, in frustration at her inability to focus on one thought, she pulled at the grass on either side of her. Questions chased each other in an unrelenting circle. Was saving an entire race of people from extinction more important than saving a single intelligent rock? She chuckled at the line of her thoughts. The villagers of Star Valley would consider locking her up for thinking that way. Of course, she hadn't known who—or rather what—she was destined to be. Her mother and uncle had done a superior job of keeping that a secret. Anger and disappointment bubbled up again alongside the incredulity of her new reality, her new identity.

She tore at the grass and flung the bits at the pair of un-ringed moons. Would she ever be normal again? What was normal? All her training to become a master blader had not prepared her for this. Glad she was alone, she drummed her heels into the ground, digging divots in a childish tantrum as she railed against her predicament.

Peeling bells from a cathedral announced the half bell. The man claiming to be her father would be waiting for her in less than thirty minutes. She stopped the selfish tantrum and scrambled to her feet. Long training and professionalism demanded she follow through on her commitments. Ani jogged down the hill to Kela, and they ran through the winding streets back to the building that housed the Stone Chamber. She pulled her bottom lip between her teeth as she thought, then pushed the thoughts away knowing she would have at least two weeks to get them in order before she stepped on Teramar's surface and faced her twin—if her twin could be found.

Though the run had warmed her up and she'd actually arrived a few chimes ahead of time, Ani shivered nervously with the prospects of the meeting.

A baritone voice brought her out of her musings.

"Was your time without observation sufficient?" Renloret asked as he strode towards her, his eyes staring at the floor instead of her, hands clasped tightly behind his back as if trying not to embrace her.

"I found the meat roll vendor and had two rolls. He wouldn't let me pay."

A slight smile softened Renloret's expression. "Did anyone bother you?"

How could she explain? "They were all so . . . polite. One woman even kissed me in gratitude."

He raised his head to face her and she almost stumbled at the depth and intensity of his gaze. She cursed her heart for wanting him, but there were more important blades to sharpen before she could declare her feelings.

Renloret frowned. "I suggested they not advertise your likeness, but they wouldn't listen to a pilot. They even ignored your father's request to wait until we had left for Teramar." He smiled again, this time more broadly. "Oh, you will be pleased to know the desired ship is a few bells away. We can leave in the morn." The pilot stopped at a door and knocked gently. "Speaking of your father, he is waiting."

He pushed it open and gave her a gentle shove. Kela followed.

CHAPTER FOUR

She didn't have to wait long for Yenne Chenakainet to find his voice. She barely listened to his rant though she was keenly aware of each time he mentioned her age and lack of knowledge of who she was and where she was from. When he finally ran out of words, the silence in the room seemed to echo. How could he be her father?

"Do I have to keep apologizing for not being five?" Ani asked. When was this man going to let that fact stand? Obviously, he was as disturbed by the age and time difference as she was, but he had known all along he was alien to Teramar and she'd just found out. He'd actually met countless aliens and traveled between stars as often as she'd driven to Gelwood's grocery. "This is not my fault," she muttered, rolling her eyes. Kela grumbled agreeably in her mind.

She watched the commander stalk about the room. It was just the three of them: Kela, this man who claimed to be her father, and herself. Renloret had left over an hour ago with the admonition that they would not be let out until they had talked. The commander did not talk, he complained. And all he could complain about was that she was twenty years older than she'd been just three of his moon-cycles ago. She corrected the time frame to months, determined to think and speak in her native language, Teramaran Northern, which he complained about as well. He wanted her to accept implantation of a bio-teacher so she could naturally speak and understand Lrakiran, but after her experience with the coma-inducing device implanted during a blade fight less than a month earlier in her timeline, she had no tolerance for another machine being placed in her body. His insistence had only strengthened her resolve, much to Kela's disappointment.

You could bend the blade a bit, Ani, Kela snipped telepathically.

Why? He's the one with all the alien experience. He should understand this better than me. He should be helping me adjust, not the other edge of the blade. She folded her arms tightly across her chest.

Kela rolled over so his stomach could be available for scratching. *You are indeed your father's daughter.*

That was uncalled for, Kela. Stretching out one foot, she tried to poke his exposed belly. The canine's comment stung.

It was not and you are.

She pushed away from the table and went to the window to study the patterns on the plaza's stone pavers, lit up for the night. A small group of normal looking people crossed under the lights. Ani turned away from the serene view. Was it really possible that the young man sitting at the end of the table, head cradled in his hands, was her father? He looked more like an older brother than a father. Tears welled up. Her father.

She wanted to blame someone, especially him. He certainly seemed to be blaming her for her mother's death and her growing up twenty years in just the few months that had passed for him. Could she blame the Stones? They *were* responsible for singing this . . . time-song, which was supposed to age everyone on Teramar forward eight to ten years. Right?

Hadn't the doctors said that she only needed to have passed into menses so she would have the correct hormones in her body to save the Lrakiran people? Why hadn't the song stopped when she reached her early teens? Wasn't that what the plan had been? Why didn't the Stones know what was going to happen? They seemed quite aware of a lot of things, including the need for The Balance to save one of the Stones. So why weren't they expecting the attack on the Anyala Stone? If they knew it was going to happen, couldn't they have prevented it? Maybe the Stones just didn't expect the assailant to be one of their own Singers.

Ani had heard rumors that her grandmother—a twisted blade of a woman—had interrupted the Stones' time-song at a critical moment by stabbing the Anyala Stone with Singer Diani's amber blade. Everyone was shocked by the turn of events—even the Stones. What little information Ani had received from the injured Anyala Stone pointed to this unknown twin being the only person who could draw out the blade. At least Ani and her father could agree on the fact that neither one of them knew about such a twin. And now, in order to save a truly alien creature, they had to go back to Teramar and find her. Once found, they would have to explain her alien identity and that she was needed on a planet in another galaxy to save the life of an intelligent crystal. Ani shook her head.

Barely two months ago, the word *alien* had been a bitter rumor that tagged along in her life like some rotten piece of fruit buried deep in the recesses of an old backpack. You could smell it occasionally, but no matter how often you cleaned the backpack, the scent wafted across your senses when you least expected it. Ani chuckled at the implausibility of being an alien, having a father barely older than herself, and having an unknown twin.

At her chuckle, the man—her father—stirred from his reverie. His dark brown eyes were intense, drawing her in.

"I apologize, Anyala," her father said in Northern. He pulled his bottom lip between his teeth.

So that's where I get it. She felt Kela's smirk and shut off the telepathic communication. Not that it made any real difference, but recognizing the habit made her mouth soften into a bit of a smile. *Perhaps* they were related. Ani pulled out a chair. He seemed ready to talk, finally, and she was ready to listen.

"You're correct. None of this is your fault, and I apologize for sounding like I blame you." His dirt-brown hands were folded against his chin and unshed tears glistened in his eyes.

"Apology accepted. I'll try not to blame you either." She could be magnanimous when she wanted to be, though she wondered how long she could refrain from blaming him for leaving in the first place.

"I think . . ." He sighed. "Ani, we need to talk to the Stones, all of them, and that won't happen until after we find the twin and return with her. We don't know the whole story and perhaps the Stones do. They might point us in the right direction to unearth answers—like why Selabec stabbed the Anyala Stone when she did. I'm confident that the wounding of the Anyala Stone caused the time bubble to swing wide of its mark, extending the aging process almost a decade."

"I've asked Selabec, and she does not understand why she did it," Ani replied. "She felt compelled to cause a ruckus of some sort to get the Stones to bring S'Hendale home." She pronounced her mother's name in the Lrakiran manner and then tipped her head toward a shoulder. "Well, after that interview, her doctors requested that I not see her again because it was too upsetting for her. Yenne, she believes I'm her daughter and your hostage." Ani noticed the flinch in his shoulder when she used his proper name instead of referring to him as her father. He would have to be satisfied with his first name and not his familial designation. She wondered if she would ever be able to call him father.

Kela harrumphed. Ani glared at him, mentally sticking her tongue out. He showed her a similar canine face. He was definitely in the same blade ring as this man. She looked around for something to throw at the animal. He laughed confidently in her head.

"There is that misperception on her part," Yenne said, bringing Ani back to their conversation.

"Did Mother ever tell you what the Anyala Stone told her before she joined your crew?"

"When she revealed her real name, she also told us she had made a blade promise to the Stone that she would go to Teramar to help us find the cure. I was drawn to her confidence. I believed in her; we all did. She was quite knowledgeable about medical research and she was constantly frustrated that technology on Teramar was hindering her. We'd been on planet for about two moon-cycles—or months—when I asked her to join-hands. She kept me waiting for three days." He chuckled at the memory.

Suddenly, Ani wished her mother could see that he was still in love with her. Ani reached out and touched his entwined hands—the first positive contact between them. "I see now that her heart was true to you and to the Stone to the end."

He nodded. "On our wedding night she told me that she would conceive a daughter who would provide the cure for our people." His eyes never left Ani's face. "When she announced her pregnancy, the two other women on the research crew feared she would die as so many of their families and friends had over the last few years. S'Hendale told us the Stone had promised she would provide a living cure in the form of a daughter and that neither she nor the child would die. When you arrived prematurely she was very concerned, but she was also confident that the Stone's promise would hold true and all would be well. Once you had made it past your original due date, she seemed to relax and became a true mother devoted to a beloved daughter."

He paused, covering Ani's hands with his and squeezing them. "You were never an experiment, Ani, if that is what you think. You were and are *our* daughter, a fact more important to us than you being the cure for our people."

Ani felt a lump tighten her throat and she fought the tears that formed. "Thank you for that," she whispered. In her heart she knew this was true. And in her heart she knew that she came from a loving family. So why had her grandmother attacked the very Stone she professed to love and want to pass on to her now dead daughter? Once again, too many questions, but did she need all the answers, now? Wasn't she under enough pressure? Could she be patient?

Kela snuggled his muzzle into her lap, and Ani freed one hand to rub his ears. His growling purr helped to sooth her roiling emotions.

When she looked up, Yenne was staring at Kela. A frown furrowed his brow. "What's wrong?"

He cleared his throat. "I've wanted to ask about Reslo. You said he was the one who enabled your link with Kela."

"Well, yes, he did. But neither of us knows exactly how he did it if that's what you want to know."

Watching him massage his bottom lip between his teeth again, Ani knew he was sorting his thoughts because she did the same thing.

"Reslo was always experimenting," he finally said. "Given a problem or task, he almost always found a solution in half the time it would have taken someone else, and it would often be . . . unique." He chuckled. "And Kela is unique."

His laughter brought a smile to Ani's face and a shiver of memory slid into place. Her father had laughed often when she was young and that was his laugh.

Of course I'm unique. Kela stated in utter confidence. *At least on Teramar.*

"How long have you had this connection?" her father asked.

Placing her hands on either side of Kela's head, she looked into those icy blue eyes with love. "Almost fifteen years. I do know that Uncle Reslo specifically chose his species because they live well into their forties, even in the wild. But while many people assume he is half my age mentally, they grow up very fast in the beginning and gradually slow to the point of matching our own aging patterns. So by the time Kela was ten, he had matched my age of twenty. He now ages one year to one of mine and will do so for the rest of his life."

"Excellent." Yenne clapped. "And he understands every word spoken?"

"Every word of Northern. He can read Northern as well."

Kela barked in agreement. *I was taught well. Tell him who taught me to read.* He winked.

Yenne leaned forward. "And he says . . ."

"I don't want to brag, but I taught him to read. Uncle Reslo was surprised when we showed him."

Eyebrows raised in surprise, Yenne sat back in his chair. "Reslo didn't know Kela would be capable of reading?"

Ani shook her head. "He only planned on Kela being able to talk to me and being able to understand what everyone in the room was saying. Reslo said it might be useful and another way of protecting me."

Yenne rubbed at his chin. "You mentioned you hadn't been in contact with Reslo for a while. Why did he go to Southern and leave you alone?"

"He was able to leave because, with Kela, he knew I wouldn't be alone. The only time I was alone was when I woke up three days ago without Kela in my head."

"My apologies, Ani."

"Well, he's back in my head and we have no intention of repeating that scenario, right?" Grabbing the ruff of fur around his neck, she pulled Kela's face to hers and kissed his muzzle several times.

Ani returned to her father's question. "As for Uncle Reslo, shortly before Mother died, Southern launched satellites as their first volley into space. Both Uncle Reslo and Mother were excited about the possibilities but didn't really explain why they were so interested. Mother's condition worsened dramatically shortly after that, and the subject didn't come up again until after the funeral when Uncle Reslo told me he was going to Southern to offer them assistance. He said that by helping Southern get into space, he might be able to use their technology to enhance the communications system at the old research center, and then he'd be one blade closer to getting home."

Abruptly, she stopped talking and clasped both hands over her mouth as she remembered the desperation in Reslo's voice when he told her that he was leaving. She spoke through her fingers. "I didn't understand, then. I do now. Oh, blades. He and Mother had been trying to send messages to Lrakira for over twenty years without success because of the time thing around Teramar. Neither one of them gave up. They were always looking for a way to get me here. He went to Southern in search of a way to—" She choked on a sob and tears spilled over. Once again, her world—or the one she thought had been her world—was cracking open.

Yenne reached across the table and gently cupped her chin. "It'll be all right, Ani. Renloret got you here in time and our people will survive. When was the last time you talked to Reslo?"

She brushed the tears off her face. "Actually talked with him? Months ago. He was excited about his research on Southern legends of some kind. Then I left him a message about Dalkey being back at the lake house and stirring up trouble about nonexistent aliens when Renloret's ship crashed." She grimaced.

Yenne chuckled. "At least they all did a great job of keeping your Lrakiran identity a secret. Do you know if he got the message?"

Shaking her head, she said, "No. I suppose that's one more thing we'll have to check on." Even with this new understanding of the man in front of her, she didn't explain that the *we* she had in mind did not include him.

The tower bells were muffled through the closed window, but they could still be heard. It was perfect timing as far as Ani was concerned. She stood. "It's late and there's much to do in the morn. I have to meet with the Singers again, and my mind is playing blade games with all that has happened."

Yenne came around the table and tried to pull her into a parental hug. Sidestepping out of range, she said in apology, "I'm not ready."

His nod of understanding chipped away at her heart.

"Kela, let's go." She waved the canine toward the door. Yenne reached it first, palmed it open, and politely let her cross the threshold ahead of him.

"Sleep deep, Ani." The rumble of his bass voice followed her as she struggled to avoid running down the hall.

The Balance

The Stone Chamber was cool in the early morn though Ani thought it was most likely cool all the time. The embroidered tapestries that hung against the stone walls were not just there as decoration, they were also there to abate the cold.

Ani studied the scenes depicted in the fading threads. The most frayed showed a night sky filled with unfamiliar star patterns surrounding what appeared to be an orange comet racing closer to the people at the bottom of the weaving. Curiously, the people seemed unaware of the danger. In fact, they appeared to be sleeping or dead. Ani stood on tiptoe and ran her fingers across the patterns. She decided to look at it positively and chose to see them as sleeping.

When she brought the hanging closer, she could see six or seven robed people in the background on a hill at a distance from the sleeping piles of people. The robed ones stood in a tight circle, their hands holding short blades aloft, tips joined in a pyramid above their heads. A rainbow rose above them and branched in two groups of three colors arching in opposite directions. There were six colors to the rainbow instead of the seven she was used to. Curious. The scene was both sad and joyous. She wondered if there was any significance to the design.

A shaft of light brightened the Stone Chamber, washing out the colors of the stitching. Ani turned to greet the pair of Singers, her questions about the worn tapestry forgotten in the urgency of the current circumstances.

Pointing to the black box on the pedestal next to the Anyala Stone, Diani raised her eyebrows in inquiry.

"Yes, the blade is within," Ani said.

"Open it, please."

Diani and Layson stared at the green crystal blade nestled against the blood red silteene fabric. Diani nodded. "Yes, that is the Anyala Stone's blade."

As Layson hovered her hand above the blade, Ani watched closely and felt a tingle of cool green slide through her mind. Somehow she knew that the injured Stone was using the blade to communicate with the Kita Stone's Singer.

Layson smiled. "The Stone greets me through the blade. The Stone is stronger with the blade here."

A humming from the Kita and Pericha Stones followed, warning the Singers, including Ani, that though the Anyala Stone was strengthened by the blade's presence, its communication would be limited to conserve energy and give Ani and Renloret time to retrieve The Balance.

Ani felt the blue and amber Stones retreat from her mind to confer with their Singers and she tried not to fidget. A questing tune snuck into her awareness. She looked at the Anyala Stone. Its dim life light flickered in rhythm with the tune. Stepping to the pedestal, she placed a hand on the Stone's surface as far away from the hilt of the amber blade as possible. Would her touch soothe the ache mirrored in the tune? A sigh escaped her lips as the physical contact increased the volume of the Stone's song. Ani glanced at the other Singers. They appeared to be meditating, their eyes closed, expressions relaxed. Matching the notes she heard in her mind, she blended her mental voice with that of the Anyala Stone. A higher-toned descant, apparently from the blade, enhanced the Stone's song.

Return The Balance and all will be well. Though softer than a whisper, the Stone's tune carried a deep sadness that wound its way into her mind before fading.

"Anyala?"

She jerked her hand away from the Stone and turned to find both Singers studying her.

"It was singing to me. I could barely hear it. As you mentioned yesterday, it was louder when I touched it. I did not know you were waiting for me."

"No need to apologize. What did it tell you?" Diani asked.

The melancholy of the Stone's statement colored her voice. "Everything will be well if I bring The Balance back. It is sad and . . . in pain." Ani reached out and pulled Diani closer. "We're wasting time. The Stone does not know how long it can survive. It needs The Balance as your people needed The Blood."

Diani wrapped her hands around Ani's and nodded to Layson to join them. Layson stepped forward and embraced their interlocked hands. "The fastest ship in the fleet has been outfitted. They await final travel orders and passengers. I suspect you can leave whenever you wish."

Ani smiled and was surprised by her own fleeting desire to stay on Lrakira so she could learn from them and perhaps even become friends. They were so different from the cold, hateful countenance of her grandmother. She bowed her head and backed toward the door. "Then I should find Renloret."

CHAPTER FIVE

About ten days later, Lrakira's fastest starship maneuvered into position behind the fifth planet of Teramar's solar system. Ani knew that Renloret had argued, unsuccessfully, that the ship was far larger than necessary for the simple search and retrieval mission. At least he had gotten his superiors to agree on this location for observation and waiting. Now there was only Commander Yenne Chenakainet to handle—or rather convince that a single star runner could do the job. The commander could not argue against the smaller ship because it would be less noticeable in the sky than the huge ship now peeking out at the edge of the gaseous planet's horizon.

Ani sighed and shifted her gaze downward as she attempted to relax her overworked mind a little. Renloret interrupted her contemplation of her feet when he entered the conference room rubbing his forehead. He was probably trying to ease the headache he'd mentioned was now a regular feature of any meeting that included the commander. She couldn't solve that problem for him.

The Balance

A frown creased her brow as Ani crossed her arms tightly. She jerked her head toward the man standing with his back to them and shrugged. Renloret sighed. Kela peeked out from under the table and winked at the pilot. Ani shoved her foot at the canine but made no comment, either audibly or telepathically.

Renloret cleared his throat to get the commander's attention. Yenne turned from the ship's view screen, pulled out a chair, and sat with a huff, glaring at Ani. Ani pressed two fingers to her lips and shook her head. It was the signal she and Renloret had come up with to indicate that neither of them had gotten the stubborn man to agree to their plan.

There was no question that her father frustrated her. Yenne's shipboard duties had made him less available to her than she'd hoped for, and this lack of contact had not enabled them to begin building any form of father-daughter relationship. She knew it did not make sense in any logical way, but it had left her feeling abandoned by the father she'd believed had already abandoned her by dying twenty years ago.

Renloret dipped his chin in greeting to Ani, snapped a proper salute to the commander, and then reached under the table to scratch Kela between the ears before taking a seat. "Commander Chenakainet, I have to supply the complete roster to the captain before she'll let us disembark. It must be okayed by you before I can submit it to her."

"I gave it to you already," Chenakainet replied. "Why are we wasting time? Do we even know how much time we have?"

Renloret shook his head. "We don't know precisely, Commander. In their last message, the Singers said that communications with and between the Stones continues to be compromised by the injury to the Anyala Stone. No one knows if it will die if the blade is not removed, or even if it *can* die. I agree with you that we need to expedite this search, but there is a problem with your list."

"You're still opposed to the number of searchers, pilot?"

"I think twenty is excessive."

Ani snorted in disgust but otherwise remained quiet. She was supposed to let Renloret handle this part of the mission.

"How many would *you* suggest?" the commander asked, sarcasm drenching the last two words.

"Three."

The commander stood. "Good, I'll meet you two at the launch bay in one bell."

"Wait."

Ani was surprised at the force behind Renloret's single word. The commander hesitated.

"The three will be Ani, Kela, and me," Renloret said. "It is the only way we can return. The three of us left and the same three will return. Others, especially you, Commander, will raise alarms about a Southern—or worse, an alien—invasion, and I am not going to march into the arc of that swinging blade if I can help it."

"You chose the canine over me?" the commander sputtered.

"Yes."

The hurt was obvious in the commander's stunned expression.

Ani turned to Renloret. "Excellent. We'll meet you in ten,"

The Balance

the tone of finality silencing further argument from her father. The whoosh of the door closing behind her as she left the room felt like an exclamation point. Surely her *father* was mature enough to understand and accept the right decision.

Ani and Kela arrived in the launch bay on schedule. She watched Renloret check over the sleek star runner. He looked in their direction, smiled, and waved them over. The trio quickly boarded and Ani was pleased when they were given immediate release. A few more hours and she would be home.

"That's Teramar?" she whispered as her planet filled the view screen. "It looks smaller than I imagined." She pointed at the equator. "The islands really do look like a necklace around the center. The few photos I've seen from Southern's satellites only show specific areas, not the whole thing."

"Southern's optics are better than the usual early attempts at satellite imagery. I'd say Teramar is off to a good start when it comes to joining us out in the stars, which I suspect will be in a few generations."

She pointed to a spiraling cloud formation. "Is that a storm front?"

"Yes, looks like a significant moisture carrier. Do you often have large storms this time of year?"

"Mid to late summer there's usually three to four drenchers, so I guess that would be one of them."

Kela whined at her side. *Can he show us Star Valley?*

She smiled. "Can you show us home?"

Renloret returned the smile and adjusted the view to show Northern's central highlands in topographic clarity. Ani gasped.

"Look, Kela, there's Starlight Ridge, Sour Water Creek, and . . ." her voice caught, "Star Valley. Home. It's beautiful. My home is beautiful."

Renloret made one more adjustment.

"Oh, my," she whispered as she grasped the pilot's shoulder. Seen from above, her family home, the lake house, stood in sharp contrast to the soft natural edges of the trees and outcroppings. The view widened as Renloret moved the optics to the small village in the valley's center. Anyala was silent as he panned over the geometric patterns of crops in various shades of green, red, and yellow, then tapped his shoulder when the sheriff's office building came into view. "Did you ever get that message to Taryn?"

"Yes. I sent it directly to his tel-com as you requested when we left Lrakira. There is no way for him to reply, so I don't know when he actually received it."

Ani nodded. It was the best they could do to forewarn Taryn of their return. She watched the screen as the visual moved down the road.

"There's the dance hall," Renloret whispered.

She chanced a glance and caught the blush that crossed his cheeks. Evidently, he remembered "the dance." Would there be another? She wished it had ended differently. In retrospect, she had mangled pretty much everything between them since then. The few times they had been alone and he had brought up their relationship, she'd changed the subject.

There was still too much to digest. Her understanding of her own identity had been wrenched into the impossible. Why hadn't she been told about being The Blood after reaching menses, or at the very latest, after achieving the continental blade championship? What exactly had her mother and uncle been waiting for? Perhaps they didn't want to tell her until they knew for sure they could get her to Lrakira. If only Renloret had arrived a year or two earlier, then perhaps her mother would still be alive and able to assist Ani in reconciling the twenty year time change caused by the Stones' ruined time-song.

Without her mother to run interference, Ani was struggling to grasp the concept of time manipulation. She knew that twenty years was a mere blink for the Stones. But for her and her father, twenty years was, perhaps, a gap too wide to cross. The fact that he had not aged more than a few months while Ani had grown into adulthood was difficult to swallow. He was hardly more than a decade her senior, yet he acted as if she was the five-year-old he'd left behind. Any progress they may have accomplished after the skills tests had disappeared once they were headed for Teramar. For the past ten days their terse conversations had either ended in shouting matches or with one of them storming off, leaving much left unsaid and unresolved. Ani pulled her bottom lip between her teeth as she realized the truth in her mother's frequent lament that she had inherited her father's stubbornness, then she expelled a noisy breath through her nostrils.

"What now?" she asked Renloret. Now that she was away from Yenne's overbearing presence, the search for her twin could commence and she wouldn't have to think about her father or the impossible explanations they would have to concoct—yet.

"I'm receiving an automated permission from the launch tower behind the old research center to complete landing procedures. Don't worry, all the signals are scrambled and wave coded. They won't know we're here."

"But the ship itself . . . won't the villagers see it?" She couldn't imagine what they might think upon seeing the star runner.

"You're not the only ones with camouflage technology."

"Oh." Ani sat back in the chair. *How silly of me to forget.* Indeed she had forgotten the holographic devices designed by her uncle that she had often used when playing games as a youth. Once, she had even used the camouflage technology to hide the mess in her room to buy some time to actually clean it up. And she had used three of the machines to protect the crash site from the prying eyes of the military when Renloret crash-landed near her cabin on his first trip to Teramar.

She crossed her arms and glared at the screen as lines of Lrakiran script appeared, replacing the visual of Star Valley. She was still adjusting to the idea that she was actually Lrakiran, though she had been born on Teramar. Technically, she had always been an alien on Teramar, though she hadn't known it and didn't feel like one. She could not even tell the difference between Teramarans and Lrakirans, apart from the difference in language and technology. They looked the same, sounded the same, smelled the same, and behaved the same. The only thing remotely alien about Lrakira was the three guardian Stones, and even that was not really alien to her. Until she had met the Stones, she and Kela were the only telepathic beings she'd known. But even with that difference between her and others, she had never doubted that she was Teramaran.

Renloret was obviously concentrating on the screen. His fingers flitted across the keyed panel in front of him. Ani scratched the base of Kela's right ear and shifted in her chair. "Teramar is my home, not Lrakira."

Renloret glanced at her over his shoulder but said nothing as he completed the landing procedures. For the moment, thankfully, her comment could not be their focus. The mission had been clearly stated. Locate and take her twin to Lrakira so the Stone would live. What would happen if they couldn't find the twin in time . . . or at all? And whether or not her twin was found, was she, Ani, required to return to Lrakira as well? Did she even want to? What about Renloret? If she stayed would he come back for her? Ani shook her head, reminding herself that she could only sharpen one blade at a time, and the most important blade was finding her twin. All other decisions had to be put off until then.

Renloret interrupted her thoughts, saying that they would be able to disembark when a certain blinking yellow light flashed to a solid green. Ani stared at the light. Her heart beat in harmony with each blink.

A slight bump and metallic clanging startled her. Had the ship landed? Ani checked the light. It was green. Renloret released his seat belt and stood. "Have to check the moorings." He paused, smiled at her, and waved at the screen. "Ready to go home?"

Ani looked out to see the actual view from the ship instead

of Lrakiran text, which had occupied the screen during the landing process. Manufactured walls with various cubbies or drawers and doors backed a bank of workstations. The view slid sideways as the ship rotated. Mesmerized by the unexpected view, Ani stared at the screen.

"I don't recognize this room. Are you sure this is part of the research center?"

"I don't think it's exactly part of the research center, but there is at least one access point between them. That's how Taryn and I found you. Actually, Kela led us to you. This launch tower was built inside the mountain behind the research center."

Ani stared at Renloret. "Whoa. Kela led you to the research center *and* to me that night?" Out of the corner of her eye, she saw Kela's ears dropped flat against his head and felt his private barrier slide into place.

"Yep, direct from the lake house to the research center."

"How?" she glared at Kela. *I'm thinking we should have talked about this.*

Kela shook his head. He did not want to discuss that topic.

"Instead of telling you, why don't we show you? Kela can lead the way in reverse." Renloret didn't seem to realize the impact of his comments.

Kela barked and headed down the central hall of the star runner to the exit ramp. He was straight-out ignoring her. When was everyone going to fess up to all that had occurred when she was unconscious? Renloret took her hand and pulled her after the canine. She stumbled along, suddenly terrified of what awaited her—and what everyone else seemed to know.

Terror was quickly replaced by the slow burn of anger that simmered as Ani walked around the hangar and launch control facility. Why had all of this been kept from her? Had her own mother and uncle not trusted her to hold their secrets safe? Safe. She knew that was their reason. They had to keep *her* safe until they could get her to Lrakira so her blood could save the entire Lrakiran race. Their people—her people.

Ani's father, Yenne Chenakainet, had managed to escape Teramar during the original attack but had been forced to leave his family behind. There had been a second ship—the one Renloret had used to return her to Lrakira. Why hadn't her mother and uncle used it? What had prevented them from escaping? Had they been under such tight scrutiny that they couldn't attempt it and by the time they thought they could escape, the time-song had somehow prevented them from doing so? So many questions and the only person who could answer them, Reslo, was hiding out on Southern.

Uncle Reslo, now he was another problem. She had to contact him, let him know what had happened, and tell him they were about to begin searching for her twin. Perhaps he would know about the twin and who and where she was. The struggle to keep her "little girl" anger—which is how she saw it—under control so she could face the realities of her new self was getting harder. Ani wanted to slash out at something or someone and she was mortified when she realized her target was her mother. If only she had been able to save her mother, all of this might have been explained. Hadn't her mother tried to explain just before she died? What exactly had she said? Ani couldn't remember. Perhaps she would later when she had time to take in all of the lies.

Well, they weren't so much lies as things never mentioned or talked about, such as this "launch tower," as Renloret called it. He said it was connected to the research center as well as to the lake house. By tunnels, no less! She felt the anger rising again. Oh, she knew about some of the tunnels—the one from the cabin to the blade room and the one from the lake house to her mother's private sanctuary near the hot springs outlet to the lake. The fact that there were more frightened her. How had she not known about them? She felt like a five-year-old.

She was startled out of her reverie by Renloret's voice. She couldn't see him and wondered where he was.

"Do you want me to explain all of this?"

"I really don't know. It's . . . overwhelming."

Kela, who had left her to her thoughts for some time, interjected. *You should have seen Taryn. I actually think he handled it better.*

"Taryn's been here?" Ani stopped in her pacing behind the consoles and looked for Renloret.

He appeared from behind the ship, sliding his hand along the sleek metallic fuselage as if he were petting it. "Well, yes. After you were injured and the Song of Healing didn't fully awaken you, I had no choice but to find a ship to get you home. This is where we found the stasis bag that helped keep you alive too. Kela helped Taryn release the star runner from storage so I could transport you back to Lrakira."

Ani considered this. Now she could ask one of her

bothersome questions. "Why didn't my mother and Uncle Reslo use that same ship? They could have waited a few weeks and then, when things had settled down somewhat, they could have flown to Lrakira themselves. Has anyone asked that question?"

A frown creased Renloret's forehead. "I haven't heard that and I didn't think to ask it myself, though I have a long list of other questions to ask. Perhaps your uncle can answer it. Once we get to the lake house or the cabin you can send him a message."

She nodded. "He usually doesn't answer right away. But maybe by the time we find my twin he'll contact us and we'll have answers. Perhaps he'll even want to return to Lrakira."

Another thought came to her. "Do you have to be trained to fly one of these? Can I fly one right now?"

Renloret's laugh was not condescending. "I don't think so. I was in training for two sun-cycles before I flew my first real mission, though I soloed in a sprinter class flyer when I was nineteen. That was considered young. That and my high marks in astrophysics and mathematics allowed me entrance into the academy before I was twenty-four." He paused. "I think your father was the only certified pilot in the research group. Usually there are at least three when you have a group of over ten, to account for possible injury or loss of life."

"Did you have a backup pilot when you came here?" Ani thought about the two men she had buried near the crash site of Renloret's original star runner.

"Sharnel."

"I'm sorry."

"So am I. Even though there were only three of us in total, that mission was deemed important enough to have a second pilot on board. Sharnel and Kiver were the ones assigned to locate your mother, your uncle, you, and anyone else from the original research team still alive. We didn't know about the time shift, so we thought it wouldn't take very long to gather everyone and return. I wasn't even supposed to have to leave the ship."

Ani chuckled. "Well, we know how that didn't work."

Kela barked for attention. *All of that is in the past and we have a mission for the future. We've got some climbing to do. Can we just get moving?*

"Okay, Kela." The canine sent her a vision of the lake house, their first destination. Ani walked to the packs with provisions sitting at the end of the ramp. She shouldered one of them and adjusted the straps. Renloret pressed a panel on the side of the ship and the ramp retracted. He picked up the remaining pack and bowed slightly to Kela. The canine trotted off, in the lead, tail waving jauntily.

CHAPTER SIX

The stairs ended at the ceiling. Renloret grabbed the handle, felt for the pressure plate on the inside of it, and squeezed. The panel slid away and a rug fell on his head.

"I think Taryn has been back to the house and covered this access." His voice was muffled as he flopped the rug off his head and out of the way. Then he scrambled up the remaining stairs.

Ani tentatively stepped into the living room of the lake house, a disbelieving look on her face. In all her years at the lake house, she had never known about this hidden entry.

I told you. Kela's voice was gentle in her mind as he emerged from the secret stairway.

I never knew. They didn't tell me anything! Her chin quivered slightly, her mind reeling under the impact of revelations clouding what she knew about her mother and her uncle.

Kela's reassuring mind voice came to her. *How could they? They were protecting you—the most important person in two worlds. They had to keep all of this secret, especially after the*

65

attack. They couldn't chance discovery, not after the accusations of harboring aliens.

Renloret seemed to know her thoughts as well. "Your mother and uncle loved you and wanted to protect you from the military until you could defend yourself. By then, I'm sure they didn't know if they would ever get you home to Lrakira. Remember that there was no communication between Lrakira and Teramar while the time bubble was present. Though that length of time was very short for us on Lrakira, it was twenty years or more for Teramar. And after so long, perhaps they gave up using their alien technology, believing it no longer functioned after the original attack. Reslo's best opportunity would have been to go to Southern when they launched their satellite. This is so messed up." He drew her into his embrace and whispered in her ear. "Parents can do the stupidest things."

His words moved her, but it was his scent, which was completely intoxicating, that stunned Ani into silence. Her anger faded to nothing. *Hells, why now?* It was as close as she had let him get in the weeks since discovering she had a twin. There had been such a fervor preparing for this return trip that they'd had little time to even discuss much beyond locating and returning The Balance, whoever she was, in order to save the Anyala Stone.

Reminding herself that she was an adult, Ani pushed away from Renloret. "I'll be okay." But would she, she wondered.

"It's complicated and perhaps too much for you to understand," he admitted. "But I know they did their best under the circumstances, and that is all we can ask of anyone, including ourselves."

Perhaps they did too good of a job, Kela whispered. *I was told not to tell you what I knew, which we now know was not enough anyway. It would have confused everyone. We needed your mother or your uncle to explain, and we had neither when the information could have helped us. Your mother was already dead and your uncle was unreachable on Southern.*

No, I still would have assumed it concerned Southern and not a far-off planet. Shaking her head, she chuckled at herself.

"Can you grab the corner and help me straighten this?" Renloret asked. He had closed the sliding floor panel and was holding one end of the rug, both eyebrows raised, waiting to be noticed.

She snatched up the corner nearest her and they pulled it straight to cover the stairwell entrance. "Why cover it at all? You can't see or even feel the seams."

Renloret grinned. "They covered the design, Ani. Perhaps they figured you would be smarter and more curious as you grew up and you would push on the design like Taryn did. That would have given you access to the tunnels and all that information before you were ready for it."

"That would be a parent for you, wouldn't it?" Shrugging, she headed to the foyer. She had to get beyond this and focus on the immediate mission. "Should I leave Taryn a note that we're going to be at the cabin or should I call him?"

"Neither. We shouldn't leave any indication that we were here. We still don't know if there has been any fallout from the skirmish when we left." Renloret followed her as they headed toward the kitchen. "If we haven't heard from him by the morrow, then we can contact him. I'd rather everyone believe we are still on Southern until we decide to let them know. Remember, Taryn has presumably been forewarned, even though I did not give him an exact date or time."

She nodded and opened the door to the back of the house.

Kela slipped through. *I'd like to do my own reconnaissance if you don't mind. I won't get as much attention when seen as either of you would.*

"All right. Go ahead. We're headed to the crash site first, then the cabin. Meet us there for the eve meal."

Kela's tail was a grey-and-white flag as he disappeared into the trees behind the outbuilding that housed the alcohol-burning vehicle.

Renloret tipped his head toward Kela's waving tail. "Scouting ahead for us?"

"Sort of. He said he had some reconnaissance to do."

Renloret opened his mouth as if to speak, then closed it without saying anything and trudged on.

Daneeha pushed the door open. "Sheriff?" Her squeaky voice carried an odd edge.

Taryn waved his diminutive secretary in without looking up. "Don't fuss, Daneeha, you may leave if you'd like. I'll close up." Taryn scribbled a note at the bottom of the day shift's report before looking across the desk. Daneeha's chin appeared to rest on the surface of the wood, but Taryn knew she was standing, impatient for his undivided attention.

He raised his eyebrows. "What is it now?"

"Melli saw Kela at the cemetery about an hour ago."

He sucked in a quick breath at her startling statement and then exhaled slowly, trying to keep his emotions from playing blade games across his face. It was work keeping his voice calm. "She's sure?"

"You know your mother."

He stood.

"I'll tell her you're on your way." Daneeha turned and followed him through the door. "Wait." She held out the magnetic lock to his hover-car.

He snatched the blue fob and without nodding his thanks, left.

In the few minutes it took Taryn to get to his mother's house, an endless stream of questions marched across his mind. Where were Ani and Renloret? Why was Kela at the cemetery alone? Should he try to make contact with them? Was there a plan he should know about?

The first words out of Melli's mouth when she saw him come up the steps were, "Why didn't you tell me they'd returned from Southern?"

"I didn't know they were back," Taryn said defensively. "You're positive it was Kela?"

"Taryn!"

"Sorry, Mother. Why don't you tell me what happened."

Melli held him at bay while she made a pot of tea, refusing to say more about it until they were settled on the front porch with cups of the spicy infusion she was known for.

"You realize that in all the fuss of their leaving we didn't celebrate the anniversary appropriately. Am I the only one concerned about this? It's not respectable at all."

Taryn did not want to talk about things that would require him to continue withholding information from his mother, but he also did not want to make his mother think he didn't care. The grave of Ani's mother, Shendahl, had been desecrated by General Dalkey, who had stolen her body as well as the green crystal ceremonial blade that had been buried with her. Of course, the military had claimed that there was no evidence of this because neither the body nor the blade could be found. Dalkey had been killed in the altercation, and there had been no official investigation because an investigation would have brought attention to some embarrassing behavior on the part of the military. And Taryn knew that Dalkey's behavior and actions were certainly embarrassing. Shendahl's casket had been recovered, repaired, and reburied, but apart from Taryn, only Mroz, Star Valley's part-time coroner and full-time bar owner, knew that there was no body in the casket. With Dalkey dead, Taryn was likely the only person on Teramar who knew where Shendahl's body actually was. And that information was just dangerous enough that he was not going to share it—not even with his parents.

"You're right, of course, Mother. But right now, I need to know about Kela."

"Fine," Melli sighed. "This morning I took more flowers to her parents' graves. When I saw Kela, I thought Ani would be there too. But he was alone." Melli twisted the teacup in the saucer.

"What did he do, Mother?" Taryn scribbled a few words in his ever present notebook.

"He came from the trees on the west side, ears all perky and tail waving. He just walked over and sat with me for a few moments. Then he looked me straight in the eyes and put one of his paws on my hand, as if he were giving me condolences, just like any person would do . . . as if he understood. Then he left. I thought you should know." Melli paused to sip her tea. "If Kela's here, then Ani is also."

Taryn picked up his cup and mumbled into his tea, "I didn't expect them back so soon." He hadn't really expected them back at all. Though it had only been about six weeks, they had been long weeks as far as his heart was concerned. He hadn't known how long the trip to Lrakira would take. And until two weeks ago, he hadn't even known if Ani had survived to save her people, or if she and Kela had even arrived on Lrakira. All he had received was a cryptic one-line anonymous electronic statement saying that all was well and they were returning. No specifics. He wasn't even sure it was from Renloret. Taryn shook his head. He didn't know enough. Actually, he didn't really know anything. "Is Father at the grocery?"

"Of course. Why?"

"If they're back they'll need supplies. Maybe they're still at the store and Father hasn't had a chance to let either of us know. I'll head there first and then go to the lake house." He stood and gave his mother a quick hug. "Thanks for letting me know. Don't tell anyone else until we know for sure."

"No worries, son. I told Daneeha the same thing."

"I'm glad we think alike, Mother." He gave her another hug and brushed his lips across her cheek before running to the hover-car.

In the rearview mirror, Taryn watched Melli's fingers ripple-rapping the porch railing. He waved as he moved the hover-car away from the house. Her response was hesitant. Then she turned and placed the cups and saucers on the tray and retreated into the house. Refocusing on the road, he shook his head, not sure how to relieve her worries. How could he? He was worried too.

CHAPTER SEVEN

Ani had stopped abruptly in the trail, and Renloret nearly ran into her. She stood her ground as he dodged and stumbled past a few steps. "Tell me again why we're checking the crash site first."

"To verify that all the signals are turned off, including the distress beacons, and to discover if there has been any military presence in the area since we left," he replied. "I also want to check the status and location of the stasis bags you used to bury my crew in so we can return them to Lrakira if possible."

Ani nodded as she flipped the long braid of black hair over her shoulder. "The cutoff to the canyon is about one hundred paces ahead." She slid by him and took the lead again. She had traveled a dozen or so paces before Renloret could adjust his pack and catch up to her.

"Ani, where did you say Kela went off to?"

"Reconnaissance. Basically, I think he wanted to check his territory. He'll see us at the cabin in time to eat."

Renloret dodged the backswing of a sapling's branch. "Is his territory that large?"

"I guess so. I never asked the size." There was a moment of silence, then she said, "I'm blocked out."

Renloret was startled at the calmness of her statement. "You cannot hear him?"

Ani slowed her pace. "Oh, I can *feel* him. I just can't *hear* any specifics. He's not sending me anything. It's not like when I woke up from that artificial coma. I hope to never go through that again. Be at ease, Renloret. Kela is right here." She touched her temple and smiled softly.

"I was verifying."

"Thank you, but truly, I would tell you if I couldn't feel him."

They hopped the small creek and moved to the canyon's opening. Renloret pulled her back as he surveyed the undisturbed view before them. "It is not possible for the land to have recovered so well in barely two moon-cycles, and where's the ship?" Renloret asked. Had the military found and removed it? That would be trouble.

Ani corrected him. "It's months here on Teramar, not moon-cycles. Remember? And you obviously forgot about the holo-cams too." Shaking off his hand, she moved confidently forward, her body shimmering slightly as she passed through the holographic barrier. She waved Renloret to follow.

He chuckled at his forgetfulness, stepped through the visual barrier, and breathed easier when he realized that not too much had changed. The marshy pond edge remained intact, but just beyond the water he could see the first impact zone of the crash path. Almost centered between the canyon walls, a wide gouge of soil skipped through the meadow. In the middle of the second gouge, two of the star runner's six tail engines jutted rudely amongst piles of soil and broken shrubs. A short distance beyond, the main body of the ship slept at an angle, its nose pointing at the rockslide on the other side of the snow-fed creek gurgling its path into the pond.

As they skirted the pond edge, a knee-high beast burst from the tall undergrowth at the tree line. The animal paused to glare at them, and with a deep chittering expletive of its own, waddled across the path to dive into the pond. The ripples became wedge-shaped as it swam to the mound of sticks and mud near the middle of the pond. Another of the creatures joined it atop their nest. Threatening squeaks, chits, and growls warned Ani and Renloret not to come any closer.

"Oh, he's finally got a mate!" Ani bowed theatrically to the pair. "We will leave you to your family." She pulled Renloret along the path. "What does your bio-teacher tell you?"

He'd already been accessing the information out of curiosity, so he recited it. "The musky dam weaver lives only in mountainous regions of Northern and mates for life around the age of four. It weaves dams and nest mounds from branches, leaves, and mud, all glued together with generous amounts of a saliva-like substance secreted from two glands on either side of its muzzle. It is from these glands that its distinctive musky odor emanates. This substance has been found to be useful as an adhesive, though the odor has a tendency to linger even after drying. A pair will raise three to five pups every two years. They can become nuisances, especially if they dam up the water sources for smaller villages or farmland. However, this trait is also useful in controlling erosion and runoff from burns. These dams serve as a form of natural flood prevention and filter the water that sifts through the intricate weave of the dams."

Renloret paused at the end of his recitation, just as they reached the tail section of the splintered star runner. "Quite an ingenious creature, really."

Mid-summer blooms jutted around the sharp edges of the craft softening the blackened ground with smatterings of green-blue foliage and splashes of red, purple, and yellow. Renloret ducked into the main cabin and just as quickly emerged. "No signals. Now to the stasis bags."

Ani led the way to the rockfall where she'd covered the two stasis bags containing the bodies of Sharnel and Kiver, after pulling the injured and unconscious Renloret from the crash. Spring storm runoffs had given the temporary burial plots a more natural look. Kneeling, Renloret removed enough of the rocks to check the readouts on the palm-sized closure latches. Satisfied with the readings, he glanced at Ani. She was staring at the wreckage of the star runner, her arms crossed tightly against her chest. "Are you all right?"

"I'm fine," she said, her tight voice belying the words. "I just don't like the idea of a person being in such a confined space."

"Ani, they're not alive. They were dead before you put them in."

She shook her head. "Doesn't matter. It gives me dry heaves just thinking about them under those rocks, untended for months. Are their bodies still . . ."

"The stasis bags put them into a type of suspension. Tests have shown no deterioration even after thirty of your years. Really, Ani, they are fine." Renloret replaced the rocks and sprinkled gravel and smaller bits of debris over them. "Didn't your mother ever explain how they worked or what their purpose was?"

"No, she just said the bags could be used to protect a person's body until they could be properly dealt with." A drawn out sigh escaped. "I did what I had to. I couldn't bring them back and I didn't know who to take them to. You needed my attention. I did for them what I was taught to do, what I couldn't do for my mother." A tear fell and her voice wavered. "I couldn't put her in one of those bags while she was still breathing. That's what she wanted me to do . . . and I couldn't. She said it would be all right. I didn't believe her. I had a bag with me but I waited too long. Alarms on the machines started blaring, the doctors swarmed in, I was ushered out, and they closed the door. I watched her die from the other side of the glass. I let her die."

Renloret heard the struggle to control her voice, but he didn't interrupt. This was the first time she'd talked about her mother's death.

"Afterwards, one of the doctors told me that her last words were, 'My daughter can save them. Tell her he's coming. She must go home.'" Tears fell unencumbered now. "I thought she meant Uncle Reslo, not you or my father. I didn't understand. There wasn't enough time. She never told me about Lrakira and her—our—people." She choked on a sob. "I still don't understand. I just saved an entire race of people and I couldn't save my own mother!"

There was nothing he could say and nothing he could do but put his arms around her. She let him, and for that, he was grateful.

The sun gilded the tops of the trees iridescent blue-green as flitters began their eve songs. Through the cabin's open door Renloret could hear Ani humming out on the porch. After a silent hike from the canyon to the cabin, they had stored the supplies and she'd taken one of the rocking chairs to the porch and planted herself within its comforting embrace. She'd been humming and rocking since. He understood her reaction to the consequences of the time bubble. He had no idea how Ani had already managed so much change since waking up on Lrakira. Her wild swings between calmness and anger were expected. That she had just saved an entire species but hadn't been able to save her mother seemed to have finally nicked her facade.

Renloret wasn't sure how long he'd held her as she cried, but she had cried long enough to make her voice ragged. When she had regained some control, she had pushed away from him and headed to the cabin without a word. That section of the trail was now littered with broken branches, kicked rocks, and even a few uprooted plants. He had followed at a safe distance, ready to defend her or whatever living thing she attacked. At least now she was making coherent sounds.

The whistlepot began its own song. Renloret made tea, carried the mugs out, and handed one to Ani before leaning back against the railing post.

Her expression was pensive as she toggled the tiny chain on the tea ball. Thankfully, she no longer seemed torn with grief. The redness had disappeared from her eyes, leaving them a deep, clear green. Closing those eyes, she tipped her head back and breathed slowly and deeply. Her lips curved slightly upward as her shoulders relaxed and the frown creases smoothed from her forehead.

He smiled. "Should I concoct an eve meal?" He sipped and the cinnamon spice brightened in his mouth. He savored the sweet sting as it warmed its way down his throat.

"Not yet. Taryn's on his way up with fresh produce. Should be here in about . . . seven chimes," she replied, choosing the Lrakiran time term.

Renloret smiled in response. "I assume that means Kela was seen doing his rounds."

Ani took a sip of the tea. "Melli, at the cemetery. She was laying flowers on Mother's grave. Kela joined her." A frown started to wrinkle her brow, but she shook her head as if dismissing the thought.

Renloret moved from the railing to the bench under the window. "I'm surprised he went that close to the village."

Ani laughed. "I think he was checking on his girlfriend."

It was Renloret's turn to raise his eyebrows. "Girlfriend?"

Giggling, she continued. "Yeah, I think it's Mroz's ovline herder, Leeshob. She'd be about three or four. Mroz started her last year."

"Started her?"

"In herding competitions. She's big enough to handle the adult ovlines, but I didn't think she was old enough yet."

"Oh," Renloret said. He let the bio-teacher fill in the information gaps. The image showed a canine with a medium length double coat that ranged in color from black to a cinnamon brown. Its structure similar to Kela's, but it had ears that hung down and a muzzle that was square instead of pointed. The breed was considered native to Northern and was most often used on large ranches to assist in the protection and control of herd animals. Renloret nodded his head knowingly.

Ani just smiled into her tea. "Oops, here he comes."

"Kela or Taryn?"

"Kela." Ani's smile widened as the canine bounded from the trees to the porch, then she pursed her lips and set her mug on the porch rail. "He's miffed that I figured it out and he's hungry." She rose from the rocker and followed Kela into the cabin.

Renloret remained on the bench, wishing he could hear their full banter. Unless Ani provided a line by line translation, no one would know they were telepathically linked, though ofttimes, Ani's speech patterns and Kela's actions hinted at it. Their telepathic connection was much smoother than that of the Stone Singers with their Stones. While the Singers often seemed to pause briefly and pull out of awareness of their surroundings with each communication, the communication between Ani and Kela flowed naturally.

Swallowing the last of his tea, Renloret contemplated the summer sun slipping behind the tree tips. Ani's one-sided comments were muffled but carried a happy tone. She was obviously glad to be in her home environment. The pilot smiled. Though they were here for serious reasons, he was also comfortable and surprisingly relaxed.

A hopper zigzagged from the underbrush near the trailhead and disappeared round the corner of the cabin. Though Renloret was fairly confident of who was approaching, he set the mug on the bench and eased his boot blade out of the sheath, eyes on the trail. He counted six breaths with no other movement visible and adjusted the blade in his hand.

"No need for that, friend," Taryn said as he stepped from the trees on the far left side of the clearing.

Renloret sheathed the blade and vaulted the porch railing. He met the sheriff halfway to clasp forearms, and then he gathered the sheriff in a firm, brief hug across the shoulders.

Taryn laughed. "Well, I'm glad to see you too. All is well on Lrakira?"

The pilot stepped back to look at his friend, retaining a light grip on the sheriff's shoulders. Taryn's blue eyes were bright with happiness, matching the smile on his face. "Mostly. The vaccine has not been proven yet, but the Stones tell us all will be well. We lost many but we will continue thanks to Ani and her blood."

Their conversation was interrupted by a screech of delight as Ani emerged from the cabin, hurdled the stairs, and ran full force into Taryn. She enfolded herself around the sheriff.

Taryn answered with what looked like an equally crushing embrace. "I thought you had died, Ani. By all the hells of Teramar, I thought you had died." His voice cracked at the end.

Covering his neck and cheeks with small kisses, she replied softly, "Without you, I would have. You sang for me." She brought her lips to his briefly, looked up at him, then resettled her lips to his.

Standing to the side, Renloret was relegated to the role of mere observer. He noted that the kiss had been initiated by Ani. He also noted the surprise on Taryn's face before he gave in and answered her kiss with equal passion. The kiss was long—uncomfortably long for Renloret. Pushing aside the jealously that threatened to turn to anger against Ani's longtime friend, Renloret reminded himself that he had not yet divulged his feelings for her and had no claim on her heart. Even so, he turned away and stalked towards the cabin.

Kela met him at the top of the stairs with unblinking eyes and his tongue lopping over his teeth in a canine smile.

"Shut up," Renloret muttered as he brushed past the canine.

Away from the reunion spectacle, Renloret took several deep breaths to regain his composure and focus before pulling out a third place setting for the table. They should share a reunion meal. Then there was much to discuss and plans to be made.

CHAPTER EIGHT

Ani kept her eyes on Renloret. The pilot had been unusually quiet while the three of them cobbled together the meal. Her own reaction to seeing Taryn alive had certainly been more than she had expected. Should she explain to both of them? No, it was best left alone. Taryn knew where her heart lay, and surely Renloret would respect her relief at seeing her best friend alive and well.

Renloret wiped a dribble of sauce from his chin and answered Taryn's question about the travel to Lrakira with only Kela as a companion. "I learned much about Kela while traveling to Lrakira. It was illuminating." He nodded toward the canine, who rolled onto his back in front of the fireplace, baring his stomach.

He kept me sane when I couldn't feel or hear you. Kela's comment touched Ani's mind softly. It contained no recriminations, just fact. *And he scratched my stomach whenever I asked!* His telepathic laugh brought a smile to her lips. He rolled completely over, presenting his stomach to Ani.

It doesn't take telepathy to understand that request. Ani pushed him away with her foot. "Grow up."

Both men stopped mid-chew and looked from Ani to Kela, back to Ani, and then to each other. They shared grins and continued to eat. Ani growled at all of them and stuffed a huge bite into her mouth.

I've been thinking, Ani. Do you think a bio-teacher would work for me?

Kela kept his belly available.

She stopped chewing in shock. *Why would you want to have a machine implanted after what I went through? Do you want to learn Lrakiran that much faster?*

Kela cocked his head to one side and raised his eyebrows. *I understand why you are resistant to getting the implantation. However, it is needed only until your mind has assimilated the knowledge. I believe it takes a minimal number of weeks. Then it can be removed and you retain what has been learned. And it might be helpful if one of us fully understood the Lrakiran language. Can you ask?*

Ani stared at the canine. *How have you researched that information?*

I was present when the information from Renloret's bio-teacher was patched into the language database so the Singers could have updated information. Renloret was kind enough to translate some of the discussion to Northern for me. The procedure did not appear to cause him any pain. I think you should consider it, Ani.

Not now for me, but I will ask for you. I promise I will think on it. Ani swallowed and shrugged her shoulders. He might be correct, but the thought of having another machine in her head disturbed her.

She put down the fork and looked at Renloret. "Kela wants to know if a bio-teacher could help him learn Lrakiran faster."

"Bio-what?" Taryn asked.

"Bio-teacher," Renloret corrected. "Hmm, an interesting thought. It works for the Slerdonians. It gave them the ability to speak telepathically with us in Lrakiran. It's something to consider when we get back to Lrakira, and if it works, it might prove to our advantage to have Kela understand Lrakiran more fully. Why don't you explain what it is, Ani?"

She sighed and rolled her eyes at Kela, then leaned forward. "Okay, Taryn, they implant a device that provides instantaneous translations and supposed pronunciations. It's a combination encyclopedia and dictionary, as well as translation device. But you have to practice using it or you can come up with the wrong word or usage of a word. The more you use it, the more accurate it is, depending on how accurate the original source is. And what's fun is that some of the slang terms are currently at least twenty years out of date."

She winked at Renloret. "And I've been told that it provides all the words but not the experience. Renloret even recited an entry on the musky dam weaver when we were at the canyon earlier this afternoon." She forked the last of her meal into her mouth.

"Was it accurate?" Renloret seemed compelled to defend his Lrakiran technology.

She nodded at Renloret and then returned her attention to

Taryn. "I also suspect that Renloret used it when I told him about Leeshob."

Her last word brought Kela to his feet. *What type of information?* Kela asked.

"Mroz's herder?" Taryn asked.

Ani nodded to Taryn, then looked at Kela. "I'm confident Renloret could tell you all you'll want to know about the breed. And if given enough time, he could give a dissertation on herding trials with a list of champions accurate up to about twenty years back."

"It is not the fault of the technology that the Stones twisted time," Renloret interjected, sounding defensive again.

"And that's why he didn't know about my blade championships or that I was all grown by the time he got here," Ani added. "Evidently, I was supposed to be only five."

Taryn waved his hands to stop the banter. "Whoa, I know he thought he was rescuing a five-year-old and it turned out to be you, but what's this about rocks twisting time? I need an explanation. Yes, I need lots of information." He pulled out his notebook.

Renloret reached across the table and placed his hand over the notebook. "You cannot write this down. Someone may read it and that would place you in more danger than you already are."

"Then I'd better destroy the other one."

"What other one?" Renloret asked. He didn't release the notebook.

"The one in which I wrote down all that stuff about the Ceremony of Passing and my thoughts on all you told me about

Lrakira and why you needed Ani and who she really is." He hesitated at the horrified look on Renloret's face. "It's in a safe place, I assure you. Not even Daneeha could find it."

Ani scorched Renloret with her own scalding look but schooled her voice to stay calm as she asked, "What is this *Passing*?" What else did Taryn know about that she didn't?

The pilot looked like a child telling secrets to his best friends as he leaned forward in excitement. "I can only tell you what I've read because the Ceremony of Passing is usually held in seclusion and only Stone Singers and the next candidate are present. In my research I found one of the older manuscripts, which contained a series of illustrations. So when Dalkey said he'd seen your mother's body turn into smoke and disappear into the blade box, I assumed a Passing had taken place.

"What I've read describes a Passing as the internal spirit of the Singer physically traveling from the decedent's body to take up residence within the blade, to share the recently deceased Singer's experiences and knowledge with the next Singer. However, nothing I read gave examples demonstrating that any of the Singers actually benefitted from that sharing or that any knowledge sharing had ever taken place, so I don't know how true the statement is."

"So what you're saying is that my mother's spirit is inside the blade?" Ani asked as she leaned back into her chair.

"Well, I don't know for sure. It may have passed from the blade to you during the Song of Healing." Renloret glanced at Taryn.

Taryn nodded his head. "I did see a greenish smoke-like wisp appear from the blade and cover your body almost like a blanket.

You mouthed 'Nana' when that happened." He shifted in his chair. "It seemed harmless and like it knew what was needed, that it cared about you . . . as if it was alive. Can smoke be alive?" He cleared his throat as if almost embarrassed. "Then it went inside you through the wound, and you seemed . . . less distressed . . . in less pain."

Kela added in Ani's head, *That was just before you left me.* He put a paw on her thigh. *I felt your mother's presence, briefly. I thought you had died and her spirit had come to take you away. They kept singing and you started to breathe again, but you were gone from my mind.*

She rubbed the base of his ears. *I'm back now . . . and forever.*

Ani looked at the men in turn. "Kela says he felt my mother just before our telepathic contact was severed by the coma device."

Renloret pushed away from the table. "I'm sorry I did not know at the time what had happened. Remember, Taryn, all we could see was the physical wound. That implanted device was rather ingenious. It has scientists all over Lrakira in a whirl. They cannot believe it came from Teramar."

"What device and why not from Teramar?" Taryn asked.

"Well, some of them still don't understand that your technology is twenty years further along than they expected or planned on. Both the medical and technical fields on Lrakira are working on what, how, and why the device did what it did. The completeness of the disconnect it created is astounding. Evidently, it has ramifications previously not considered." Renloret shook his head and started to reach for Ani but let his hand drop to his lap. "Not that it matters now that you are safe."

"So the assailant in the cavern was the person who developed this little machine?" Taryn asked.

"Well that's one of many possibilities," Ani said.

Taryn scrunched his face. "Would you recognize him if you saw him?"

Ani shook her head. "He was wearing a full body mask, and we were in a poorly lit cavern at the time, if you remember."

"I assume you asked him some questions while you were waiting for us to appear."

"Of course," Ani said testily. She knew Taryn was in full sheriff mode and was digging for answers, but her memory of the incident was becoming less clear with each passing day. "Listen, Taryn, he'd managed to cut my cheek with a poison-laced blade just as I arrived in the cavern. He spent most of his time running me around, waiting for me to succumb. So whatever questions I may have asked or answers he may have given after that are disappearing from my memory. However I do remember him saying something about his wife and Shendahl."

Taryn leaned forward. "He knew your family?"

"Evidently, but I can't remember enough of what he said to put the pieces together."

She realized she was crying in her frustration to remember and brushed her cheeks. "I wasn't thinking straight to begin with, Taryn. After I figured out who had taken Mother's body from the grave, all I could think about was finding Dalkey and getting her body back. That man in the cavern stole my revenge by killing Dalkey. That's why I ran after him. I had to find out why."

More tears blurred her vision as she wiped her nose across

her sleeve. She reached down and clutched the fur around Kela's neck. He sent her comforting thoughts. "To tell the truth, my memory of what happened in the cavern is slipping away, Taryn. Sometimes all I remember is what others have told me I said just after waking from the coma. Could my memory be altered or damaged by that device?"

Taryn sat back in his chair shaking his head. "I don't know about that. It seems to be a very sophisticated machine, but that sounds improbable. Perhaps it was the poison."

He paused. "I will just have to accept that you can't remember though the lack of definitive information is not going to help the investigation we started. My report lists your assailant as 'unknown.' I really was hoping you would return and be able to identify him. At the moment, we're looking for a phantom." His sigh was heavy with frustration.

He looked at Renloret. "That's not the only reason you returned, is it?"

Renloret ran a hand through his hair. "No, but Ani should explain that." He dipped his chin at Ani, giving her a chance to tell her side of the past six weeks and explain why they had returned to Teramar.

She shifted uncomfortably. "Taryn, there *is* a more important problem."

CHAPTER NINE

Taryn locked eyes with Ani and waited for her to continue. But she just held his gaze silently. "Another disease?" he asked. How many more people were going to die? Was Star Valley in danger?

"Not exactly."

He sighed. Was he going to have to handle more than one problem at a time? Well, no matter, it was always best to get everything out so it could be sliced up into manageable pieces. "Go on."

"We thought you might be able to help with a family matter, unofficially." Ani glanced at Renloret, who gave her an encouraging smile.

Taryn raised his eyebrows. "Unofficially a family matter? What are you dancing around, Ani?" He turned his notebook to a blank page and glanced at Renloret. "Can I take notes on this?"

This time Ani placed her hand on the notebook. "I'm not sure you need that yet. Let's outline the problem first. You can make your notes later."

Taryn put down the notepad and folded his hands. What could be so important that it needed explaining before she garnered his agreement to help? Didn't she know he would do anything for her—even believe in aliens? He shifted to a more comfortable position. "So, outline."

"You know about the Stones?"

"Generally speaking. But since I have no solid proof, I'm not sure I believe in them. Still, I have an open mind. Go on."

Her green eyes sparkling, Ani whispered, "They're real, Taryn. They sang to me. I couldn't *not* believe."

"This is about them, then?" His tone was wary. Had they brought one of them to Teramar? Had they stolen a priceless alien object?

Renloret interrupted. "One of them is injured."

"A rock can be injured?" Taryn choked on his laugh. "I'm really trying not to judge, but give me a little help!"

Ani slapped his shoulder. "Yes. Someone stabbed it."

Taryn looked at their serious expressions, gave up, and let the laugh bubble over. Ani threw her napkin at him.

Renloret shrugged, gathered up the plates, and took them to the sink. "I told you he wouldn't believe us."

Ani rolled her eyes.

"Yes, someone stabbed the Anyala Stone. We're fortunate it's still alive, though it is weak and has difficulty communicating," Renloret said.

Taryn held his hands over his head, surrendering to the

preposterous idea that a rock was not only alive, but had been stabbed. "I apologize, but can you be serious?"

"We *are* serious, Taryn," Ani said gravely. "One of the guardian Stones is dying. *My* Stone is dying." She retrieved the napkin from the floor and slapped the back of his head as she returned to her seat.

"Ow!" He rubbed the spot.

Ani glared at him. "Stop being such an idiot."

"I'll try. But you're the ones talking about living rocks being stabbed." Trying his best to get back into his sheriff's mode, Taryn started drawing on the paper. At least that made him feel like he was doing his job.

Renloret harrumphed, obviously unconvinced, and moved back to the sink to wash the dishes.

"I need you to think, really think, about this, Taryn." Her tone was as imploring as her stare was intense.

"What does the wounding of a rock on Lrakira have to do with *us*? Isn't that *your* problem?" Taryn tried not to smile, pointedly looking at Renloret. "I still don't understand the whole intelligent pebble thing."

Ani swiped at him again. "Stones, Taryn, not pebbles. I assume Renloret told you a little bit about the Stones. I mean, he told you about the Ceremony of Passing—which he didn't tell me." She glared at the pilot.

"I just know that these Stones have something to do with government or religion or some such thing," Taryn admitted. "Renloret said he'd explain in detail later, if he had a chance to come back." There was a slight pause as he raised his eyebrows. "So, you're back."

Renloret returned to his chair. "First, let us agree that there are such things as alien life-forms—some very different from our own or what we might suspect or expect."

Renloret pointed at Kela. "Take him for example. To many, he is an alien. He can converse in at least two languages that I know of and he is learning a third."

"Excuse me, but how do you know?" Taryn asked.

"By his reactions to speech. Any intelligent being would react the same way. Body language is universal, with some exceptions you do not need to know about. And the two languages he is fluent in are Northern and his own species' method of communication. The third is Lrakiran. I started working with him on the trip to Lrakira while you, Ani, were in the coma. But we ceased the lessons when we arrived, and events on Lrakira distracted us from that process. On the way back, I thought it would be better to do everything in Northern for your comfort, Ani, in part because you are still struggling to think of yourself as one of those alien life-forms you have been told do not exist. And they are far more numerous than you could have guessed."

To bring the conversation back to the topic, Taryn interrupted. "Do you know who committed the crime?" He saw Ani's face immediately bloom into a blush.

"My grandmother," she whispered.

Taryn stared at her. "I assume the culprit is in custody."

"Yes, she is being cared for appropriately," Ani said.

Silence settled between them while Taryn considered the information, rubbing his forehead, as if that would improve his thinking. No wonder she was hesitant to talk about this. "This still doesn't answer my question about how Teramar can help a wounded being on a planet we cannot even see in the night sky."

Renloret pointed at Ani. "The solution is also related to her, actually."

"What? Did you bring your grandmother here?"

"This is not about Selabec, Taryn. It seems I have a twin."

"What? Now I'm really confused. Again, what does that, even if it is true, have to do with saving an alien's life or you coming back?"

Ani shrugged. "Well, it's a bit confusing on our side, as well. Evidently, my father didn't know about a twin, either."

"Your father? So you met the old bastard? Why didn't he come back for you?" The look on Ani's face told Taryn he had opened a barely healed wound.

"You knew he was alive?" Ani snapped.

Renloret and Taryn shared looks.

Taryn spoke first. "You two have not done enough talking, have you?"

Renloret grimaced. "We've been interrupted too many times, and it's kind of hard to decide where to start."

"What about Kela? Couldn't he have done some of that explaining?" Taryn asked.

Kela growled and glared at Taryn in warning. Apparently, he wanted to be kept out of it.

Ani shushed the canine with a wave of her hand.

Renloret turned to Ani. "Kela was not there when I told Taryn that your father is alive. I believe we were at the cemetery, just before you *escaped* from Melli and Gelwood's home."

Taryn fended off further accusations. "Things kind of got out of hand after that, Ani. There wasn't time to tell you much of anything while we were trying to save your life."

"Oh, all right," Ani said, the sputter and edge in her voice having turned to begrudging defeat.

"And since you woke up, we've been a little distracted with everything that has happened," Renloret added, still defensive.

Ani raised both palms to the pair of men. "I said all right!"

Taryn returned to his seat on the couch. "That brings us back to why you've returned. You have a twin?"

Ani sighed. "That's what I've been told by three rocks."

"Do you believe these rocks?" Taryn asked.

She rolled her eyes. "Taryn, I realize this sounds absolutely unfathomable, but I absolutely believe the Stones. They say that there is a twin who is alive, or at least was alive a few weeks ago. The Stones are adamant that only The Balance—that's what they call her—can pull the blade from the Anyala Stone." She held up her palm to Taryn, forestalling his question. "Perhaps I should explain what happened after we arrived on Lrakira."

Taryn nodded, more than ready to hear her story.

"It's my understanding that Renloret and Kela had difficulty explaining why I was twenty years older than anyone was expecting when they arrived on Lrakira. At the time, no one but the Stone Singers knew about the time-song. Evidently, to ensure I was old enough to provide the correct hormones, I needed to be in early pubescence. And when my father arrived at Lrakira and announced that I had been born and was a healthy five-year-old, the Stones had their Singers bring them together so they could twist time around Teramar to age me and everything else on the planet.

"Of course, the Stones didn't fully explain what they were doing or why, just that the song would ensure the success of my retrieval. From what I was told, the Anyala Stone's Singer, my grandmother, was unhappy with her assigned Stone because my mother left without her permission and brought the Stone's blade with her to Teramar. I'm not sure I have the whole story straight on what happened. In short, suffice it to say that my grandmother stole one of the other Singer's blades and interrupted the time-song near the end by stabbing the Anyala Stone. This threw off the time shift attempt, and instead of being about twelve or thirteen, I was twenty-five before the song ended. Fortunately, I was still young enough to provide the hormones needed in my blood to create the vaccine against the plague that was killing all the women. At least I was not beyond childbearing. And no one knows if my blood would have worked if I had already gotten pregnant or had children."

She paused and Renloret took up the story.

"And it was this warping of the time-song that caused my crash. The injury to the Anyala Stone now inhibits full communication between all three of the Stones and their Singers, and it is assumed that the injury will eventually kill the Anyala Stone, thus crippling Lrakira's way of life. Ani and I both tried to remove the blade without success. Actually that's when we were informed of the twin."

Taryn felt overwhelmed by all the information.

"Even the Singers were surprised to hear that The Blood and

The Balance were two different people," Ani said. "The Blood and The Balance are supposed to become Stone Singers, so they had always assumed the legend referred to one girl—me." Her laugh took on a nervous edge. "Yeah, Taryn, I'm a legend on Lrakira. More like a prophesy. Can you believe that?"

Taryn chuckled. "That's more believable than talking rocks. Do you realize that you're a legend in Star Valley as far as the blade ring goes?"

"So I've heard. But seriously, Taryn, even if you don't believe this twin thing, I am fairly sure something like a twin is here. We could use your help to find her and convince her to go to Lrakira so she can pull that damned blade out of the Stone. Then perhaps we all can go back to our real lives, alien or not."

Taryn could barely keep up with the questions caroming around in his head. "Why didn't your parents take you home to Lrakira after you were born? Surely, the Stones could have made a much smaller bubble to age just you. Wouldn't that have been safer and more accurate? I mean, your father had two ships available. He used one to escape in when the research center was attacked. Why didn't he take you with him? What was or is so special about Teramar that you had to grow up here?"

"These are all good questions, Taryn," Ani said. "I don't know the answers."

"Perhaps your father does. Can you ask him?"

"We're only supposed to contact the main ship if we need help or we're on our way back with the twin," Renloret stated. "Any other communication is deemed an unnecessary risk of detection."

Ani shrugged. "Your questions are worth asking, Taryn. But I'm not sure Yenne Chenakainet has the answers. He's still having trouble with the fact that twenty years have passed. The further this goes, the more I think only the Stones know the whole story, and for some reason, they didn't tell us. Maybe they don't think we could handle it all at once, so they just give us information one piece at a time."

Taryn grinned. "You mean like a scavenger hunt? We can start looking for clues." He had always enjoyed that game and he was excellent at it too.

"While we are searching, we can leave out the part about traveling to another planet to save a 'talking rock,'" Renloret said. He looked at Taryn. "There are some educational programs on the history of Lrakira available from the star runner's computers that explains the Stones if you are interested. They've been designed for visiting dignitaries."

"I've seen them," Ani added, "and while they are informative, the real thing is better. To have them sing in your head is a powerful experience. Their language doesn't have to be translated because they speak or sing in whatever language you're most familiar with. They don't need a bio-teacher."

"Have you actually used a bio-teacher?" Taryn asked. He wondered how she would react to having another machine implanted in her body even if it helped her rather than put her in a coma.

"No, though several people have been pressuring me to do so, but I'm not too enthralled with having another machine put inside me yet."

Renloret frowned. "Who's been pressuring?"

"Commander Chenakainet."

The pilot was openly surprised. "After what you've been through, he's pressured you to have a bio-teacher?"

"He said it would be easier for me to learn the Lrakiran language. I told him no. Since then, I've tried to discern words, structure, and meaning without artificial help. Depending on the outcome of this search, I might change my mind, though I'm fairly good at languages anyway, so it's been fun on my own. I haven't tried to practice with Renloret because he's been busy with the plans to return and all." Her voice trailed off.

Taryn thought Ani looked frustrated, wistful, and sad, all at the same time.

Ani pushed herself out of the rocker. "I don't know. I feel isolated. So much happened without me. No one even talked to me about how I felt about having a twin. They just kept asking me why I didn't know about her and why my own mother would lie about it."

She knotted her hair in both hands and turned away from the men to face the fire. "Why would she lie? How would I know she lied? She never, *ever*, said anything about having twins!" Ani turned to face Taryn. "How can I have a twin that even my mother wouldn't talk about? Something horrible must have happened to her. Maybe she was deformed or there was brain damage. I *was* born early. I almost died. Mother did tell me that."

"Wait, you almost died?" Renloret's voice slid up in surprise.

Ani waved him down. "Almost, Renloret, almost. I was born during an early spring blizzard, along with a lot of other children.

So something must have gone wrong if mother never told anyone about a twin."

Renloret interrupted, directing his comments to Taryn. "All right, let's assume Ani is correct and the twin was also born early. There were obviously complications. If the twin did not die—and I believe the Stones' assertions that she is still alive—and she was disabled in some way, then perhaps S'Hendale gave her to some hospital to care for while she raised Ani until she could be tested to verify that she was, indeed, The Blood."

"What if the twin had been The Blood and Ani was The Balance?" Taryn asked.

"No. Commander Chenakainet believed S'Hendale when she told him, shortly after Ani's birth, that *she* was The Blood. He also mentioned that S'Hendale said they had to wait until Ani was older before she could be tested and returned to Lrakira."

Renloret turned to Ani. "Isn't that what the commander said?"

Ani nodded. "Something like that. Evidently that's why they waited until I was five before they tested my blood for the first time. I'm sure I was attentive to every word *he* had to say," she muttered.

Renloret ignored her comment and focused on Taryn. "They had argued about waiting longer. The commander had wanted to leave as soon as his daughter was identified as the cure. But S'Hendale was adamant about waiting. Then the research center was attacked and Commander Chenakainet escaped to bring back help."

Taryn pulled out his notepad again. "Look, I have to take some notes. And whereas all this information is good, this speculation is not. We should focus on who might have information that is twenty-five years old. And pardon me but I have to use the Northern pronunciation of your mother's name, Ani. That S'Hendale stuff isn't as easy as Shendahl and that's the only one I've known your mother by."

He started scribbling down information as he verbally recapped. "Say we believe the Stones and Shendahl gave birth to twins. We know Ani was premature and there was concern for her survival. There should be some records at the research center because back then it was used as a hospital when there was an emergency. Only very serious patients were moved to the hospital in Saedi City. So we should check out what we can here first. We should talk with Melli too. She was pregnant with me at the same time. Ani, our mothers were best friends, even then, so they would have talked about everything."

Ani and Renloret each nodded.

"No wonder you're the youngest sheriff the valley has ever had. Good thing you didn't turn to opera for a career or we'd never get answers," Ani said.

"There was also less competition in the sheriff department than on the opera stage. I may not earn as much, but I don't have the travel expenses, either, or the publicity . . . unless aliens really do become a problem." He looked up from the notebook. "And you two are not going to be problems, are you?"

"No, sir." Ani and Renloret answered in unison.

With his sheriff face in place, Taryn stood. "Now that we have places to investigate and people to talk to, let's get some rest." Before either Ani or Renloret could comment, he took Ani's hand and pulled her toward the door. He waved at Renloret to remain seated. "I need to talk to her alone. Finish your tea before it gets cold."

Once on the porch, Taryn pulled her around to face him. In a harsh whisper he demanded, "Why in all the hells of Teramar did you kiss me like that?"

Ani tried to back away. He shook his head, keeping her close. Her eyes were wide, and he read only innocence.

She stuttered, "I . . . I . . . didn't know if you were alive or not. Even Renloret didn't know. We had no idea what kind of situation we would find here. I . . . missed you."

"Oh, Ani. You broke his heart with that kiss."

She jerked her hand out of his. "I did what?"

"He's in love with you, Ani."

"He is not."

"Yes, he is. If you haven't . . ." He sighed. "Hells, you haven't. Have you kissed him, really kissed him?"

"No!" The truth came out in a breathless whisper. "Oh, sure, we've hugged once or twice and even held hands, but nothing else."

"Have you even wanted to?" Taryn's voice was tender. "I thought after the dance that you would have."

She blushed. "Don't bring up the dance. It just confuses things."

He took her by the elbow and led her off the steps. "That dance made everything quite clear to all there. You even sang the duet with truth in your voice."

"I know, Taryn. But he had a mission to save an entire race of people. He couldn't get involved. We talked about it. I asked him to be my partner, several times."

"Really? And he turned you down?" Taryn nodded thoughtfully, respect for the pilot rising even higher. "He's a true soldier. He sticks with the mission in spite of his own feelings. I like him even better now." He placed a hand on Ani's shoulder. "After that welcome home kiss he's positive you love me."

"I do love you," she admitted.

Taryn smiled. "I know, but not the way he wants you to love him."

Silence slipped around them.

Taryn lifted her chin so he could look into her eyes. "Is Kela talking to you?"

She tilted her head toward the cabin. "No, though he's listening." She paused. "I can't just announce that I love him, Taryn. There's so much to do. A relationship will get in the way. We have to wait. My life has changed. I've changed. Taryn, I'm an alien!"

"And so is Renloret. Blades, you Lrakirans are about as slow as we Teramarans. He should have had time to say how he feels by now."

"No one is interested in that topic. They're all focused on the Stones now that my blood has saved them."

She frowned a bit petulantly, reminding him that even though she had reportedly saved an entire planet, she was still the Ani he had known all his life. "Are they really talking rocks?"

"They sing, not talk. It's an amazing feeling. It's different from the connection I have with Kela. Similar, certainly, but different.

I can feel Kela all the time . . . except when I woke up. That was terrible."

She shivered. Taryn put his arm across her shoulders and moved them back to the steps. When they sat down, Ani put her head on his shoulder.

"I thought I'd lost all of you—even Kela, because I couldn't feel him."

Taryn sat with his thoughts for a time. The situation was complex and fraught with problems. He realized that he had accepted the fantastic and implausible events of the past few months as real, and he knew he could handle anything that might happen in the future. He shifted into sheriff mode again and broke the silence. "We'll have to concoct some kind of story about why we're looking for your twin."

"True, and it could relate to her needing the vaccine." She looked back at the window. "I'm going to have to talk to Renloret, aren't I?"

"Yes. Not right now, though. We all need some rest. Take the bed. He can have the cot and I'll take the couch. Unless you want to bunk with him."

Her elbow hit fast.

"Ow! It was just a suggestion, Ani. It would answer some of the questions he won't ask."

"It would also be unfair, to all of us. You have no idea what I might do if I were in a bed with him." Ani stared out across the dark clearing.

Taryn stood and offered her a hand. "Oh, I can imagine, girl. Oh, and as soon as you get the chance, you should kiss him like you did me." He winked and nudged her toward the door.

He followed her inside just as Renloret straightened from readying blankets on the cot on the far side of the room.

"I located this and thought it would be appropriate to set it up. I also reinstalled the hanging to give you two some privacy."

As Renloret turned back to the cot, Taryn winked at Ani and whispered, "I told you so."

Ani rolled her eyes. "Thank you, Renloret, but Taryn will be on the couch, where he belongs."

CHAPTER TEN

The early morn sun warmed Renloret's face. Seated on the porch, his hands cupped around a steaming mug of tea, Renloret inhaled the freshness of the dawn. Kela arrived at his side and appeared to survey the clearing between the cabin and the trees. Yellow and blue flitters chirped and warbled their summer greetings. Soft sounds of conversation eked their way through the open door. The comfortableness of it all brought a smile to Renloret's face as he sipped his tea. He had chosen the piney-leafed concoction this time, wanting the taste and smell of trees instead of the invigorating sting of the cinnamon tea Ani often served.

He knew he could live on Teramar. After less than one mooncycle on the surface of this planet, he already knew it for home. It was more home than the Sancharos Mountains where he'd grown up.

Ani's laugh warmed him. He still hadn't figured out the relationship between Ani and Taryn. He had fully expected them to take the bed and leave him with the cot. Their morning behavior did not include any little touches or looks that one might expect of lovers reunited after several months. Perhaps he still had a chance at gaining her heart.

He took another swallow of tea and contemplated their mission. They had laid out a multipronged plan to find information on Ani's twin as quickly as possible, though they were going to delay the start of the plan until Taryn had checked on the number of people who were currently at the research center. Evidently, the scare of a plague that was decimating entire villages in Southern had spurred the Star Valley citizens into reactivating the medical research side of the center that had been abandoned for years.

While breaking their fast, Taryn had explained that the attack precipitating Ani's father's return to Lrakira had badly damaged only the front portion of the building, and after some months of basic cleanup and equipment moving, Ani's mother and uncle, along with some assistance from locals, had reopened a new clinic and regional hospital closer to the village. Whatever research they had been pursuing had been scaled back, and S'Hendale and Reslo had managed to curtail the number of advances coming from the research center, thereby making it seem as if the attack had worked. The military had left them alone to attend to local needs.

Kela nuzzled Renloret's arm, requesting attention. The pilot obliged. A low rumble of contentment issued from the canine's throat.

"I assume all is well with Ani?"

Kela winked once.

"Good," Renloret said. She had seemed nervous about being assigned to learn more about the circumstances of her birth by talking to Melli. No one wanted to speculate on her mother's thought processes until more was known about the actual event. Renloret knew Ani worried about the lives this news would change. She had already received a dramatic amount of information that had forever changed how she understood herself and her family. Renloret swallowed more tea.

Kela placed a paw on Renloret's leg and slapped a lick across the pilot's cheek.

Renloret heard Ani's voice before he saw her. "Kela, what have I said about licking?"

Renloret almost laughed at the glare of indignation the canine gave her.

"Pah!" Ani stomped her foot and made shooing motions with her hands. Without a look behind him, Kela pushed away from the pilot and trotted down the stairs as Ani took his place and rocked gently against Renloret's shoulder. "Good morn."

He felt his breath catch at her simple greeting and turned to look at her. The smile on her face lit her eyes. He recovered by sipping more tea and pretending to observe Kela as the canine made his rounds of the clearing perimeter before slipping between trees and disappearing from sight.

Ani nodded at the last wave of Kela's tail. "He'll be back in a few hours—I mean bells. Excuse me." She corrected her terminology to match Lrakiran standard.

"No need for that, Ani. I am now quite adjusted to Teramaran syntax and word usage." He didn't look at her. Instead he tried to concentrate on the piney tea or anything else other than how close she was to him and how hot his shoulder was.

"Really?" She giggled.

"Yes." He did not understand how being with her on the ship had been so different from this. They'd had plenty of time and proximity to each other during the trip back to Teramar to work out some reasonable understanding of their feelings about each other. Somehow they had failed to do that.

They sat silently sipping their tea, but Renloret was palpably aware of Ani's close proximity.

Taryn leaned against the doorjamb. Kela had long since left, and the pair of confused lovers sat next to each other, most likely contemplating the mission to find the mysterious twin and ignoring the need to resolve their mutual attraction. He shook his head. Melli was correct. Renloret was perfect for Ani and she for him. Hadn't his mother said theirs was a match ordained by the stars? He smiled at that. Melli didn't know they were both from the stars, aliens so like Teramarans that there were no apparent differences, right down to the blade culture and reverence for music and dance. Taryn had promised himself he would broach the subject of these similarities once the twin was found. He knew Renloret had similar questions, but they had all managed to stay focused on the mission during their conversations that morn and the previous eve.

The Balance

How was he going to get these two to acknowledge their mutual attraction *and* find the twin? Surely, other topics could be brought forward and dealt with when they had successfully completed their mission. He wanted Ani to be happy. In fact, he would do anything to support her happiness, even if it meant he would lose her—possibly forever. And he was positive that Renloret would make her happy. Having the pilot's stability and personal support would enable her to deal with the family consequences that were sure to be even more complicated with the addition of a sibling.

The sun topped the trees and the porch was fully bathed in its rays. Taryn walked up behind the pair and reached over their heads to take the empty mugs from their hands. Without a word, he reentered the cabin and began to wash the dishes, leaving the pair to soak in the brilliance of the sun and the songs of the flitters.

Ani finally shook herself from the reverie. "We'd best review Taryn's plan again." Placing her hand on Renloret's thigh, she pushed herself to a standing position, held out a hand to offer Renloret assistance, and steeled herself for the skin-to-skin contact. Why did that cause her heart to beat faster? She had just spent almost an hour shoulder to shoulder with him as the sun rose above the trees. They hadn't talked much, which was fine with her. Just being next to him was an odd mix of pleasure and wariness.

She released his hand to keep him from feeling her tremble. Again, the frustration welled up. Taryn's comments about her and Renloret had touched a nerve last eve. Oh, she certainly wanted Renloret. But how could she encourage such an arrangement when she was unsure of her own identity or the makeup of her family? Too many unresolved issues were making her personal life miserable. She'd barely slept thinking about it all.

She was at least relieved that Taryn not only harbored no jealousy towards Renloret but also approved of her feelings towards the pilot. She had not considered how it would look when she had kissed Taryn so fervently upon seeing him, but she had been so relieved to actually see that he was alive and well, it had been an instinctual response. She grimaced. Taryn was no longer her lover. She had made sure of that even before she had recognized how attracted she was to Renloret. Taryn was a good friend. Perhaps her twin and Taryn would wind up on the same blade. That was a comforting thought. But she also wondered how the girl would react when she was found.

Had she and her twin been identical or fraternal? Would they look alike? How would the twin feel about having her life turned inside out with the knowledge that not only did she have a different "real" family, but that she was an alien from another galaxy so far away you could barely discern its star through a telescope.

Ani was excited to show off her knowledge of the reality that was beyond Teramar's simple star, asteroid belt, and five planets. Would her twin believe the truth? Would she willingly come to Lrakira to save the life of a true alien? If she didn't come on her own, Ani knew that she would find a way to abduct her, take her to Lrakira, and demand she pull the blade from the Anyala Stone. Then the twin would understand, and they could begin to build a relationship between themselves and their father.

Ani shivered. *Her father.* Due to the time bubble the Stones had sung, he was barely eleven years older than she. Ani found it interesting that this bothered her more than the knowledge that she was an alien. How would the twin feel about it? This was a mess.

"Oh, there you are!" Taryn said, greeting them when they came inside as if they'd been gone for hours.

Ani glared at him. Renloret did not respond but moved to the table and began sifting through the sheaf of papers Taryn had placed there.

She perused the room. The dishes had been done and the cot and other bedding had been put away. She couldn't hide a grimace as she realized they'd been sitting on the porch a fair piece of time.

Renloret looked up from Taryn's notes. "Do you think we should do this today?" He tapped the stack of papers.

"No. There's still some prep I need to do." Taryn gathered the papers into one stack and stuffed them into a pack.

"What kind of preparation?" Ani asked.

"Well, I need to find out just how many of the old research center staff have returned since you three left. Quite a few of those who worked alongside your mother fifteen to twenty years ago have returned and they might remember something about a twin—if Shendahl said or wrote anything about her in the work environment.

"I also want to do some background checks on the newest employees to be sure they are not connected with the military. After what Dalkey did at the cemetery and research center, I doubt that the military would risk stirring up more trouble. Even so, I want to be sure that a spy has not slipped in."

"Did you have any trouble with the milits after we left?"

"All of them were present when Dalkey showed them the blade box and talked about aliens disappearing into it, so they weren't too reluctant about leaving." Taryn grinned. "And I made sure no one actually saw Dalkey's body. They all took my word for what happened. I took down their names and said that if I ever found out they were back in Star Valley I would arrest them for aiding and abetting Dalkey in his disobedience of the restraining order. They left quietly, and I haven't heard a snitch since.

"And with them gone, Star Valley got back to normal quicker than I thought it would. The official report states that the general had burned your mother's body to get rid of evidence but had retained the blade and its box as a form of trophy. I mentioned that the ceremonial blade was returned to its rightful owner. Mroz was outraged about the casket and illegal cremation and kindly offered to rebuild the casket. We held a simple ceremony to rebury it about two weeks after you left. Mother has been taking flowers to the grave every week since to honor her friend until Ani returned from Southern to participate in an official ceremony." He turned a questioning look at Ani.

"I guess I'll have to schedule one now that I'm back from *Southern*." She bit her lower lip.

"It doesn't have to be right now. Mother will expect you to

discuss the arrangements with her at some point, and she'll want to be part of the ceremony. She will also want to hear your impressions of your family's Southern village. Your parents and their coworkers were always rather tight-lipped about details."

"Of course," Ani said as she sat down. "But what should I say? I've never been to Southern, only to a planet in a galaxy way off out there." She waved a hand above her head. "She'll know if I lie."

Renloret shook his head. "You don't have to lie, Ani. You can even mention seeing some rockets because Southern has been launching satellites, and everyone on Northern knows about them. In fact, I bet Northern is trying to duplicate the feat. You can say I took you to one of the launchings as a tourist. I'm sure Taryn would enjoy hearing about that." Renloret looked encouragingly at Taryn.

Taryn nodded but cautioned, "Just don't tell her about the Stones. Talking rocks won't go over very well. And don't say a thing about your father, either. She'll think you really are sick or something."

"What do you mean, 'really sick'?" Ani asked.

"Well, you weren't exactly in the best frame of mind when you ran away from their house to kill an insane military general."

"Oh, that." She grimaced and shrugged her shoulders. "What did you tell your parents when I didn't return with you?"

"Um, I thought it best that Mother and Father know you were still alive, so I told them you were just not thinking straight. They were okay with Renloret taking you to Southern to recover from Dalkey's stalking you and digging up your mother's grave, as well as checking to see if your blood could save members of Renloret's village. Oh, Renloret . . . you will have to use the same story or this won't work. You took her home to Southern where her extended family assisted in her mental recovery and her blood stopped whatever disease was the problem."

Renloret nodded. "Well, I did take her home. That basic story is general enough to be correct, but how do we explain this twin thing?"

Taryn shrugged. "I'm working on that. But I've got to check on how deep the new staff has explored before you, Renloret, can get to the records room." He turned to Ani. "Or we need to come up with a reason for Renloret to have returned with you, Ani, to find the twin. I think it will take a few days to set everything up. I'll forewarn Mother and Father as well. They'll cooperate with anything we come up with—unless it has to do with aliens.

"So, Renloret, where did you put the ship?" Taryn was obviously ready to move on to other subjects.

"In the launch room."

"Did you run across any people?"

"Nothing appeared to have changed since we left and no one confronted us. Kela did not find any trace of other intruders either."

"Good. All right, I need you two to stay up here a few days while I prepare the residents for the return of a healthy Ani and her . . . blade partner." He smiled at the expression on Ani's face. "I think I have this figured out. Both of you will be training for the regional blade ring competition, which is scheduled for the last week of summer."

Ani tried to interrupt, but Taryn stopped her. "You can't complain about this, Ani. You're the one who introduced Renloret as your student at the spring dance." He looked at her as a parent would look at a child he was instructing. "You're healed now and your parent's village is safe, so you've come back to finish what the two of you started. Got it?"

"Got it, Sheriff," she said with a heavy sigh, resigned to follow the plan. It was not often that she could shake him from a plan.

"Finally! Now behave and start practicing. I'll work on the twin angle and let you know." He grabbed his pack and headed for the door.

"But this won't—"

"Ani, this is the only way it will work. Renloret, I'm relying on you to make it work. You're blade partners now. I'll make sure to enter you both. There is a mixed pairs division this time, so it's perfect."

Under her breath Ani said, "Hopefully, we won't be here that long."

"Ani!" Taryn got her attention. "It will work on a lot of levels. You've got to play along with your original announcement as to why Renloret was with you."

She held her hands up in surrender.

He turned to Renloret with narrowed eyebrows and determination in his eyes. "You, pilot, will pay attention to the differences in competition rules. I expect to witness a mock match in the village by the end of next week. Star Valley has several participants, and we will be running full practice sessions for the coming months. You both will be there."

Renloret smiled and offered the proper Northern blade salute.

"Nice start," Taryn replied.

"How long will it take you to set everything into motion?" Ani asked. She doubted she could last more than a few days of constant contact with Renloret before she cracked and told him how she felt. That would be a heavy distraction, and the Stone needed the twin more than Ani needed to reveal her feelings to Renloret.

"A couple of days at the most. I'll let you know." Taryn stepped onto the porch. "Keep that tel-com on and check it at least once a day."

"Yes, sir," Ani said, giving a sharp salute.

Taryn rolled his eyes. "Love you too." Then he waved and jogged across the clearing to the trailhead.

CHAPTER ELEVEN

Sweat dripped down his neck, soaking into the fabric of the exercise tunic and expanding the dark stain that would soon reach the middle of his chest. Renloret shifted to the next position, holding it for three full breaths. He lowered his torso, touching his forehead to his knees, and wrapped both arms around his calves. He could hear Ani's slower breathing and envied her control. It had been a long time since he had performed a full Jinma set. He relished the feel of his leg muscles and lower back lengthening. They had been tight after the run.

Ani's voice came muffled through her leggings and the tightness with which she held the pose. "Release and finish."

A glass of water and a small towel appeared at his feet as he extended upward and out to return his arms to his sides. "My thanks."

Ani raised her glass to him. "Well done, pilot. That was the warm-up. Let's go choose the arsenal." She stepped lightly up the stairs to the cabin.

Renloret toweled off the sweat, drained his glass of water, and followed. It had taken Ani only a few chimes to outfit both of them. He assumed he was wearing the same tunic he had worn during their first workout. How long ago? At some moments it seemed an eternity and at others it seemed they had just met. Renloret decided it was most likely both. He entered the cabin.

Ani was sorting through the drawer in which she kept a variety of blades. She took some out and placed them on the table. One had a blade with two slicing edges and a nasty row of curved hooks designed to make removing the weapon either impossible or extremely painful. He swallowed and grimaced at the imagined pain and damage it would cause. He picked it up.

"I thought so," Ani said.

"What is this?" he asked as he examined the unique blade. It was masterfully constructed.

"Uncle Reslo's invention. I don't think he gave it a name. He's a highcraft blade maker. The milits pay a tremendous amount for custom blades—mostly officers, but he's had a few foot soldiers with wealthy families who wanted them to have the best. His are the finest on Northern."

The weight and balance of the unusual blade was exquisite. "May I?"

"Here." She handed him a sheath. "Boot, thigh, bicep, or waist strap?" She reached into the second drawer.

Renloret tried to imagine using such a weapon. He knew he did not want to face a similar one. "Bicep."

"Also guessed correctly." She tossed him two straps. "You'll have to practice with it so you don't injure yourself. It's an unknown weapon, and I would not suggest using it in the blade ring unless you want to inflict lethal damage. To my knowledge, there are only three in existence. I've never had the opportunity to use it, though I wish I had thought of it when I went after Dalkey at the research center."

Renloret shivered at the memory. "The sword was weapon enough, Ani."

"I suppose. Oh, you can strap it for top or bottom draw." She returned to the first drawer, pulled out a pair of triple-pronged hooks, and after a brief hesitation, put the hooks back. "I'd suggest you try a bottom draw. There's a magnetic lining in the sheath, so no catch is needed. I'll set up some targets for throwing practice later. In the meantime, let's go with straight blades." All her leg and wrist sheaths were loaded as she grinned up at him. "Ready?"

He slid the unusual blade into its magnetic sheath and set it next to the straps for fitting later. Then he quickly made his choices and followed her to the clearing in front of the cabin.

She stood with her back to him—still and loose. He watched her hands tighten to fists and waited. She turned to face him, a frown on her face. "This won't work. To get this right, I'll have to show you the blade room." Her bottom lip pushed out in a pout.

"More tunnels," Ani said, brushing past to enter the cabin. She went directly to the necessary room, and he watched her press a tile to the right of the door. The towel cabinet retreated and slid silently out of the way. "I always thought these were the only secret places we had. I never imagined the tunnels from the lake house to the research center. Come on. I'll take you to one of my childhood training facilities."

Renloret followed. The cabinet closed on its own. A set of stairs led down several flights in near spiral formation to a landing Renloret assumed was directly under the cabin. The short hallway ended in a double door covered in intricate carvings. Renloret recognized the similarity to the designs on the doors at the lake house and on Lrakira.

"Who carved the door?" he asked, curious.

"Probably one of the members of the original research team. I'm pretty sure it was neither of my parents nor my uncle. I have in mind who it might have been but I can't remember her name. She got sick and I think she died a couple of years after Father left. Mother was quite upset. She said something about wishing the woman had waited a few more years."

Renloret contemplated that. "Do you suppose she got pregnant and you weren't old enough to provide the correct blood for a vaccine?"

"Perhaps. Mother only said that if everyone had patience, time would fix everything."

Renloret shook his head. "The Stones were working on time as fast as they could. I think they were expecting to be told the moment you were born. They would have sung the time-song then and aged everyone at the same time. But communications were not always good, and when your father returned to Lrakira six years later, he was surprised that it was the first anyone knew about you. And you were already five."

"So if the Stones had known about me sooner, my family

might have aged at the same time and my mother might not have died?"

"As you said, *might*. I guess we'll never know," Renloret said, his voice soft. He changed the subject. "Do you know when this was completed?" An arm sweep indicated the secret passage and room ahead.

"I assume around the time the cabin was built. I've known about it all my life." She pushed the doors open. "This is where I had my first blade lesson. Where I blooded my mother and heard the Song of Healing for the first time. Where I learned everything my mother and my uncle could teach me about blades and the 'Southern' methods of competitions. Of course, I now assume all that talk about Southern was a lie and it really was Lrakiran traditions I was being trained in. But they were similar to Northern styles." She walked across the room, the lighting brightening to show the expanse of it.

Renloret gave a low whistle as he took in the three full training rings. There were rows of audience seating around the central ring. Traditional Lrakiran weapon stands flanked each ring. Long and short swords alternated with sabers and foils in the racks. The room seemed to be waiting for activity, inviting combatants or trainers and students. Though on a smaller scale, this could have been any training room on Lrakira. Renloret gazed upward. Along one wall, banners hung proclaiming Lrakiran championships with names, places, and records. On the opposite wall, Teramaran banners were similarly draped, though they did not spell out the individual accomplishments.

Renloret pointed to the first set. "Those are Lrakiran, Ani."

She glanced up and harrumphed. "I grew up being told they were from my parents' home on Southern. They called it the Lrakira District. They never said a thing about an alien planet called Lrakira, and I never questioned them." She shrugged. "Now that I've been to Lrakira, I see the similarity to the banners that were hanging in the ring where my blade skills were tested. I guess that's yet another point to discuss with Yenne." She walked to the other side of the ring, shaking out her arms.

Renloret tried to get rid of the sudden unease that shivered through his body. The similarities between the two distant planets were unnerving. It could not be mere chance. How could the original research team not have questioned the similarities? He tried to push his own questions aside. Only one problem at a time could be solved. Perhaps that was why the original team never asked—they were trying to solve one problem, the survival of their species, first and foremost. They made the best decision for the immediate circumstances and they took advantage of the opportunities those similarities offered. Renloret had to commend their efforts. He needed to do exactly what he suspected they had been doing—stay focused and solve the problems in front of him. He could turn his attention to the shared societal traditions once they successfully completed their immediate mission to find Ani's twin.

Ani stepped into the central ring. "This is how it will go. Wait there until I announce you, then walk to the center of the blue section of the ring and give me the salute."

Renloret adjusted his blades and watched in fascination as Ani became a competition referee.

The Balance

She stood quiet for a few breaths, then she raised her arms overhead and turned slowly, acknowledging an imagined audience. He could almost hear the cheers. She then saluted and bowed to the four directions.

"Gents and ladies, welcome to today's first game. From the red I give you Anyala Chenak, a district and regional youth champion in all age brackets in staff, sword, and short blade. She placed second in foil at her last regional youth competition at the age of seventeen. She was a pairs champion at the age of twenty with Taryn Avere in sword and short blade. They qualified for and won the continental championships pair's competitions in sword in the twenty-three to twenty-eight age bracket two years ago. That same year, Miss Chenak became Northern's first female singles short blade champion. She now instructs hand-to-hand, staff, and short blade at the Saedi City Military University. Please welcome her back to the competition ring."

She pointed at the red section of the ring, giving a salute to the currently invisible combatant. She then turned around several times using her arms to encourage applause from the make-believe audience before turning to face Renloret. He smiled widely at her showmanship and acting ability.

She now waved her hands to quiet the imagined crowd. "Gents and ladies, it is my honor to introduce Miss Chenak's first opponent. From Southern's Lrakira District and the village of Awarna, please give a big Northern welcome to Renloret." She grinned. "He's so famous there, he does not have a familial lineage name. He's an award-winning troubadour in opera and folk, and from what he tells us, he has placed well in several blade ring battles in both local and district games. We don't know if he even qualified for Southern's continental competitions, but we will take his word for it . . . this time." She waved her hands from side to side. "Now, now, folks. The boos are uncalled for. Let's try this again." She motioned for him to enter the ring.

Renloret clucked his tongue against his cheek trying not to laugh. He leapt into the ring, skidding on the thin layer of sand covering the surface. Regaining his balance, he executed a Northern blade salute to Ani, then turned and waved exuberantly at the audience, bouncing from foot to foot.

Ani rolled her eyes and chuckled. "All right, Renloret, you get the gist of the introduction phase. You'll have to provide a lineal name and list of awards or placements in competitions they can read, even if we have to invent them. If you don't, you'll get something close to what I did. Announcers can be painfully creative. Fortunately, I performed with enough skill that the disparaging remarks were short-lived.

"After the introduction, the bladers approach the referee for instructions and salute their opponents. You'll keep your mouth shut during this even if you're taunted, understand?"

"No different than on Lrakira. Taunting is unsporting behavior anywhere."

She nodded sharply. "I'll give the instructions and then we'll commence with hand-to-hand. Ready?"

Renloret straightened. Giving her as steely a look as possible, he matched her salute with some level of decorum.

She did not smile. "This is hand-to-hand. No weapons will be pulled or shown. This is a timed bout and single points will be earned for honest contact. A takedown is five points, a pin is ten, and a knockout wins regardless of point totals."

"Really? Regardless of total points?"

She didn't laugh. "Yes. Am I to assume that if you knock out your opponent it does not necessarily mean you win on Lrakira?"

"Knockouts are twenty-five points on Lrakira. Though it is rare, I have seen a few matches where the one getting knocked out actually wins in total points."

She shrugged. "Don't get knocked out here."

"All right."

She saluted again and backed away. He mirrored her movements.

"You didn't say how long the bout is."

"Long enough." She took two small steps and launched her feet at his head.

He staggered backward just far enough to avoid a blow to his head, but not far enough to avoid the impact on his shoulder. He felt rather than saw the next kick coming. He tucked and rolled into her rather than away from her, and as she recovered, he swept his foot, hitting her at the ankles. She crashed to the sand, her breath rushing out. Renloret stood up and watched her struggle to breathe.

"Five points to you. That's the second time you've done that." Her voice was barely a whisper and tight with pain.

He offered her a hand. "Practice, remember." He remembered the takedown in front of the cabin barely two days after meeting her.

A tight smile graced her lips as she took the proffered hand.

Once on her feet she said, "Hand-to-hand until the next takedown, then thirty with short blade, then thirty more of running. We'll end with stretches and maybe a soak."

He agreed with an abbreviated salute. They squared off and began again.

CHAPTER TWELVE

It was well past midday when they started down the path leading to the lake house. But Ani veered off shortly after entering the trees, pushing through several lengths of heavy underbrush toward an outcropping of rocks. The trees gave way to a spectacular view of Star Valley from the edge of a substantial cliff below the boulder field. A faint trail wound along the edge of the rockfall for several paces before crossing to a narrow slit between boulders from which a small waterfall cascaded.

Renloret paused briefly to take in the view. A silvery road snaked through the patterned patchwork of cultivated fields, outlining the farms on the outskirts of the village. Towering peaks surrounding the valley were dusted with a warning of snow, reminding him of the Sancharos Mountains on Lrakira.

A few loose rocks on the edge of the path threatened his footing. He had been caught up in the view instead of watching where the path went and now had to catch his balance against the large boulders that formed the uphill side of the path. They were warm to the touch though they were shadowed in the late afternoon light. He reasoned that only an internal thermal spring large enough to heat a section of the mountain could account for that. Ani had said something about a hot spring after he'd recovered from the crash, but time had not allowed a visit. He hadn't soaked in a natural hot spring since he'd left home to become a pilot and eagerly turned his attention to Ani and the anticipated soak.

The spicy scent of minerals tickled his nose, and he noticed that the rocks closest to the waterfall displayed mosses and ferns usually seen in more tropical environs. Multicolored stains painted the rocks and pebbles under the clear water. He categorized the minerals and salts by color and smell. The combination would be therapeutic and quite enjoyable if the temperature wasn't too high.

Ani motioned him to follow her into a large slit in the rock face where the stream exited to make its run down the mountain. Expecting the coolness of a cave, he was instead wrapped in comfortable steamy warmth as he entered the darkness. Ani lit a torch, illuminating the narrow passageway that looked to have been artificially enlarged. The stream ran along one side of the tunnel before spilling out across the boulders. A stack of torches lay on a long shelf carved into the tunnel wall. Renloret reached for one.

Ani smiled, shaking her head. "One will do." She moved off down the tunnel.

Renloret shrugged and followed.

The burbling chatter of flowing water became louder as the

tunnel turned left and widened dramatically to reveal a large cavern with several steaming pools. Ani moved along the right wall, jumped the overflow from the first pool, and stopped at the much larger and deeper second. She pointed at several stone benches. Closer inspection revealed that the simply designed seating had been masterfully carved out of the rock. Niches at shoulder height had also been cut into the cavern wall, each holding several folded wraps. The lone torch gave out a soft light, which reflected off the white crystals coating the ceiling and was diffused by the steam clouds rising from the numerous pools.

"We came here after most of our training sessions and sometimes just to relax. Mother loved it. Always said she felt like she was at home here. It's been in use since I was very little, but it's been a while since I was last here. Not much has changed, and fortunately, no animals have moved in." She gave him a crooked grin as she removed her jacket and footwear.

Renloret waited. Desire welled as he wondered if she'd remove anything else while he watched. He quickly pushed away the thought. They were here only to ease the stress of overworked muscles. He took a deep breath of the moist mineral laden air.

"What are you waiting for?" She'd turned arched eyebrows at him.

"Do you really want to know?" He didn't know if he was sweating because of the heat or because of her.

She shook her head, blushing. "No." She pointed at the larger pool. "You can use this one. Swim a few laps."

"And you?" He sat on a bench and slipped off the shirt, now damp from the steam.

She turned her back on him, the blush deepening. "An upper pool, over there." She gestured toward the heavier steam billowing in the back of the cavern. "It's smaller. Don't stay in too long. I'll let you know when I am coming back so you can get out. Use these towels to dry off." She gestured to the niches, then climbed up a series of wide terraces, her bare feet sluicing through the runoff from the upper pool.

He watched the steam wrap around her as she climbed. When he could no longer see her, he disrobed, grabbed one of the towels, and moved to the edge of the pool. After tentatively testing the temperature, he slipped into the waist deep water and sucked in a breath as the salts found their way into every scrape and cut. Thankfully, the sting was quickly numbed by the heat. He moved toward the center, testing the depth. When the water reached chin high he relaxed, leaned back to float, and closed his eyes. A deep slow inhale and exhale helped him center his thoughts on the present state of his muscles enough to nudge out the flickers of desire that continued to tickle at the edges of his mind.

This single pool was larger than any of Lrakira's Sancharos' mineral springs. It would take ten or more strokes to swim across this one. The temperature was perfect, though it increased the closer he floated to the upper pool's spillage, indicating a much hotter spring above. He opened his eyes to study the area Ani had disappeared to. Steam wafted thickly in the soft torchlight.

He wondered who else knew about these springs. Did Taryn? Had they been here together? How was he, Renloret, going to tell Ani how he felt about her? He genuinely liked Taryn and didn't want to intrude on their relationship. From his observation they seemed very comfortable with each other—more comfortable than he felt when he was around Ani, especially when it was just the two of them. He tried to convince himself it was just because Ani and Taryn had grown up together. But how could he compete with a relationship that already spanned twenty-five years?

Renloret flipped to his stomach and took a few strokes. Muscles complained slightly but settled down again as he continued across the pool. It felt good to stretch in the heated water. He grabbed the edge and pulled himself out, turning to sit and dangle his feet. He examined his shin and calf. The line of stitch scars puckered now with moisture. He'd have these reminders for a very long time. The medics on Lrakira had offered to remove them, but he had refused. They were a visual reminder of the mission that had saved his people, and he did not want to forget. He slipped back into the pool and stroked smoothly across to the bench. After wrapping the towel and tucking the end firmly at his waist, he began a slow series of meditation moves.

Ani floated on the gently bubbling surface, trying not to think about the pilot in the pool below. It was more difficult than she'd imagined. Her thoughts turned to the sense of attraction rather than the object of the attraction. She tried to analyze it. Why now? Why him? Why here? She felt her body heat rise with desire at the very thought of him—not from the heat of the pool.

Trying to push him out of her mind, she concentrated on the changing pattern of steam in the pale, soft light reflected by the single torch. The steam and light had taken on an unusual green tinge.

What was it about that color that bothered her? She had seen it before. It had surrounded the crash site when she had pulled Renloret out as well as when she had retrieved the info vials and readers he wanted. How many weeks ago? So much had happened since then. As the water rippled across her back, she sighed, wanting to ask him to join her—in more ways than this simple soaking. She considered an image of him laying across the office desk at the lake house, reaching for her, his eyes evening blue with desire.

Careful, little one. I can hear you.

Kela! Stop eavesdropping. She stood up brushing the water from her face.

I wasn't even trying, Ani. Your thoughts are so loud and you're so . . . relaxed. He chuckled.

Ani slapped the water. *Can't I think without getting interrupted?*

You call that thinking? Oh my, girl, we do need to talk. He laughed again, his mind voice full of caring and teasing.

She returned the tone in kind with a hint of defensiveness. *Yes, we do need to talk, but after we've found the twin. We need to resolve this situation and then, with luck, he'll want to come back to Teramar and we can explore these unreasonable feelings.*

These are not unreasonable feelings, Ani. They are real and you will have to face them before too long. Your experience with Taryn has not prepared you for this pilot.

Ani swiped at the water again. *And just who's supposed to prepare me? You?* She waded to the pool's edge and climbed out. After toweling off and wrapping the damp towel firmly around her body, she threw the pile of clothes over her arm and stomped toward the lower pools.

Aren't you forgetting something?

What?

The pilot.

The simple statement stopped Ani in her tracks, halfway down the stairway.

"Oh," she whispered as she looked directly at Renloret's back. He was walking toward the bench, water glistening off his skin in the diffused torchlight. For some reason, seeing him nude while unconscious and injured after the crash was completely different from what she was seeing now. She could hardly get a breath and her heart seemed to be leaping and bucking erratically, like a freshly caught fish. As her eyes rested on his chiseled waist and tight buttocks, her hands ached to test their firmness. Movement of the towel drew her eyes up to the muscles rippling across his shoulders and arms as he dried off, wrapped the towel about his waist, and began to stretch. Biting her lip to keep from verbally expressing the wave of desire that rushed her blood through her veins, Ani tried unsuccessfully to avert her gaze.

Back up, girl, before he turns around.

Kela's order cooled her like a dip in the lake at mid-winter. She hastily did as instructed until steam concealed what she desired and common sense prevailed. *Where are you that you can see what's going on?*

She was perturbed when he wouldn't tell her but again followed his advice when he suggested she warn the pilot of her impending return. "Renloret?"

The steam concealed his reaction from her though she felt Kela laugh. *What's so funny?*

Nothing.

"I'll be ready shortly, Ani."

Over the sound of the running water, she heard him muttering in what she now knew was the Lrakiran language, not Southern. He seemed to be using a list of curses she did recognize.

You could get dressed, too, little one. Kela still sounded smug.

Right, I could. But perhaps I want to know what he'd do if I walked over to him with just a towel wrapped around me. She didn't want to follow commonsense protocol.

That would be cruel.

More like interesting, I think. Maybe I will. She was warming up to the idea, getting excited about the possibilities. Why should she obey a dog?

Don't do something just because you are frustrated or angry with me.

With a sigh she pulled on her pants, dropped the towel, and slipped into the wrap top.

Kela snickered. *Better.*

"You can come down now." Renloret sounded as if he was talking through clenched teeth.

"Are you all right?" she asked as she emerged from the steam.

Renloret was seated on one of the benches holding a foot. "Stubbed my toe."

Giggling, Ani walked over, knelt in front of him, and pulled his foot out from his grasp to look it over. Sure enough, the tip of the largest was red. She rubbed it. A hiss issued from Renloret. "Poor thing. It didn't have a chance. Maybe this will help." She leaned close and gave the toe a gentle kiss.

A different kind of hiss came from Renloret as he jerked the foot from her grasp.

Kela's comment was immediate. *Talk about cruel!*

She knew it had been a foolish move but hadn't been able to stop herself. Now she sent a blistering list of curse words to Kela in two languages. Then before she could kiss more than his toe, she stood and slapped Renloret on the shoulder. "Buck up, pilot. We should get back to the cabin and check in with Taryn. He'll be wondering where we are."

Ani turned her back on Renloret and strode toward the stream outlet. "You can bring the torch." She disappeared into the tunnel without daring to turn around to see if he followed.

It was all she could do to not turn around and show him exactly what she desired. She pushed the pace while forcing her thoughts away from her attraction to the man behind her and tried to keep them on the mission she had promised to fulfill. Using as few words as possible once at the cabin, she directed Renloret to set the table while she fixed the eve meal. Fortunately, Taryn arrived shortly after, and Ani was able to relax a bit.

The dinner conversation revolved around Taryn's process of setting up the residents of Star Valley for Ani's and Renloret's return from Southern. The sheriff had also adroitly dropped hints at the newly reopened research center that Ani and her

Southern companion had returned from Southern and would be doing some research of their own in older records to see if her mother had mentioned the virus to which Ani had immunity and whether there had been concern of it showing up in Star Valley. They wrapped up the eve with a basic plan to visit the research center in the morn.

Throughout the eve, Ani had managed to evade direct questions from Taryn about the blade practice by saying she had introduced Renloret to the blade ring procedures and that he had executed each exercise well enough to avoid being a disgrace in the ring with an opponent. The noncommittal smile that accompanied the reddening of Renloret's face had, to Ani's dismay, momentarily focused Taryn's attention squarely on *her*, and to escape another porch lecture or interrogation, Ani pushed the need to move forward with the search for her twin. That managed to redirect Taryn's attention to the mission at hand and away from her, a critical diversion because she was finding it more and more difficult to hide the raw lustfulness of her attraction to Renloret.

When Taryn conveniently suggested they retire for the eve, she could barely excuse herself fast enough to hide behind the blanket curtain that separated the bed from the rest of the room.

She heard Renloret's "Sleep deep, Ani," before snuggling under the blanket and closing her eyes, wishing for quite different circumstances.

CHAPTER THIRTEEN

Isul Treyder looked up when the door knock disrupted his focus on the work in front of him. The sheriff entered, followed by two people.

"Doctor Treyder?" The sheriff asked.

He stood. "Yes?" Had he been found out already?

"My apologies for the interruption. I need to introduce you to some people."

Treyder froze a neutral expression on his face when he offered a high bow to the young woman at the Southerner's side as she was introduced.

Thanks to extensive practice, he was able to keep his voice even and his face neutral as he greeted her. "You're all grown up, Miss Chenak." Perhaps that would throw her off.

"Should I know you?"

He pasted on a smile meant to relax his opponent even as his mind raced toward panic. What in all the hells of Teramar was she doing here? Would she remember anything about the cavern?

"I think it unlikely, though we did cross paths at company gatherings occasionally when you were still in local schooling. I worked with your mother until about five years ago. She was a gifted physician and researcher. I was sorry to hear of her death. We will miss her." He could allow her to know he had once respected her mother even though he had celebrated her death, which had come too soon for his purposes. "I didn't get a chance to offer my condolences. Please accept them now." He bowed a second time, more deeply.

She responded with a similar bow and thanked him. She didn't seem to recognize his voice. Good. When he bought the contraband, he had been told that the poison would impact her memory as well as slow her reaction time. Just how much did she remember? Not even the sound of his voice seemed to set her off. But would the missing memory effect be permanent? He fervently hoped so. He noticed her eyes flicking to the two men as if asking permission for her next words. Both men smiled at her, and when she turned her attention back to him, she asked what projects he had worked on with her mother. He gave her a rather brief and vague explanation about how her mother had steered him towards mechanical design because she had noticed his expertise in that area. Then he smoothly changed the subject to avoid further disclosure. Too much information might spoil his cover.

When he asked how he might assist them, the nosy little sheriff answered, "We're looking for Doctor Tezak Ganevek. I was told you might know where he is."

Treyder thought a moment, trying to place the local physician who had allowed him to return to the valley not fully aware of the reasons he had left or of the reasons for his desire to return. "Ah, I believe he is ensconced in the third lab on the right, across from his office. At least, he stated he was headed there this morn." He wondered why they were searching out the local doctor. Had he assisted in the removal of the device?

"Doctor Ganevek agreed to help us locate some notes from Miss Chenak's mother. We may need to access some of the older sections of the building for that research. I also wanted to make you aware that Miss Chenak and Renloret will be in and out of the building over the coming weeks."

Treyder did his best to cover his fear with professionalism. "Will you need access to all the labs?" The last thing he needed was for them to discover his little collection of machines and deduce his connection to the green-eyed Miss Chenak's near demise.

"Don't worry. They're not interested in bothering anyone's current research. It's a personal matter."

"I'm only just beginning to renew my research. If you are interested, I could show you." He wasn't sure he could keep the waver from his voice as he offered to show them his life's work, work that Miss Chenak had unexpectedly participated in so recently. Even if she didn't remember a single thing, the reputation of the sheriff was enough to cause some concern. Maybe if he was willing to show things to them, they would view him as just another member of the research team. After all, they were at the facility to see Doctor Ganevek, not him.

Thankfully, the sheriff declined the offer by saying they were on a tight timeline and gestured his two companions towards the door.

"Yes, yes, of course. Perhaps you will find the time later. In fact, later would be better. I will be further along and able to demonstrate its uses."

He tried not to seem too eager to get them out of his office. When they left, closing the door behind them, he took a breath and concentrated on slowing his racing heart. He was happy that the chance meeting had provided some proof that even in tiny amounts, such as those administered through his nick to Miss Chenak's cheek in the cavern, the poison could profoundly impact a person's memory. His imagination began to race almost as fast as his heart. He inhaled slowly and refocused on his interaction with the trio. Though entirely too close for comfort, he had at least demonstrated just the right amount of interest and eagerness to avoid arousing suspicions. The money spent on blade training had paid off in steadying his temperament and reactions. He was calmer now than when he had faced Ms. Chenak in the caverns. He opened the door a crack and checked the hallway. Empty. Before returning to his desk, he locked the door.

He would have been delighted to have some time alone with Miss Chenak to discuss her experience with the device, even though he knew this was impossible. But how could he get the answers to his questions without involving the victim of his experiment? He needed another specimen. He pulled out a sheet of paper and began to make notes.

If the poison had mangled her memory, why wasn't she in a coma? Had the device malfunctioned? When he'd left her lying on the cavern floor, she had appeared to be slipping into the coma as expected. But he'd left before he was sure because he had heard her friends approaching the cavern. If he had stayed longer, he would have been caught. And that was not part of the plan. He stopped writing.

Tapping his pen against his teeth, he tried to remember what the gossip was concerning Miss Chenak's whereabouts. He'd only arrived at the research complex two weeks ago and had been busy with moving equipment into his new lab space, so he really had not paid much attention at the time. He thought that if he expressed too much interest in the Chenak girl, his connection to the young woman's coma might be discovered. It was something about her being taken to Southern to assist with a disease. But if the device had been working, she would not have been much help. And no one had mentioned her being in a coma.

He smiled as he concluded that the disease story was more likely a cover-up by her uncle to have the comatose girl taken to Southern for care and treatment. Treyder wondered when the doctors on Southern had found and removed the device. The Miss Chenak who was in his office moments ago had exuded health. He beat down the frantic need to know. Why hadn't Reslo come back with her? He obviously had sent the Southerner here as a bodyguard to prevent a similar attack. How had Reslo managed transporting his niece and a bodyguard back and forth between the continents? Hadn't the senator said that the two governments were at war or nearly so? Wasn't that why the senator wanted the long-distance delivery system?

Down the hall, the trio began perusing the notebooks Doctor Ganevek had laid out. They had divided the stacks between the four of them. Each was muttering dates and occasional partial entries when Ani finally spoke. "He's a bit on the odd side, wouldn't you say?" She couldn't shake the feeling she'd met Isul Treyder before, and recently, but where and when eluded her.

"Who's odd?" Ganevek asked, not looking up from the document in his hands.

"Doctor Treyder." She turned a page and glanced at each paragraph's first sentence. So far, nothing. She started to roll her bottom lip between her teeth. Grimacing, she stopped the action. Every time she caught herself doing that, she was reminded that she shared the nervous habit with her father.

Ganevek laughed. "For a mechanical genius with an advanced degree, he's not so odd. I've met others who are much quirkier. While he was here, he invented a number of machines and tools that became quite useful and much in demand. He left about five or six years ago when another company offered him more income and recognition. Don't know much about it, but your mother was upset at his leaving. There was a rumor his wife passed away a year or so after he left."

"Why's he back now?"

"He'd heard we were looking to rebuild and he offered to return and help set up the new labs," Ganevek replied. "I thought it would be good to have some of the old staff in place before bringing in new ones. We wouldn't have a lot of training to do if we brought in people who had worked here previously, and he knew what types of machines might be needed and which ones were destroyed in the raid twenty years ago."

The Star Valley doctor shook his head. "Oh, he may be scattered at times, like most geniuses, but once you give him a project, he works on it until it's done and done right. Treyder's like your uncle in that way, Ani. A bit of a loner though. He's not much into social interactions, even when he was here before the raid on the center. He would show up at company parties for only the briefest amount of time and then he'd disappear into his lab. I don't know how his wife managed."

Doctor Ganevek stopped talking for a moment and looked wistful, as if remembering something important from the past. "Treyder invented some marvelous things." He crossed the room, pulled an object with multiple joints and arms out of a cabinet, and placed it carefully on a table. "This is one of them."

"What is it?" Renloret asked, a skeptical tone creeping into his voice.

"He called it a remote surgeon."

"What's it supposed to do?"

"He said it could perform certain surgeries without the actual surgeon being in the room. He thought it might be good on the battlefield as a way to keep the medical staff safe and save lives at the same time." Doctor Ganevek pulled out a section, adjusted a few other parts, and flipped a toggle switch. "Here, look at this screen."

They turned to see a view of the desktop with its stacks of reports. He began striking keys on the keyboard below the screen. The machine on the desk moved. Taryn, Renloret, and Ani watched in amazement as two of the "arms" reached out and, using pincher-like appendages, pulled a notebook from the middle of a stack, opened it, and turned several pages before stopping. All the while, he typed.

Ani was impressed. "Amazing. And you don't need wires to connect the keyboard to the machine?"

"Nope. Treyder said it uses radio signals. As long as the lens is in the right place, the person on the keyboard end can make it do quite a bit of stuff. It does take some practice, though. That's about all I can do with it. You also need someone to set it up, monitor the radio link, and lay out the supplies and tools needed for some tasks. It needs some refinement, I think, before it can be used in actual operations. But I see the potential.

"It would have been a convenience to have had something like this during the attack on the research center. It probably could have saved Gelwood's leg. By the time we got him to the hospital in Saedi City, the damage to his leg could not be repaired, but they managed to save his life. Even so, that was a couple of years before Treyder came up with this contraption."

Doctor Ganevek toggled the machine off and returned it to the shelf in the cabinet. "Like I said, he's a genius. I don't even know if he knows I have it and it still works."

"Why don't you take it to him? He said he was just getting started up on some projects. Maybe this will help him."

"I'll do that, but not now. I've been thinking, Ani. The notes you're interested in may be in the research vault."

"Research vault?"

"It's a large room a few floors down and at the back of the building. Actually, the room is in the original building. The hallway may actually be blocked by debris from the attack. I didn't see a need to go that far because all the information there is at least twenty years old and outdated by now anyway."

Renloret and Ani looked at each other. Ani wondered how much of the old section was even accessible.

Taryn stood up. "I can get the original building blueprints for Renloret to use as a map. Some of the original parts of the building may have signage in Southern as well, and I think he's the only one able to read it." Smiling, Taryn moved toward the door. "Would it be all right with you if Renloret does this research on his own? Ani and I have our own research parameters."

The valley's doctor nodded. "I don't see why not. As I said, no one has been in that section for quite some time. I'll let the staff know he has permission to come and go as needed. He shouldn't have any problems, other than dodging around some rubble."

They made their good-byes and got ready to leave.

Ani stood and offered her forearm to Ganevek in thanks, and he clasped it with a smile on his face. "Thank you, again. May I take a few of the older files to review tonight, just in case the information is there? I'll return them in a couple of days." Maybe this would be all they needed to identify the twin.

"Have at them, Ani. If there's anything else I can do, let me know." He tightened his grip on her arm and smiled. "I'm glad you're back and that you're feeling better."

"My thanks again, Doctor Ganevek." She smiled as she gathered up several folders and left.

Hours later, a heavy sigh from Renloret told Ani that even he was discouraged with the lack of enlightening information in the notes she'd borrowed from her mother's compatriot. Closing the file in front of her with a smack, she stood up and stretched. Three pairs of blue eyes watched.

"What?" she asked. "Can't a person stretch?" She grinned at the realization that all the important males in her life had some shade of blue eyes—with the exception of her father, whose blackish-brown eyes actually reminded her of Uncle Reslo.

She turned away from the three pairs of blue eyes and pulled down the tel-com. Punching in Reslo's code, she muttered under her breath, "Now that I think about it, I should have done this as soon as we returned." A message box appeared on the screen.

"Hey, Taryn? Do you know anything about Southern's Tianet Mountain Region?" Ani did not turn from the screen as she began typing a message.

"Which mountain range and why?"

She heard the chair scrape across the floor before Taryn joined her at the screen.

"You trying Reslo again?"

"Trying is the operative phrase. He hasn't actually responded to any of my attempts from a couple of months ago and there's notice that he was notified of waiting messages but he has yet to pick them up. His away message says he is at an archeological research station in the Tianet Mountains."

"Well, there was a bit of news just after you left about some ancient artifacts discovered in Southern's central mountains, but

I don't remember specific names. Archeologists all over Northern tried to get permission to go down."

"I wonder why Uncle Reslo is there instead of at the satellite base." She finished typing her message. "Well, I asked him if he'd heard anything about my having a twin sister. Do you think that might be enough to get a quicker response?"

Taryn chuckled. "If I were him, I would call as soon as I got something like that."

Renloret shoved his stack of papers to the center of the table. "Well, whether he knows anything or not, I suspect he will contact you as soon as he is able. These notes and reports from Doctor Ganevek's office have nothing. We need to get on with the search, and it can't wait weeks for your uncle, even on the slightest chance he may know about your twin, Ani. We'll have to rely on our own knowledge and sleuthing abilities."

"I know, but it's frustrating that he's in such an isolated area and apparently can receive notification that I've sent messages, yet cannot read them. Sometimes I wonder if these computers are even progress. Paper may be more reliable. This time I included the fact that contact was made and the Lrakiran people will survive. You know the main reason he went to Southern was that they were building things like your star runners. He was continuing to try to contact Lrakira and get someone here to fly that last ship. Now at least I understand why he left. It was looking like Southern's space endeavors would be his only chance to get me to Lrakira.

"As far as the plan to find my sister, I think we have it down, and I'm actually thinking that it won't take us too much longer.

It's not such a daunting task now that the infamous Star Valley sheriff is on the task." She dodged the jab from Taryn and closed the tel-com.

Ani moved to the stove. "Anyone want some tea?" The nods confirmed her guess that the two men were, like her, ready to set aside paperwork, concerns about the search, and questions about Reslo. She turned on the stove and stepped out onto the porch.

Kela padded to his usual place on the woven rug between the fireplace and one of the rocking chairs. *How do you feel about talking with Melli about the twin?*

Ani was dragging the rocker back into the cabin from the porch. *I'm trying not to think about it right now. We have a reasonable plan and each of us has a part to play. Right now I just want to relax. I want to forget about being an alien who's looking for a secret sibling.* She brushed off a couple of six-legged beetles from the cushion and ground them into the wood with a mild crunching sound. She winced once. She hated doing that but she just couldn't abide touching them, and squashing them was her only defense against Taryn's teasing that she, a blade ring champion, was even slightly horrified by such a small creature. She checked the underside of the cushion and finding none under it, nodded in satisfaction.

Kela rolled his eyes. *You could have let me eat them. Now they are all mashed and unappetizing.* He had made his way over to examine the bits of bug and snuffled loudly in disappointment.

She pushed Kela away from the remnants. "You cannot eat the beetles."

Both Renloret and Taryn laughed. "Kela eats sap beetles?" Taryn asked.

If you lick them right off the bark, they are sweet and crunchy with a bit of zest that lingers most satisfyingly. Kela rolled onto his back and let his tongue lop over his jaw.

"Oh, for blades' sake, Kela!" She thumped the cushion hard, fervently hoping no other crawly things were nestled in the creases.

"What did he say, Ani?" Taryn asked with a wide grin.

She put her hands on her hips. "Do I need to translate everything?"

"I'm just curious."

"Yes, Ani, please translate," Renloret said.

Her sigh of resignation was loud. "He says they're sweet and crunchy."

Almost like dessert. He scrambled to his feet and maneuvered behind the couch so Ani couldn't reach him.

A whistle from the pot on the stove interrupted the levity. Ignoring the snickers from both men and Kela, she poured the hot water over the tea balls. The bite of cinnamon drifted from the mugs as she handed them out. Cradling their mugs, each sought out a seat facing the fireplace and a comfortable silence settled between them.

Kela yawned and placed his head on his paws. His eyes perused the trio. *This is good.*

She covered her smile by sipping the tea. *Yes, it is.*

Renloret shook his head and sipped his own tea, a smirk settling on his lips.

"What are you thinking?" Ani asked softly.

He closed his eyes and answered. "This is home, Ani. I just

realized that an alien sheriff, a real heroine, and a telepathic canine are far more *family* than I have on Lrakira."

Ani swallowed a mouthful and began rocking. Taryn smiled at her and began tapping his hands on his thighs in syncopated rhythm to the steady creaks from the rocker runners. Ani began to hum and tilted her head at Taryn in silent suggestion. He nodded and began singing. The old folk song about a lost child longing for a family connection and finding that the definition of family, as varied as the shapes of snowflakes, seemed to solidify Renloret's comment. After the first phrase, Ani joined in, watching Renloret's reaction out the corner of her eye.

Renloret had closed his eyes. At the beginning of the second verse, he softly added monosyllabic background baritone notes. The chorus was simple enough and he sang the words. The trio sang it four times through and Renloret whisper-sang the last line of the chorus to a satisfying close. Then the only sound was the crackling of the fire.

Another one please, Kela requested.

Ani obliged the silent request with a sideways glance at Renloret.

The pilot set his mug down in astonishment as Ani launched into a Lrakiran song. He waited for her to begin the chorus and joined in. Ani occasionally stumbled over pronunciation, but she held the melody line while Renloret played with descants.

Taryn applauded at the end. "Well done. Did you practice that on your way back?"

Ani smirked. "I have to apologize to Renloret. I found some music files on the starship and entertained myself when I couldn't sleep. I don't know the meaning of most of the words, but the tune is catchy and . . . I liked the feel of it. I hope the words aren't offensive or lewd."

Waving her off Renloret said, "No apologies from you are needed. I apologize for not making you aware of the files in the first place. On a ship, I have a tendency to concentrate on the mission at hand. I certainly did not want to botch up this one. It's an old folk song children are taught in schools. I'll get you a translation, if you want."

"Perhaps later. Now, do either of you want anything else to eat or drink before we settle?"

Crunchy sap beetles? Kela offered.

Ani nudged the animal's rib cage. "Beetles, bah!"

The two men laughed. Ani snatched the mugs from their hands and placed them in the sink. "We have a lot to do after we break fast in the morn. We should get a good eve's rest. Taryn, you set up the cot and I'll get the blankets."

When she tossed the blankets from the shelf, Taryn missed and the blanket landed on Renloret's head, making her snicker. He pulled it off and ran his fingers through his hair to smooth it out. Ani turned away to hide her smile. The three of them had been together most of the day, so perhaps she should accept that they got along and appeared to like each other. Nothing bad about that. She felt the agreement from Kela, whose tail thumped softly against the floor.

Yes, you are right, she admitted silently. *This is good.* She nodded at the canine's wink. She was more relaxed than she'd been in months. Together they would find the twin and save the Stone. Then all would be well.

CHAPTER FOURTEEN

Renloret pushed down on the door handle a third time. It did not open. There was no palm pad, no key opening. He leaned against the wall thinking that it might require a verbal command to open.

No one was with him to enlighten him about the storage room lock, so he would have to figure it out on his own. Ani and Kela had gone to Melli's house, as planned. Taryn had probably checked in with his office before heading to the library to do some research. And he was standing in front of a locked door at the research center.

He tried all the Northern words for open or unlock the bio-teacher offered. It did not open. He cursed in Lrakiran. That gave him the idea. "Abren." The bar of the handle glowed green. "Ha!" He pushed it down and the door swung in.

Lights automatically hummed on as he entered the records room. Drawered cabinets lined three walls. A rectangular table with six metallic chairs occupied the center. Renloret turned around. The wall with the door also displayed a large writing surface. There were no windows to the hallway. He set his pack on the table and looked at the drawer labels. Bolded words were in Teramar's Northern. In smaller script beneath, the words were Lrakiran. Obviously, workers from both had used the records. He pulled open a drawer.

More labels, all in Northern, delineated categories of information. The bio-teacher supplied basic translation as he perused the paper contents. Such a waste of space and resources. He shook his head and closed the drawer. He didn't have time to search each drawer's contents. He finished reading the exterior labels. Nothing suggested he'd find what he needed in any of the drawers. Was there another records room?

He sat down and pulled the pack close. The outer pocket held the layout of the research center Taryn had retrieved and printed from the tel-com at the cabin. Renloret had been more than surprised at the technology hidden amongst the cabin's rustic appearance. Before they had slept, Taryn had sent a message to his secretary to send the schematics and architectural features of the research center in the morn. Within the first bell of the workday, the papers had printed out, and after a quick study, they had targeted this room for Renloret's first search. He leaned closer to the paper and then studied the room. The dimensions on the blueprint were incorrect.

Paper in hand, he strode to the back of the room and ran his hands across all the cabinets. They were all solid and heavy with paper. The labels gave away nothing. What had he missed? He returned to the corner where there was a gap between the cabinets and ran his hand over the sides of the last one, stopping at a slight imperfection in the surface. To most people it would have felt and even looked as if the metal had been scratched. Renloret smiled knowingly. How clever. He pressed the scratches and spoke, "Abren."

The entire wall moved away from him and slid to the side. In the room beyond, a row of screens with Lrakiran keyboards appeared. Now this was what he really needed. He ran back to the table, retrieved the backpack, and entered the hidden space.

He set the pack next to one of the keyboards, returned to the false wall, and examined the surface until he located pressure switches for sealing the wall. A smile crossed his lips as he also discovered alarm settings. Obviously, only Lrakiran personnel worked in this section. He made a few adjustments and the wall slid back in place. Comfortable he would not be discovered if someone wandered into the deserted portion of the complex, he turned his back to the wall and went to a keyboard and screen. Would it initiate? He pressed the pad and when a small blue light appeared, he expelled the breath he'd held and began typing.

Ani had dropped Taryn at his home so he could use his own hover-car to get to the library, then she continued to his parents' house. She sat in her vehicle and stared at the home, her second home now that her mother was gone. The wide porch with its iron railings welcomed her as they always had. She had sipped many a cup of tea with Melli on that front porch.

"Okay, Kela. Let's go in," she muttered aloud, as much to herself as to the canine. "I'm not sure I'm prepared for this. She's going to have a lot of questions, especially after the way I left." The last time she'd been here, Ani had sneaked out of the house through an upstairs window with the intent of finding and killing the man who'd stolen her mother's body from the cemetery.

Kela snuffled in her ear. *Not as many questions as you have for her.*

"I guess I can bluff my way around the alien stuff. Everything else is true. I just have to remember that everyone here thinks I left to save a single village, not an entire planet of aliens."

That shouldn't be a problem. Just don't mention you met your father.

She ground her teeth. He was the last person she wanted to talk about.

A curtain moved in the large window. Ani could see the silhouette as it moved toward the door. Melli came out and waved, her smile radiant. Ani responded in kind.

"Come on, Kela. Time to get this search rolling." Ani held the vehicle door open for Kela and watched as he bounced up the stairs. His tailed waved with pleasure as Melli bent to rub the top of his head.

"Good morn, Kela. I see you convinced her to come."

Ani raised her eyebrows. *Does she suspect our connection?*

No. But I bet she knows you talked with Taryn after we saw each other at the cemetery. She had asked me then if you were also in the area, but I had no way of actually telling her. Let her believe what she wants. I think she's delighted that you are back and have chosen to see her first.*

"Yes, he wanted to come with me and I couldn't refuse. I can put him back in the wheeler if he becomes a pest."

I heard that.

I know. Now, behave like a normal canine.

Kela gave a pleasant rumble as Melli continued to massage the base of his ears. He sat down and placed a paw on Melli's thigh. She took it and leaned closer to place a small kiss on his muzzle, and he beat his tail on the porch floor in response. Having greeted Kela, Melli straightened and held her arms out. Ani stepped into a fierce maternal hug.

"So glad you're back, Ani. Did your friend return with you?" Melli stepped back and held Ani by the shoulders to look into her face.

"Renloret?" She was surprised by the question. It wasn't on her list of possible first questions at all.

Melli nodded encouragingly.

"Yes, he did. He's staying at the cabin right now."

"Why not at the lake house?"

"We weren't sure of the reception he would receive after nearly abducting me from the valley. What did you tell them?" Ani maneuvered Melli to sit on one of the chairs. Kela followed and lay at Melli's feet.

"Oh, there was quite a stir about the cemetery scandal, and we used that as an additional excuse for Renloret to take you to Southern to recover until the mess could be straightened out."

Melli leaned forward and took both of Ani's hands in hers. "Did Taryn tell you we reburied your mother? When you are ready, we can discuss a proper remembrance ceremony."

Ani could only nod. She felt her chin tremble with an onset of fresh grief. She couldn't tell Melli her mother's body had truly disappeared and the casket was empty.

Patting Ani's hands, Melli reassured her. "It's appropriate to be upset. I cannot imagine what you've been through. So horrible that someone would do such a thing. That it was General Dalkey just makes it worse. And just to steal your mother's blade. I just can't understand the reasons."

Kela gave a low, approving growl. *Ah, that's how Taryn explained it. Good thing.*

Close enough to the truth. "I apologize for behaving the way I did, Melli. I didn't know how to handle what had happened."

"Taryn said you were in a real state when they found you."

"Yes, that's what I was told."

Melli sat back in the chair. "How did that turn out?"

Ani cleared her throat, readying the story. "It was a good idea to go to Southern so I could come to terms with what happened at the cemetery and what I did afterward. Plus it turns out that my parents were indeed from the village that needed help, so when I got there, I was tested and it was confirmed that I had some immunity to the virus. They created a vaccine from my blood and everyone in the village was inoculated. They lost quite a few before we could get there. I'm embarrassed to say that part of the problem was that my parents had changed their names, so Renloret didn't recognize them from the list. Apparently, there had been some trouble between the medical and political factions early in their careers and moving to Northern allowed them some freedoms they didn't have in Southern at the time. Things have changed in the past twenty years, things we didn't know about until my uncle returned to Southern. He's located in a different part of Southern and didn't know there was a problem in their home village, so he couldn't help."

Melli patted her hand again. "People should talk things out. Miscommunications cause more problems than anything else. We are not all that different from them."

Kela gave Ani a canine grin. *No lie! It's only a matter of technology and time.*

Ani ignored Kela. "No, we are not that different." She paused, uncomfortable with changing the subject but knowing she had to.

"Listen, Melli. While I was there I learned some things about my own family and I need to talk to you about them."

"Why me?" Her surprise was genuine.

"Well, you were mother's best friend."

A wary look crossed Melli's eyes and the smile disappeared. "Yes, we were close."

Ani stood and placed her hands on the railing, looking away from Melli. "I don't know how to broach this. I'm still not convinced it's even true. If it is, then I have to reorganize my whole understanding of my mother and her side of the family."

Ani received a telepathic scene from Kela's point of view. It was disconcerting because she was in it, standing as she was, but she could also see Melli. She watched Melli become still, as if hesitating to respond, her face studying Ani's stiff back.

Kela explained. *This way you don't have to sneak a peek and perhaps not see what you need to see.* He continued to project the scene from his point of view.

Melli finally gave a sigh and firmly stood up. "Why don't we make some tea? I do know your mother was very conflicted about her relationship with your grandmother. There was some event neither could overcome or reconcile. Shendahl never explained. Let's go inside and see if I can answer some of your questions."

Ani turned, grateful for Melli's intuition. This would be a start to finding out if there had been a twin. And maybe she would discover more information about the relationship between her mother and grandmother. She and Kela followed Melli into the house.

There's more to Melli than even I suspected. Perhaps I should consider becoming a frequent visitor, a nonverbal listener, a confessor of sorts. There are advantages to being a canine. Plus, I could beg for snacks and actually get them.

Yes, you do have advantages no one else has. That's a good idea, except for the snack part. Ani reached down and ruffled the fur on his neck.

CHAPTER FIFTEEN

Running his hand through his hair, Renloret pushed back from the desk. He had looked through so many files he could barely think. And still no leads. He hoped the other two were having better luck. He pulled out a meat-stuffed roll from the backpack and absently took a bite, chewing while he stared at the scrolling screen. He wondered if he had entered the best search criteria. Next to the screen, the insulated container of tea seemed to whisper his name. He poured the tea into the cup-like lid and breathed in the scent of cinnamon. He blew across the still scalding liquid before sipping. The spicy bite tingled pleasantly. He studied the screen. It had stopped scrolling. One file was highlighted and he selected it.

Renloret read the entry again. It was just one faint line, scribbled in the margin within one of S'Hendale's personal notes on her research for a cure. It looked like she had tried to erase it. Magnifying it, he read it aloud. "What if I'm wrong and I chose the wrong twin?" This was the first true evidence that there had been a twin. He let out a shout of jubilation and scanned the report for any further explanation. He found none and backtracked to check the date of the report. It was several months before the attack on the research center. Ani had just turned five and her mother had finally started to test her daughter's blood.

"Thousands Trapped or Stranded. Eight Feet of Snow Blankets Mountains." The headlines caught Taryn's attention. He scanned the front-page article from the capital's main newsline and remembered the stories of rescues retold many times over the years. There had been unusually heavy spring snowstorms the year he was born, storms that had buried Star Valley and the neighboring mountain ranges. So many children had been born premature that spring that the local hospital officials had jokingly called them low-pressure babies or storm-front babies. Taryn and Ani had shared birthdays with a higher than usual percentage of school classmates. Old tales of barometric pressure changes setting off labor in pregnant women came under scientific scrutiny that year. Instead of the three or four birthdays a month, he could count at least ten within the same week as his. They were considered survivors.

In the details of the article, all births were listed, along with where the births had taken place. He found his own birth listed at the Star Valley Hospital. The valley actually had a hospital back then. He could not find a listing for Shendahl and Yenne Chenak welcoming even one daughter, let alone two. He checked the lists again. A surprising number of infants had not survived the long hours of cold or the lack of medical attention. He checked several weeks on either side of the blizzard without success. Ani's birth was not listed or announced in any of the local bulletins or the regional newslines. Where had she been born? He was fairly confident she had been born in Star Valley. Perhaps her mother had been moved to a special medical facility because of an imminent premature birth. But the commander hadn't said anything about a troubled pregnancy, and Taryn had gotten the impression that the premature birth had been a surprise like so many others. Maybe Shendahl had been in another district giving a lecture, or maybe Ani's parents hadn't wanted official notice because Ani was not really from Northern. The search for the twin would have to rely on personal accounts and that meant Ani's discussions with Melli were even more important.

"Here, try this." Melli placed the mug in front of Ani. "You're my first victim."

It was not the cinnamon tea Ani expected. A decided exotic scent wafted from the steamy tendrils. She blew across the liquid's surface before carefully sipping.

Melli didn't bother cooling hers but took a mouthful and inhaled through pursed lips. She then swished the liquid from cheek to cheek, held it in her tongue, and inhaled again before swallowing it. She set the mug down, pulled out a pad from a pocket, and scribbled a few words. Ani smiled. The note-taking habit of Taryn's obviously came from his mother.

Melli didn't look up. "What is your first impression?"

Ani considered. "Curiosity."

Melli looked up. "Curiosity? Haven't heard that one before. Tell me more."

"Well, it's better than the sheren leaf and chard."

Melli giggled. "Yes, that was a mistake I won't repeat."

The slight bite of udi root reminded Ani that she had forgotten to bring the package of tea from Layson. It was still on the star runner. Ani made a mental note to retrieve it at the next opportunity and present the "Southern tea" to Melli. Hiding a brief smile behind her cup, Ani sipped again, rolling the tea over her tongue, swallowing and inhaling the residual aroma, and tasting for other familiar flavors before commenting. "A suggestion of udi root and luris seed."

Melli nodded.

Finally recognition of the main flavor hit Ani, surprising her. "Whirjerata?"

Melli laughed. "And only you would pick that out. Your uncle shipped me a batch of dehydrated fruits shortly after he arrived on Southern. I think it was his way of thanking Gelwood and me for kind of looking after you while he was down on Southern. You know, it took almost two months getting here. I haven't had any response to my note of thanks, so he must be far from a communication source. I used about half in pastry fillings right away and stored the rest for later use. Well, you know me. I had to experiment with the newest food. Funny thing you using the word *curiosity*. I was considering naming this batch Southern Curiosity. I'm still working on getting a consistent taste. I'm not sure about the amount of luris seed. I think there's too much. It almost hides the whirjerata." She added to her notes.

Ani took another swallow, appreciating the juxtaposition of the citrusy luris seed against the Southern fruit. "Perhaps that's why I had trouble identifying the whirjerata, Melli. Besides, I've only had them twice since Uncle Reslo discovered them. But they do have a distinctive flavor. I agree that the luris seed hides that specialness. You are a master tea designer, Melli. You should market these on a wider scale. Your teas are the best kept secret of Star Valley." She hesitated and then added, "With a few exceptions." This was a perfect segue to the topic she really wanted to discuss.

Melli pocketed the notepad. "True enough. Now, what do you want to know about your mother?"

"As I said, I don't know how to begin. It seems so wrong to not know your own family."

"Well, I always try to appreciate directness. I may not like it but getting a topic out in front makes it easier to discuss and handle than keeping it inside and letting it fester or get muddled." Melli sipped her tea.

Kela needled. *Except when it comes to the love life of her son. You know she's trying to set Taryn up with Keci's youngest sister.*

Ani poked a foot at Kela. *Stop it. You should not be talking. I need you to listen and observe.*

Yes, master. Kela sighed and sidled up to Melli, bumping her hand, asking for a petting.

Melli rubbed the base of the canine's ears as she waited for Ani. Ani adjusted her seat. "Melli, Mother lied to me."

A frown accentuated the wrinkles between Melli's eyes. "About what, dear?"

"Oh, blades, this is more difficult than I thought." Ani looked at the ceiling because she couldn't look at Melli. Then she took a slow breath, bent her head to her chest, and expelled the breath into her mug, studying the pattern the rippling tea made.

Melli leaned forward, her face neutral, nonjudgmental. "Just say it."

Ani's whisper was barely audible. "I have a twin."

Melli froze.

Ouch. Kela sent the sensation of Melli's fingers clenching the roots of his fur at the base of his ears. Ani felt him struggling not to wince or whine as Melli's fingers began to pinch the skin. *Ani, do or say something. It hurts.*

"Melli?" Ani looked up and saw the shocked expression in her friend's eyes.

"I . . . I was not expecting that." The older woman's voice shook with uncertainty. She brought both hands to the mug and drank deeply.

Kela shook his head. *My thanks.* He lay down where Melli couldn't reach his ears.

"At least I am not the only one." Relief colored Ani's comment.

"A twin?"

For the first time Ani heard a guarded tone. Melli might be hiding personal knowledge or suspicions that there was a twin. "Did Mother ever say anything about having twins?"

Melli pushed away from the table. "Anyala, there is . . . are often things that are too painful to discuss. And when one promises to abide by a friend's wish, it is—"

"Melli, you must tell me. I have to know." Melli had used her formal name instead of the diminutive, something she seldom did. This was serious.

"I promised her, Ani. I don't want to break that promise."

Reaching across the table, Ani grasped both her hands. "It's been twenty-five years since I was born and mother's been gone more than a year. It will do more harm for you to keep this secret than reveal it. I need to know." Ani scrambled to find a reason for Melli to explain. "It is a matter of life and death."

Melli finally looked straight at Ani. "I thought you had saved everyone in that village."

Ani almost breathed a sigh of relief. "The family records in Southern mentioned that Shendahl had birthed twins when she was here in Star Valley. I need to know where she is so I can give her the vaccine—if she has not already died."

"Is this disease contagious?" Melli's alarm was evident.

"No, it's confined to a particular genetic pool. I would feel responsible if my twin were to die because I didn't know who or where she was. It will be up to her to decide to have the vaccine, but I must offer her the choice." This was a true statement . . . unless the twin also carried the correct hormones to cure Lrakira.

Ani rushed on. "Even if she was born with a disability, I have the same responsibility. Perhaps Mother could not care for both of us." How did her mother make the choice? Why was Ani chosen and not the twin?

Melli was shaking her head. Ani assumed it was in disbelief.

"Melli, don't misunderstand me. I don't hold a grudge for the choices my mother needed to make. I want to understand them so I can manage the consequences. Do *you* understand?"

"Oh, Ani." Melli started to cry.

Ani walked around the table and embraced the sobbing woman. In her heart Ani realized Melli knew about the twin. But what exactly did Melli know? She began to cry too.

"Melli, it'll be all right. Please tell me."

Wiping tears from her face, Melli sniffled into a kerchief from her pocket. "It was supposed to be a fun trip, to get the two of us out of the village. Gelwood and Yenne had wanted to stay with us, but we made them go home. We were fortunate they had brought up enough food for a week, though we had intended to stay only for the weekend. It was useful, what with the blizzard and all."

Ani pulled a chair around the table and sat next to the now calmer woman. "Where did you go?"

"The cabin."

"You two went to the cabin?" Ani was surprised.

"Oh, we were younger back then and not so wise in the ways of weather or babies." Melli shook her head. "We were foolish and it nearly cost us our lives—and the lives of our children. Yes, Ani, there was a twin, but she died. I'm so sorry. It's complicated. You need to hear the whole story." Melli sniffed again and straightened her bodice. "Dear, could you pour more tea, please?"

The tension left Ani's shoulders at Melli's words but quickly returned as she considered Melli's tone of voice when she said "the whole story." No matter how long it took to hear this story, Ani was determined to let Melli tell it at her own pace. At least now she knew, and that brought about a sense of relief. Her mother had not lied to *everyone*—Melli knew. And even though this was different from what the Stones believed, it was what Melli believed.

Ani complied with Melli's request for more tea while Melli launched into her story. "It was mid-spring, you know. The weather was wondrous and it had been weeks since the last storm. We thought we needed one final adventure before becoming mothers. Your mother was a little further along than me, so we had carefully planned our weekend escape to be at least a month before your mother's due date. It was planned for two eves, and the men promised to come get us. Yenne was so sweet. He insisted on filling the food cooler to the brim. He had just installed it, you know, and he made it fully functional. He also made sure the pump worked so we wouldn't have to carry buckets of water from the stream. Gelwood chopped almost a month's worth of wood so we'd be as warm as possible when it cooled off after the sun went down.

"We practically kicked them out so we could have our girlfriend time. We had brought up crafts to finish. Shendahl was putting the finishing touches on a crib wrap and I was needling a yarn blanket. This was going to be our last time to be just girls, not mothers." Melli halted her dissertation to swallow more tea. "Where was I?"

"You had kicked our fathers out."

"Oh, yes. We had a fabulous aftermorn, so warm. The birds

sang so much. Turned out to be a warning about the coming storm. We just sat on the porch and talked girl stuff while we stitched our projects. By the next morning, the weather had chilled quite a bit. It was overcast and windy." Melli shook her head. "We still didn't heed the warning. We thought it was just going to rain.

"Ani, we didn't have the fancy weather satellites back then, so we had no idea it was going to snow so late in the spring. So much has changed in the last twenty years."

"It's not as bad as that," Ani said, though all she could think about was the twenty-year time shift in the time it took the Stones to sing a song and the knowledge that Melli's best friend was from another planet.

Kela rose from the floor to nuzzle Melli's hand for more attention now that the shocking news had been exposed.

Melli laughed. "Oh, I'm not complaining. Technology is a good thing, Ani. It gives us hope. It was Shendahl who complained about the lack of technology. She was always pushing the scientists at the lab to create new things, thinking of wild and hard-to-imagine ways to make life better.

"You know, just before you entered your teens, she once told me that you were very special, that you were going to save lives. At the time, I thought she meant you were going to become a doctor like her and discover new treatments. Now I think she knew you were going to save the lives of those in her village down in Southern.

"She was grief-stricken after your father died, but she tried to raise you in the Southern traditions. All that blade training and such. She always said she needed to uphold her end of the bargain, hold to her promise, and make sure you were respected for who you were, not just for being a girl. It was because she and Reslo trained you that so many girls are getting better educations and participating in all sorts of athletic competitions. Perhaps there will be blade competitions between Northern and Southern athletes someday, and we'll crown a planet-wide champion. That was her goal for you, I think." She drained her cup. "Your mother was so proud of you when you won. It was worth all that work."

"And all the teasing," Ani said, remembering that most painfully.

Melli turned to her and took up both of her hands. "Oh, she saw that and hurt for you, but she knew you would overcome it. She always said you were the rock she could lean on."

"What?"

"She always said she could trust and rely on her Anyala stone." Melli smiled. "You were the stone base for her beliefs, the reason she kept going even when she missed Yenne so much and even with everyone telling her she should quit the doctoring because she was alone with a youngster. She said she had to keep her promise to her home and family and she'd do whatever was needed."

The Anyala Stone. That's what she talked about, and because she named me after the Stone, Melli thinks she was talking about me. Ani sent the telepathic thought to Kela.

Perhaps she was, Ani. Kela answered back.

There was a knock on the screen door. "Melli? You home?" a woman's voice drifted down the hall to the kitchen.

The Balance

Melli scooted her chair back. "Oh, I completely forgot, Ani. Nonnash was bringing Brenlee over. I was going to watch over the baby while Nonnash took a walk."

"That's all right, Melli. It's been twenty-five years and another eve won't change the results. It's a lot to take in. I just wanted to know if it was true. Thank you for telling me. We can continue this tomorrow." Her head was spinning and she needed some time to internalize this new information.

Melli nodded and patted Ani's hand. "I have so much to tell you, and I have to find some things from your mother that might explain even more than I know, but tomorrow will be better. We'll have more time. Now that you know, can you wait for the reason your mother asked me not to tell?"

Ani nodded. She tried to remind herself that another day wasn't that long, and she really needed to approach this with care. At least now she knew the Stones were partially correct—there actually was a twin. Melli patted her hands again then leaned toward the front door and raised her voice. "Nonnash, I'm in the kitchen. Come on in."

Nonnash arrived with her youngest daughter snugged in the carry seat. "Thank you so much for watching her. All the other girls are in school, and I just need some time by myself." She recognized Ani.

"Oh, you're back from Southern! Did you find the cure for your village?"

Ani smiled and greeted the woman with a respectful nod of her head. "Yes, we were fortunate to get there in time. Many lives were lost but the rest are well now."

"What was the cure?" Nonnash talked as she uncovered the sleeping infant, now almost a half-year-old.

"It turned out to be me. Well, my blood. Apparently, members of my family have a natural immunity to whatever bug is down there, and it took them a while to locate us. Renloret was kind enough to get me down there to assist. They drew enough blood to create a vaccine and they inoculated everyone."

"Will you have to go back?"

"Maybe. Depends." Ani shrugged. She drew her finger across the sleeping infant's cheek. "All the baby girls are safe now."

Nonnash looked at Melli for an explanation. Melli offered, "Something about the virus affecting only the women and girls."

"Oh. Can we catch it here?" Concern flashed across Nonnash's face.

Ani answered as honestly as possible. "I don't think so. This was an extreme outbreak and not likely to happen again, especially now that they have stockpiled the vaccine."

Ani gave Nonnash a hug. "You and Keci make beautiful daughters. Have a nice walk. I've got to get back too." She nodded to Melli. "I will see you first thing, all right?"

"Yes. I'll have your favorite tea ready."

Ani walked herself to the door leaving Melli to hear care instructions from the mother of six. She left knowing without a doubt that her mother was the mother of two, and in the morn, she would find out why only Melli knew.

CHAPTER SIXTEEN

This time they met at the lake house. During the eve meal Renloret revealed the note he'd found. It was dated a few months before the attack on the research center and it questioned S'Hendale's choice of twin. While it did not reveal the identity or whereabouts of the twin, it implied she was still alive at that time. Both Taryn and Ani sighed with relief.

They moved to the living room with its larger table so Taryn could lay out copies of the newslines announcing all the births and deaths that had been registered during and shortly after the unprecedented blizzard. Taryn voiced his concern about the lack of notice of Ani's birth, let alone a birth of twins anywhere near Star Valley, but he also said that official notices hadn't been required at the time.

Settling on the couches, Ani and Taryn took turns reading selections of the newslines aloud. Renloret needed to understand the magnitude of the storm and its aftermath. The pilot had been preparing to build a fire when he noticed the family photo on the mantel. He took it down and showed it to Ani. After staring at it for several minutes, she passed it on to Taryn, battling tears as she began chewing on her knuckles.

"So does he still look like this?" Taryn asked as he reached over and pulled her hand out of her mouth. "Well? This was taken when you were about five, wasn't it?"

She wiped the trace of tears off her cheeks. "Yes and yes. Mother kept it on the mantel. It was the last image she had of him."

An uncomfortable but respectful silence settled around them until Ani sighed deeply and refolded the newsline papers. Tucking her feet under her, she stared at the crackling fire for a breath or two.

"I admit he's my father. Now can we get on with our mission?"

The defeat and frustration in her words kept the two men silent.

She motioned for Renloret to take a seat. "My turn and it's good news, sort of. Melli admitted that there was a twin, but she said the twin died." She waved off Renloret's attempted interruption. "We know that the Stones said the twin is alive, and contrary to Melli's statement, I am inclined to believe the Stones. There is also the note Renloret found. I need the whole story to understand why Mother never said anything about her. Melli had just started to tell the story when Nonnash arrived at the house and interrupted us. I'm supposed to go back to hear the rest in the morn."

"She couldn't have asked Nonnash to come back later?" Taryn asked.

"No, she had offered to watch the baby for a while. And

after twenty-five years, I can wait another day. Besides, even if we had all the information right now, we couldn't do anything until tomorrow. Plus, I don't know how much information your mother has, Taryn. She said she promised to keep Shendahl's secret. But since I told her I know about the twin and Mother is gone, she has no reason not to tell me."

Taryn rubbed his hands together. "All right, here's the plan. Ani, obviously you are back with Mother. Renloret, do you think there may be more notes in the storage files, perhaps in more recent material?"

"There are definitely more files to go through," Renloret replied. "I mean, she made one note five years after the birth, so she might have expressed other doubts later on, especially as Ani approached her menses. I have no difficulty with returning to my assigned area."

Taryn nodded. "Renloret, why don't you ride down to the center with me? I want to interview some of the other workers who have returned and may have been around twenty to twenty-five years ago. Surely, someone saw or heard something, especially after the attack on the facility twenty years ago. Perhaps Shendahl slipped up somehow."

Ani stood, stretched her arms over her head, and yawned. "The plan sounds good to me. I'm headed for some sleep. Renloret, you know which room you can use. Taryn, take the middle guest room. I'll see you both in the morn. Now that we know Mother shared the secret with Melli, I feel a bit more optimistic. In the morn I'll know why the twin was a secret." She moved toward the foyer, Kela following her.

"Sleep deep, Ani," Renloret called after her.

"Sleep deep yourself."

Kela trotted back into the room, carefully grabbed the handle to one of the tea mugs, and dropped it onto Taryn's lap. He laughed and patted Kela's head, understanding that the dog was telling him to clean up. The canine barked once at Renloret and retraced his steps.

"What do you suppose Kela wants *me* to do?" Renloret asked Taryn, grinning.

"Probably bank the fire," Taryn said, dipping his chin toward the logs as he gathered the other mugs and took them to the kitchen.

Renloret replaced the photo of Ani's family on the mantel and banked the fire before climbing the stairs.

Ani tried to calm herself as she approached the front door. She shouldn't be this frightened. What was she afraid of? She already knew there was a twin. It was just the reasons for not telling that bothered her. She suddenly wished Kela was at her side providing commentary that would keep her calm. She felt his reassuring presence behind the privacy block they'd agreed to put in place so she wouldn't be distracted. That was what she wanted now—a distraction. This was worse than the blade ring championship finals. She took a calming breath, but it didn't stop her hand from trembling as she knocked.

"Coming, Ani!"

Ani rubbed her temple. Even after the discussion last eve, she was not as ready as she had assumed she'd be.

The door opened. "Come in, dear one. Oh, there's nothing to be afraid of—perhaps a bit sad, but nothing to be afraid of. And I have some of your mother's things for you too." Melli took Ani's hand and drew her into the formal sitting room.

Ani's smile was tentative as she followed Melli's lead, but her smile widened when she noticed the tea setting with biscuits and jam. She took the indicated chair while Melli poured the tea and then offered the tray of biscuits. Ani made her selection, spooned the jam onto a piece, and took a bite. Her eyes lit up at the gednium-based jam. Melli grinned and placed two biscuits on her own plate. After a sip of tea and a second bite, Ani picked up the napkin, hesitating to put it to her mouth when she recognized her mother's needlework. She glanced at Melli for assurance and then patted her lips.

"I was not prepared for such a formal tea, Melli. You didn't have to go to all this trouble with your best service and even my mother's embroidery." She shook her head. "It has been too long since my last formal tea. I believe it was with you and Mother before I headed to the university."

Melli bowed her head slightly in acknowledgment. "It's my pleasure to offer a bit of ceremony to you, Anyala. You are not only my best friend's daughter, you are as a daughter to me. I felt this occasion needs to be handled with respect." Melli took a bite of biscuit. As she chewed, she nodded. Evidently the biscuits had come out exactly right. She chased the biscuit with a swallow of tea.

"Ani, you asked about your birth and the fact that you have a twin." Melli fidgeted a moment before continuing. "I'll tell you what I know, though it may not be what you want to hear."

"It's all right, Melli. I'm prepared for almost anything."

"Please be patient with me, Ani. I've never told the whole story, until now. As I said yesterday, your mother and I had gone to the cabin for what we called a girls' getaway about a month before Shendahl's due date. I was a couple of weeks behind her but wasn't having any of the troubles I'd had with the previous pregnancies, so I wasn't worried. Besides, Shendahl was there and she had her medical bag, just in case. We had plenty of food and plenty of activities planned. We expected the usual warm spring days and chilly nights, especially that high up the mountain, and we had a marvelous first day and eve. The second day the sunrise was almost as red as blood. We should have heeded its warning. By late morn, the clouds came in and the wind picked up. We assumed—or rather hoped—it would just rain. Midday, the temperature began to drop. By our eve meal, it had snowed several hands deep. To be honest, we were already in trouble." Melli picked up her teacup and swallowed. "Then her water broke."

"Oh, no." Ani covered her mouth.

"I won't go into detail, but several hours later, you arrived all squalling and mad about leaving the warmth and safety of your mother's womb. The afterbirth took a long time to come. She worried about that. She said she didn't feel right and felt that something was wrong. She was correct." Melli took a deep breath. "It got a lot worse because I went into labor shortly after you arrived."

The Balance

Ani sat back in the chair, stunned. She had never heard this version of her birth. She'd assumed she'd been born at the hospital like most of the other babies, though she remembered that Taryn said her name had not been on any of the official lists in the newslines.

Melli leaned forward, her face serious. "Your mother tried to stop my labor with the medicines she had brought up. I think she always had them within arm's reach after I told her I was pregnant. Twice before, I had miscarried before the sixth month, and she was determined that I would go full term this time. But her ordeal wasn't over and she was in no condition to care for me while she tried to pay attention to you, considering how early you were.

"About two hours after I went into labor, Shendahl's contractions resumed. And because of the medicine she'd given me, I wasn't able to help her. But I heard her. Your twin was born about four hours after you. The baby didn't make much noise. Shendahl was angry that the technology here hadn't prepared her for twins.

"While she was fussing over your sister, my contractions started up again, despite the medication, and Taryn arrived just before dawn. He was so small and he barely cried. Your mother had stayed awake all that night dealing with you two and with Taryn. I'd never seen her cry so much before that day or since. She was frantic to keep all of us alive until our husbands could rescue us. By then the snow was almost up to the windowsills and the wind was a constant howl."

Ani gulped down the remaining tea. "So what happened to my twin?"

Melli wiped away a tear that had spilled down her cheek. "I want you to know that your mother tried everything to save her, but she evidently stopped breathing while your mother was attending to me and Taryn. I feel responsible, Ani. If I had not insisted we have a girls' escape, we would have been closer to the hospital and your twin would most likely have survived." She sniffled and blew her nose into one of the napkins.

Ani bit her lip to keep from contradicting Melli's words. Obviously, Melli was completely convinced the twin had not survived. But why did the Stones believe otherwise? Perhaps there was a clue in the story. If she listened closely, she might discover how the twin survived and why Shendahl had kept it a secret.

Melli nodded. "Shendahl wrapped her up in one of the blankets and put her in the tinderbox. From where I was on the bed, she looked like she was asleep, at peace with such a short life. I'm not sure she ever opened her eyes. Your mother made me promise to keep it all a secret. I've kept my promise until now."

Ani was quiet for a couple of breaths, then she frowned. "Where did she bury the baby?"

"I don't know. Probably somewhere near the cabin. She never told me. I was still under the influence of the medication, so she may have mentioned it, but I truly don't remember. I tried for a long time afterward but Shendahl kept telling me it wasn't my fault and everything was going to be all right. She said other babies died that week, not just her own." Melli wiped tears from her cheeks.

Ani reached across the table to take Melli's hand. "What else do you remember?"

"The storm lasted three days. We managed to clear off the porch and steps by taking turns watching over the babies and shoveling. Shendahl may have buried the baby during her first turn at shoveling. She was gone a long time. It took two more days for the men to arrive. They had Tezak with them, and he checked both you and Taryn. He said it was a miracle both of you had survived. All the credit goes to Shendahl. We never talked about it afterward. We were just two women who had given birth during that awful storm. Several of our friends in the valley also lost their babies, so your mother was not alone in her grief. She seemed to come to terms with her loss when she knew Taryn was going to survive. I don't think she would have recovered if I had lost him too."

Melli paused. "I'm eternally grateful for all Shendahl did to ensure I still have him. Her skills saved him, and I grieve that those same skills were unable to save your sister, Ani."

Turning to the chair nearest the fireplace, Melli pulled a small embroidered blanket into her lap. "I saved two things for you. Shendahl had originally wrapped the twin in this, but after Taryn was born, she must have changed blankets because when she presented Taryn to me, she said it was the least she could do for her best friend. She wanted me to have this one so we could share the memory of our children's birthdays. I put it away when he turned two. I was saving it for the next one. I never had another one. So I thought I would give it to either you or Taryn depending on who had a child first." She passed the blanket to Ani. "You deserve the blanket that hugged your twin."

Ani buried her face in the softness.

"It's also time you had this."

Ani looked up from the blanket to see Melli push the thick leather-bound journal toward her.

"It was my gift to your mother when she announced her pregnancy. It's called a mother's journal. It's a traditional gift to a first-time mother here on Northern. I know Shendahl wrote in it often, before and after your birth. It's written in Southern, so I've not been able to read any of it and, well, it's a personal thing and I didn't want to show it to anyone who might be able to translate it. Can you translate it?"

Ani shook her head. She'd have to ask Renloret.

"I do know that there are several long entries around the date of your birth," Melli added.

Ani ran her hands over the pliable creamy softness of the much handled leather. "I remember this. She wrote in it at least once a week. I didn't know you had given it to her. She treasured it. She told me someday I would be able to read it and then I would understand her. Where did you find it?"

Melli looked guilty. "It was in the bottom drawer of the dresser. I found it when you and I were closing up the bedroom after she died. I didn't think you were ready for it then, and I thought you might dispose of it before reading it. You were so upset at the time and wanted to throw away everything that belonged to her."

"Yes, I was very angry," Ani admitted. She had been angry that she had been unable to save her mother, angry that she was now alone. She'd felt responsible for her mother's death. Now Ani shoved the memory aside.

"I decided to keep it safe until you were ready. You're ready now, Anyala."

Ani placed the journal on top of the blanket and embraced Melli. "Thank you so much."

"I only wish your twin had survived."

"At least the mystery has been solved. I'll see if Renloret can help me translate the journal. It'll be a pleasure to get to know my mother and what she thought and hoped for—though for all we know it will contain just a list of things she did or a list of groceries to be bought." She forced a laugh to make light of a situation that was still freshly painful. Tracing the worn embossing on the journal cover, she wondered what her mother had written about the birth and what had really happened to the twin. This eve, with Renloret's help in translating, they would finally know.

"I need to get going, Melli. Renloret is expecting me to pick him up at the clinic. He was helping Doctor Ganevek and a few others with some of their research on the medical crisis on Southern. They are trying to avert a similar one here or at least be prepared for the possibility. I'm guessing the doctor will want some of my blood—in case."

Melli returned the hug and placed a kiss on Ani's cheek. "Don't let him take too much. Oh, thinking of doctors, Taryn called me before you arrived. He said to tell you that he won't be at the eve meal with you and Renloret tonight because he has a meeting with one of the doctors."

Ani frowned. "Did he say which one or why?"

"No. Is it important?"

Ani shrugged. "Probably not. If you see him before I do, let him know we're staying at the lake house for the next couple of days. Since we're back in time, Taryn registered Renloret and me for the summer regionals and wants us to participate in the practice bouts next week."

Melli's smile lit up her face. "Oh, that's wonderful, Ani. Will you compete as a pair?"

Ani stumbled on her words as she tried to cover her embarrassment caused by the inadvertent double entendre tied with the word *pair*. "Well . . . I . . . I can't remember what divisions Taryn suggested. We've been sort of focused on other things."

Melli patted her shoulder. "There's no hurry, dear. You have at least a month to decide which ones to enter. Will Renloret be eligible even if he's from Southern?"

"Taryn was having Daneeha look into it. Anyway, Melli, speaking of Renloret, I need to pick him up." She made her way down the porch stairs.

"Of course, dear. I'm sorry I didn't have the news you wanted to hear." She squeezed Ani's arm. "If you want to talk more, I'm available to listen."

"Thanks." Unaccountably, she felt tears welling up as she hurried to the vehicle. As she turned out of the driveway she smiled and waved to Melli, who could not see the tears now streaming down her cheeks. Alongside the relief of knowing, worry was building as the end to the search seemed to have slipped out of her grasp.

CHAPTER SEVENTEEN

It was obvious to Renloret that Ani had been crying when he slid into the passenger seat and moved a book and folded piece of embroidered fabric onto his lap.

"Bad news?"

"Not exactly."

"What's with the blanket and book?" The embroidery on the blanket had a familiar look about it. He studied it while he waited for Ani to answer.

"They were my mother's. Melli gave them to me." Her voice trembled.

"Why did Melli have them?" Renloret made the connection on the embroidery. The style matched the stitchery on the bed coverlet in the guest room. He began examining the book. The animal hide binding was worn smooth and pliable with much handling. The bio-teacher translated the embossed Teramaran script on the front cover. In surprise he announced it aloud. "A Mother's Journal."

Ani bit her lower lip. "It's a traditional gift to an expectant woman, so she can write down her thoughts and wishes about the child, especially chronicling occurrences late in her pregnancy and the first year of the baby's life. Most women just write up to the child's first day of school or start over when they get pregnant with the next one. It's sometimes read aloud at significant birthday celebrations to remind the child how he or she came into life."

Renloret considered that and thumbed to the last entry. It was written in Lrakiran, though the date was Teramaran. If the bio-teacher was correct, S'Hendale's last entry was written a few weeks before her death. He glanced over it. "And some obviously write until they can write no more."

Ani glanced at him. "Is that her last entry?"

"Yes, a few weeks before she died." He saw her chin quiver as she rolled her lower lip back and forth between her teeth.

She whispered, "I'll need your help to read it."

He silently read the last line and closed the journal. "Whenever you are ready." The last words on the page seared through him. *I know I won't survive this. Tell your father I love him. He will return and take you home to save our people, for you are The Blood and The Balance. I'm sorry I won't be there to explain.* There was no mention of the twin.

The rest of the trip was silent.

Kela was noticeably absent when they entered the lake house kitchen. Renloret asked where the canine was as he placed the journal and blanket on the kitchen counter.

Ani flipped her long braid out of the way and grabbed items from the cooler for the eve meal. "Kela's with Melli, comforting and listening like only he can. He stopped by to check on her a few minutes after I left. He's getting biscuits and a lot of hugs."

"There are advantages to having the right telepathic connections." Renloret went to the cabinet and selected three plates and mugs.

"Oh, Melli said Taryn won't be joining us tonight because he scheduled an evening meeting with one of the doctors. I think it may be that Dr. Treyder."

"The one you felt was off somehow?"

"Yeah, I probably got him in trouble by saying that. I just didn't like the way he acted, like he was hiding something. Taryn must have picked up on the same thing. If Taryn *is* talking with Dr. Treyder, the meeting was probably scheduled at Treyder's convenience."

"Do you want to tell me about the blanket now or after the eve meal?"

"After, if you don't mind. I'm still trying to understand everything Melli said." She resumed slicing vegetables.

Renloret set the whistlepot on the stove to heat. Both the tea and dinner came together quickly, and they talked about everything except Ani's conversation with Melli.

After the meal, they renewed their mugs of tea and took the blanket and journal to the more formal study rather than the living room. Renloret ran his hands over the intricate carvings on the doors. A deep nick marred the design on the left-hand door.

Ani blushed. "My mistake. If I'd thrown the wrist blade a bit earlier at the correct person, perhaps all this would have turned out differently."

"Who did you intend to hit?"

"General Stubin Dalkey."

"Who did you miss?"

"Taryn."

"Wow. Good thing you missed."

"Yes. If it'd been anyone else I would not have missed, and Taryn would have been required to arrest me. Then where would we be?"

Renloret shrugged. "It doesn't matter now. We're here." He put the journal on the desk and handed Ani the blanket.

She hugged it to her chest, and he waited for her to tell him the story about it.

"I . . . I don't . . . understand the significance of this blanket. According to Melli, my twin and I were born at the cabin during that spring blizzard." Ani fingered the blanket.

"Go on." Renloret encouraged.

Ani retold Melli's story ending. "Melli remembered my mother crying a lot."

Ani stopped to wipe off renewed tears and Renloret sat still. He recognized the incongruity between Melli's story and what the Stones had told them on Lrakira. They were as sure that the twin was alive as Melli was that the twin was dead.

A ragged breath signaled Ani's willingness to continue her recitation of Melli's account. "Mother wrapped Taryn in the twin's blanket saying it was the least she could do." Tears were running freely down her cheeks, dampening the blanket. "Melli has kept it since. She said she was going to give it to whichever one of us had a child first, but I think that even though she seemed to understand that Taryn and I were never going to be a couple, she harbored the fantasy that he and I would marry and have a child. In that way, she could return the blanket to Mother.

Renloret shifted in his chair. "But if Melli says the twin died, then why do the Stones believe the twin is still alive?"

Shaking her head Ani said, "I don't know. Unless . . ." She sat upright in the chair, her eyes bright with hope.

"Unless what?"

"A stasis bag! Mother could have used a stasis bag to ensure the baby lived long enough to get her the care she needed to survive."

He sat forward. "That's been done before, Ani, especially with premature births."

"Mother wouldn't have been able to explain the stasis bag to Melli so maybe she lied about the baby dying, all the while keeping her safe until she could get the baby to a hospital. But why wouldn't she have told my father? Do you suppose the baby was deformed or suffered brain damage? By using a stasis bag, Mother could have waited weeks before she took the baby to a hospital in the capital, right? You said the stasis bags could hold a person in suspension for months without harm. Would a premature infant continue to grow and develop if placed in a stasis bag right after birth?"

"I don't know. It sounds plausible, but I doubt it. Let's find out what your mother says happened."

Renloret put his hand on the journal. "This may have the answers to our questions."

Ani stared at the journal, obviously unsure she really wanted to know. Renloret was also uneasy about knowing, but the Stones had been adamant that the twin was alive. However, all indications on Teramar pointed to a twin who had died shortly after birth. Hopefully, the answers were in S'Hendale's handwriting.

Renloret studied Ani's expression. Did she really want him to read her mother's journal? This was a private thing, wasn't it? Weren't journals supposed to be for the writer's own eyes? By mutual heartbreaking consent, the two women had kept the knowledge of the twin a secret for twenty-five years. No one else knew.

"I think I need a drink." Ani got up and opened the cabinet doors behind the desk to reveal a number of bottles. "How stiff do you want yours?" She turned to face him with a narrow-necked gourd bottle in her hand.

"I'll have what you are having."

She poured two fingers of an azure liquid into multifaceted tumblers, raised her glass, and gave a deep blade salute combined with a bow. "To Mother!" As she straightened, she put the tumbler to her lips and knocked the contents to the back of her throat. She shut her eyes and shivered, then set the tumbler down and poured another two fingers.

Renloret followed suit. "To S'Hendale!" Tears stung his eyes at the burn of the alcohol. He inhaled through his mouth, the vapors biting into his sinuses, and suppressed the need to cough. Whatever it was, it was probably the strongest liquor he'd ever had. It suited the situation perfectly. He set his glass on the desk.

Ani poured him another two fingers and sat down. This time she took a sip and seemed to savor it. "Start reading from the date of my birth."

Renloret was still trying to get his breathing under control, but he nodded and opened the journal. He looked up at Ani before beginning. She tossed the rest of her drink into her mouth and waved at him to start.

"'After two miscarriages prior to the sixth month, I thought Melli would carry this one full term. I promised her a healthy baby. I could not break her heart. I have fulfilled my promise to the Stones by giving birth to The Blood and The Balance. My Anyala will save my world. And the Stones have blessed me with a way to honor my friend and make her family whole. May Yenne forgive me—I gave the twin to Melli. She named him Taryn.'"

There was silence for several breaths.

"Read that last part again." But before he could, Ani slapped her hand over the page. "On second thought, don't. I need another drink." She stopped pouring at three fingers and raised the bottle to Renloret in question.

He dipped his chin but held up two fingers. He wasn't sure how much he could handle. The first serving of liquor had softened his vision already and he thought his words might have slurred just a bit towards the end. Ani acquiesced with a grim twist to her lips. After pouring his service, she raised her glass. "To the Stones of Lrakira. They were correct. The twin lives."

Renloret joined the toast and added, "May they rot in the hells of Teramar for not telling us the twin is a boy."

With bitter laughs, they both downed their portions.

CHAPTER EIGHTEEN

Sparks snapped out of the fireplace landing harmlessly on the stone hearth. Ani swirled the last of the liquor and contemplated the fire's flickering through the liquid pattern. She sipped. Her stomach complained only a bit; it had been numbed into submission. She knew she had to think about the journal's revelation but right now, she wanted to forget she'd ever heard the words "and she named him Taryn." She glanced at the pilot. He was staring at the ceiling, a finger tapping the edge of his now empty glass. What impact was this information having on him? Ani sat up.

"Fortunately, we never did anything together for which I am ashamed of or regret."

His finger stopped tapping but his eyes remained on the ceiling. "It's all right, Ani. I've been thinking about the behavior between the two of you. Your statement about Taryn being your best friend was the truth. I believe you. At the spring dance and sing, even Melli said your relationship was never going to be more than friends and that was what it should be." He straightened up, and the intensity of his eyes gathered her in. "That's what she told me at the dance. Could she know or suspect?"

Ani didn't answer right away. The tone of the journal implied that Shendahl had not told Melli that it had been her child, not the twin, who had died, but . . . Ani remembered a conversation, or had it been a warning, between her mother and Melli when, as teens, she and Taryn had been caught kissing on the porch. Her mother had said something about a friendship being the only way to keep from breaking hearts and possibly ruining families. Could Melli have guessed? If she had, wouldn't she have mentioned it somehow? Ani wasn't going to ask straight-out. Hells, this was a mess.

"Perhaps, but she sounded positive that the twin died. However, unlike Gelwood, Melli never pressed us to become a couple. Gelwood can hardly wait for me to join the family, though since your arrival, I think even he will back off." She muffled the last words, not wanting to broach the subject of where her affections might be focused.

Nodding, Renloret stood. He stretched, teetering a bit. "What does Kela think about all this?"

Harrumphing softly, Ani turned her gaze to the canine who was laid out on the rug between the couches. He had arrived shortly after the identity of the twin was discovered. Soft snoring indicated he was sleeping deep. "He told me before he fell asleep that he is marvelously entertained by the news. He insists on being included when we tell Taryn."

"Hmm, that will not be until tomorrow," Renloret mused,

staring at the softly snoring beast on the rug. He rubbed his chin. "I think we ought to follow Kela's example and get some sleep. Perhaps the morn will bring us solutions. Hopefully, Taryn will have more information on this Doctor Treyder and how or if he is connected to all this. Then we can figure out how to tell the sheriff *he* is the twin we're looking for."

Ani shook her head. "I'm not sure which he will find more difficult to ingest, the fact we are sibs or that he's an alien, like you and me." She slowly rose from the couch and reached for Renloret's glass. Her vision veered and blurred as she shuffled toward the kitchen. "Bank the fire, please. I'm going to bed." She hoped he heard her because she wasn't sure she actually said it aloud.

Once in the kitchen, she splashed cool water on her face. It wouldn't sober her up but it might help her make it to bed without falling down. She chastised herself for imbibing to that extent. She was already feeling guilty, so she knew the hangover headache would be gruesome.

A glance into the main sitting room showed Renloret leaning against the mantel, his head on his arm. The fire had been properly banked and Kela was still asleep on the rug. She turned to the stairs. They looked very long and steep. Taking the steps one at a time with both hands on the bannister, she considered how she was dealing with this change. It probably did warrant the massive drinking session, but she was not convinced that the alcohol would help her understand that she not only had a twin, but a brother. A slight shake of her head almost sent her tumbling backward down the stairs. The last step brought a sigh of relief and her hand slid heavily along the wall to her room.

The Balance

She closed the door and slid down to the floor, finally allowing the tears to come. Ani gulped in air and struggled to reach the bed. She crawled in and curled up tight. She'd always wanted a brother and now her best friend *was* her brother. It wasn't like that should be a problem because they were practically family anyway. Stifling the desire to laugh hysterically, she realized that now they were indeed family—siblings—and in the quiet of her room, she was actually not too upset by that.

But the question of why The Balance was a boy instead of a girl flashed like a bright warning light. Wasn't there something about only girls being Singers? The Singers had mentioned it, hadn't they? Even Renloret had said that when he was younger, his mother had been concerned that he had wanted to become a Singer, and she had dissuaded that interest because only girls had been Singers. Ani realized that the possibility of the twin being male had never been mentioned. The entire social structure of Lrakira revolved around female Singers for the Stones. Perhaps things on Lrakira were about to change and the Stones needed a male Singer.

She considered the title that Taryn would bear, The Balance. Balance. Brother balanced sister. Male balanced female, didn't they? Would that fact be enough for an entire world to change their social structure? Would Taryn be up to that? How would this simple yet monumental change affect Lrakira, Taryn, and Taryn's parents? How would it change the relationship between Taryn and her? How had this knowledge already changed her? Ani gave in to emotional exhaustion and closed her eyes. Tomorrow she could figure it all out.

Several hours later, Ani pulled the blankets over her head and snuggled deeper, trying to ignore the telepathic call from Kela. When she couldn't, she growled, threw off the blankets, and stomped to the door.

Kela was sitting neatly centered in the doorway, the very tip of his tail waving in front of his white paws.

Good morn, Ani. Kela sauntered into the room.

There's nothing good about this morn. Her headache was blistering. After shutting the door gently, she made her way to the edge of the bed and rubbed her face with both hands, feeling the dried tear tracks on her cheeks.

You look terrible.

Peeking between her fingers, Ani glared at him. "Ah, thanks," she mumbled.

You'll feel better after a shower. He cocked his head and gave her his impression of a smile. *Did you sleep in your clothes?*

Her words were muffled through her hands. "Evidently." She sighed. Did she even have a change of clothes here? What about Renloret?

Kela pushed his muzzle under her clasped hands to swipe her chin with his tongue. *It'll all work out, Ani. Taryn's understanding of his world is broad. Remember, he helped Renloret save your life by singing an alien song. He saw what the blade did. He saw the ship Renloret flew to get you to Lrakira. You've told him about your experience on Lrakira. Did he reject these facts?*

"No," she said.

If I know Taryn, once all is explained, he'll even help tell his parents. And Gelwood and Melli are *his parents. He's never known otherwise. The only difference is that the two of you are related.*

"That's a big difference, Kela." She flipped her hair out of the way.

Not as big now as it would have been two years ago. Remember?

Ani yanked off the boots—evidently she'd slept in them as well—then stripped the rumpled shirt and pants and tossed them in the basket outside the washroom. "I remember, Kela. You should remember I told him it wasn't going to work out between us other than as friends. He was hurt then, but fortunately, he seems to have come to accept it over the past few months. You heard the lecture he gave me a couple of days ago."

Oh, I did indeed. Well said too. You should give Renloret a chance. He would be willing.

She started the shower. "Right now, it's more important to tell Taryn who he is than to tell Renloret how I feel about him."

Are you sure of that?

Ani stepped into the water and began scrubbing with the soapcloth. "Yes, I can wait. The Anyala Stone can't." As suds sluiced off her cinnamon skin, she began to wake up.

Hurry, the tea should be ready by now, and whatever he's fixing to eat, I want to be first in line. Meet you in the kitchen.

Ani finished her shower, tucked the towel around her, and let Kela out of the room. Then she turned her attention to finding appropriate clothes for the upcoming disclosure. What did a person wear when they told a friend they weren't who they thought they were? She had to chuckle. Even the question didn't make sense.

What words should she use to explain? Confidence was

quickly fading as she considered the overwhelming skepticism he was sure to voice. How much time would be wasted in trying to convince him? The idea of simply abducting him and traveling to another galaxy was enticing but impractical and decidedly unfair. And what kind of reaction would Melli and Gelwood have when they were informed that Taryn was not of their blood . . . and an alien on top of it?

Ani paused at the top of the stairs and shivered. Could they handle all of that information? No. It was bad enough to subject Taryn to being her twin and therefore an alien. His parents, however, should not be told about the alien stuff, only that Ani and Taryn were twins and that their mother had freely given Taryn to them out of love and respect.

The fact that Shendahl assumed The Blood and The Balance was a single female child and not separate individuals was beside the point. Shendahl had been focused on saving her entire species and knew that a female child was the only solution. She had obviously not understood the significance of having twins, let alone the significance of one of them being male. It appeared that her mother had believed she could give Melli and Gelwood the child they dreamed about without endangering her home world. Now it was up to Ani and Taryn to face the consequences of Shendahl's mistaken belief and choice.

Kela thought that Taryn would be able to handle the fact that he was an alien without any hesitation, but she wasn't as sure. Would he go willingly to Lrakira to save the Anyala Stone? What would happen after that? Would he become the Anyala Stone's Singer? She was surprised at the flare of possessiveness that wrapped around her heart at that thought. She'd only just discovered she was a Singer and now she might have to relinquish *her* Stone to her brother. If Taryn became a Singer would he have to stay on Lrakira? How could that be explained to Melli and Gelwood?

Renloret interrupted her thoughts by calling her to join Kela and him. She followed his voice and met them in the kitchen.

"I've constructed the morn meal and the tea is still hot." He smiled and bowed his head in greeting. "Let's break our fast and face the day."

"I'm impressed, Renloret. You're not mangling Northern's language as often as you did right after the crash."

"The fact I understand the difference between *day* and *suntime* leads you to that conclusion?"

"Mostly. You're also using contractions more frequently. Not that I minded the lack of contractions. At least your accent is still noticeable."

"I'll work on that." He handed her a mug and pointed to the table set with a pair of plates.

Once seated, Ani perused the contents of her plate: gedniums, plantains, a scrambled pile of seared meat pieces and tacara root topped with a pair of cushawk eggs, their blood red yolks barely paled by the thin albumen. After sipping the spicy tea, she sighed. Perhaps the day would go better than she expected.

CHAPTER NINETEEN

"Why did you bring him here?" the woman demanded. Because she was in the back corner of the room and in the shadows, Treyder could not see her face clearly. In fact, Treyder had never clearly seen her face. She was usually quiet and always stood where she could not be seen. But when she spoke, her Southern accent garbled some of Northern's words and syntax. Outside of his wife and some of those who had worked at the research center, this woman was the only other Southerner he'd been around. While she appeared to be trusted by the senator and occasionally offered worthwhile information, she was actively working against her own Southern government by associating with the senator, and Treyder wanted nothing to do with a traitor.

At least his former employers had the ethics to work on things that benefitted everyone, not just those living on Northern. And when his wife was alive, so had she. Their shared employers just hadn't believed he could make robotic machines so small. But Senator Nelham did.

The senator sat on the government's space protection committee and had originally contracted Treyder over twenty years ago when Treyder was looking for a job in mechanical research and development. Treyder had leapt at the chance to work at the best research center on Northern so quickly after completing his university courses. All he was asked to do was pass on information about the projects that were coming out of the remote Star Valley installation. The only problem had been that he'd been assigned a military overseer named Stubin Dalkey. But Treyder had solved that problem a few months ago. He smiled at the thought of discovering that his laser beam, which he had invented as a distraction device, worked beautifully as a killing weapon.

He pushed away those pleasing thoughts and focused on what the woman had said. As far as he was concerned, she didn't have the authority to question his actions. Dismissing the woman, Treyder turned to the senator. "I couldn't very well keep him in Star Valley, Senator Nelham. Since you requested proof that the device worked and I could not produce Miss Chenak, I have brought you the next best subject, Sheriff Taryn Avere. The entire valley's population is probably looking for him now. They'll turn every building inside out, and anyone new to the area may be under suspicion. I need to get back. The clinic's guard knows I was meeting with the sheriff last eve, and I obviously am not at work as normal right now."

Treyder pulled the blanket up closer to Taryn's chin. He lifted each eyelid and flashed a small beam of light across the eye's surface, then entered his observations on the chart before turning to the senator. "Keep an observer in the room at all times," he said. "I don't know how that Chenak woman recovered so quickly. With the facility as it was when I left after my wife died, they should not have been able to even locate the device, let alone remove it. It should have taken them years to develop appropriate equipment. I took everything with me when I left the first time. Perhaps there was a malfunction.

"However, with your assistance, Senator, I now have this second facility for furthering your requested research projects. I will soon be able to give you what you desire: unequalled military power over both continents."

He smiled to show the senator how much he appreciated the sponsorship, even if it was not yet widely known. The senator smiled back. They both knew Treyder had returned to the Star Valley Research Center to renew his undercover observations and to look for proof that the Chenak family was now using Star Valley as a secret base from which Southern could launch an attack on Northern territory.

The disappearance of the infamous girl blade champion so quickly after he had successfully implanted the coma device worried Treyder. There had been no word about her return to Star Valley until she had walked into his office. The fact that she did not show any ill effects, with the exception of her impaired memory, made him think that, perhaps, the first prototype had malfunctioned, and he wondered if the device had failed at some point. Had the device failed and was still in her or had it somehow been removed? He would consider those possibilities as he studied the effects of the second device on the sheriff.

Treyder frowned at the realization that he had possibly made an error. "There was no indication from the villagers that they even knew she had been in a coma. All they talked about was her going to Southern to help develop a vaccine for some sort of virus she was immune to that was epidemic in a Southern village. Or at least that was their cover story for her disappearance."

"She went to Southern?" the senator asked. He seemed surprised.

Treyder nodded. "I assume so. Her parents were from there. Evidently, Southern secretly sent a man to Star Valley to find a woman and her daughter from Southern. You might look into whether or not the political pressures you have been exerting on the relationship between the continents required Miss Chenak's removal from Northern for possible spy training since she won the blade ring championship. With that title, she has wider access and notoriety than expected. But I don't think she has any feelings against Northern because she stayed and even took on that recruit training position at the university. It was inopportune timing, that's all. And not for the first time. I was so close to being able to use it on Shendahl Chenak when she died."

The shadowy female figure in the corner stepped forward. "Someone came for the Chenak girl?"

Treyder saw the senator scowl at the intensity in her voice, as if he didn't appreciate her interruption.

The senator faced the woman. "Were you aware of the Southerner's impending arrival when you suggested we use Dalkey as bait to get that Reslo character back on Northern territory?" The senator's tone was accusatory.

"Of course not."

Retreating into the corner at his scrutiny, she spoke directly to the senator. "When you told me about the radio signals, I suspected her uncle, whom you allowed to leave, was trying to contact her by using some of Southern's new technology. I thought Dalkey's reappearance in Star Valley would bring Reslo Chenak running back to protect his niece, and then you would be able to *invite* him to share his knowledge of Southern's space technology with your committee. You could have used his knowledge to your advantage, and with Dr. Treyder's assistance, Northern would quickly exceed Southern's attempts to explore beyond our atmosphere. You, sir, would have been instrumental in the development of a space-worthy army."

Treyder saw the senator puff out his chest at the compliment. This woman knew the senator and how to manipulate him. He would have to watch her.

"You did tell me you wanted Reslo Chenak and his knowledge of Southern science, not his niece," Treyder said. "I want him as well. The girl is nothing more than a freak of nature who was manipulated by her mother and uncle into the blade ring. Even so, she knows nothing about her uncle's work. I do. Reslo Chenak will come running at her request, now that I have the sheriff. Once Chenak is here, you can extract the information from him and I can show him just how small I can make things. The sheriff here is proof of what I can accomplish, with your support, Senator, both in the device itself and in the distance delivery of it." He patted Taryn's chest to bring the senator's attention back to the reason they were holding this meeting.

A grin on his face, the senator rubbed his hands together. "Yes, yes, Isul, the projectile weapons you are developing will allow us to overcome any enemy. When can you start mass production of the device?"

"Another few tests should do it. Then you can have all you want. The assembly-line process has been designed. I just want to make sure all of them work the same as the prototype." He didn't explain that he'd only had two of the devices, the first now either in the hands of Southern scientists or nonfunctioning within Ms. Chenak and the second presently keeping the sheriff quiet. He wondered just how the senator saw the device being used in warfare, but decided not to ask, at least not yet.

"Good. And how is the work on the distance launcher I suggested? The need to get so close to the opponent risks too many of my soldiers." The senator's smile was without mirth.

Treyder patted Taryn's chest again. "I have developed a second delivery system. This one worked as well as the sliver blade. It's a small handheld weapon rather than the large multiple barreled cannons you requested. It would be far more manageable and more accurate in the field."

There was interest in the senator's voice. "At what distance were you?"

Treyder studied the room. "Approximately the length of this room. There are only a few problems."

"Such as?"

"The explosion made a horrible racket and the smoke was intense. Both alerted the guards. I was able to dissuade them from entering the lab and finding the sheriff's body by explaining it had been a chemical reaction I was not expecting. I had burns across my lab coat as proof. I will look into the ignition process to see if it can be quieted and still get the syringe to travel the desired distance. It has to hit the body with the appropriate amount of force to pierce any fabric *and* go deep enough to release the device into the blood stream. Once in the blood stream, the device has its own instructions, telling it where to go and what to do."

The senator grasped the doctor's shoulder and shook it gently. "Fine. Fine. A fine job, Treyder. I look forward to reading your full report. Let me know when you are ready for official presentation." He frowned as he looked at the sheriff's body. "Is there any special method you want me to use to dispose of this body?"

Alarmed, Treyder replied, "Oh, he's not dead, senator. We can't dispose of him. There is much I can learn from him, now that he's cooperative. I'll get started on a list of things I am anxious to know when I return."

A harsh laugh came from the woman in the corner. "Such as?"

Treyder was all too ready to share his excitement. "How much stress or pain can be inflicted before the heart is affected, for example. Without the subject's ability to express pain, experiments can be run without the examiner getting squeamish. The sheriff is virtually a stone with no sensations. Essentially, most of his brain has been disconnected from the physical body, allowing only automatic functions to continue. He's been pithed without cutting the brain stem. He'll feel nothing until the device is removed and he awakes, unfortunately." There was disappointment in his voice. "However, this will allow my assistants to work dispassionately and therefore longer."

The senator shivered slightly. "How long can you keep him in this state?"

"As long as I want or need to."

"A stasis bag would be better," the woman muttered just barely loud enough for him to hear.

"A what?"

"Something a genius like you could come up with if given the idea and enough time, I am sure. Perhaps we will have the opportunity to discuss it later. Much later." The shadowy figure waved him off like an insect.

"Very well, Treyder," the senator said. "I'll set up guards and attendants. We'll await your return."

Treyder paused briefly in the doorway and looked back at the body on the metal examination table. He wasn't sure how he felt about all this but he did believe it was going to be worth all his investment. Perhaps this tiny device would even be able to protect Teramar from the aliens he suspected were waiting to pounce on an unsuspecting populace. If he had anything to do with it, Northern would survive, and to hells with Southern. They were the ones who had brought the aliens here in the first place by launching those damned satellites. Treyder knew he could hold the sheriff hostage to gain Reslo Chenak's knowledge of Southern's designs and now, with this secret research facility in Northern's capital, Saedi City, he could make good on his promise to the senator with regards to the coma device and its handheld launching mechanism without discovery of the device's connection to Anyala Chenak's nearly two month long absence. He could use the Star Valley site to further his study of lasers and their possibilities.

The woman laughed as he closed the door.

"What do you mean he's not here?" Ani hissed through her teeth.

"He's not here." Daneeha repeated. "He didn't come in this morn. It's not like him at all. He usually calls if he's going to be late or is on a case or decided to sleep in." The petite woman smiled up at Ani and her Southern companion. "I checked his calendar and all he had listed was a meeting of some sort with a Doctor Isul Treyder at the hospital last eve. Is he sick?"

"No, but he's going to be," Renloret muttered.

Ani smacked her hand across his back. "Stop it. We'll talk about it afterward." She leaned across the desk and whispered, "Were there any notes about the meeting?"

Daneeha looked at the door to Taryn's office. She appeared uncomfortable. "I don't remember." Her eyes shifted away from them.

The frown on Ani's face turned into an encouraging smile. "Oh, come on, Daneeha, any secretary worth their blade steel would remember more than just a name if there was more. Am I right?"

Daneeha jutted out her chin. "If he finds out I told you, I

might get fired. I'm not supposed to be in his office unless he's present or personally directs me to locate something for him."

Ani was not intimidated by the tiny woman. "Daneeha, this is a life threatening situation. We must talk to Taryn, now!" Ani slapped her hands on the desktop, bouncing papers and making the mug of tea jiggle. The deputies looked up from their desks; one of them stood up to see what the problem was.

Holding her palm up to forestall the deputy, Daneeha said, "It's all right, Yantel. I can handle this. They're just anxious to find the sheriff. When did he last speak with you?"

"Last eve about eighteen. He was on his way to the hospital to question a witness about an attempted attack on Miss Chenak a few months ago." Yantel remained standing and attentive.

Daneeha looked at Ani for an explanation. "What attack?"

Ani glanced from the secretary to Renloret to the deputy. "I agree with Daneeha, what attack? I wasn't attacked by anyone." She hoped she had said that with the appropriate amount of surprise.

"He said *attempted* attack," the deputy replied. "I did ask him if it might be someone new to the area who didn't know about your connection to Southern and that you only went down there to help your parent's home village. Taryn said the attempt occurred just before you left for Southern. He mentioned possible new evidence he needed to check out before bringing charges." A shrug of his shoulders said that was all he knew.

Ani also shrugged. "Well, this is news to us. Something must have come up since we last spoke with him yesterday morn. When I talked with Melli yesterday aftermorn, she mentioned that he wouldn't be having the eve meal with us because of a scheduled meeting. She didn't know what it was about, either. Obviously, Taryn thought it was important to keep his suspicions to himself until he'd checked them out thoroughly, as usual."

"Did you check your messages?" Renloret asked the secretary.

"Of course I did! I check them every morn when I arrive and several times during the day. Are you questioning my ability to do my job?"

Ani grinned when Renloret backed up a step in the face of the diminutive woman's indignation.

"No, ma'am. My apologies. Taryn has spoken highly of you and the invaluable work you do."

Daneeha relaxed a bit, climbed off her chair, and pulled a key from a pocket. "Do *not* tell him I let you in." She glanced at the deputy. "Thank you for the information, Yantel. I apologize for keeping you from checking with Mroz about the fistfight at the bar. From his tone of voice, I don't think he's going to press charges, but he wants us to know who was involved in case of a repeat offense. Here's the initial report."

The deputy nodded. "Glad to help." He snatched the report off Daneeha's desk and scurried out the door.

She shook her head as she unlocked the door. "I better not get into trouble for this. The calendar is on the left side of the desk. There were some notes—not many, but you might get an idea of what exactly he was looking for or hoping to get from this *witness*. Maybe you can understand what he meant by 'the device.' I'll call the hospital and see if I can talk with Doctor Treyder." She closed the door, leaving Ani and Renloret alone and unobserved.

Ani and Renloret stared at each other. "Device?" they said in unison.

After a brief hesitation, they both scrambled to the left side of the desk. Ani found the note first.

"Here. It says, 'Doctor Treyder, engineer and physician. Worked with and for Shendahl. Said could show me updated device.' Renloret, the word device is underlined. Do you remember Treyder saying anything about an updated device?"

"No. What else does Taryn say?"

She pointed to the bolded script. "He's got the word *same* with a question mark, also underlined."

"Are you thinking what I am thinking?"

"Taryn is in more trouble than he thought if Doctor Treyder is the man who attacked me. And I am fairly certain whoever attacked me was also the one who killed General Dalkey with that light weapon."

"Laser," Renloret said, correcting her.

"Didn't you say it was illegal?"

"Just because a weapon is illegal does not mean no one has them or uses them, Ani. Many illegal things are still present in most societies, no matter what planet you are on. And there are many positive uses for lasers."

"What does it mean if this Doctor Treyder even had access to a laser weapon?"

Renloret's voice was soft. "Let's not conclude anything until we talk to the doctor or Taryn . . . or both. We can only pick up one stone at a time."

Ani smiled at his metaphor, though she would have referred

to sharpening one blade edge at a time. "Agreed. Let's get to the hospital and find Doctor Treyder. I knew there was something not quite right about him, but I didn't imagine it would be this. Hells, what if he kills Taryn?" She felt her chin tremble at the thought of losing Taryn. This was not the time for her to start crying.

Renloret pulled her into a quick embrace. "One stone at a time, Ani."

She nodded against his chest.

When she pulled back and they turned to leave the office, he took her hand. The physical contact was reassuring and comforting. Whatever they encountered at the hospital, at least she was not alone. It was a relief to have Renloret with her.

Ani acknowledged the curious look from Daneeha. "We have what we need. When we find Taryn, we'll let you know. If he contacts you, let us know."

"Will do," she said, waving them toward the door. "By the way, I couldn't reach Dr. Treyder."

They might have needed to take it one stone at a time, as Renloret had put it, but Ani was apprehensive about this particular stone. They hurried to the hospital. Once there, she glanced at the attendance board in the hospital's front lobby. "Doctor Treyder has not checked in for today. I suppose that explains why Daneeha couldn't reach him."

Renloret took her hand and dragged her down the hall. "Let us hope he just forgot and he's in his office or lab."

The office was dark and the door was locked. Ani removed the stylus from her handheld tel-com unit and inserted it into the lock. In less than three breaths she smiled up at him and opened the door.

"Another talent I didn't know you possessed," Renloret said, smiling at her. "Does Taryn know you can pick locks?"

"No and don't tell him. I've a few secrets I'd like to keep to myself."

They entered cautiously, easing the door closed. Keeping the light off, they visually scanned the room before separating to check the perimeter. Ani pushed a button on her tel-com and a dim light appeared.

In the low light, Renloret opened all the cabinets. "Nothing," he announced in a whisper.

From behind the desk Ani said, "I think I have something."

Renloret joined her as she rubbed the flat edge of a writing implement across a pad on the desk. Words made their appearance in white relief under the spot of light and she read them aloud. "'Distance firing design needs work on explosive sound. Implantation was successful. 45-9004-87.'"

Renloret pointed at the series of numbers. "What are those?"

"Tel-com connection. Let's see who it goes to." She pushed the series of numbers.

"Are you sure that's a good idea?"

"Too late." Ani started at the sound of the message. She repeated it to Renloret. "It's the Military and Space Protection Department, Senator Nelham's office." She closed the connection. "Hells, I'm going to have to get rid of this now. They'll be able to track it to me by the end of the day if they bother to check contacts."

"You had better destroy it then."

"Not yet."

He pointed at her tel-com. "Wait, does Taryn carry one of these?"

"Yes, why?"

"If they can track you, can Daneeha or one of the deputies track him?"

Ani's mouth formed a circle in surprise. "I didn't think of that. Back to the sheriff's office. Daneeha is very good with stuff like that and she'll be delighted to be involved."

They started to leave when the ball of light from her tel-com passed over a piece of fabric stuck to the corner of the counter. Renloret pulled on Ani's sleeve and pointed to it.

Leaning close she examined it. "That's from a sheriff's department jacket. At least, it is the same color and fabric type."

Renloret worked it back and forth until he could pull it free and pocketed it. "Let's go."

Ani was beginning to feel that they were going in circles with every circuit more troublesome than the last. Apart from the bit of clothing, there was no concrete reason for her to be worried, but her earlier apprehension had given way to deep concern for Taryn's safety. Fortunately, she was right about Daneeha. Once back at Taryn's office, the diminutive secretary needed only the barest of requests before jumping in to help.

When the longitude and latitude lit up on the screen, Daneeha jumped up and shouted, "What's he doing in the capital?"

"Perhaps the doctor took him to see someone else about what he witnessed," Renloret offered in response. "A lawyer, maybe?"

The secretary's response sounded skeptical. "Why didn't he leave me a message to that effect? He didn't tell either Melli or Gelwood. Oh, on his way back from getting Mroz's report, Deputy Yantel checked Taryn's house. Nothing's been disturbed and his personal hover-car is still there. No lights on. The bed's not been slept in either. Oh, and the sheriff's vehicle was still in the research center's parking lot, so Taryn and this doctor must have left together last eve after their meeting."

"That would time out correctly. Can you tell when he arrived in the capital?" Renloret asked.

"We're not that sophisticated yet. Can you Southerner's do that?"

Renloret smiled. "No, but it's a nice idea."

Ani was entering the coordinates of Taryn's tel-com into hers. "All right, we can locate him or at least his tel-com. Again, Daneeha, keep us informed. Tell his parents we've gone to the capital and that everything's okay. I don't want them to worry. Oh, and if Melli asks, tell her the journal was interesting and I'll talk to her about it when we return."

"Will do. Now go." Daneeha made shooing actions with her hands.

CHAPTER TWENTY

As they were stopped at an intersection, Renloret looked out the open window and up at the glass-sided buildings of Saedi City that reminded him of Awarna's business district. Though the buildings were not as tall, they reflected the same cold and sterile feel onto the streets and walks they loomed over. There was a similar lack of character in the architectural details.

Ani checked the geographic location again. "It should be around here, within the next block or two."

Ani turned left into an opening marked with a symbolic hover-car. She pulled up to the ticket kiosk, snatched the mechanically offered token, and pulled into the first available slot.

"Now where?" Renloret asked.

"Fifth floor or thereabout since the tel-com appears to be hanging at around sixty to seventy feet above us. It's probably in someone's office. Let's see if Senator Nelham works there."

Five flights of stairs left Renloret slightly winded while Ani seemed unaffected. He needed to work on his fitness level. A double door on the landing opened to a large well-appointed lobby with a semicircular desk at its center. Three attendants manned screens and keyboards. When Ani approached the oldest attendant, Renloret assumed her choice was based on previous experience. She was less likely to be seen as an adversary by a more mature woman. He pasted on a smile.

"We'd like to see Senator Nelham," Ani said.

The woman looked up from her screen and perused the pair. A second, longer look made Renloret think the woman might have recognized Ani as the only female blade ring champion on Northern until he realized the woman was actually admiring him. He offered the woman an acknowledging smile.

"He's in the council offices today." The woman continued to hold Renloret's gaze.

"Um, has he had any visitors recently?" Ani asked.

"As in this morn?" The woman took her eyes off Renloret just long enough to glance at the screen in front of her. She shook her head and directed a sultry smile back at Renloret.

Renloret decided to use her obvious interest and leaned over the screen and put all he could into his voice. "What about last eve, miss. We were supposed to join them, but the traffic from the western districts was impossible. He wasn't answering his tel-com and he has yet to respond to our personal message." He knew he was bluffing but it wouldn't hurt to insinuate that the senator had a private tel-com she did not have access to.

Ani turned away from the woman and, after rolling her eyes, glared at him. She was going to hit him very hard for flirting so outrageously. He hoped it would be worth the pain.

The woman blinked at his intensity and her skin flushed. "Last eve? Yes, he met with a Doctor Isul Treyder."

Renloret continued, dropping his voice into the throaty range of his baritone. "Excellent. They did get together. Did the doctor mention where he was staying? We might be able to connect with him instead." The woman frowned and shook her head, seeming unable to take her eyes off him.

Ani covered her mouth and coughed. Renloret was confident she wanted to smash him into the wall. He hoped she would wait until they were out of sight.

The woman graciously answered, "I'm sorry. My shift ended before their meeting did. But the senator is at the committee meeting as we speak. They'll be breaking for the midday meal soon. I can alert him of your arrival."

"Oh, you don't need to bother him during the meeting. We will wait for him to conclude his business. Then we can take him to his favorite restaurant and conduct our meeting there. It will be a disappointment for me that you will be unable to join us, though I know you are dedicated to your position here. Can you remind me of which committee room he's in again? I didn't write it down." Renloret let honey drip from each word and was amazed the woman didn't see through the farce.

The woman checked her screen again, wrote a few things on a piece of paper, and then handed the paper to Renloret. He took it from her slowly, letting his hand linger on her skin.

The woman turned her head away and giggled.

He straightened and grabbed Ani by the elbow. "We can see ourselves out." He pushed Ani through the door into the hallway, and as soon as the door closed, Ani's fist landed on his shoulder.

"I can't believe you!"

He staggered. This would bruise.

"But I got the meeting room number." He showed her the paper and she snatched it from him.

"Oh, and hers too." Disgusted, she shoved it back into his hand. "Here. You might need this later. Come on." She jogged to the lift.

He glanced at the paper and noticed the second set of numbers. It was probably the secretary's personal tel-com. He grinned at Ani's obvious jealousy and followed.

It didn't take them long to find the room.

"Can you identify this Senator Nelham?" Renloret asked as they peered through the pair of windows on the door.

"Third from the left, on the dais."

Renloret studied the man. He sat forward, mouth almost touching the microphone, arms extended, waving to emphasize each of his words. Was he angry or explaining his position on the current topic? Renloret looked at the reaction Senator Nelham's speech was getting from the rest of the men in the room. There were no women visible. "Are all your politicians and leaders male?"

"On Northern, yes. But women are making inroads faster than some of them want. It will take a few more elections before we reach numbers comparable to those we know about on Southern. My championship in the blade ring rubbed salts in many eyes. And they couldn't do anything about it." Her tone was smug.

Politics was one thing he couldn't do anything about, so he

changed the subject to something he thought he could. "Do you have a plan for how we're going to find the doctor or Taryn?"

"Working on it." She continued to stare into the conference room. "Hopefully, the senator can tell us where the doctor went after their meeting."

Renloret rejoined her at the window. "Looks like a team blade ring contest where the weapons are words."

Ani gave a short laugh. "Never thought of it that way, but it's a good analogy."

The man at the central seat stood up and hit the desk surface with a small hammer, stopping the discussion. In unison, they all rose, executed a semblance of a blade salute, and then bent to close up notebooks and straighten stacks of papers. While several exited through a door behind the platform of desks, others gathered in groups of two or three in apparent conversations.

Renloret watched Nelham as he moved methodically off the platform and worked his way towards the doorway. He greeted several of the observers with a smile or a nod of his head, the image of a practiced politician. As such, Renloret decided he couldn't be trusted. One of the observers pulled on the senator's sleeve and whispered something in his ear. The senator frowned and indicated that the observer could accompany him. The pair pushed through the remaining crowd. Pulling Ani with him, Renloret backed out of the way as the door swung open. The two men paused just outside the door, unaware of Renloret and Ani.

"Are you sure the sheriff is alive?" the senator asked. He seemed so focused on the man who had whispered in his ear, he didn't check to see if anyone was listening. Renloret and Ani were invisible.

"Oh, yes. His body seems to be functioning as if he was in a deep sleep, but he doesn't move. No eye movement either. Even coma patients have some eye movement. Is Doctor Treyder still here? I want to be sure this is what he expected."

The senator shook his head. "He left early this morning after delivering the patient. He should be back at the research center by now. Here's the tel-com number he can be reached at." He scribbled on the bottom of a notepad and tore the corner off.

"My thanks, sir. I wish to serve you to the best of my abilities. This experiment will not be a waste." The man saluted and hurried off down the hall.

The senator watched after him, then muttered, "It better not. I won't be able to hide the expenses much longer." There was a bitter undertone to his statement.

Renloret glanced at Ani. If her look had been a blade, the senator would have died on the spot. He whispered, "Leave the senator, Ani. We should follow *him*." He tipped his head after the unknown lackey as he disappeared around the corner.

She grabbed his arm and pasted on a too-wide smile. "Come, darling. Enough of this waiting. He'll be in there for hours yet. I'm hungry. There's a café on the roof. It has the perfect view of the city and it serves vishon." Her voice was shrill and whiney.

"Vishon? Oh, that's wonderful," Renloret replied as he allowed himself to be pulled past the senator, offering the man an apologetic grin as he brushed by him. The man acknowledged him absently and turned in the other direction to call after someone leaving the conference room.

Renloret contained a chortle. Ani's improvisation had been

priceless. He tucked her arm through his and rounded the corner to the lifts as the bio-teacher inside his head extolled the culinary virtues of the freshwater animal that was supposedly being served at the rooftop café.

The lift doors slid open and they could see their target moving forward.

"Sir, please hold it," Ani said, using the falsetto voice. She hurried toward the lift, pulling Renloret with her.

A hand waved and held the door so Renloret and Ani could enter. Renloret raised his eyebrows at Ani, wanting to ask why they had used the stairs to climb to the fifth floor instead of this lift. She shrugged and gave him a tense smile, then turned to the man they had followed.

"What level?" The man had already pressed one of the symbols.

"That'll do nicely," Ani replied. "Are you headed for a café? It's our first time in the capital and we've no idea which one offers a quick and reasonable meal. Could you suggest some place nearby? Garrend and I have about two hours before the lawyers are finished with my father's estate. Then it's a long drive north back to Doven."

Working to keep a straight face, Renloret merely nodded.

The man gave a noncommittal greeting. "There are numerous options. Several buy 'n carries are within strolling distance along the plaza. If you want to sit for a while, I'd suggest Wither's. It's on the other side of the street from the east side of this building."

"Our thanks for your kindness." Ani had softened the shrillness in her voice but kept it in the soprano range. She leaned closer.

The man almost shivered in delight when she placed her hand on his sleeve.

Who was flirting with the unsuspecting now? He didn't trust himself to speak, fearing he would laugh. Fortunately, the lift bumped to a stop. All three stepped out, and after he gave Ani a direct smile, the man headed to a phalanx of doors whooshing back and forth as people exited and entered the building. Ani held Renloret back for about two breaths, then released him to follow.

The man's green jacket was visible amongst the crowd on the walkway, making it easy for Renloret and Ani to tail him. They followed him discreetly for several blocks until he crossed the street to a park. Ani jogged across the mowed grasses at wide angles while directing Renloret to pause behind a tree, then waved him to run to a small structure near an area with play equipment. He was momentarily enthralled by the laughter and hijinks of the children on the playground, then glanced toward Ani's last location to find her frantically pointing at a fountain surrounded by small groups eating the midday meal off their laps or out of bags. As he approached the fountain pool's edge, Renloret caught sight of the jacket on the opposite side. The man was walking with purpose toward an exit gate.

Ani arrived at his side. "I don't know who is the bigger idiot, him for not being aware of his surroundings or me for thinking he'd be looking in every direction to see if he was being followed. Come on." She tugged at his sleeve.

Once out of the park, they followed him into an older business area where the streets were narrow and the rough-textured stone buildings with flat roofs reached two to five stories. Unsavory individuals lurked about the doorways. Renloret mentally checked where each of his blades was strapped.

The man they were following stepped into one of those doorways. Renloret and Ani continued past it. Renloret glanced at the sign that hung overhead. In the time allowed he only recognized one of the words—*medical*. When he hesitated, Ani pulled him forward and resumed her inane chatter in the falsetto whine. She turned after passing the first store entrance and guided him into an alcove used for deliveries.

Ani pressed two fingers to his lips, forestalling his questions, and pointed at the door. "This is the delivery entrance for the building he entered. We can probably get in without notice." She pushed the door open. Warmer air leaked out, and he could hear muffled conversation and the clatter of machinery.

"You're confident that we won't be noticed?"

"We only lose our advantage if we fail to take the risk." She winked and entered.

Renloret followed.

Chapter Twenty-One

The hall became a ramp into a large storage area. They stopped to study the behavior below them. Shelving stacked three or four times Renloret's height formed a grid with passageways between, giving the impression of a maze. Rolling carts fronted by forked levers maneuvered crates or boxes onto or off the shelves. Renloret recognized the conversational buzz as instructions, questions, and replies issuing from the workers' handheld devices. Clicks and pops punctuated the noise as each worker spoke or paused to listen. None of them glanced up at the delivery ramp. Ani tugged on his sleeve and pointed at a door adjacent to a counter at the end of the ramp.

Renloret offered Ani a smile after they slipped through the door—apparently without notice. She acknowledged his smile by mouthing, "I told you so," then hurried toward the front of the building.

Signs directed them to a kiosk listing the businesses within the building. Ani ran a finger down the list as she mumbled each entry, then tapped a particular line. "Would this be an option?"

Renloret read it aloud. "Medical Equipment Research Foundation. Well, it is more plausible than Home Craft Supplies or Employment Clearance Center." Another perusal of the list showed that the Medical Equipment Research Foundation occupied the entire fourth floor. "Is there a lift or do we take the stairs?" He was hoping for a lift.

"The lift to the fifth, then main stairs to the fourth."

Renloret moved around the kiosk toward the lift alcove, but Ani held him back. "Wait." After a quick look around the lobby area, she undid the elegant bun that held her hair off her neck and stuffed the beaded clip in a jacket pocket. Then she quickly worked the loose tresses into a thick single braid. The simple alteration changed her appearance from a noticeable businesswoman to a casual working girl, just like all the other girls Renloret had seen on the city walkways.

"Now it won't get in my way if we get in trouble," Ani said, flipping the braid over her shoulder and demurely tucking her chin before strolling to the lift.

Renloret paused to check the lobby for witnesses to her transformation. No one had passed through while they had been at the kiosk. She had timed it perfectly. He jogged up behind her as the door swished open. Two men exited, brushing Ani out of their way as if she was unworthy of their notice, though they both acknowledged Renloret. He gave them a tight-lipped smile and stepped into the lift.

Ani had mashed herself into a back corner, arms folded protectively, head down. Beads of sweat began to appear on her forehead. She did not look up until the doors closed and the lift rose with a tremble. "They might remember you, but I was invisible," she muttered, tight-lipped.

The sudden change of behavior surprised him until he remembered the story Taryn had told him of how everyone discovered she had claustrophobia. The story had come out after Renloret had asked Taryn to help him put an unconscious Ani in a stasis bag for transportation to Lrakira. It had been Taryn who, on a dare, had locked her in a tiny closet to keep her from attending a blade training class. She probably didn't need reminding of the incident, even though it was fifteen or more years in the past. This elevator compartment was much smaller than the one in the government building—just small enough to set off a claustrophobic reaction. He had to keep her talking.

"Who taught you to be invisible?" Renloret really did want to know because Ani had been demonstrating some pretty impressive impersonation skills since their arrival in the city. There was more to her than he imagined, and the topic would distract her from the confining feel of the small elevator.

"Uncle Reslo. After the blade ring championship, he decided I should know how to disappear in public." She shifted her stance but kept her arms wrapped tight. She seemed to be consciously taking slow, deep breaths, and her eyes were locked on the floor indicator as if staring at it would make it rise faster. "We had worked on several techniques when mother got sick. After that, we concentrated on her, not me."

"You'll have to teach me some of those techniques," he said.

The elevator bumped to a halt. She closed her eyes and inhaled, breath wavering as if coming across a washboard. The door slid open and she pushed past Renloret. Once in the hall, a shimmy of her shoulders seemed to release the anxiety and her stance straightened.

"Those tactics will have to wait until we've found Taryn. And if they've implanted him with the coma device, as I fear, based on what we overheard, he'll be incapacitated. It may not be easy getting him out of this building." She moved toward the stairway.

They made their way down the central stairs to the fourth floor. Renloret heard an audible sigh from Ani when they met no one in the stairwell and another after she cautiously opened the door to the fourth floor. The two soft-footed their way past several office doors. Lights brightening the sliver of space beneath one closed door gave them notice that at least one was occupied. They slipped by without notice.

The corridor ended in a double swinging door that signaled the entrance to a large open room. Looking through the windows, they took in the lights that glared over an array of tubing, wires, and metal cabinetry surrounding a solitary platform. Renloret mentally paced out the length of the hallway they had come down and surmised that the space beyond the double door was laid out across the back of the building. He could see the lighted emergency exit in the far right corner. It would logically be in the corner of the building away from the street entrance and not connected to the elevator shaft in the center of the building. He craned his head to see what lay on either side of the swinging doors. Several doors lined the walls, indicating more rooms or offices of some type. A second set of swinging doors on the left side of the space announced the possibility of a second hallway with rooms like the one they were hiding in. He perused the rest of the room. There was something under a white sheet on the platform between the long bank of equipment and monitors and the doors behind which Ani and Renloret hid. Renloret placed a firm hold on Ani's arm as she began to step forward. The gleam of a wrist blade was noticeable against the palm of her hand. He shook his head and pulled her away from the door.

"It may not be Taryn," he whispered.

"And it may be." The hiss of her response sent a chill down Renloret's spine.

Voices from the room brought them both to attention. Ani shook off Renloret's restraining grip and stepped back to the window. Renloret looked over her shoulder and saw several men enter the spot-lit area from a room to the left.

"There he is." He could barely hear her words.

Two uniformed men strode across the open area and took up positions facing the bank of equipment, their backs to the doors Renloret and Ani were peeking through. Flanked by two yellow-coated, file-bearing attendants, the man who had discussed the Star Valley sheriff's condition with Senator Nelham followed and paused to study a screen of blipping lines. The attendants scribbled notes, and then they turned to the sheet-covered form.

When a gasp issued from Ani, Renloret clapped his hand over her mouth and pulled her close to his chest, dragging her away from the doors to keep her from charging through. She kicked him in the shin with her heel and though it had been almost three months since the crash that sliced that same shin to the bone, Renloret experienced a flash of concern about whether it had totally healed.

"Blades, girl, stop it, or we'll never get him out," he whispered into her ear.

She stopped struggling and he released her.

"Now what?" Her question was barely audible.

He glanced up and down the length of the corridor, and when he saw the darker opening of a recessed doorway, he began to slither along the wall, pulling her with him. A short sigh pushed past his lips when he saw the door lacked a window. There was barely room for the two of them, though it gave some concealment so long as no one opened the door or came down the corridor. For several breaths they just stared at each other.

Placing both hands on her shoulders, he gave her a gentle shake. "I know what you want to do, but neither one of us is prepared to execute a snatch and flee. Do you agree?" Despite speaking in a whisper, he put as much command as possible in his voice.

Her chin trembled and a quick swipe of her arm across her face soaked up the first trickle of tears as she swallowed and nodded. She straightened and shrugged off his shoulder grip. "Need a plan." She checked the hallway, rolling her bottom lip between her teeth. "Maybe some help."

Renloret hadn't seen any more than the two uniformed men he assumed were guards of some type. Were there others? He needed verification. "How many guards did you see, Ani?"

"Guards?" Her eyes widened, then became slits as she frowned.

"How many?" he asked again. Silence accompanied a green-eyed stare. He counted two slow breaths. Perhaps it was the shock of seeing Taryn on the table that delayed her response. He knew she would have noticed.

The frown dissolved into a tight-lipped grimace. "Two, both with scabbards and slings. There were none at the emergency exit behind the bank of equipment and obviously there are none at either end of this hallway. Even so, we're going to need help. Gotta change appearance again." She pulled the hair clip from the pocket, twisted and wrapped the braid into an artful bun, and fastened it into place.

The door Renloret leaned on opened inward and he barely caught his fall into the room.

"What! I'm sorry, I didn't hear you knock." The woman was garbed in yellow and had one arm wrapped about a stack of files. She backpedaled into the room.

Renloret nodded a greeting at her. "Didn't have the chance." He moved forward, backing her to the desk, hoping to give Ani time to finish whatever transformation she had in mind.

"Is Dr. Treyder here?" Ani asked as she strode up behind him. She had turned under the collar and unbuttoned the shirt, showing off what he considered to be an alarming amount of skin.

The woman winced from the high pitch of Ani's falsetto. "No, he went to the valley to pick up some equipment and notes. I expect him back in the morn. Do you have an appointment?"

Ani cleared her throat. "Senator Nelham sent us. Something about the doctor's latest test results. The senator needs them for his report. Are those the reports?" She reached out offering to take the files.

Renloret kept his mouth shut. How could Ani think so fast?

The woman hugged the files. "No. These are for the payroll department. I think you were sent to the wrong room. Let me get Dr. Treyder's assistant." She started toward the door.

Renloret and Ani shook their heads in unison.

"Don't bother him. He seemed quite busy when we came through," Ani said before the woman could make a move.

Renloret added, "We'll come back in the morn."

They edged out of the room and into the corridor.

"Our thanks," Ani said as they headed away from the central laboratory.

"Wait. Let me show you the way out."

"No need, really." Ani pushed Renloret. "We'll let the senator know he'll have to wait another day or two." She started walking faster.

Renloret chanced a backward glance. The woman was standing just outside her office frowning at them, her mouth working. How long before she figured out something was awry? They had almost made it to the lifts when the woman's screech sounded. Ani broke into a run and skidded around the corner, slapped at both call buttons on the lift, and pointed to the stairway. They double-stepped down two flights and slipped through the door onto the second floor. Ani punched the down button on the elevator, and when it whooshed open, she pulled Renloret in with her. Apparently, any fear of small spaces had been supplanted by the need for quick action.

They had just enough time to catch their breaths and make sure they didn't look disheveled from the run before the lift bumped to a stop. Ani finished adjusting the hair clasp in the twisted braid just as the door opened.

He watched as Ani nodded to the trio of men waiting. They returned the acknowledgement and all hesitated to watch her move into the hallway, her hips swaying just enough.

"Come along, Wiak. We're going to be late." She kept walking without looking back at him.

Renloret put on a fumbling assistant act and excused his brusque exit from the lift to follow a demanding wife. He heard the three men chuckle. Renloret caught up with Ani as they passed the directional kiosk. "Now where?"

She pointed across the street. They were almost out of sight of the building when a mass of sword carrying semi-milits or private guards spewed from its doors. The shout from one of them confirmed that the woman in payroll had given a good description. Without a word, they increased their speed and barreled through a grocer's careful display of fresh goods. Renloret grimaced. The guards would have them pinpointed now even though they were almost two full blocks ahead. He hoped Ani knew her way amongst the towering buildings of the city as well as she knew her mountain property.

Scrambling into a narrow passageway between buildings, they slid to a stop at a trash bin barrier. Renloret cursed at their bad luck. He turned to look back down the street. The soldiers had just rounded the corner and spread out, methodically checking each doorway on both sides.

"Take off your shirt," Ani said.

"What?"

"Take off your shirt!" Urgency hissed in her whisper.

He glanced behind him. Ani had already shed hers and was struggling to pull her pants down over her boots. Frustrated, she removed one of the boots and tossed it out of the way. "By the Stones, what are you doing?"

"Misdirection." Leaning against the building, she jerked the remaining boot off with the pants. She tossed them under the trash bin. She stood brazen in only her undergarments. "Turn the shirt inside out and give it to me." She unbuckled the wrist blade sheath and slid it under the bin, then unclipped her hair and began unwrapping the braid.

"Ah, brilliant." If they changed what they were wearing, the soldiers might not recognize them. Buttons flew in all directions as he tore his shirt open. These garments did not have the smooth release closures of his usual Lrakiran attire. He pulled the sleeves through as he removed it and threw it at her. Pushing away from the wall, she caught it, spread the sleeves out, and whipped the body of the fabric over and tied it low around her hips. Following her action he removed his arm sheath and tossed it under the bin alongside hers.

He managed to look away from her long enough to see that one pair of guards had reached the alley on the other side of the street. "Hurry, we can just walk out. They won't expect that. They're looking for us to be running." He felt a tap on his shoulder. Turning he found her green eyes bright with adrenaline and a sly smile on her lips.

Her hands clasped his head and she gave a slight push, slapping his bare back against the stone wall. "I have a better idea. Plus, Taryn told me to do this at the first opportunity." She pulled his head down and pressed her lips to his. With a slight jump, she wrapped her legs around his hips. His attempt to protest ended as her tongue slid into his mouth. Sliding his hands up her back and under the cascade of her hair, he accepted her idea.

Two guards edged their way around the corner of the building and into the alley, blades first. The ardent couple earned stares from both. One sniggered. The other gave a disgusted snort and pulled his partner back to the walkway. "They must have taken the next turn, Napav. These two have other things on their mind." He waved his blade to those behind. "Dead end, sir. Nothin' but a guy gettin' what he paid for."

As the pounding boots and occasional shout faded, Renloret immersed himself in Ani's distraction. The fierceness of her kiss changed to an urgency he didn't want to stop. They should have done this moon-cycles ago. Her skin was hot and smooth under his hands. She loosed her legs to stand on tiptoes, lacing her fingers into his hair and crushing his attempt to take control. His heart raced for a different reason now. He thought he heard a whimper. Then her tongue entered his mouth again, asking for response. He answered by entwining his hands in her hair and taking control.

CHAPTER TWENTY-TWO

Ani?

Not now. Hells. She'd let down all her barriers and Kela knew.

Whoa, this is your idea of a distraction? I thought you were looking for Taryn, not having a meeting of tongues. Kela's tone was hard, thoroughly destroying her mood.

The distraction worked. Now get out of my head. She tried to reclaim her enthusiasm. Blades, what was Renloret doing with his hands? Arching her back, she gave him permission to move them lower.

No. Stop it! Now! That scientist is here, but not for long. He's collected some of his equipment and boxes of things and has packed them into his vehicle. I can't keep him here. You've got to come back.

She had sent Kela to do some surveillance while she and Renloret were in Saedi City and it had evidently paid off. She sent a clipped thank you to Kela and pushed Renloret away. She could see the mirror of her frustration in his expression. "Sorry, shouldn't have done that. Kela says Treyder is in Star Valley—packing."

Scrambling away from where she wanted to stay, Ani began searching for her clothes. She couldn't look directly at Renloret. Out of the corner of her eye she watched as he slid to a seated position. He'd cupped his face in his hands. Was he embarrassed or was he as frustrated as she was? She found her pants and one boot, then untied the sleeves of the shirt she wore as a skirt and flung it at him. He caught it and stood up, his back to her. A twinge of guilt washed over her at the red scrapes from the wall that marked up the smooth muscled surface of his back, but she didn't dare touch him.

She cleared her throat, making sure her words were not laced with unintended desire. "We're two hours away. We're going to miss him."

A stream of vulgarities whipped off her telepathic tongue to Kela. He only laughed now that she was back on task. She fastened her pants and, leaning over the edge of the mostly empty trash bin, spied her shirt. She pulled herself up and reached unsuccessfully, then hooked her bare foot on the edge, hoping to slide into the bin. The foot slipped and she fell in with enough noise to cause even Kela to wince in her mind. She stood up, kicked the metal side of the container in anger, and voiced her emotions in a growling scream. Thrashing through the bags, she located her shirt and after shaking off some debris, managed to pull it on.

She glanced at Renloret over the edge of the trash bin. He now stood nonchalantly leaning against the stone wall fully dressed, though his buttonless shirt was teasingly open to his waist. He was apparently in perfect control. He held her wrist blade sheaths out to her, a wicked smile on those delicious lips.

"Such a bad idea," she muttered. There wasn't time to wipe the smile off his face, so she hopped out of the container, recovered and shoved on her boots, and stomped over to snatch the sheaths from him.

"Your shirt is inside out," he said, his tone husky and suggestive.

She pulled one of the blades out and pointed it at his middle. He backed up several steps, hands high above his head. "We're not talking about this," she snarled as she stalked passed him. In silence, they carefully worked their way back to the wheeler and left Saedi City.

The first half of the ride back to Star Valley was painfully silent. Ani had refused to talk. Every time he tried to speak she had held the palm of her hand up. It was not until they reached the most wheel-screeching curves on the mountain road that her tongue loosened. Then he was bombarded with a list of things she thought they would need to effect the rescue of her brother. Fortunately, he was used to receiving long orders without benefit of notes.

It was only when she finally ran out of words that he noticed the tears on her cheeks and the white-knuckle grip with which she maneuvered the wheeler. He chanced her anger by touching her shoulder and to his relief, she tipped her head, pressing his hand between cheek and shoulder. A few breaths later she asked if he thought there was a way they could use the star runner to help with the escape.

He was thinking the same thing and suggested they stop at the lake house where he could use the tunnels to get to the launch tower and prepare the ship while she gathered rope and weapons. He also suggested that a third person would be helpful in carrying Taryn and providing protection. They discussed some of the possibilities, but when Renloret mentioned Mroz, a ghost of a smile flickered across her lips.

Before she could argue against it, Renloret defended his choice. "Mroz seems well-balanced and can certainly handle himself in stressful situations. He managed me at the cemetery when I discovered your identity. He knows blade work and, if I remember correctly, he still competes in age-group competitions on occasion. Beyond those things, his size and strength would be an asset in moving Taryn to the roof."

"He is the most skilled in the valley outside of Taryn and myself," she admitted. "He is also trustworthy and levelheaded and not easily shocked. I think he's our only real option. My only question to you is, are you sure you want to bring in a native?"

"In spite of what my superiors might say, we need Mroz."

When they were back in Star Valley, they made a single stop at the research center to check on the whereabouts of Treyder and then picked up Kela before heading to the lake house. Once there, Ani penned a note to Mroz requesting a private meeting, slid the note into the slim tube of a message collar, and latched the tube around Kela's neck. Kela would deliver the message to Mroz while Renloret and Ani finished their preparations. They planned to meet Kela at Mroz's bar.

Renloret took the tunnel from the lake house to the launch tower, leaving Ani to collect items from her list. Less than half a bell later, Renloret emerged from the tunnel and found Ani nearly ready to go. It didn't take long for them to finish loading the wheeler and head for the village. A few chimes later, the antique wheeled vehicle rolled into the parking lot of Mroz's bar. Kela was on the porch, waiting for them.

As the engine ceased its rumble, Ani turned to Renloret and stopped the nervous habit of rolling her bottom lip between her teeth with a reluctant grin. "Ready?" She unbuckled the safety strap across her chest but did not open the door. "There's still time to contact the ship and get reinforcements."

He shook his head. "No, we don't really have the time. Besides, your father would be the first to come, and once on Teramar, he might decide to get involved again. We can't clear that path for him. I'm more confident of Mroz than I am of your father."

"Me too." She got out of the wheeler and ruffled the fur on either side of the canine's head as she headed into the bar.

Renloret paused outside the entrance. Neither of them really knew how Mroz would react to the message Kela had delivered. Bringing in a Teramaran native to assist in rescuing Taryn with alien technology was a dangerous gamble. He hoped he had judged Mroz correctly. With a sigh and shake of his head at the impulsiveness of their plan, Renloret followed Ani into the bar.

Mroz nodded to him and pointed at a table with three chairs.

The Balance

"Welcome back. Ani's note said we'd *all* be needin' some bolstering without the hangover before and during this conversation, so I pulled one of the energy brews I sometimes use before a competition. Oh, it's not illegal, just some extra vitamins and a few herbs. Also, just so you know, we have about an hour before customers start arriving, so we don't have too much time."

Mroz came from behind the bar and set a tray in the center of the table. He indicated the two pale red containers, a trio of glasses, and a single sauce bowl. Then he poured two fingers of the red liquid into each of the three glasses, splashed some into the bowl, and set the bowl on the floor.

Ani selected a glass and drew it slowly past her nose, checking the blend. "Good choice, Mroz. Just enough caffeine to brace ourselves but not enough to impede reactions or thoughts. Now for the toast." She raised her glass overhead.

"To the Stones of Lrakira and their misunderstood prophecies." Her voice was clear and soft.

"To Taryn," Renloret added.

"To friends in need," Mroz said, a questioning tone lifting the last word.

Kela's single bark punctuated the toast.

"Now, what's this about?" Mroz asked, setting his empty glass on the table.

Ani glanced at Renloret then cleared her throat. "I asked Taryn to investigate something for me, and now he's in trouble and we need your help to get him out."

Mroz slapped his hand on the table making the glassware tremble. "Ha! Between the two of you, Taryn the Terror's been in trouble ever since he locked you in the cabinet when you were nine." Mroz hesitated at the look on Ani's face. "Okay, I'll take the blame for the cabinet since I knew about the scheme and didn't stop him, but he's been in trouble before and since, Ani."

"This is not a child's prank, Mroz, this is serious. Lives depend on Taryn and his life is being threatened."

"All right. What kind of trouble is he in now?"

"He's been kidnapped by Dr. Isul Treyder and is in Saedi City being used to test one of the doctor's experimental devices."

"You're sure he was kidnapped and didn't go willingly?"

They both nodded. Renloret took the piece of fabric from Taryn's uniform out of his pocket. "We found this in Treyder's office at the research center." Frowning, Mroz fingered it, handed the swatch back to Renloret, and nodded for them to continue.

Ani lowered her voice, even though there was no one else in the bar. "Briefly, this is what we know. Taryn didn't sleep at his house, he didn't call in to work, and no one has seen him since last eve. This morn Daneeha showed us some notes concerning a meeting with Dr. Treyder at the research center last night. When we checked, the doctor had not signed in for his usual morning shift. His office looked a shambles, and we found some notes there that made us suspicious. We punched a number from the notes we found into my tel-com and it connected with Senator Nelham's office in the capital."

She paused to make sure that Mroz was following her. The bar owner was hunched a bit toward her, clearly intent on what she was saying. "So we returned to the sheriff's office and had Daneeha trace Taryn's tel-com. It was located at the government center in Saedi City. We went there and discovered that the doctor had met with Senator Nelham late last night. The doctor was not with Nelham when we saw the senator, but one of his associates was, and as the two of them left a committee meeting, we overheard enough to follow the associate."

She took another sip of her drink. "We followed him to a building in the industrial section that seems to be housing a medical research business. Once inside we saw Taryn on a gurney in a guarded laboratory. He was hooked up to all sorts of tubes and wires." Her voice was shaking and her chin trembled.

Renloret continued the story. "Before we were able to discern if he was alive or not, we were discovered and had to run. We escaped the guards only because of Ani's ingenuity."

A blush warmed his face and he noticed Ani averting her gaze. He smiled just a bit and then continued. "We returned to Star Valley as soon as we could to find the doctor so we could question him. Upon arrival, we were informed that the doctor had checked in much later than usual and that he'd left soon after with several boxes of papers and a couple of pieces of unknown equipment. Doctor Treyder didn't tell anyone where he'd been, where he was going, or when he was coming back. Taryn's life is in danger, Mroz. We need your help."

"Hells of Teramar," the bartender whispered. He poured another two fingers of fluid into his glass and swirled it around, obviously contemplating the information. Mroz eyed each of them, even Kela. "So, why do you need me? You two are very capable individuals, and you know what you're up against. Kela here can be a good lookout. Can't you figure out how to do this by yourself? Why not involve his deputies? Why do you need an old man like me?"

Renloret cleared his throat, again hoping he'd read Mroz correctly. "Forget about the deputies. The plan they will come up with will take too much time and involve too many people. And they'll want to barge in and carry him out through the front door. I want to take him off the roof this eve."

Mroz's eyebrows raised but he didn't say anything. He just tipped his glass toward Renloret indicating he wanted more information.

"He's on the fourth floor of a five story flat-roofed building. I'd rather go up one floor than down four. Ani and I could possibly handle an unconscious body, but if you were with us, it would be faster and there would be less chance of injury."

"How are you going to get on and off the roof?"

"This is where I need to know how you really feel about aliens," Renloret replied as he sat back in his chair.

CHAPTER TWENTY-THREE

Mroz took the news about aliens far better than Renloret had imagined. In fact, the bartender practically fell to his knees in excitement when he fully understood what he was asked to help with. It turned out that he was more than eager to do something out of the ordinary and delighted that Renloret had shared such sensitive information with him. The fact that Renloret, Ani's entire family, and even Taryn were aliens seemed to be the least of Mroz's concerns. The childish grin on his face had only gotten larger as he peppered Renloret with questions about why the two species were so similar in looks and in the blade culture. And even though Renloret emphasized that such similarity was extremely rare, Mroz seemed comfortable with the overall idea of aliens, so long as they didn't sprout wings or other extra appendages. Renloret suppressed a smile at that and purposely neglected to mention the Stones, only saying that Taryn was needed specifically to save the life of one of Lrakira's rulers.

The tavern owner became pensive and serious when Ani mentioned that Taryn was her twin. After a long, searching study of Ani—which made her visibly squirm—he silently topped off her glass, raised his to her, and tossed the contents down his throat.

Mroz reached across the table and took her hand, giving it a squeeze. "Do Gelwood and Melli know?"

Ani shook her head and explained that even Taryn did not know because they had only discovered his identity the previous eve. Mroz sounded a soft whistle, then poured the last of the fortifying drink out and silently tossed it back as if it were alcohol.

"I always knew there was something special about your family—aside from being good people. I now understand a bit more about your parents' reluctance to talk about their home in Southern." Mroz chuckled. "Southern. Blades, we never questioned that. All the nuances and accents in our language, the blade techniques, and even the music and dancing seemed to fit with what we know about Southern. Their dedication to the research they were doing, respect for our Northern ways, and willingness to befriend me, teach me . . . is . . ." He shook his head. "I wish I'd known before they died. It would have been fun having an alien for a friend back then. Hells, it was fun. Six years of knowing your father was not long enough. He was a good man, Ani." He patted her hand. "If it hadn't been for the attack on the research center, would your family have stayed?"

Ani shrugged. "All I know is that the original plan was for me to be returned to Lrakira when I reached puberty. Things turned

The Balance

out differently for reasons I can't explain right now."

"Well, other than losing both your parents, I'm pleased with how it worked out . . . until this. Do you have any idea why Isul Treyder has done this? I mean, he was always a bit odd, but he was focused on his machines and how they would help. Why would he resort to kidnapping anyone, especially our little village's sheriff?"

Scooting her chair closer, Ani focused on Mroz. "It's been noted that he had issues with my uncle. Would you know anything about that?"

Mroz nodded. "I remember Reslo fussing about Treyder working on his own projects rather than those he was assigned. And when Treyder wouldn't drop work on them, he was asked to leave the research center. Unfortunately, the dismissal came around the time Treyder's wife died. She had been in a coma for a number of years. It probably didn't set well with the doctor."

"It didn't. We think Taryn is under the influence of one of those little devices."

"So all we have to do is unhook Taryn from the machine and he'll be all right? Why do you need me for that?"

"Because it is not an external machine. Treyder has made it *very* small and it has put Taryn in an artificial coma." Renloret pinched his forefinger to his thumb to demonstrate the size of the tiny device that had been removed from Ani's brain two months earlier, shortly after arriving on Lrakira. "It will take a special surgeon on Lrakira to remove it."

"We have to take Taryn to Lrakira," Ani said.

Mroz shook his head and looked at Ani. "Why would the

doctor want to put someone through that ordeal after he spent over a decade caring for his wife?"

"My guess would be that he wanted to demonstrate it first on my mother to get back at my uncle for firing him. He wants Uncle Reslo in particular to suffer having a family member in a coma, just like he had. But my mother died before he could inject it in her, so when he had a chance, he injected it in me." She shrugged a shoulder at Mroz's shocked expression. "Yeah, it's a long story that can be told *after* we get Taryn out of the mess he's in. The important thing is that we are sure Taryn is under the influence of a similar device and is being held against his will in Saedi City."

"So will you help?" Renloret asked Mroz. "You'll get to be the first native Teramaran to fly in a spaceship." He silently amended his statement to first Teramaran *biped* when he saw Ani push her foot into Kela's ribs. Of course Kela was truly the first Teramaran on a spaceship. He would have to apologize to the canine later.

Unaware of the exchange, a smile lit up Mroz's face. "Absolutely. Count my blade in. This will make an interesting new chapter in my memoir." He winked at Ani. "Now, let's see this plan of yours and how it matches mine." Mroz cleared the table and brought out a pad of paper. He gave Renloret and Ani several sheets so they could sketch out a basic building plan while he called the bartender scheduled for the evening shift to tell him he would be on his own that night. Renloret smiled at Ani when Mroz added a couple of coughs to polish off the lie that he was sick.

The Balance

Renloret was surprised and relieved at Mroz's calm reaction to the existence of aliens. Mroz seemed to take it all in, shrug off the unbelievable part, and just get on with life and the rescue plan. He was more comfortable with the mere idea of aliens than Ani had ever been, or still was, though she'd been to Lrakira and had spent weeks traveling amongst the stars. Renloret decided Ani's mother and uncle had been too successful in protecting Ani's identity.

Once they arrived at the launch tower and control room, Renloret watched Mroz carefully, just to be sure he was really as accepting of the information shared with him and the plan as he appeared to be. When he finished the sequence of codes to release the hidden star runner from its storage space and it slid out of its holding stall, Mroz gawked at it, muttering, "So you really could exterminate us if you wanted to."

"Perhaps." Renloret couldn't lie but he was not certain how much he should say.

They had added the items from Mroz's list to their supplies and then, at Kela's telepathic suggestion to Ani, they had taken the tunnel from the lake house to the research center. This allowed them to escape notice and possible questions from the eve staff at the research center.

As for Mroz, he accepted Renloret's simplified explanations of how the alien Lrakiran technology had created the underground passages between the residence and the research center with its ship storage and launch areas. Renloret kept hoping the decision to include the tavern owner in this escapade would not endanger the future of Teramar in some way. Until this moment, Mroz seemed to have no hesitation about fraternizing with aliens. Now, at Mroz's question, Renloret guessed the reality of an alien presence on Teramar had finally made its impact.

"Do you want to continue?" Ani's voice was tight, as if she was afraid Mroz would answer negatively. Evidently, she'd been thinking the same thing.

Renloret didn't blame her. He waited for a response as Mroz walked around the ship, sliding his hand across the metallic shell. His behavior reminded Renloret of watching Taryn doing the exact same thing barely two moon-cycles ago when Renloret had to take the then comatose Ani back to Lrakira. Would Mroz continue to react as positively as the sheriff had to this glaring announcement of alien technology?

The ramp slid out as Mroz's hand crossed the touch pad, and he stood calmly until it had settled. Then he strode up into the ship. Mroz hadn't yet responded to Ani's question. Renloret and Ani shared concerned glances and Renloret started for the ramp. There were things inside that shouldn't be touched.

"You said you can make this thing invisible?" Mroz asked, his voice drifting down the hall from the bridge area.

"It has a type of camouflage screen or field. You'll only see it if you know what to look for," Renloret replied as he headed for the front of the ship. "Trust me, we won't be seen and since we will be executing this in the dark, after the city's usual work hours, there should be an even smaller chance of discovery."

Mroz stepped out of the control bridge to stand in front of

Renloret, his face serious and adrenaline lighting his eyes. Two large hands gripped Renloret's shoulders. "Then let's hone this blade. We're wasting time."

CHAPTER TWENTY-FOUR

As they hovered over the roof of the building, Ani watched the screen for the structural scan to complete. This whole escapade would be worthless if the weight of the star runner collapsed the building. Renloret had expressed relief that the buildings were crowded up next to one another and that their frames were of metal. She now understood his explanation of how the ship's magnetics would assist the physical braces and allow the star runner to settle without shaking a single building. When everything was ready, he nodded to Ani and Mroz and they gathered equipment, a folding stretcher, which Mroz had suggested, and their weapons.

Once on the roof, they ran to the service stairs. Mroz turned around to stare at the hidden ship.

"Glad we're doing this in the mid-eve and no one is looking up. As you said, Renloret, if I didn't know where it was, I'd never know. Just like those hand-sized holograph units Reslo designed but on a larger scale. I always wondered what good those things would be other than just for entertainment. Now I wonder what Reslo was trying to keep us from seeing." He glanced at Ani.

She shrugged and gave him an innocent smile. "They're perfect for playing hide-and-find. Didn't you ever wonder how I always won? I knew where Uncle Reslo stashed them and I always got one before we played."

Mroz laughed softly. "Didn't your mother ever explain about cheating, girl? One or more of those small units would be handy for this game."

She winked at Mroz. "Sorry. I didn't think about the advantage they might have given us. There really wasn't time."

Ani pulled the fitted hood over her face and opened the roof maintenance door. "Let's grab the sheriff. I expect more guards have been posted since we were chased away."

Renloret put his black assassin hood in place and pulled out his boot blade. "Blades ready?"

Mroz jerked his chin down in answer as he slid a hand to the inside of his jacket and revealed a forearm-length, narrow double-edged blade. "Always."

Ani paused on the fourth floor landing to roll up her shirtsleeves, baring the set of wrist blades. Then she drew a short blade from her thigh scabbard. Renloret helped Mroz tighten the straps holding the folding stretcher to his back while Ani eased open the door. "Ready?" Both men nodded in response.

Stepping through the door, she began checking the other entrances where guards might be stationed. But before she could finish her assessment, the well-lit image in the center of the room immobilized her.

Taryn was no longer lying on a gurney with a sheet covering him. Years of training drained away leaving her near empty except for the blood-chilling need to destroy whoever was responsible for what hung in front of her. All she could think of was killing the doctor, then the senator. She shuddered and enough of her training trickled back to suppress the instinct to scream.

Curses in two or more languages erupted from the men behind her. A hand gripped her shoulder preventing her from bolting blindly to the body hanging from a four-cornered frame in the middle of the room. She was shocked to find herself unsure if she wanted Taryn to be alive or dead. She couldn't close her eyes.

"Wait." Renloret's voice was tight with the kind of control Ani didn't feel.

She tried to shrug out of his hold.

"Think, Ani."

She shook her head. How could she think? Her shoulder hurt as he applied more pressure.

"Breathe. You're in the ring. Where's your opponent? Breathe." The whispered instructions—demands really—reminded her of Uncle Reslo. She straightened up, inhaled for five counts, and forced her mind to see the scene before her as one of the special situation blade rings used to train the recruits at the university. She perused her surroundings. They were similar to one or more of the many holographic blade games Reslo had invented to keep her sharp. A predatory visual search of the room verified opponents had not yet set foot inside the ring, but her goal hung in the center, spotlights showing every bruise and cut. Wires trailed from patches strategically placed on his chest, extremities, and shaved skull. Each line was connected to a machine.

"Mroz? You okay?" Her raptor gaze had come full circle. She'd never seen that expression on his face. They were all going to have nightmares.

"Barely." There was anger and horror in the word. "Let's get him down before they figure out we came in the back way."

Taryn's abdomen rose and fell in an irregular rhythm. Blood oozed from crisscross cuts on his chest and all five fingers of his right hand appeared to be broken. His left knee was swollen and cockeyed while his foot hung at an odd angle, the ankle also broken. Saliva dripped from slack lips. Ani and Mroz vomited on opposite sides of the spot-lit centerpiece of Dr. Isul Treyder's experiment.

"I will kill him," Ani hissed as she wiped her mouth.

"Then I get to," Mroz growled.

Renloret stood in front of the bank of machinery staring at the screens. "I don't think he can feel any of it."

"What?" Both Ani and Mroz chorused.

"He's been implanted with the device, Ani," Renloret said.

"Then why torture him if he can't feel anything?"

"The doctor's notes say he wants to find out how much the body can take before it dies, and if the *patient* can't react, then the ones executing the work won't get squeamish before Treyder gets the results he's looking for."

"I guess I should thank the doctor," she whispered, wiping tears off her cheeks. "At least we found him quickly."

Mroz unstrapped the portable stretcher. "Let's cut him down."

While Ani helped Mroz set up the stretcher, Renloret pecked at a keyboard. "According to this first report, there is no sign his brain is registering any discomfort, only his heart, lungs, and other organs. The meticulous doctor notes that he is delighted with how long the process may take and will continue to experiment—until the body gives out. He plans to wait until some of this initial damage has healed before renewing his efforts. He states that the device works better, and yet differently, than originally planned. There's more here. Should I read it all?"

Ani shook her head. "No. We have to get Taryn to the star ship so the medics there can begin to fix things and then get to Lrakira to have that hells-cursed thing removed."

She could not take her eyes off her brother. His stretched and mangled body brought to mind the back room of the butcher shop she had mistakenly wandered into when the Star Valley school had taken the then ten-year-olds to Saedi City to see how farm produce was processed and packaged. It had been a hot day and Ani had wandered off in search of a cooler place—arriving at the overlook to one of the slaughtering rooms. She remembered watching in shocked fascination as carcass after carcass of ovlines swung on hooks around metal tables where men gutted, skinned, and carved off quarters.

Ani now realized that Doctor Isul Treyder was treating Taryn as less than an animal raised to feed people. At least those ovlines had not suffered injury before being compassionately euthanized for butchering. What she saw hanging before her was a product of a deranged mind. Now, even though her stomach was empty, bile rose up from the depths of her intestines, burning the back of her throat. She swallowed against the gag reflex as she allowed anger to replace the horror her eyes and mind had difficulty processing.

Mroz placed the gurney beneath Taryn's tortured body and was studying the straps that held him upright. "We can cut these and then disengage the lines."

Ani kept surveying the edges of the room. She'd expected a certain number of guards, especially after being chased away from this location just hours earlier. Why were there none? Perhaps they were just waiting. Or even better, she supposed they were expecting a more obvious entrance through the main street-level doors. Appreciation for Renloret's idea to use the star runner and enter the building from above eased some of her tension.

Renloret turned from the screens that continued to record the information fed to them by the sensors on Taryn's body. "I think we ought to take all of this, not just Taryn."

"Why?" Ani asked.

"Our researchers on Lrakira could use this. Maybe they can figure out a way to deactivate the device remotely. According to these notes, Treyder was going to offer thousands of devices like this to the military for use in a war against Southern, and he was developing a method to deliver over a hundred of them at a time at distance—without endangering the soldier firing the machine. According to Treyder's notes, Taryn was the first to be *shot* by this machine. Seems it would only take a nick to embed it and then it would travel to the brain and shut everything off. What would happen if every Southern soldier was the recipient of this?"

Ani shivered as the question hung in the air. "I wish I could remember more of what happened when I encountered Treyder in the tunnel and he inserted the coma device in me," Ani admitted. "I remember the beginning, when he nicked me with the poison on the blade. But everything after that is gone."

Ani felt Mroz's stare but ignored it as she sliced the restraint above Taryn's left knee. "All right, Renloret, but we get Taryn out first. Then we can come back for the rest."

Eardrum piercing whoops shattered the air and flashing lights rotated about the room making it difficult to see.

Mroz leapt on the folding gurney and whacked at the bindings of both arms. Taryn sagged across his shoulder as Ani swung her blade through the remaining leg strap. Without regard for possible further damage to his body, she pulled on both legs to stretch him lengthwise on the gurney. Mroz dropped to his knees and eased Taryn's chest and head into place.

Shouts could be heard from the corridors. Obviously, they had been waiting for a frontal attack. Soldiers spilled into the room, blades and swords unsheathed. Ani grinned at Mroz across Taryn's body, then turned away to face multiple opponents. Yes, just like some of Uncle Reslo's scenarios.

She didn't bother yelling as she dodged the first swing of a sword. The overeager soldier staggered three steps past her as her short blade caught the back of his neck. One down. Two more advanced, a bit more wary. The blaring sirens ceased. Ani heard the ring of blades sliding against each other behind her and to her right, but she did not look to see who engaged with whom. Renloret and Mroz were qualified.

Instead of coming at her singly, the pair in front of her separated and rushed her in a coordinated formation. Recognition of the tactic brought her blade perpendicular to the floor and out of the way as she snapped both wrists backwards releasing the flick-blades towards the assailants. They didn't have a chance to react. They were not wearing vests. Three down. She chanced a glance behind her.

Mroz grappled with an opponent as large as he, though Ani thought the tavern owner was in control. Renloret appeared to be sparring against a well-handled long blade, retreating and advancing the length of the machines. All the sensor wires hung limp, having been blade severed rather than unplugged. One sparked every time Renloret's opponent brushed it, causing him to flinch. Unfortunately, he wouldn't last long, though his technique was more than good—almost familiar. She wondered if she'd seen him compete.

A whistling sound brought her attention back to one of the corridors. She turned her head to see the slingshot release a projectile. She raised her left arm in front of her face, and the solid metal ball smacked the back of her wrist blade sheath. At least one bone broke with the impact. A curse slipped past her lips. She wasn't sure she'd be able to use her hand. The man in the corridor loaded a second time. She grimaced. It was his turn to pay for Taryn.

A cry from Mroz swung her around in time to catch a descending blade against hers. She kicked at this new opponent's knee. With a cry of his own, he dropped his blade and crumpled around the ruined joint. Ani kicked the weapon away and struck the butt of her blade on the man's temple, silencing him. Four down.

The high-pitched whirling of the sling signaled that another ball was on its way. She flattened her body on the floor. The ball passed over her and ricocheted off several pieces of equipment, pinging almost musically until it rolled to a resting point on the room's central drain. Ani noticed that the drain was stained red with Taryn's blood and anger boiled up, renewing her adrenaline. She rose from the floor, refusing to be pinned down by a rock thrower. Wasn't he man enough to meet her one-on-one?

Another metal ball thunked into her side, making her grateful they had all worn vests. The strike was sure to cause a bruise, but it did not break a rib.

The sling wielder stepped out of the shadowed corridor with a sword. Ha! He was out of throwing ammunition. With her left wrist disabled, she didn't waste time. Instead of meeting him blade-to-blade, she ducked, rolling into his body to bring the short blade up into his chest as he tried to leap over her. She was jerked backward along with his fall. Twisting to her side, she wrenched the blade free and jumped to her feet.

Movement on the other side of the room caught her attention. Renloret was withdrawing his blade from his opponent's gut. Turning in her direction, a grimace on his lips, he pointed his blade at the gurney. Mroz was buckling a strap across Taryn's chest. Blood dripped from Mroz's mask. Ani ran to him and pulled up the edge above his eyes. The skin had been split in a powerful glancing blow, possibly from an elbow. It would bleed a lot at first, but the mask would act as a bandage until they could get to the ship. She released the mask and patted him on the shoulder. He gave her a bruised and bloody-lipped smile and reached for a second strap.

Ani listened for additional soldiers. How many had entered the room? Had any left to get reinforcements? They couldn't wait. They had to get Taryn to the ship.

"Renloret?" Ani glanced over to the machines he had been looking at when the soldiers arrived. He was stacking whatever papers were on the work surfaces into a box.

"I'm unscathed. You?" he asked.

She tried to move her wrist. Up and down was not too painful but twisting it caused her to suck in a breath through clinched teeth. "Possible broken wrist. Mroz?"

"A nick or two. I think he bit my arm too." The bartender wiped his blood off Taryn's stomach, then looked at Renloret. "I'm assuming Ani will provide rear protection as we transport the sheriff to the roof." He cocked his head toward the emergency exit.

"I'll return for the research," Renloret said, stuffing a handful of notebooks into the box and then taking up the grips on the gurney.

After depositing the gurney with Taryn's body in one of the sleeper alcoves in the star runner, the three rescuers returned to the lab. Bodies lay where they'd fallen. Mroz gathered all the loose computers and tablets into a second box and ran back up to the ship. While Ani stayed at the door checking for signs of reinforcements, Renloret crawled under the long console counter and tried, without success, to figure out how to remove the entire assemblage of hardware from its floor bolts.

"We've got everything we can, Renloret. Let's go. You'll have to carry the box." A groan from the soldier Ani had knocked unconscious added urgency to her order.

Renloret crawled from under the desk and kicked the almost conscious man in the head. "We have more time now." He started to duck back, but Ani grabbed at his shoulder.

"No. Get the box. We're leaving now." She jerked her head toward the stairwell door and grabbed one of the swords abandoned by a fallen soldier. It might be useful.

Renloret straightened with a sigh, embraced the box of files, and followed her. The sound of boots and raised voices echoed through the corridors. Ani shoved Renloret up the stairwell and jammed the extra blade in the stairwell door before running down one flight and pulling the door open a crack. Let them think the intruders had escaped by going down to the third floor rather than up. Taking the steps two at a time, she reached the roof with minimal sound. Once out the roof door she made sure it was firmly closed, then dashed for the ship.

She crossed into the camouflaged surroundings at a run and at the wrong angle. When one of the ship's supporting legs grazed her head, she automatically slapped her free hand, the injured one, on top of her head. The double shock of pain brought tears to her eyes and curses rolled off her tongue.

"Over here."

She stumbled into Mroz, who dragged her up the ramp and examined her scalp once they were inside.

"No harm. There'll be a lump. Now let's look at the wrist."

"Later, Mroz. Did you strap Taryn in?"

"Not fully. Renloret told me to watch for you."

"Let's tuck my brother in and get out of here." They moved toward the sleeping alcoves.

"Can I go with you to this Lrakira?" Mroz asked as he tightened the strap across Taryn's chest. "Not sure I like being here anymore."

Ani placed her uninjured hand on his shoulder. "Sorry, Mroz. I don't think we have time to concoct a story to explain your absence so I think we should stick to the plan and take you back to Star Valley. But you will need to be careful. If the milits find out you've aided aliens, you won't be safe."

Mroz nodded in agreement and tucked her into a tight embrace. "Yah, I know."

Ani returned the hug. She was thankful they had managed to get Taryn out and thankful none of them had sustained serious injuries. She patted Mroz's shoulder before running up the central passage to tell Renloret he could head for Star Valley.

"Mags are holding," Renloret said as she joined him. "The bracing struts have retracted and are locked."

Mroz joined them, and Ani tapped him on the shoulder and pointed out the front window. The roof maintenance door burst open and soldiers stepped out onto the roof cautiously, preparing a first line of defense. One waved more soldiers onto the roof's surface and all held their blades ready as they attempted to cross to the far side of the building. Near the center of the roof, the magnetic force holding the ship above the building abruptly pushed their swords and short blades down. Their confused antics were amusing as they looked around trying to figure out why they could not lift up the weapons.

"They'll never figure this one out," Mroz said. He tapped Renloret on the shoulder. "Homeward, young man."

"Buckle up, people."

Ani's stomach flip-flopped when the ship rose swiftly into the darkness above the city. The city's illumination gradually blurred to a singular blob and then disappeared as the star runner moved toward the mountain range that separated the capital city from Star Valley.

CHAPTER TWENTY-FIVE

On the way to Star Valley, Mroz wrapped Ani's broken wrist and gave her a large dose of painkilling tablets. It would suffice until the medics on the star cruiser could attend to it. After dropping Mroz off behind the bar, Renloret flew them to the cabin to meet Kela. The canine relayed through Ani that Taryn's disappearance had been noted and official inquiries were being made. Gelwood and Melli had been informed and were reportedly distraught. The sheriff's office wanted to talk with Ani and Renloret as soon as possible about the results of their investigation.

Renloret suggested that they stay in Star Valley until some sort of explanation for their departure could be constructed. They decided to keep Taryn in the star runner tucked safely in a stasis bag, but they knew they had some creative storytelling to do with the authorities, not to mention Melli and Gelwood. First they needed to contact the sheriff's office to report that they had information about Taryn and needed to meet as soon as Ani and

Renloret could get to Star Valley. Ani planned to suggest that the acting sheriff get the capital police involved.

What the capital police would find at the laboratory would probably be enough to bring the doctor's methods of experimentation under scrutiny and government oversight. Ani wondered if they had left enough information to incriminate the doctor for kidnapping and hint that the senator was involved. It would be interesting to see how deep his influence ran. In the meantime, the investigation could be directed by the local deputies.

When Renloret stated that they wouldn't have to tell anyone, including Melli and Gelwood, that they had actually rescued Taryn, Ani nixed the idea, not wanting to put the couple through that kind of mental anguish. She insisted on talking to them in person. Renloret reluctantly agreed.

Though it was very early morn, Daneeha picked up the call before the second buzz when they called her at home. Ani told Daneeha that she and Renloret needed to talk to her and the acting sheriff, whoever he was, as soon as possible because they had important information about Taryn. And despite Daneeha's probing, Ani remained firm that details could wait until they got to the sheriff's office. Though completely flustered, Daneeha relented and promised to contact the acting sheriff and then head over to open the building. Ani lied when Daneeha asked how long it would take them to get to Star Valley by saying they were still a couple of hours away. Fortunately Daneeha accepted that, and Ani disconnected the com-tel before she could pry more information from her.

With a sigh she turned to Renloret. "We still can't tell anyone that Taryn is my brother. Not only will I not take away their only child when they are under this kind of stress, but Taryn needs to know who he really is before even they are told. Agreed?"

"Agreed," Renloret said.

Kela barked his assent.

"Now I have to eat something or I'm going to faint. And we have a couple of hours to figure out what exactly we're going to say." Ani began pulling out leftovers from the food cooler, wincing as she unconsciously used her injured wrist to keep the cooler door open. She heaved an audible sigh when Renloret gently pushed her to the couch and completed assembly of the meal. The pain tablets had enabled her to function though she was still aware of a deep ache. She cradled the injured appendage, confident that the medics on the waiting cruiser hiding behind the fifth planet could repair it on the way to Lrakira.

So, what are you going to do about Taryn's physical injuries? Kela asked.

Ani repeated the question aloud for Renloret's sake and then took a deep breath as she considered her answer. "I am not a doctor, Kela. We bandaged his wounds and made his body as comfortable as possible until we get him to Lrakira."

No, you have not done everything, Kela whispered in her head.

She responded verbally without translating. "What do you mean I haven't done everything? What else can I do?"

Use the blade.

"Use the blade? To do what?" Her voice trembled with agitation. She counted the number of cuts she and Renloret had already bandaged before sealing Taryn in the stasis bag. She'd almost thrown up at that point, her claustrophobia tearing at her own lungs at the sight of a living, breathing being closed up in one of the black and silver bags. As much as she wanted to, she didn't think she could even sit next to Taryn until he'd been removed from the bag.

You could heal his wounds with the blade.

"*I* could heal him?"

Ani glared at Renloret. He had come from the stove with a plate full of leftover scramble. He took a step back, raising his free hand in surrender as he faced her, the plate just close enough for her to grasp. Fortunately, he wasn't smiling, or she would have shown him the meal side of his offering in minute detail.

"What makes you think I could heal him?" she asked. Her stomach growled at the enticing smell and she snatched the plate. "I'm going to eat. Don't talk to me. I have enough on my mind." She shoveled a portion into her mouth.

Kela sat directly in front of her, his ears at full attention, his eyes locked onto Ani's. She chewed, swallowed, and tried to scoop up a second spoonful. The spoon stopped just outside her open mouth. She could not blink to break his scrutiny.

"Oh, hells." She set the plate on the cushion next to her and stomped out of the cabin, slamming the door. She didn't want to consider what Kela was requesting. She just didn't.

You know the song. You've heard it twice and you've sung it at least once.

His gentle reminder brought tears to her eyes. The first time she'd heard the song was the only time she'd actually seen what it could do. She'd been a mere seven years old when her mother began her blade training. About halfway through her first lesson, Ani had managed to cut her mother's arm, and though her mother had been calm and praised her for ingenuity, the copious amount of blood had frightened Ani. In fact, she'd been so frightened she'd almost forgotten how her mother had used the blade and a song to staunch the blood and heal the wound to a faint line running the length of her forearm. The memory of causing her mother injury had nearly foresworn her from ever touching a blade, let alone the green crystal blade her mother so reverently spoke of and handled.

She defended her reluctance to try. *The blade is just a blade. It's a tool, not a physician, Kela.* Ani sat on the top step, chin in her uninjured hand. Not much discussion had been held in her presence about the second blade healing. From Renloret and Kela's accounts, as well as what she had gathered from the medical records on Lrakira, her wounds from the fight in the cavern had supposedly been healed by the Anyala Stone's crystal blade and a song. *Supposedly* was the catchword. It was too much magic for her sensibilities, though she could not discount the fact that her wounds had healed to a barely discernable ripple in her skin in less than two weeks.

She had, of course, not witnessed this healing because she had been incapacitated by the poison and coma device at the time. She'd been told that Renloret and Taryn had used the green crystal blade and an ancient Lrakiran song of healing to rid her body of the poison and heal the physical wounds. Evidently, the song and blade combined to keep her alive, but it was unable to remove the tiny machine lurking at the base of her brain.

When she had awakened on Lrakira upon removal of the device, the lack of contact with Kela had terrified her. It had taken her singing the remembered healing song to break through the lingering effects of the device.

She rubbed the back of her head where the Lrakiran surgeon had said the tiny machine had lodged. The scientists and doctors on Lrakira were still studying the device, amazed that such an advanced piece of technology had come from the backward world of Teramar. She had seen it, once. Now she shivered, though she hadn't then when she was just curious about how such a minuscule item could bring about coma. Merely thinking about the impact of that *thing* on her—including its ability to suppress her mental connection with Kela—angered and frightened her. What would it do to Taryn? Could it enable Treyder to manipulate Taryn in some way? Could the Lrakiran physicians really heal him? Could she?

Ani studied the clearing in front of the cabin. If she looked close enough, she could see the edge of the holographic camouflage hiding the ship, Taryn's tortured body inside. Could his injuries be healed by the song?

"Ani?" Renloret had followed her to the porch.

Without turning around she asked, "Can I heal Taryn's body?"

He settled next to her on the step. "I was just thinking about that myself. As a Stone Singer, you have a better chance than Taryn and I had in the cavern. You won't know unless you try."

Uncomfortable silence filled the space between them for several breaths.

Kela joined them. He placed a paw on her shoulder. *You must believe, Ani. You are the Anyala Stone's Singer, even here on Teramar. You were healed by the blade* after *the Stone was damaged and the blade allowed Renloret and Taryn to sing for you.* He paused. *I believe you can heal your brother's injuries.*

Wiping the tears from her cheeks, she knew she had to try—for her brother, for the Stone. She stood. "Let's sharpen this blade now, before I can talk myself out of it."

She marched toward the star runner being careful of where the dawn light shivered around the camouflaged struts. The camouflaging fit the star runner tightly, so she traced her hand across the surface until she reached the boarding ramp pad. After slapping open the ramp, she headed to her sleeping quarters to retrieve the blade. Renloret and Kela trailed after her.

Blade box in hand, Ani led the way to the long-sleep section, and it took them only a few minutes to prepare Taryn's body. Ani stood opposite Renloret, her eyes shifting from the box in her hand to Taryn and back to Renloret. She was afraid and swallowed against her reluctance to prove her identity as a Stone Singer as she keyed the blade box unlock sequence.

Opening it, Ani sighed at the sight of the bejeweled handle and the faceted dark green crystal blade nestled on the blood-red silteene fabric. She felt a mental call not unlike the telepathic communication with Kela. The blade was expectant, eager to be in her hands. She hesitated. Was it alive like the Stone?

Kela's voice came as a whisper. *May I listen with you?*

Surprised, Ani spoke aloud. "You can hear it?"

He barked in assent.

She looked at Renloret, who was standing ready on the other side of Taryn's body. "Kela can hear the blade through me."

It is more emotions than words. It knows you and Taryn. It is eager to assist you in the healing.

"He says the blade knows me and why I need it to heal Taryn."

Renloret nodded. "I assumed you were blade-bonded in some way, though I had not seen the tattoo scars on your arms at the time of your healing. They would have confirmed you were the Singer. I took a great risk assuming you were bonded and the blade would not harm me or Taryn when we sang for you.

"I didn't know the rules of how a blade healing should be performed, but neither do Diani or Layson. They will need to review the oldest texts. The Singers have been complacent in their communication for too long. They no longer study the past and prepare for the future. It wasn't until after your father returned to Lrakira with news of your birth that the Singers even asked their Stones about the prophecy. They hadn't bothered to research it until then, even though the Stones had mentioned it before your parents left Lrakira. The Singers did not understand the importance of that first song." He shook his head.

"The first song?" Ani asked, rubbing her wrist. The pain relieving aspects of the tablets were wearing off and the ache of the broken bone grated against her ability to concentrate on what Renloret was saying. She wasn't sure how much longer she could manage but she wanted a distraction, at least for a few minutes, and the first song sounded like a good enough distraction option.

"The first song in the first book of *Stone Singer History* mentions The Blood and The Balance and how they will each save one. I only saw the words once before coming here but I was able to write it down over a month later, and yet neither Layson nor Diani could place it."

"Why not? Surely they would be instructed on the history of the Stones when they became Singers."

"You would assume that, though under the circumstances, I doubt your mother was, and you haven't had this instruction either."

"Now wait," she said. Ani wanted to defend her mother and herself, but his expression and tone of voice said he was not judging, just stating facts. The facts were agitating. "I guess Mother had the excuse that she was doing what the Anyala Stone requested, and my excuse is that I didn't know until I woke up on Lrakira. I've probably been a Stone Singer since Mother died."

"No one expected you to be the Anyala Stone's Singer when you'd never been on Lrakira," Renloret admitted. "We have all these ceremonies around the bonding between the Singer and her Stone. Now they seem to be inconsequential."

"They aren't inconsequential to Selabec," Ani replied. "She still thinks I'm her daughter instead of her granddaughter, and the last time I talked with her, she was actively planning some elaborate ceremony to officially bond her daughter to the Anyala Stone. I'm not sure she even remembers stabbing the Stone."

Waving his hand and shaking his head, Renloret dismissed her comment. "Let's keep that blade dull until we're on Lrakira."

Ani agreed with a decisive nod. Looking at Taryn now, Ani felt a compelling need to heal all of his wounds, and she did not want to wait even a couple of hours to get him to the medics on the waiting ship before she attempted it. If she could heal him now, that healing would be immediate and complete instead of taking weeks on Lrakira, even with the skilled doctors there. She knew she could not remove the device, but if she could heal his wounds, the device could be removed as soon as they returned to Lrakira. He needed to be healthy and strong enough to pull the blade from the Stone, and the sooner he healed, the sooner he could do that. She turned a quizzical expression toward Renloret as a thought came. "How does a crystal get stabbed? I know what we both saw in the chamber but I still don't understand it."

He shrugged. "I don't either. We can ask the Stones once Taryn does what he is supposed to do. It's just one of many questions I want answers to." He pointed at the blade box. "Since we don't know if he has internal damage, I suggest you start by holding the blade near his chest and begin singing. I think the blade will lead you the rest of the way—or at least that is what happened when Taryn and I used the blade over you in the cavern. I will join in as Taryn did. I think multiple singers, not just Singers, make stronger medicine."

Ani raised the blade to her lips and whispered, "Though the Anyala Stone is injured and very far away, if I am truly bonded through you, show me the way to heal my brother."

Inhaling deeply, she searched for the starting notes of the song. Memories flooded in of her mother singing. The half-remembered vision of the green blade glowing in concert with her mother's delicate alto warmed Ani. The melody came.

Light from the blade bathed the room in a soft green haze.

The Lrakiran words, foreign to her tongue but not her

memory, came to fit the music. The blade was hot and glowed with an internal green fire. She was surprised when the green haze gathered first about her broken wrist. Warmth spread out and back, the pain eased, and she actually felt the bone mend.

As she continued to sing, a green fire leapt from the blade, centered itself over Taryn, and appeared to lick out and into his body. Tears coursed multiple paths to drip onto her hands. White knuckled, Ani gripped the blade hilt as it moved. She seemed to see each injury under the bruises mend within a green haze, and she knew, without doubt, that alien magic—the combination of song and connection with Taryn through the blade—was causing an unimagined miracle.

Her hands trembled uncontrollably, but larger hands covered hers, halting the tremors. Renloret picked up the song. She followed with a descant and felt the power unleashed through the blade. She took a breath and added joy as she sensed what the blade was doing. Together, they shared the healing of Taryn's knee, the straightening of twisted intestine, and the calming of his heart. They sang until their voices cracked and the blade allowed her to release her grip.

When Ani opened her eyes, Renloret was staring at her, his eyes filled with wonder. Then he bowed almost to his waist and touched his left index finger to his forehead. "This salute, the oldest I can verify, is given to acknowledge a Singer as is proper when she has shown the truth of her bonding."

"I sang the song and the blade directed the magic. You assisted when I faltered. I did not accomplish a healing on my own. How is that a sign that I am a Singer?" She wondered if she would be accepted as one because she'd needed help in accomplishing the healing.

"A successful healing is the strongest and oldest sign of a true Singer," Renloret said. "And this healing is not the only one. Ani, you have succeeded four times in healing."

"Four?"

He nodded at Taryn's body. No bruises showed, his heart and lungs seemed to be functioning with ease, and only a few scar lines were visible, marking where the flesh had been cut or torn. "Taryn was your fourth. The third was when you healed your broken wrist, just before you healed Taryn. The second was when you healed yourself after the coma device was removed. The first and most important was after you were poisoned and implanted with the device. If you had not been blade-bonded, I am not sure Taryn and I would have been able to save you. The blade allowed me to use it to heal you. That would only have happened if you were a Stone Singer." He repeated the honorific gesture.

Ani lowered her head in acceptance and relaxed her grip on the blade. It no longer glowed with internal green fire. It was no longer hot. It was a plain, green, crystal blade. Ani studied Taryn's still form. Had she and the blade truly succeeded?

CHAPTER TWENTY-SIX

Ani gingerly removed the bandages from Taryn's body. All the cuts and bruises were gone; even the twisted knee was straight. Renloret tucked a blanket around Taryn's form and pulled the sealing tab up the length of the stasis bag. Ani backed away, arms crossed, and Renloret noticed the shiver of her shoulders as he secured the stasis bag's lock.

"He will be fine until we reach Lrakira," Renloret said. "The device will be removed, and then he can save the Anyala Stone."

"Will he become its Singer?" She seemed afraid of losing her newly accepted title.

"I . . . I don't know. I suppose the Stone will tell us when it has healed. When I was younger, I once asked if I could be a Singer. The answer was a simple and emphatic no. Instead, I read all I could about them. In all my explorations of the history of the Stones, I have not once read of a male Singer."

"Not a single one?"

He shook his head. Renloret did not know how this part of

The Blood and The Balance prophecy was supposed to end. He knew only the first verse of the song, and like all songs, it was cryptic enough to cause a multitude of arguments. The Singers would have to read the whole song. Perhaps this incident would encourage the Singers to communicate more closely with their Stones. Hopefully, the Singers would then pass on their rediscovered past to the entire population of Lrakira and not just to the next generation of Singers. He allowed a smile to soften his face.

Admitting that the Singers did not know everything about their crystalline charges would cause ripples of disbelief and trouble across his home world. Some portion of the populace would not trust the Singers to guide them if they could not be honest about the knowledge gained from their connection with the Stones. Perhaps the Singers had never been "in charge" of the Stones as was commonly believed. Perhaps—and this made Renloret a bit uncomfortable—the Stones were really in charge of the Lrakiran people, not the other way around.

Seeing Ani frown, he asked her if she was worried that she might not be the Anyala Stone's Singer once Taryn was healed.

"Perhaps a little, but it's a subject I haven't really had time to digest. Since no one seems to know what's going to happen next, I think we'll all have to wait until the Stone is saved," she confessed.

With that comment, she turned to the long-sleep compartment, gently lowered the sliding door, and pressed the sealing pad. Her shoulders shivered slightly but she maintained a straight, calm face as she double-sealed Taryn into the confining space.

With her brother cared for to the best of their abilities, Renloret could now send a message to the waiting ship and Ani's father, letting them know that the twin had been found and they would be leaving Teramar after picking up the bodies of his original team from their temporary burial place in the canyon above the cabin. His thoughts on those two things, Renloret started toward the star runner's bridge, expecting Ani to follow. She did not.

He backtracked. Ani was crouched beside the compartment with one hand on the transparent barrier and the other covering her mouth. She was crying. Kela had wedged himself between Ani and the compartment, bracing her, his icy blue eyes staring accusingly at Renloret.

The pilot settled on the floor and pulled Ani into a cradling embrace. "For the second time, I am sorry, Ani. We don't know how much time the Stone has and we need to get Taryn to Lrakira as fast as possible."

"I have to tell his parents something." Her words were blurry through her crying.

"Stones and blades! I have forgotten Melli and Gelwood. Aren't we supposed to let the sheriff's office know when we will be there so they can meet with us?" Renloret wondered what Ani would—or could—tell them at this point. A great deal had happened within a very short time, and neither Melli nor Gelwood had been privy to most of it.

She sat up, wiping tears away with fists like a young child. "Isul Treyder may have tried to take him away but we found him, and that Lrakiran doctor, Sholoret, or whatever his name is, can take that thing out of his head and bring him back. Right?"

"I am confident, Ani. The surgeon has done it once already with great success."

"I thought I had this all figured out before we healed him. Now I'm not sure. What are we going to tell Melli and Gelwood? I can't tell them he's an alien and is needed to save the life of an intelligent crystal. And I can't tell them he's my brother. I won't, not when even he doesn't know."

Kela whined.

She grabbed the canine by the scruff of his neck and pulled him close to kiss his muzzle. "Yes, Kela, that's a good idea." She scrambled to her feet and headed toward the exit ramp.

"What is Kela's idea?" Renloret asked as he hurried to follow.

"We're going to lie . . . sort of. I'll explain on the way to the sheriff's office. The Anyala Stone will have to wait a few more bells."

Before heading into the village, Ani called the sheriff's office to inform them of their target arrival time. During the dash down the mountain to the village, Ani talked through the plan with Kela and Renloret, occasionally pausing to hear their input and answer questions. She was thankful that the drive to the village took about twenty minutes because it gave them time to collect themselves and get their story straight.

Daneeha looked up from her desk as Ani and Renloret strode into the reception area of the sheriff's office, Kela padding close to Ani's side. The secretary flipped the switch on the interoffice com. "Yantel, they're here."

Taryn's office door opened and the acting sheriff, Deputy Yantel, beckoned them in. Ani nodded approval when Yantel asked Daneeha to come in as well. Daneeha moved a chair close to the door so she could keep an eye on the reception area then climbed up and sat—her face serious, a notebook and pen at the ready.

Yantel offered his forearm in greeting to both Ani and Renloret then sat on the edge of the desk. Like Daneeha, he had a notebook and pen poised. Ani felt her lip curve upward at the similarity between the deputy now in charge of Star Valley's security and the missing sheriff. If needed, she knew that Yantel would make a fine sheriff, having learned from Taryn.

Yantel cleared his throat and looked directly at Ani. "Miss Chenak, I'm glad you've recovered from the trauma caused by General Dalkey. The sheriff said that your parents' village is safe and healing because Renloret here," he nodded at the pilot, "was able to get you to Southern in time.

"Now, as to our immediate concerns, I've told Gelwood and Melli that we had news of Taryn's whereabouts. I will send a deputy to pick them up when I have the details. Start talking." He was ready to take notes.

Ani found herself rolling her lip between her teeth. She took a breath and began. "Well, I'm sure you've read Taryn's report of what happened at the cemetery and the research center." Yantel nodded, and Ani explained that when Taryn and Renloret found her, she was only able to tell them that she'd been poisoned before losing consciousness.

Renloret then took up the narrative and gave Yantel the story he and Ani had agreed to about rushing Ani to Southern to counteract the poison and see if her blood would save the village. "But when she did not regain consciousness after the antidote was administered, the Southern doctors ran a complete body scan and found a very small device lodged in her head."

He paused, and when he did, Yantel looked up from his note taking.

"Once the device was removed, Ani quickly recovered and appeared to have no ill effects from either the poison or the miniature machine, with the exception of memory loss, which was attributed to one of the side effects of the poison. The doctors then tested her blood for signs of the virus and when they confirmed she was immune to it, they were able to create a vaccine."

When Renloret paused again, Ani continued. "Renloret and I stayed in Southern until all the women of my home village were inoculated and deemed safe. Then I spent the ensuing weeks researching the genetic implications of the disease and found reference to my mother having twins. But only my name was in the record."

Yantel stopped the telling at that point. "So that's what Taryn was helping you with? To find your twin?"

"Yes. Mother had never talked about a twin, and I had no idea if she was even alive. If she was, I wanted to find her—not only because she was my twin, but because she would need the vaccine if she was not also immune. I thought that perhaps Mother would have made notes somewhere about the disease and my immunity. And maybe she had written something down about what had happened to the twin. So we needed access to her old notes at the research center."

"And that's why you and Taryn were working at the new center." Yantel nodded. "That makes sense. Go on."

"Well, we went to see if Doctor Ganevek had any of my mother's old records and ended up talking to a Doctor Isul Treyder. He seemed to recognize me but I have no specific recollections of him, though he did say he'd been gone for a number of years and only recently returned. While we talked, I got a creepy feeling about him. I mean he, well, ah, just acted a bit odd." Ani paused and grimaced. "I mentioned it to Taryn and Doctor Ganevek a bit later, and Ganevek agreed that the man was odd but that he was also a mechanical genius. Then Doctor Ganevek showed us one of the amazing machines Treyder designed. Well anyway, I'm thinking that the combination of Treyder's behavior and the machine must have triggered something in Taryn—suspicion or a gut feeling—and that's why he went back that eve." She pointed at Taryn's open notebook on the desk. "He probably made notes on it."

"Yes, I've already read them. Now I understand the references." Yantel added to his notes. "So now I want to back up a bit. Did you ever discover the identity of the twin?"

Ani glanced at Renloret, and he gave her a short nod. "Yes, but according to Melli, who was present at the birth, the twin died shortly after birth. The baby may never have taken a breath. My mother asked Melli to keep it a secret, but when I told Melli that I knew about the twin, she told me what had happened. Melli also told us that Taryn was meeting with a doctor that eve, so Renloret and I decided to wait until morning to tell him that the twin had died. Then when we got here, Daneeha told us Taryn hadn't checked in yet, so we went to the research center to see if Treyder might know where Taryn was, but the doctor wasn't in his office either."

"All we found was a note on Treyder's desk with a tel-com number on it and a piece of fabric we think belongs to the sheriff's uniform jacket," Renloret added as he pulled the scrap from his pocket and handed it to Yantel.

The acting sheriff took a step toward Renloret, shaking the fabric evidence in his face. "Blades, man, why didn't you leave it there so we could have found it? I could charge you with destroying evidence in a possible criminal investigation." Yantel looked at Daneeha, who grimaced and nodded.

Renloret shrugged and added that they had entered the number from the doctor's note into Ani's tel-com and it had connected to Senator Nelham's committee office in Saedi City. They wondered if Taryn and the doctor had gone to the capital to discuss something with the senator but couldn't figure out just what, so they had asked Daneeha to trace Taryn's tel-com to be sure.

Yantel nodded and said he remembered, then asked to see her tel-com. Glad she had not yet disposed of it, Ani pulled it out and showed the coordinates to Yantel. When Yantel said he was keeping the tel-com as evidence, she pursed her lips and was about to protest when the stern expression on Yantel's face convinced her to back down.

"At the government building we were told that Dr. Treyder had met with Senator Nelham very late that eve and that we should speak with the senator if we had questions. We were directed to a committee meeting room to wait for the senator to conclude his business. He came out of the room with another man. We overheard him asking the man if the sheriff was alive, and the man answered that he appeared to be in a coma and was concerned that his condition wasn't what they expected. When he asked if Treyder was still in town, the senator said he wasn't and gave him a number to call. Then they went in opposite directions. We decided not to waste time confronting the senator and followed the man he'd been talking to." Ani took a breath. "He led us to a medical building in the warehouse district of Saedi City. We found Taryn already in a comatose state in a guarded laboratory on the fourth floor."

Yantel and Daneeha both scribbled in their notebooks as Ani gave a bare blade account of the rescue, leaving out Mroz's participation and anything that smacked of alien devices or vehicles.

Yantel listened and added notes, his frown deepening until he apparently couldn't hold back his reaction. "What in all the hells of Teramar made you think you could—or should—pull that off without any assistance or backup?"

Ani shrugged. "Well it worked, Yantel. We got him out, and he's prepped for evacuation to Southern so that machine can be removed. I wanted to go right away but Renloret suggested, rightly, that you and Taryn's parents should know what happened before we left. I promise we'll bring him back as soon as we can."

"You better," Daneeha said, breaking her silence.

Yantel threatened to arrest both of them for taking matters into their own hands and not informing him of what had transpired until after the fact, then grudgingly admitted that if the blades had been turned the other way, Taryn himself would have committed the same hotheaded caper. The difference would have been that he would have taken the deputies. But his straight-lipped smile did not bode well for Renloret and Ani.

"Please, Yantel. We're positive Taryn has been injected with a device similar to the one removed from me. We should get him to Southern as soon as possible."

Yantel closed his notebook. "Daneeha, please ask the deputy to go pick up the Averes. I'll want to pass on this information to them." Daneeha left the room, and the acting sheriff turned his attention back to Ani and Renloret. "How long do you think it will take to get to Southern, have the device removed, and return Taryn to health and home?"

Ani glanced at Renloret. "I'm guessing about a month. At most six weeks. I'm sure the doctors there will want to make sure he was not subjected to any unseen abuse or injected with anything else." She hoped he wouldn't ask to be given examples.

Yantel pursed his lips and rubbed his hand across his forehead. "Okay. I will fill in the Averes. While you're gone, we will get some help from the Saedi City department and track down the *doctor* and see if he has any connection to the senator. If you're wrong, I will hunt you both down, no matter where you are."

She didn't dare smile at the knowledge that they wouldn't be anywhere on Teramar.

"Bring him back, Ani."

She stepped close and hugged him. She was relieved, but she also felt a large amount of guilt rise up as she realized that Melli and Gelwood would hear from Yantel about the coma device and that she had been the first recipient of it—something she had deliberately kept from Melli in their earlier discussions. They would be alarmed that Taryn had such a device in him, taken aback by his quick removal to Southern, and probably furious with Ani for the lie of omission. She couldn't imagine what they would think or how they would feel if they knew the full truth. As much as she wanted to be the one to tell Melli and Gelwood, she appreciated the acting sheriff's sense of urgency and understood that, in any event, it was his prerogative to be the one to tell them. And she knew that getting the device out of Taryn as soon as possible had to be her priority.

Yantel pushed her toward the door. "Now go before I can figure out why I should arrest you."

With Renloret on her heels, she made a swift exit. She would have to make amends to Melli and Gelwood later.

CHAPTER TWENTY-SEVEN

Before the star runner left Teramar, Renloret stopped at the canyon crash site to retrieve the two stasis bags. The bodies of Kiver and Sharnel were secured in separate units next to Taryn's and the star runner, once again camouflaged against visual detection, bolted from the planet's atmosphere.

A brief message outlining the successful completion of the assignment with some complications was sent ahead to the waiting cruiser. Commander Chenakainet's demand to know the identity of the twin had been ignored, along with a request for explanation about the complicating circumstances. As far as Ani was concerned, her father could wait a few more hours to learn that he had a son and not another daughter, and the full account of what had happened would take some time.

A grin from Renloret as he flipped off the communication switch in the middle of Chenakainet's third attempt to get the identity of the twin elicited a sharp guffaw from Ani as she stopped pacing and flopped into the copilot's seat.

"He's known about the twin for a few seconds less than me and he can't wait until we dock?" Her tone was harsh. "I've known Taryn as my best friend since birth, and Chenakainet probably barely remembers him because Taryn and I were only five when he left. I'm trying to figure out which one of us should be more upset. Hells, Renloret, I considered marrying Taryn."

Was the reason she turned down Taryn's proposal because she subconsciously sensed that they were related? It didn't seem likely, though she had to admit that she had always been closer to him that anyone else besides her mother. Thanking all the gods, three parents, and an uncle for their influence on a pair of teenagers and young adults, Ani let loose a relieved sigh that Taryn and she had, together, decided to remain celibate, though breaking that celibacy had crossed their minds on occasion. Ani remembered one particular night they had come terribly close. She shook her head in wonder. How was it that both of them had felt it wasn't quite right? Was their attraction to each other more about the fact they were twins than anything romantic? Was that why they never consummated the relationship?

They often seemed to know what the other was going to say or do. How many times had one or the other of them said or done exactly what was needed in a way that seemed more than usually intuitive? Was this how being a twin was supposed to feel? Would this newly discovered connection help Taryn come to terms with the change in their relationship?

Kela laid his head across her thigh and she rubbed the base of his ears. *Will he be embarrassed to be around me? Will he be disgusted?*

He should know his heritage so he can decide who he truly is.

I am not sure of my own identity, Kela. Am I Ani Chenak, first female blade ring champion of Teramar's northern continent, or Anyala Chenakainet of Lrakira, Singer of the Anyala Stone?

Why not both?

Her laugh was not the happy sort. She waved off Renloret's look of concern but decided to explain at least a bit. "Kela and I are discussing the identity problem my twin and I are going to be dealing with. We'll need time to adjust our understanding of who we are, how we define family, and even what we consider to be alien."

Thankfully, the pilot nodded and did not press her for details. She considered kissing him. That would distract him—and her. Kela groaned heavily, letting her know his thoughts on her thoughts. Ani ruffled his fur and pushed him away. Evidently, he didn't have a sense of humor. She considered the action and possible consequences, especially in light of the kiss in the alley, which had almost gotten out of her control. Yes, kissing him would be distracting and fun, but not a good idea this time.

"Let me know when we've docked." Ani said. "I want to be alone until then, okay?"

"I can put it on autopilot, if you want to talk," Renloret said.

Oh, she wanted to do more than talk. She felt the blush heat up her face at her totally inappropriate thoughts. "Not yet. I need time alone. Kela, stay here and don't try to listen." She felt him slide the privacy barrier into place. She sent a thankful note to him before it fully closed and then she headed back to the long-sleep compartments. It was safer for her to be with the comatose and dead. She needed to be away from Renloret's presence so she could focus on the dramatic changes that had disrupted her life.

After leaning against the compartment holding her brother for a few minutes, Ani slid down to sit on the floor. She firmly pushed away thoughts of everyone except Taryn, tipped her head back, and closed her eyes. Scenes of the last twenty years rolled across her memory: the barefoot hunts for the gold and red amphibians native to Mineral Creek; the blade training sessions that had often ended in sibling-like shouting matches and scuffles, especially when they were young; even the locker incident during which Ani and everyone else discovered her claustrophobia. Now she tried to laugh at the bloody nose she'd given Taryn after being released from the locker, another sibling-like squabble. Then there were the late night study sessions while preparing to enter the universities. No, she didn't want to think about those, especially with what she knew now, because some had ended badly . . . uncomfortably. More than anything else, she feared that in gaining a brother, she might have lost her best friend.

To keep the tears at bay she eased into thinking about the situation, not the emotions. Pragmatism would serve her best. Ani shifted gears and began planning.

There was most likely going to be an uproar when the identity of the twin was announced. The biggest hullabaloo would be over the fact that her twin was male, not female as everyone—*everyone*—was expecting. Perhaps the history book in Awarna's library would be helpful to have on hand before the news leaked out. She should ask Renloret to send a message to the librarians to locate it and have it ready for them when they landed. The

Singers, at least Layson and Diani, could read it beforehand, and then they might have answers to the many questions that kept erupting and interrupting her thoughts. Plus, it would give them something to do besides worry. In theory, the book might help them figure out the prophecy and come to the conclusion that the twin was male. Perhaps they were already looking into the details of the prophecy by now.

She also had to plan how to handle Yenne Chenakainet—her father. Even after more than two weeks, she was uncomfortable about the idea of him being her father because he was hardly ten years older than her. Her last childhood memories of him were in a smoke-filled hallway, kissing her mother on the cheek before taking boxes of files from her and disappearing down the staircase. Ani paused in mid-thought. It seemed important to understand her last impression of her parents together.

Long forgotten words and images came forward. Yenne had said he would return with help if S'Hendale couldn't get to the ship in time. He wanted to take Ani, but S'Hendale said no and handed him a second box. Ani remembered that in the stress of the moment, her father had pronounced her mother's name in what she thought of as the Southern way, not the blended soft way of Northern. The tone of their hurried conversation carried so much love, though Ani now knew that they had spoken Lrakiran to one another. They had kissed again before her mother pushed him toward the stairway door. The face she saw in this memory was the face of Yenne Chenakainet—the same ebony skin, well-shaped nose, brown-black eyes, and wide high cheeks she saw each time she looked at the commander. Even her memories confirmed that he was her father, and until that moment, she had not realized it. How was she going to handle this new awareness and tell him he had a son, not a second daughter?

The memories began to flood back to her, unbidden. She made no attempt to stop them. After her mother had pushed Yenne to the stairway, she had picked up Ani and had run back into her lab to gather the remaining box of files. They had made it partway back to the stairway, Ani holding tight to her mother's hand, when Ani had been yanked away from her mother by a man. Ani now knew he had been a much younger Stubin Dalkey. The stranglehold of his arm around her waist had pushed all the air out of her lungs. She had struggled to breathe, even while kicking and scratching at the man's chest. Her mother had screamed, dropping the box, the papers scattering. Another blast of explosives rocked the building. People were running toward the exit, past the trio in the middle of the corridor. Ani remembered the blood on sleeves and faces of her parents' friends and coworkers, and she remembered someone practically dragging another man whose leg was terribly mangled—Gelwood.

Her mother's pleading words to Dalkey to just let the child go to her father had been answered with near hysterics by the man crushing Ani's five-year-old body to his chest. Her mother had relented and followed the man out the exit. Once outside, Ani saw her mother look at the mountaintop and smile. Dalkey had followed her gaze and loosed his grip on Ani as a flash of light erupted at the peak. In the present, Ani sucked in her breath at this memory. She, too, had seen the star runner her father piloted breach the trees before the camouflaging had engaged.

Ani had run to her mother, trying to hide from the smoke of the burning building and the sound of the walls crashing in as they surrendered to the fire. Leaving Stubin Dalkey staring at the mountain rather than the wreckage of the research center, Shendahl had taken her daughter into a firm hug and whispered, "I will keep you safe and make you strong. He *will* come back for you. You are The Blood and The Balance, my sweet Anyala. You will save our people and the Stone."

The memory of those words took Ani's breath away. Even in that terrible moment, her mother had believed Ani was both The Blood and The Balance. Shendahl had made a mistake. She misunderstood the prophecy by thinking only a female would be able to save the Stone, and when she gave birth to twins and one was male, she assumed the girl was both The Blood and The Balance. By assuming this, Shendahl had felt safe in giving her son to Melli and Gelwood. Shendahl would then be able to focus on her daughter while being assured her son had parents who loved him without reserve. Plus, there was the added advantages of seeing her son every day and knowing she had brought joy to her best friend.

Ani shook her head. How had her mother been strong enough to keep the secret, even from Melli, and even after Ani and Taryn had hinted they wanted to get married?

She began remembering snippets of gentle lectures about not marrying lifelong best friends, the hints that it would be better to find a man who did not come from the same small town and that potential life partners were more likely to live outside Star Valley. One conversation came rushing to the forefront of her memory.

The Balance

Her mother had been making dinner after the last regional blade competition prior to the continental championships.

"You know Taryn too well, Ani. He makes a good pairs partner, but he's starting to protect you in the ring. If you're not careful, both of you will find that your skills are suffering because you rarely work with others. Try to spice up your acquaintances. What about the young man from Zocanel Province? He was definitely interested in you at the regionals. He attended all your matches."

At the time Ani had almost gagged. Oh, sure, she had noticed him. He was good-looking enough to draw the eyes of most of the women—though not near the number that hung around Taryn like long-tailed sippers around a bouquet. Kursal Ceri had been a presumptuous fool, but she hadn't told anyone then and wasn't about to tell anyone now how he'd tried to accost her in the training room right before the championship round. It had been his folly. After a brief scuffle and a blade at his throat, he'd confessed to being instructed to connect with her and slip some kind of numbing drug into her water. He claimed it would only slow her reaction time so her opponent would be guaranteed a win.

Ani sat up with a jolt. Something was beginning to make sense. Ceri had said his sponsor, a politician, had bet heavily on her losing. To make sure the competition ended in his favor, he had ordered the young man to collect a small package of powder from a doctor to dump into her water. She had been irate and had tied and gagged him before placing him inside one of the lockers with a statement to the effect that, if she lost, it would be in a fair and worthy fight and she would not allow anyone to demean her or her opponent in such a manner. Ani had been determined to win or lose on her own skills. She had decided to tell no one to avoid sullying the competition.

This new memory suddenly became more important than how her mother had kept the relationship between Taryn and Ani a secret. Wasn't Doctor Treyder tightly connected to a politician and hadn't the doctor been the one who used a poison to slow her reactions in the cavern so he could implant his coma machine? The likelihood the two incidents were related was extremely high.

But she was not on Teramar anymore so she really couldn't do anything about it until she and Taryn returned from Lrakira. And she had no doubt that they would return. She would have to remember this bit of information because it might provide the link between Treyder and the senator. In the meantime, she would have to trust the Star Valley Sheriff Department and the Saedi City police to do everything possible. Her only concern about the investigation was that Renloret might have been too thorough in absconding with as much information as possible and there wouldn't be enough evidence left to propel an investigation. She thought about her last look at the laboratory. How many papers or files had remained? She had not paid any attention to that. Renloret had not been able to bring all the computers or files, and there were surely samples of Taryn's blood and saliva on the floor and near the drain. She hoped the Saedi City police could get there before Treyder or his assistant could get it cleaned up. In any case, Ani figured that the Lrakiran scientists could make copies of everything and she and Taryn could take them back to Teramar as evidence.

And when she and Taryn returned, Melli and Gelwood would know that Taryn was healthy and safe. Then when things had settled down, Taryn could decide how much to tell them. But she wondered what life would look like if Taryn's true identity was revealed. Ani was not sure. She worried about what would unfold once the Anyala Stone was healed. Were there other prophecies yet to come?

A long sigh pushed past her lips. She could not speculate what was to come, but she could manage the moment. Ani stood and saluted her brother's unmoving form. "I think I understand our mother's reasons, however mistaken they were, and I am beginning to see that Teramar has almost as many problems as Lrakira. If you save the Stone, perhaps we can solve a few other mysteries. I believe the Stones have answers, or at least clues, to those mysteries. They certainly seem to know more than two worlds of people."

She stared at the compartment containing the stasis bag, wishing Taryn were by her side with his little notebook. She needed him and his sheriff's mind. "Let's get you to Lrakira, dear brother, and begin the unraveling of this tangling so we can see things straight and true." She leaned close and kissed the compartment's covering. "I just need to talk to our father first."

During the short walk to the bridge, she composed her side of the coming conversation. Once there, she slid into the seat next to Renloret. "How much longer 'til we settle into the landing bay?"

"About twenty minutes. I requested a medical team to meet us. Do you want me to run interference?"

She reached for the communication switch. "Already have a plan to distract Yenne while you explain to the doctors about Taryn." She reached for the communication switch.

"I need to speak with Commander Chenakainet, please."

"This is Chenakainet."

So, he was more than just monitoring the communications from the star runner—he was in the seat. She smiled. "Is there any alcohol on the ship?" She ignored Renloret's questioning look though it probably mirrored her father's expression.

"Um, yes," Yenne said.

"Get a flask or whatever container it comes in and meet me in the flight debriefing room outside the landing bay. What I need to tell you should be said in person and in private."

She waited almost three breaths before he responded.

"Done. How far out are you?"

"Renloret said fewer than twenty Teramaran minutes."

"Good. Oh, I heard the request for a medical team. Is she—"

"I'd rather wait on that topic until after I talk with you. I'm fairly sure my twin will be fine. I will see you in the debriefing room." She snapped the switch before he could wheedle out more information, sat back in the chair, and let out a noisy breath. Now all she had to do was wait.

CHAPTER TWENTY-EIGHT

"A son?" The incredulity in his voice brought a wry smile to Ani's lips. She nodded and poured two fingers of liquor into the fist-sized glass in front of him. Without hesitation, he tossed down the contents, swallowing with only the barest cough.

Ani sniffed at hers and took a tentative sip, then chuckled. "Almost as good as your twenty-year-old vaquin." She raised her glass in salute and took a hefty swallow. Nodding his thanks, he pushed the empty glass forward and she refilled.

"When we found out that Taryn was my twin, Renloret's toast was to the Stones, sending them to the hells of Teramar for not telling us outright that the twin was male," Ani said.

"Well, here's to the Singers whose ignorance of their own teachings brought about the near extinction of our people." This time Yenne sipped the liquor. "So, how did you discover his identity?"

"Do you remember the mother's journal Melli gave Mother?"

Yenne nodded. "She wrote in it almost daily. She said that you would need to read it at some point to understand what being a mother was like." He paused. "I honored her privacy and never attempted to read it. Where did you find it?"

"Melli gave it to me. She had saved it for me. After Mother died, all I could think to do was throw away everything that belonged to her. It was grief behavior, not good sense. Melli was holding it safe for me until she thought I was ready. She never read it either, but then, it was written in Lrakiran." She waved him silent. "Yes, I realize that having a bio-teacher would have enabled me to read it, and I might yet change my mind. Let me adjust to one alien thing at a time, okay?" She saw him catch his bottom lip between his teeth before he nodded. This was one choice she could control, and she wasn't ready to make it yet. "I asked Renloret to read the entry around the day of my birth."

She hesitated, her hands on top of the journal, and then explained that she'd never once heard mention from her mother or anyone else that there had possibly been a twin until Melli's confession that verified the Stones' announcement of a twin birth. She assured Yenne that Melli seemed confident that the twin had died shortly after birth and that Taryn was her own child. These things would have to be dealt with in some manner once they returned to Teramar. She then opened the journal to the flagged page and slid it across the table, poured more liquor into her father's glass, and watched him read the entry.

He cried for a bit before whispering that he could forgive his wife for her decision. Even the Singers assumed The Balance was female, and he knew how much S'Hendale had wanted her friend to have a successful full-term pregnancy after her miscarriages. It was so like her to make such a sacrifice. Some moments of shared silence followed.

More liquor was ingested as Ani told him about the kidnapping and subsequent torture while Taryn was in a mechanically induced coma. The identity of the culprit stunned Yenne.

"He is a brilliant man," Yenne admitted, "but something always made me hold him at blade length. I was unwilling to get too close."

He seemed pensive for a moment before continuing. "You know, Fairaden, Treyder's wife, was one of the three Lrakiran women from the original research team. I tried to dissuade her—unsuccessfully—from joining hands with Isul the year before the attack on the research center."

"She died after an eleven-year coma," Ani said.

"I'm sorry to hear that. Something highly irregular happened not long before the attack on the research center. S'Hendale . . . that is, Shendahl, as you knew her . . . told me that Fairaden was pressuring her to create a vaccine from your blood, even though you had only just turned five. The woman was eager to have a child and hoped the vaccine would allow her to do so safely."

Though this new information was intriguing, Ani thought the subject could be looked into later, after Taryn was cured and had saved the Stone.

Ani then told Yenne how they had enlisted Mroz in the successful snatch and grab caper. A knowing smile lit his face at the mention of Mroz, and Ani wondered what kind of stories Yenne could tell about the Mroz he had known years earlier. She filed away that thought for a later discussion as well.

Ani shared information from Treyder's notes that confirmed he'd used a second coma device on Taryn. At first Yenne sat back in his chair in amazement and then he leaned forward to catch every bit of her narration about the blade healing. "So you could feel each of the wounds healing?" He was examining her once-broken wrist.

She nodded. "It was surreal, but I had to do what I could. I was not going to let him heal slowly and possibly badly. It seems like magic but it worked, and for that I'm grateful, though I hope there is no need to do it again."

"Well, magic or not, considering the alternatives, I am indebted to you and Renloret." Yenne shifted in his chair and took another sip of his drink. "What explanation did you give to the local authorities about their missing sheriff, and what did you tell Melli and Gelwood?"

She got up from the table and paced the room as she gave him an abbreviated version of how she and Renloret had left things with both the local authorities and Taryn's parents. Of course, that raised the issue of how Taryn's true parentage would be divulged and whether or not Yenne should be near Taryn after the device had been removed.

"Yenne, I have an important request."

He sat back in the chair, a neutral expression on his face. The look reminded her sharply of Taryn when he was in full sheriff mode. Not to be intimidated by this, Ani plunged on. "I think you should wait to meet Taryn until after he removes the blade. He's going to be under enough stress that meeting you, face-to-face, any time before he removes the blade from the Stone may be just too much for him. Removing the coma device comes first, then telling him who he is, and then, hopefully, he will believe us and save the Anyala Stone."

Yenne was silent for a few breaths, a frown scrunching between his brows. "From your tone of voice, this is not a request but a demand?" His voice rose slightly making the statement a question.

She pursed her lips and gave her head a firm nod. "No matter how he reacts to his identity, I have promised the Stones that my twin will remove Diani's blade from the Anyala Stone and give it a chance to live. And we will not overwhelm Taryn in the process. He may be more open to change than I am but . . . this is more change than anyone, alien or not, should expect a person to accept all at once. Don't you agree?"

"Personally, I would prefer to meet him when he wakes from surgery, but you state the situation clearly and yes, I will agree to wait to meet my son. But may I have your permission to visit with him during our return flight to Lrakira? There should be no harm in that, should there?"

"Ani? Is Commander Chenakainet still with you?" Renloret's disembodied voice over the communication speaker filled the room, startling both.

"Um, yes. I think we have just finished our discussion." She tipped her head toward her father in silent question. He nodded and sipped the last of the alcohol from his glass.

"The captain has given the order for us to proceed directly home to Lrakira."

"Good."

"The report from the medic center states that despite being

in a coma, Taryn is otherwise healthy and has been made comfortable."

"Do they have the results from the genetic test we requested?"

"Yes. Commander Chenakainet is to be congratulated on his son. And you, Ani, can be congratulated on having a brother." Ani heard the smile in his tone and raised her glass to her father. He responded with a smile of his own.

The com speaker crackled once again as the ship's commander requested that all be made ready for departure. Yenne rose from his seat, arms stretching out to Ani, and she quickly grasped both of his hands, holding off a full embrace, but giving him a small smile. "I'm not quite ready." Her voice was soft with regret.

He nodded in understanding. "I should get back to my station, Ani. Ten days to home." Yenne gave her hands an extra squeeze and left.

"Your home perhaps, but not ours," she said to the door as it slid closed, and she knew she meant hers, Kela's, and Taryn's. It was also ten days until Taryn's life changed forever, and there didn't seem to be any way of stopping that. At least Yenne would stay out of the way until after the Anyala Stone was saved. She realized that they were putting the life of an intelligent crystal, a species of creature Ani had never before considered, ahead of their own desires.

She contemplated the fact that she had accepted the importance of the Stone to the society of Lrakira to the point that she would threaten Taryn's life if he refused to save it. Was it duty or something else? Perhaps she was beginning to accept herself as a Stone Singer. She realized it wasn't really a new identity—just something added. And she found she was okay with that. She wasn't quite ready to look ahead. Her brother had yet to save her Stone. Then they could look to the future—together, as a family.

Two days into their travel, Ani found Yenne sitting next to the long-sleep capsule containing his comatose son. She hadn't seen her father since that first stunning conversation in the debriefing room and to be faced with the man's raw grief over the situation troubled Ani to the core.

Over the next eight days Ani made it a point to have several conversations with Yenne. With each discussion she understood more about the pain and loss he could no longer hide. They often cried together. She told him how it had been to grow up without a father, even though she had been surrounded by a loving mother and uncle. She even confessed that she had difficulty accepting him as her father, mostly because the time bubble had created a mere ten-year difference in their ages, though she also confessed that the age difference was becoming less of an issue.

They also discussed how close she and Taryn were. Ani told him about Taryn's proposal and explained why she'd broken it off, describing their relationship as more like that of siblings than lovers, though Taryn had been upset. Yenne was quite relieved at that news and seemed to be less shocked about their overall relationship when he realized that nothing more than some kissing had transpired between them.

By the time they were halfway to Lrakira, their scheduled discussions had wandered away from immediate familial concerns to why there was an apparent need for a male Singer and if it had anything to do with the disease that had killed so many women. While there was the logical thought that at least one male Singer would bring a sense of *balance* to the Stones' connection with the people after a thousand years, Ani didn't see any way the Stones could be responsible for the disease. Her impression was that the Stones were only interested in the health and well-being of their charges, much like parents with their children.

Both were confident that their many questions could be asked and answered after Diani's blade was removed from the Anyala Stone. Though Ani wasn't as confident, Yenne seemed to think that neither Layson nor Diani would have a problem with a male Singer. The only thing they couldn't figure out was if Taryn would replace Ani as the Anyala Stone's Singer or Diani as the Pericha Stone's Singer once the blade had been removed. They assumed that the Stones would inform them of the next step. Then, depending on what that next step was, they, Taryn, and the two Singers would help the Stones break the news to the rest of the Lrakiran population.

They surmised that though there had been early indications of impending changes, the Singers had not paid appropriate attention to their own history. If they had, they would have known that The Blood and The Balance would be twins, one a girl and the other a boy. And S'Hendale, as Yenne continued to pronounce his wife's name in the Lrakiran manner, would have made a different choice the eve Taryn and Ani were born. The only way to get through the situation was to be objective.

"We need to think like the Stones, Yenne." She blushed. Though she knew he was her father, after almost nine days traveling, she still could not yet call him that. It would take more time and many more conversations.

He cleared his throat as if trying to speak, but no words passed his lips. He was clearly uncomfortable. He closed his eyes and sighed. "Think like the Stones? What exactly are you suggesting?"

"We can ask them all sorts of questions after Taryn removes the blade. If we ask them direct, clear questions, I believe they will give us direct, clear answers. They are not emotional in the same way we are. We have to remain neutral while holding firm to the belief that the Anyala Stone will survive and we can get those answers."

Yenne gave her hands a firm squeeze and stood. "The last communiqué stated that the Anyala Stone's condition appeared unchanged, but the Singers remain anxious and are adamant that The Balance—I mean Taryn—must remove the blade for the Anyala Stone to survive and recover. Even though I sent them a message asking that they locate the book Renloret had found in the library, they don't seem to be unduly concerned, so perhaps they are prepared for a male Singer. Perhaps we are overly worried for no reason." He gave her a thin smile and, continuing to hold one of her hands, edged around the table to embrace her.

Ani stepped into and finally accepted the fatherly action she had missed since she was five. There were still plenty of problems to be worked out, but this was a start. She squeezed his chest.

"We should be arriving on Lrakira soon. I am guessing we will need to speak with the Singers immediately. I will send a request that they meet us." Her father planted a kiss on her forehead before releasing her and leaving the room.

Ani was halfway through a sigh of relief that he had not called her "little one" when she realized she had been *wanting* him to say it. She touched the damp spot on her forehead where her father's lips had left a healing impression.

Renloret watched Commander Yenne Chenakainet pause to wipe his cheeks as the door slid shut to the conference room Ani and the commander had used almost every day while traveling. For the first time, he saw a smile on the commander's lips as he turned away. Perhaps, finally, there had been a breakthrough in the relationship. That would help Taryn with his upcoming transition. Renloret waited at least a chime before moving to the door. Ani had not left. Was she upset? He palmed the announcement pad. "Ani? It's Renloret. May I enter?"

After three breaths of waiting, the door slid open and Ani pulled him in. They hugged and she led him to a pair of chairs facing the observation panel. He took one and she claimed the other. A surprisingly comfortable silence followed as they watched the myriad of stars streaming past. Ani clasped his hand, her thumb stroking across the back of his. He heard a sigh but didn't turn to look at her, just squeezed her hand to let her know that he was attentive. He wanted Ani to be the one to speak first.

"Yenne is sending another message to the Singers telling them to meet us when we arrive. We expect they will want to discuss the book you were reading prior to your first meeting with them, particularly that part of it relating to the Blood and The Balance prophecy. We're hoping they will be prepared to accept Taryn by then. Yenne also has a copy of the genetic testing in case the Singers question our word. Do you think they will demand a second genetic test to confirm his identity?"

"Perhaps," he said.

Her chuckle made him turn his head to look at her.

"Now that I think about it, Mother was always frustrated with how slowly people embrace technological advances. I well remember an argument with Uncle Reslo about a year before the Northern Blade Ring Championships. She wanted to announce some type of research results before Uncle Reslo thought it prudent.

"His reasoning was that Northern politics would not allow such breakthroughs to become general knowledge until the Star Valley Research Center shared *all* of their technological advancements with the military. Mother was furious that politicians could govern advancements in health and medicine, and Uncle Reslo cautioned her about bending blades beyond repair with her obsession. Oh, that really set her off. I had never heard Mother curse before. Back then, I thought she was cursing in Southern, but now in retrospect, I recognize some of the words as Lrakiran. By the blades, she was angry.

"They were in the kitchen at the lake house. You could hear them even though the back door was closed. I waited until she had stopped shouting before bursting in as if I hadn't heard a word. Uncle Reslo was hugging her, telling her they would figure out how to get *her* home even if they had to appeal to Southern for help. I thought he was referring to getting Mother home to Southern, not getting me back to Lrakira."

"You were about twenty then?"

"I was twenty-two, and I had come home from the university to tell her that after months of thinking and talking with Taryn, I wanted to enter the next year's spring continental championships in the short blade singles divisions. You had to be over twenty-one to enter as adults, and both Taryn and I had aged out of the youth divisions. The two of us were overconfident then, having won many competitions. We planned on celebrating our twenty-third birthdays with shared adult championships. I also mentioned that Taryn and I had decided to enter the pairs division. I was afraid to tell her the pairs entry was Taryn's way of proposing." Her voice had dropped to a whisper. "Or that I had told him I would consider accepting his proposal on the grounds that the topic of marriage would not be discussed until after the championships. Mind you, I hadn't officially accepted his proposal in any way. I just said that I would consider it."

Renloret didn't know how to respond so he just kept listening. This helped explain the marriage proposal she had mentioned earlier, which she had said she had refused. So it had been Taryn, not Ani, who posed the question, and Ani had subsequently refused it.

She sighed. "In the end, I never told her about Taryn's proposal, though I think she suspected. She kept introducing me to all sorts of other bladers and young men of good reputation. Once, she even mentioned we should go to Southern to meet 'the rest of the family.'" Ani laughed.

"Well, suffice it to say, my competition news seemed to overshadow frustrations with government pressures, and she never mentioned it again. Within a few weeks, she and Uncle Reslo had designed a rigorous training schedule for both Taryn and me, starting after my last semester. Taryn had just completed law enforcement training and had been appointed the new sheriff of Star Valley. For the previous couple of years Star Valley had been using the same sheriff as the next valley over, but Sheriff Driton really wanted to stay in his home jurisdiction and not split time between the two. Once he found out that Taryn was interested, he encouraged Taryn to apply and offered to mentor him through his first year. The other deputies were also young and neither of them wanted the responsibility of the office at the time. I found it interesting that no one ever brought up how young Taryn was. Everyone seemed to like the idea and it just seemed right, like Taryn was meant to be the sheriff of Star Valley."

"Does Commander Chenakainet know this?"

She cocked her head at him. "I've told him about our growing up. He was relieved when I told him that I refused Taryn's proposal."

"Why did you refuse when you didn't know your true relationship?"

Her hearty laugh said much about where she was emotionally. "During the blade ring competition, I watched all the women, and I mean *all* the women, watch Taryn with lust in their eyes, chasing after him to get his attention or even kiss him. And I realized I was never—not even once—jealous. I even encouraged a few of them behind Taryn's back. I was surprised that I saw him more as brother than possible lover." She shook her head. "I didn't feel the kind of love for him I thought a life partner should feel, so I rejected his proposal. Taryn was disappointed, but we've managed. That was just before Mother got sick.

"It was a good thing I broke it off because I was able to focus on her afterward, including trying to figure out what had made her sick. A few days ago, Yenne and I speculated that if we had her body, the doctors on Lrakira might be able to find out why she died. Now that her body is gone, I doubt we'll ever know."

Renloret wanted her to continue talking. The shock of learning who her twin was had actually allowed her to see part of what her father was struggling with. Life was not what they had understood it to be, and to survive with their own identities intact, they had to find ways to face and accept reality as it was, with all its surprising and surreal components. This would make them better people, a better family, and better able to support Taryn.

Ani looked down for a moment, avoiding direct eye contact. Then she raised her head, met his eyes, and gave him a crooked little smile. "I'm not sure that gaining a second child will stitch together Yenne's battered and bruised soul. He has lost twenty years of his family's life, his wife is no longer around to love, and he now has two children who are adults. His son doesn't even know he's his son and his daughter has been resisting the idea of being his daughter, until now." She looked directly into Renloret's eyes. "Yes, I've fully accepted it, but the notion of my father being barely ten years older than me still strikes me as uncivilized." She broke into a full grin. "But you will be relieved to know that I am more rational about it all now—as if there is anything rational about any of this. I guess I've been learning how to accept the impossible as possible ever since I met you, or at least, ever since I discovered you were alien."

Renloret joined her in a laugh. At least she was able to see some humor in the situation. He was not sure he would handle it as well, even with his knowledge that time could be twisted. He looked around the room. Where was Kela? Renloret assumed the canine would have attended all the conferences between father and daughter. He leaned over to see if Kela was under the table.

Ani's head appeared next to his. She smiled. "No, Kela is not here. He is in the infirmary, keeping an eye on Taryn for me. Even when Kela is not in the room with Yenne and me, he always listens in on the discussion—at least my side of it. He's still listening in, and he is laughing right now because he sees you through my eyes, upside down under the table."

Renloret straightened in his chair. "I was wondering."

"He appreciates your concern."

"That brings up a question of mine. Just how much can Kela see or hear?"

Her green eyes took on a distant, inward looking appearance, and she was silent for a few breaths. "He says I can tell you that, in general, without any of our shields in place, he can feel my emotions, hear my thoughts and spoken words, see what I am seeing, and, are you ready for this? He can read the lips of the person or people I am with as long as I can see their mouths. He cannot actually hear them speak unless I think about what they said or he's in the room with us. He understands Northern, and I'm guessing your instruction time with him on the first trip to Lrakira has given him impetus to continue learning Lrakiran as well. So be careful what you say around him. That talent has proved quite useful if I want to know what's being discussed and can't or shouldn't be present, such as when I sent Kela to be with Melli before we obtained the journal.

"In fact, he's using his knowledge of Lrakiran to keep me informed of what the doctors and other crew members talk about. Oh, he's just heard that we're approaching the Lrakiran system and that the doctors on board have requested the same surgery team that removed the device from my head to report to the hospital to prepare to remove the device from Taryn."

Ani tipped her head toward the door. "Let's get the coma device out of his head." She palmed the door panel to open it and Renloret followed her.

CHAPTER TWENTY-NINE

Ani tucked the blanket around Taryn's shoulders and placed a kiss on his forehead. She was relieved he was out of the confines of the stasis bag. And though she knew he could not hear, she whispered in his ear, "Renloret said you wanted to come with him when he brought me to Lrakira but you opted to stay behind to do what you could to protect Star Valley and my family. Thank you for all your help in finding my twin. I hope you won't be disappointed with the results. I guess your reward for being who you are is a secret trip to a faraway land where you can save the life of a true alien."

Ani stepped back, allowing the attendants access to the floating stretcher. She hugged herself as they guided it out of the ship and into the medical building. The same surgeon who had removed the coma device from her brain walked beside them after promising Ani she would be allowed in the recovery room. He wanted a familiar face to be present when Taryn awoke. An extensive medical staff would be present throughout the removal operation to learn from and support Doctor Sholoret. The staff was excited about having a second device available for research, and they were ecstatic about the boxes of research notes, which would be in their offices soon. Ani had been treated like a hero for bringing them another opportunity to get their hands on the device. None of them had been told the patient was The Balance.

Ani glanced back at the ship. Her father and Renloret had reached the end of the ramp and were in animated conversation. Kela followed them and sent her a quiet message saying that Renloret had delayed Yenne to give her a few moments with Taryn before he was escorted to surgery. Yenne was still struggling with the time loss and subsequent age difference between him and his now adult children. She wasn't sure she understood it all herself, but she did understand how difficult the circumstances had to be for him.

He had left his wife and young daughter at a moment of crisis and had every intention of returning as quickly as possible to retrieve them. The Stones certainly had not cared whether the father of The Blood and The Balance had been on Teramar or not. They had been focused on the time-song, which should have aged the twins to pubescence. The time bubble around Teramar had evidently blocked all communication with Lrakira during the ensuing years, thus explaining why her mother and uncle had not been able to communicate with Lrakira even to request another rescue when Yenne had not returned in the expected timeline. And then Selabec had attacked the Anyala Stone, shattering the bubble and jumping the time forward. At least that was the line being thrown to those who needed an explanation.

"Ani?" Renloret's voice eased her out of her ruminations. She turned to see that her father and Renloret were now within arm's reach and held out her hand. Renloret grasped it and pulled her close. She felt her father's hand on her shoulder. The three of them huddled wordlessly for several breaths, each offering and accepting comfort as the hovering stretcher disappeared beyond the doors on the way to the hospital. To Ani, the huddle felt *almost* like a family.

Still, she was the one who pushed away first. "While Taryn is in surgery, the Singers wanted to discuss their findings with us in the hospital conference room."

"Selabec is coming?" Yenne asked.

Ani shook her head. "No, just Diani and Layson. My grandmother is still in protective custody until the blade can be removed and the survival of the Anyala Stone is guaranteed."

"As she should be." He patted her shoulder.

Kela's snarky agreement flashed through Ani's mind. "Stop that, Kela."

The canine sneezed and glared at her. *Well, I do agree with him.*

"You don't have to be quite so spiteful." She bent down and stared into his icy blue eyes.

Yenne chuckled. "I'm guessing he's in agreement with me."

"You could say that."

I did say that. Kela swiped her cheek with his tongue. *She needs to be there a very long time. She tried to kill it, Ani. What happens if Taryn can't remove the blade?*

"I don't know. I'm still trying to figure out why Selabec did it in the first place."

"Now that is a good question, little one," Yenne said.

Ani, Kela, and even Renloret stared at Yenne. Ani swallowed. *Little one.* He had finally called her *little one.*

"What did I say?" He stepped out of the huddle, consternation clear on his face.

Ani shook her head. "It's not important, Yenne."

Ani pushed Renloret toward the building. The last time Yenne had said those words to her, she'd been five years old, and even though she'd been waiting for him to say it, she was perturbed by how important hearing those two words from him again actually was. Waffling between giving her father a hug and smacking his shoulder for treating her as if she were five, Ani grabbed his hand and pulled him toward the door. She tried to convince herself it really was not significant, especially since she was finally beginning to accept him as her father. It was just that she was too old for such a childish nickname. She motioned to Kela to lead the way. He complied with a muffled grumble in her head about puppies always being puppies and he could commiserate with Yenne on this topic.

In all the conversations they'd had on the trip from Teramar, Yenne had never once used the term. Why had he used it now, and was it as important as part of her wanted it to be? This time slip and age difference or lack of one was going to drive her crazy. She released her father's hand and increased her stride to get ahead of the two men. Somehow this would get hammered out and her self-understanding would be straight and clean as a newly annealed short blade.

The hospital conference room was the same one she had been

interviewed in after her own surgery to remove the first coma device. She had also been introduced to her father in this very room. A small amount of guilt wiggled up as she remembered slapping him. She watched her father rub his cheek. He also must be remembering. She looked away. Much had changed in the past couple of weeks, and circumstances were very different now.

While they waited for Diani and Layson to arrive, Ani silently ran through all the messages that had been sent to the Singers during the trip back to Lrakira.

"They did get Yenne's message about the book, didn't they?" Ani asked.

"I received acceptance notification from Diani," Renloret said. "Hopefully, they found it and have deciphered its meaning. I guess we will have to wait until they get here."

"Did we ever receive confirmation that the vaccine made from my blood is actually working," she asked. She had been told that it would be distributed quickly, but it didn't seem possible that any country, let alone an entire planet, could vaccinate millions of women and girls in such a short time.

Renloret turned from the window and gave her a heart-melting smile. "Oh, we would have been told quite soon after landing on Teramar if the vaccine was not working. I mean we *are* more technologically advanced than you folks on Teramar." He winked at her to keep her from defending her birth world. "The vaccines were divided by provinces and every female on Lrakira was probably vaccinated before we were halfway to Teramar. It would only take a few test subjects to verify the authenticity and effectiveness of the vaccine. Any female off world would receive their dose in their next supply deliveries. So there is the possibility that, truly, all is well for our people, thanks to you."

Ani shook her head. A thought brought a frown to her face. "How many women have died in this plague?" she whispered, stunned by the impact the blood of one person had on an entire planet. Was she really their savior?

Renloret pulled out the chair next to her and grasped both of her hands. "As I told you, it took us several sun-cycles—years—to figure out exactly what was going on. Those who became pregnant during the last six years all died, though the last year or so, the number of pregnancy related deaths dropped considerably. By the time I left for Teramar, I heard that close to fifty-eight percent of the women of childbearing age had died. The remaining women had gone to great lengths to prevent a pregnancy, and any man foolish enough to get a woman pregnant was dealt with harshly because it was the equivalent of committing murder. It has been cataclysmic to our way of life. Basically, no children have been born to the Lrakiran people in almost five years."

The impact of his words stunned Ani. "Five years? No children, anywhere, even if they were off planet?"

Renloret brought her hands to his lips. "So, do you see why you are heralded as the savior of our people?"

"Why couldn't I have been born on Lrakira if it was just my blood that was needed?"

"Diani said The Blood had to be a Stone Singer's child, conceived, born, and raised to puberty on another planet. It had to be a specific planet too. It had to be Teramar."

"Why Teramar?"

"We don't know yet. When the Anyala Stone is able to communicate fully, perhaps . . ."

The door slid open to reveal two of the Singers. Ani toggled the room's translator before she stood and offered a Teramaran Northern salute to Diani and Layson.

They touched their foreheads in a Singer's salute and swept in, their gold robes rustling. She noticed tears on Layson's cheeks before being tightly embraced by the woman.

Layson whispered in Ani's ear, "I can start thinking about a child of my own. Thank you." Then Layson released her and stepped back, smiling. "And now you have saved your Stone, as well as your people."

Ani motioned for the Singers to take seats. "Before we talk about who is saving what, we need some answers."

"What are your questions?" Diani asked.

"Did you find the book?"

"Renloret had already given us the song verse, which revealed the trueness of the prophecy. In our review of the verse, we verified that The Blood and The Balance are twins and not one individual." Diani smiled at Renloret.

"But did you find the book?" Renloret asked. "We need the rest of the song."

Diani seemed unconcerned. "Why? The verse you remembered told us what would transpire. Each of the twins 'will save one.' Ani's blood saved the Lrakiran people and her twin will save the Stone. The twin is here and she will pull my blade from Anyala. Then we will be whole again—in balance."

Shaking his head, Renloret continued. "You still don't

understand that the early songs were to prepare us for different circumstances. Have either of you read the whole song?"

Both shook their heads.

He slapped the table surface, and Ani reached out and touched his arm. "It's not their fault, Renloret. We're going to have to tell them."

He turned a frustrated face to her. "But the song would have prepared them, Ani."

"They saw all the answers they thought they needed in the first verse," Ani replied. "They didn't think they had to read the entire song to understand the immediate circumstances. Even we assumed that, Renloret. Even we."

"Excuse me, we *are* present," Layson said. "What else should we know? You have returned the twin, thus you are to be doubly honored. Your actions will save—"

"I am not the one who will save the Anyala Stone," Ani said, interrupting. She was tired of trying to ease the shock. "It will be Taryn, my brother." Ani had to cover her mouth to stop a laugh from bubbling out into the stunned silence. She felt Renloret move to stand behind her and Kela. Kela, who was mumbling in her mind that he couldn't resist looking, put his paws on the table so he could be eye to eye with the Singers. Ani noticed his comical expression and again struggled to control a burst of laughter.

The Singers' jaws finally started to move up and down though no sound came forth for several more seconds.

Deciding not to wait any longer, Ani jumped right in. "Believe me, I was just as shocked as you are. I think we got wholly drunk after we discovered the twin's identity."

"A man?" Diani's voice slid up an octave. She seemed to be having trouble breathing.

Ani turned a concerned look to Renloret. He retrieved the pitcher of water from the center of the table, filled two glasses, and placed one in front of each astonished Singer.

"But, I thought . . ." Layson took a swallow and shook her head. "It's supposed to be a girl. It *has* to be a girl!"

"Well, he's not a girl," Renloret said. He filled two more glasses, giving one to Ani. "And he does not yet know he is her twin."

"How can he not know?" This time Diani's voice had regained some of her calmness. "Why haven't you told him? You had more than enough time to discuss this as you were traveling."

Layson interrupted. "Isn't Taryn the name of the sheriff of your village?"

Ani nodded. At least Layson was putting together the little details that made the discovery so . . . interesting . . . and life-changing.

"Where is he? He should be here." Diani's voice was taking on a demanding edge. "What's wrong?"

"Weren't you two lovers before you met Renloret?" Layson asked, again seeing the personal ramifications. She covered her mouth with both of her hands, eyes wide with sorrowful shock as she stared at Ani.

Now Ani let the laugh escape. Diani seemed to have lost her voice again as Layson's question sank in.

"They were never lovers," Renloret said, coming to Ani's rescue.

This time, Diani recovered her poise more quickly than the younger Singer. "Are you so sure?"

Ani stopped laughing. Turning stony green eyes on the Singer, she said, "I am. Nothing more than teenage kisses passed between us. And the topic will not be brought up again, understood?"

Layson closed her eyes in acquiescence and solemnly brought her glass of water to her lips. She took several swallows and composed her expression. "Why doesn't he know?"

Renloret spoke first. "He's in a coma."

"Like I was when I first arrived," Ani added.

"I don't think I want to visit Teramar. Half the people there seem to be in comas," Layson muttered, bringing smiles to Renloret's and Ani's faces. Ani was reminded of Mroz's comment about not wanting to stay on Teramar because of the behavior of a few people.

"How did it happen?" the ever-practical Diani asked.

Renloret took up the narrative. "After Taryn agreed to help us find the twin, his plan was for us to split up to make the search go faster. One particular person's behavior was suspicious enough that Taryn met with him the evening Ani and I read S'Hendale's journal and discovered the identity of the twin. We decided to wait until morning to give him the news."

Ani jumped in. "He wasn't at work and neither he nor the man he went to interview had been seen since that eve's meeting. We traced his location to the capital city, where we discovered he'd been kidnapped after the interviewee injected him with another of the coma devices. He was being tortured while under the influence of the device. We were able to rescue him with some assistance from a family friend."

"Didn't he have *parents*?" Layson asked. Once again, Ani was pleasantly surprised the younger Singer cared about the personal side of the situation.

"Yes, Gelwood and Melli Avere. As far as we know, neither of them knows that Taryn is not their genetic child." Raised eyebrows and skeptical looks greeted this statement. "It's too long a story to go into at the moment. What is important is that Taryn is The Balance. We brought him here to save the Anyala Stone. What happens afterward is unknown because you did not read the rest of the song." She wanted to get back to the task the Singers had been asked to do but had not completed.

Both Singers flinched at her accusing tone. Ani didn't care. Hadn't they been asked to find and read the entire piece to prepare them for what was to come? How could they assume the meaning of a prophecy when only the first part was read? Were they that naive? But by their own admission, they hadn't even attempted to find the book, assuming the remembered verse given to them by Renloret was all that was needed. So now they weren't prepared. And now Ani and Renloret did not have the information they were hoping for before meeting with Taryn to tell him who he really was and what he was destined to do. Ani turned her back on them, rolling her eyes at Renloret. Kela grumbled in her mind as well, echoing Ani's frustrations.

She turned back to look each Singer in the eye and pointed at Kela. "Even Kela understands how entrenched Lrakiran society is. If Taryn is supposed to be the first male Stone Singer, it's not me who's going to tell everyone. It's you two. And you're going to tell them my grandmother, Selabec, tried to murder the Anyala Stone!"

When protests began bubbling forth from the two Singers, Ani held up her hand to still them. "After Taryn saves the Stone, we will fashion a single statement to inform the Lrakiran people—together. Nothing is to be released until we *all* understand the prophecies within the first song." She stopped and tipped her head to Renloret. "And there are multiple prophecies, right?"

"There was something about the number seven and a reunion," he replied. "I certainly don't understand those parts. We should read the whole thing, and preferably before Taryn is out of surgery. I'll assume his recovery will be rapid because of the blade healing."

"Another blade healing?" Diani shook her head.

"Yes, Renloret and I performed it to heal the injuries inflicted on Taryn while he was in the coma. The surgeon was told. He wants me, in particular, to be in the recovery room. So we best be about the business of gathering the information we need to explain this to my brother." She walked to the door, which slid open, and allowed a smile at the Singers as Kela took a muzzle full of gold fabric in his teeth and tugged Diani out of her seat.

A shout from an attendant running down the hall stopped them. He pointed at Ani and waved at her to follow him. He babbled something in Lrakiran. Ani remembered she was no longer in the conference room with a mechanical translator, but she heard the surgeon's name somewhere amongst the sounds.

Renloret touched her on the shoulder. "He says your brother is being moved to recovery and Doctor Sholoret wants you there. They don't know exactly how long he will be under. The attendant will take you to him. Oh, take Kela so Taryn will have two familiar faces in the room."

Ani realized he was able to switch languages in the same breath and his Northern was getting smoother every time he spoke, though his accent still revealed that he was not a native speaker. She wondered if she would be able to do as well if she decided to have a bio-teacher installed.

Kela barked. *Thank Renloret for thinking of that. I most certainly want to be there when you tell Taryn he's an alien. Maybe that's how he will figure out he's your brother. He's intelligent enough.* Kela's snicker brought a smile to Ani's lips.

"All right, let's meet in the Stone Chamber when we get together again, and bring the book when you find it. Okay?" Ani nodded to the pair of Singers, placed a quick cheek-side kiss on Renloret without a thought, and hurried after the attendant.

CHAPTER THIRTY

Stunned by the freely given kiss, Renloret could barely inhale. Too many things were happening. Life was not as ordered as he wanted it to be. Why couldn't he just be a pilot? Would there ever be a time when he could tell her how he felt? Once again, circumstances were forcing Renloret to suppress his attraction to the green-eyed girl so he could focus on the most pressing exigencies. He frowned. Now what were those exigencies? Rubbing his temple, he headed toward one of the chairs in the hospital lobby and slumped into it.

"Have you told her?"

He looked up to find that both Singers were standing in front of him.

"Told her what?" he mumbled. Which Singer asked? It didn't matter.

"That you love her."

"No."

"Why not?"

Now that sounded like Diani. He ran both hands through his hair. The tiny ridge where Ani had stitched his scalp together after the crash made him smile briefly. How could such a small act as a kiss on the cheek throw him so far out of the blade ring?

"How can I, with more important things always needing attention?" Anger and frustration at himself for not taking the initiative and just saying it aloud in her presence bubbled through his words. "We've only known each other for . . . what . . . barely three moon-cycles? And she was in a coma for almost a third of the time. She's been through too much change to expect her to take me on, at least at the moment."

Singer Layson leaned close to stare directly into his heart. "You underestimate her, Renloret. She is far stronger than you believe, and from her expressions and tone of voice when you are around, it is clear that she loves you."

"And you know this how?"

A smile crossed her lips. "The Kita Stone told me."

Diani stepped up behind Layson, adding a supportive smile. "Be at peace, Renloret. There *will* be time to tell her which side of the blade your heart is on. Now, we should follow through with her request and find the book." Diani pointed to the hospital's front door with a dip of her chin.

Kela laughed in Ani's head.
What's so funny?

You don't even realize what you did, do you? Kela's tone was smug. Ani didn't like it when he thought he knew everything.

She asked anyway. *What did I do?* The attendant was almost running down the hall in his urgency to get Ani to the recovery room before Taryn woke. He stopped at a door, slapped a hand to the entrance pad, and disappeared into the room.

You kissed him.

"I did not," she said aloud. Had she? Even if she had, why had she? She peeked into the room, not really seeing anything because her mind was reviewing what had just happened. Ani ran her tongue over her lips. She tasted Renloret, and the distraction in the alley came rushing back.

Kela snickered. *Granted, it was only on the cheek, but it was a kiss in front of others.*

"Oh, hells of Teramar." A blush darkened her neck and face. How would she explain? Was it a careless mistake or an unconscious need to let him know how she felt?

You'll have to make time to discuss it with him—after Taryn saves the rock. Kela trotted over to the bed where the attendant stood, his hand holding a small disk to Taryn's bare chest.

The attendant smiled at Ani, pointed to a rolling chair, and then stepped out of the way. Following his hand motions, she scooted the chair close, sat down, and enfolded one of Taryn's hands in both of hers. His chest rose and fell evenly as if he slept.

How am I going to explain all this, Kela?

You'll find the words. His muzzle wedged under her arm.

But how is he going to react when he finds out our mother gave him up because she assumed I was the only one needed—that he was extra?

Melli and Gelwood needed him. He is not an extra to them. You've known each other your whole lives, Ani. He won't act any differently toward you. He already knows your heart belongs to Renloret.

She started to laugh but couldn't. Had her attempt at misdirection in the alley revealed her true feelings? The truth, she realized, was in her desire to be back in the alley, kissing Renloret, not here holding Taryn's hand.

A squeezing pressure on her hands brought her back to the recovery room on Lrakira.

"Am I sick?" Taryn's voice crackled with dryness. "Got any water?"

The attendant silently came forward with a small glass of water and again retreated into the corner. Ani was fairly confident he did not understand Northern but was just paying attention to his patient.

Ani held the glass to Taryn's lips. He swallowed once then grasped the glass on his own and raised his body up to drink from it.

"I'm not an invalid, Ani." His blue eyes were bright with no sign of the trauma his body had been put through. He downed the rest of the water.

"Obviously not," Ani replied. She took the glass from him and sat back in her chair. Crossing her arms, she studied him as he looked about the room. His eyes stayed on the attendant momentarily and moved on just before it became apparent he was scrutinizing everything. He was probably wishing for his notepad.

"Don't get too attached to the place. You'll probably be excused by the end of the day."

He cleared his throat. "How long have I been in the hospital?"

"Actually, not too long." She wondered if he would feel the difference in time and location before she told him what had happened over the past ten days. She was pleased that the larger ship meant a faster travel time.

His perusal of the room completed, he touched his upper right shoulder, his fingers rubbing across the tiny indentation beneath the fabric of the wispy gown that all hospitals seemed to think was appropriate no matter the planet. "What kind of throwing blade did he use?"

"We're not exactly sure. We were hoping you would know." Outside of the sketches and research reports she had read, she had no idea what the weapon might have looked like, though she was positive the coma device had not entered his body through a hollow sliver blade, as had been used on her. "Can you tell me what happened?"

"Well, you know me, I'm always looking for the reasons behind people's behavior. And Doctor Treyder seemed quite surprised to see you—stunned, really. He kept staring at you the whole time we were in his office, like you were a ghost. I couldn't tell if he was just uncomfortable, nervous, or maybe even a bit intimidated by your presence. Didn't you hear the tremor in his voice?"

Ani shook her head. Had her desire to get her mother's notes overridden her usual observations?

"Well, I thought he would be more forthcoming without you around, so I arranged a solo interview. Plus, I thought he might show me some of his newest designs. My father always had praise for his handiwork. Father couldn't figure out why Treyder had left a couple of years ago and yet asked to return only a month after you had left for Lrakira. Some of the other scientists who returned had mentioned him grumbling about your mother's death being too soon for him to show her his new invention. They assumed he thought it might have saved her in some way. He also expressed disapproval of your uncle's . . ."

"Defection to Southern?"

Taryn shrugged with a crooked grin. "You said it, I didn't." He sat straighter. "Listen, Ani. There are definitely some bad feelings between Treyder and your uncle, and Treyder considers Reslo a coward for running to Southern after your mother's funeral. Treyder also said he'd tried to balance the sword with Reslo by using you instead of your mother to test that coma device. I was surprised he admitted accosting you."

She clucked her tongue on the roof of her mouth. "He's even crazier than Stubin Dalkey. At least Dalkey died knowing he was correct about aliens being on Teramar. Isul Treyder killed Dalkey because he wanted to put me in a coma and feared Dalkey would ruin that plan by killing me."

Taryn leaned forward. "I don't think he planned on killing Dalkey, only distracting him. That light beam weapon is so far beyond even his capabilities that I believe he didn't know it could kill. He was considering using it as a distraction device that would allow our armies to get closer to Southern's forces so he could use the upgraded coma delivery system he was designing. Ani, I think he got that light beam weapon from someone else, maybe even another alien."

"Another alien? What do you mean by that?"

Kela whined. He pushed his head under Taryn's hand, which immediately began to massage the base of his ears. *Remember Yenne saying Treyder was married to one of the original Lrakiran research team? Maybe she told him some things before she died.*

You're right. He may be on to something here, but it's a bit off topic, isn't it? She really just wanted to focus on one problem at a time.

Take notes now and remember to read them later.

She gently swatted at Kela's head, but the canine ducked away from her hand in time to remain unscathed.

"Has anyone considered someone didn't want the Lrakiran people to survive the plague and was hoping to take over those crystal stones once the Lrakiran people were gone?" Taryn asked.

Ani looked at the attendant. He was sitting with his hands folded, unperturbed by the patient's speculations. Taryn followed her glance, but he immediately refocused on her, dismissing the attendant.

"Well? Those rocks are priceless, right? They could be sold for a lot of money and . . ." Taryn frowned. He stared at the nonreactive man in the corner. "Does he understand Northern?"

Finally.

Kela's flat comment brought a smile to Ani's lips. She shook her head. "No." She waited as Taryn again examined the room. It would be more fun for her and better for him if he figured this out on his own. She reminded herself that her brother was more open-minded than she had been and would probably be delighted he was on a different planet. In fact, being on another planet would most likely be easier for him to understand than the fact that he was her twin and had been living a lie of sorts for the past twenty-five years.

A laughing agreement came from Kela. The canine nuzzled Taryn's hand again, for he had stopped rubbing the base of the dog's ear. *How long do you think it will take?*

Shrugging, she answered silently. *Not as long as some people expect.* She watched the expressions dance across her brother's face. Each time she thought of Taryn as her brother it got more comfortable. Her past feelings for him seemed to be sorting themselves out, making more sense. She realized she was finally coming to terms with their altered status.

Kela made a low rumble in his throat. She looked down at him and received a wink. She returned it.

"Ani?" Taryn's voice was a whisper.

"Yes?"

"You won't laugh at me, will you?"

"No."

"We're not on Southern soil, are we?"

"No." She couldn't hide the smile any longer.

"All the hells, girl, why didn't you tell me right off?" His expression was endearingly hurt.

"It was more fun this way." She couldn't help it.

"Fun? You think this is fun? How long were you going to . . . ? Hells, girl . . ."

Ani realized he was getting angry. The attendant had stood up and looked ready to interfere in any altercation. She waved him off, confident she could handle the coming wrestling match.

Taryn jabbed her in the shoulder. She flinched but grabbed

his wrist as he tried to administer a second punch. They glared at each other for a full four breaths before Taryn wrenched his hand from her grasp and turned his gaze to the floor. The expected fisticuffs did not happen. Perhaps they were too old for that childish method of resolving disagreements between them. Hiding her disappointment, she allowed Taryn to work through his thoughts.

"Lrakira?" Taryn finally whispered as he looked up at her.

She nodded.

"Renloret?"

"Hopefully, he's at the library looking for a book that should have answers we need."

Taryn swung his legs to the side of the bed, keeping the sheets across his lap. "Shower? Clothes?"

Ani pointed at the small privacy chamber. "All you need is on the shelves." Taryn wrapped the sheet securely and padded into the chamber, slamming the door closed. She could hear him talking to himself. Was he still angry? She couldn't tell.

Well, that was fun. Kela's mental voice sounded disappointed.

Shut up.

I was expecting something a bit more melodramatic—like vomiting and a rousing fight with the attendant.

"I said shut your muzzle, Kela." She did not want to be reminded of her reaction when she figured out she was on another planet.

My muzzle has nothing to do with my talking. He managed to dodge the pillow she threw.

"Ani?" Running water barely softened Taryn's voice.

"Yeah?" She moved the chair to be closer to the door.

"It was Isul Treyder in the cavern. He was the one who designed the poison to slow you down so he could get close enough to insert the coma device. It was so bizarre when he showed me the drawings of the modifications he made to the blade he used. After his near failure with you, he was encouraged to figure out a long-distance method of injecting similar devices into people."

"Really? How was he going to do that? The only method I can think of to project something a long distance is to use a throwing blade, and there's a lot of variation amongst soldiers in arm strength and accuracy. They'd still have to be fairly close." This was not the thing she thought he would be thinking about.

"He showed me another sliver-blade design, which he said would revolutionize war itself. And he said soldiers could be hundreds of yards apart. He just had a few more tests to run before he could go to the senator." There was a pause. "Oh, he wouldn't say which one. I asked."

Ani grimaced. She knew exactly which one they'd be talking to when they returned to Teramar.

"And he said he'd originally hoped Reslo would want to protect his niece from further alien accusations and return from Southern. Treyder planned to personally demonstrate the new delivery system of the coma device on Reslo when he came to rescue you from General Stubin Dalkey. When Reslo didn't come, Treyder decided he would use you to demonstrate the device. He even admitted to using someone who was close to the senator to get Dalkey out of the hospital. I don't think he suspected it was real aliens who muddled his plans. He still doesn't believe in aliens, which makes me wonder about that light beam weapon. But it's not important now." He became silent as the water continued to run.

"Hey!"

Taryn's stuttered exclamation brought Ani to her feet, her hand reaching for the boot blade, which was not there.

"Are you all right?" She moved her hand from her calf to the door's lever.

"Where'd all these scars come from? And who cut my hair so close?" He sounded curious and on the edge of being frightened.

She tried to put surprise in her voice as she replied, "What scars?" He had pointed out the one on his shoulder where the coma device had been forcefully injected, so she thought he would have noticed the torture scars when he got into the shower. He had apparently been so focused on telling her as much as possible about Treyder and his plan that almost five minutes had passed before he saw or felt the scars.

"On my chest and back. Ani, there are even some on my legs. And they all look like they've been there for years. I would have remembered getting most of them from what I can see. These are not just scratches, Ani. These would have caused serious pain and a long healing time. And I have never wanted my head shaved."

Hells. She decided to tell him. "You have Doctor Isul Treyder to thank for all of those. Finish your shower and get dressed. We have a lot to discuss and I'd rather not do it through the door."

The water stopped and she could hear more muffled cursing. The door opened shortly thereafter. Taryn stepped into the room, his hands running over the black stubble on his scalp.

"First, Ani, I've got to finish this line of thinking before I get distracted again. Treyder was quite talkative, I guess because he was confident he wouldn't suffer any repercussions from his actions. Maybe because of the senator's support."

Or because you were in a coma and he was planning on you dying before regaining consciousness. Ani couldn't keep her thoughts quiet.

Kela cocked his head at Ani. *Are you going to say that out loud?*

No. She folded her arms across her chest.

Taryn paused and shook his head. The action brought a frown to her lips. It would be a while before his hair was long enough to even comb through.

"Treyder is planning to make hundreds, maybe thousands, of those coma devices so Northern's armies can use them against Southern's. Once he gets the delivery system perfected, he's expecting the senator to authorize a huge payment and all the accolades Treyder craves. But the senator wants to see a real victim of the device before he'll fully fund the project."

Taryn settled on the side of the bed while Ani returned to her seat in the rolling chair. She was becoming amused with her brother's fast-paced rundown of his conversation with the doctor.

"Treyder was planning to use your mother as the first victim, but she died before he could implement his plan. He tried to lure Reslo back from Southern by setting Dalkey on you, but Dalkey went off-track, messing up the timing even worse. And Reslo didn't show up as expected. You were available, so he used it on you. Then you disappeared without a trace, and his little inquiries met a solid wall. He was without a physical victim to use in demonstration and he didn't have the device, so he created a second one. He'd heard rumors you'd been taken to Southern to help cure some disease, and he was confused that no one said anything about you being in a coma like he expected. So he took advantage of the open invitation to former researchers and staff that Star Valley issued to come help restart the hospital. He was using the opportunity to find out what had happened to you and to build more of the devices and to develop a faster long-distance method for delivering them. I'm guessing that's what he demonstrated on me when I went to interview him."

Crossing her arms, Ani smiled slightly as he continued his long-winded account. She wasn't sure if she'd ever heard him talk this long without taking a breath. She smothered the urge to even chuckle because she didn't want him to stop.

"I have never heard of a possible suspect talk so much and give such damning information so freely. It doesn't make any sense." He scrubbed his hands over the stubble of his head. A frown crossed his face briefly and then he seemed to get back on track. "Treyder said the device would work with his modifications, even if the victim was just grazed, and it would take only a few heartbeats to get to the brain and put a soldier in a coma. They wouldn't be able to raise a blade in defense. They'd just fall over and go to sleep. He didn't act like he was going to throw it, so I wasn't worried. Then there was a loud noise, like a small explosion, and my shoulder hurt real bad." Again he rubbed at the shoulder, fingering where she knew the small round scar was.

Taryn took a breath. "He laughed and said he would finally get all the recognition he deserved after so many years and he'd have paid back Reslo for not believing he could make it so small. That's when I started having trouble hearing him. My vision got foggy and my shoulder sort of stopped hurting. Then I fell . . . I think." Taryn took another breath. "I don't remember anything after that until I woke up here with you holding my hand."

"Wait a second, Taryn. Why can you remember everything up to the point of being struck in the shoulder by the weapon and I can barely remember what happened to me in the cavern from the time Treyder cut me?"

Taryn cocked his head to the side. "You're correct. Hey, that's direct evidence that your memory problem is associated with the poison, not the coma device. I'll take that as a good sign."

"Um, so I guess you won't be pestering me about details anymore. Taryn, I have another question for you." Ani tried to refocus on a single important point. "You're saying Treyder is planning to mass-produce the coma device and give it to our military?" Taryn nodded. "Why would the military want to put enemy soldiers—and maybe even the enemy public—in a coma state instead of killing them? Perhaps they want to avoid killing so they can take them prisoner for some reason. Or do they want Treyder to develop something that gives them control of those implanted—out of a coma state but within their control? Something else?"

Taryn shook his head as he sighed and leaned against the pillows. "I have no idea. I'm not sure he knows what the senator has in mind. Treyder might just be interested in getting recognized for his genius, however misguided it is." Deep creases between his brows told Ani he was considering her questions.

The consequences of such an action were horrifying to Ani. She envisioned fields of comatose soldiers. Would that really be possible?

Taryn sighed. "But I don't have an answer for it. We'll have to go back and stop Treyder and this unnamed senator, but first you've got to warn your uncle." He reached out and took her hand. "His next target is Reslo. Treyder wants to personally prove his genius to Reslo."

CHAPTER THIRTY-ONE

Before we return to Teramar shouldn't Taryn know who—or rather what—he is and save the rock?

Kela's question made Ani raise her hand to stop Taryn from continuing his dissertation. "One blade edge at a time, Taryn. Before we run off and commandeer a ship to fly back to Teramar, we need to attend to circumstances here on Lrakira, whether or not we want to and whether or not we believe our own world and people are more important."

Taryn was quiet. He stared at the floor and then ran his hand over his scalp, a rueful smile on his lips. She thought he missed his hair. Then he gave a crisp nod as if making a decision.

"Did you just bring me to Lrakira to get a machine removed from my brain or did you and Renloret also manage to find and retrieve the twin?"

Ani cocked her head to the side and gave him a mischievous grin. "Well, yes, we did find the twin—"

"Great!" Taryn interrupted. "When can I meet her? What's

her name? Where does she live?" He stood up and started for the door.

Ani pulled him back. "Whoa, you have to hear this first. Now sit down and listen."

Taryn sat. Under his stare he suddenly was at a loss for the right words. This was not going as planned or expected. But how had she expected this conversation to go anyway? She realized she hadn't had expectations. By mostly dealing with her feelings on the matter she had not *really* thought about how Taryn would react to the news. She now knew that she assumed he would react as she had, by getting angry. She prepared herself for that side of Taryn, which she rarely saw.

Honesty would be best, Ani. As they often did, Kela's words brought some semblance of order to her thoughts.

She cleared her throat. "Taryn . . ." For some reason, tears stung her eyes. She blinked several times. Would he hate her, hate their mother?

His hands encircled hers, giving her physical support. "Ani, I'm listening. I understand this is difficult for you. Is she injured or disabled in some manner?"

How could he be so blade straight logical when none of this was logical? Shaking her head, Ani tried again to find the words. "The twin is not a girl . . . it's you," she whispered. Why was she so terribly sad? She clutched at his hands, afraid he would pull away in disgust and rejection. Silence echoed inside her heart as it settled between them.

His hands were very still and his breath came long and deep, as if he were preparing for the blade ring. It cooled the skin of her cheek and neck as she felt his head gently press against hers. Failing to match his breathing, she allowed her tears to fall, splashing on the clasped hands in her lap.

Kela's paw scratched at her knee. No words came from him, only a sense of comfort and caring. The three of them huddled in near silence for a very long time.

"I'm sorry," she finally whispered.

She felt his head rock back and forth and he chuckled softly. She looked up to find him smiling.

"Sorry that we're actually related?" he asked.

How could he be happy about this? She wasn't sure she was, and she'd had time to get used to the reality of their relationship. She'd talked about it with Renloret, Yenne, and Kela. There'd been a lot of yelling and crying the past ten days. And he was smiling! Anger boiled up and she struck him hard on the shoulder. Why wasn't he angry?

He backed away and motioned for her to come at him. That was fine with her. His stupid smile begged to be bloodied. She ignored the shout of warning from the attendant and silently called to Kela to keep the attendant from interfering. She and Taryn settled into hand-to-hand positions. He was still grinning.

Advancing toward him, Ani executed several stylized movements, warming up her muscles. Taryn responded with similar moves. He did not flinch from pain or stiffness. Good, Ani thought, I can forget about being gentle. We don't have time for this. Curses on him. She kicked.

He slapped her foot away and used his longer reach to grab at her braid. He pulled as she knew he would. It worked every time. Tucking and rolling she came forward under his guard and shoved a hand straight up. Taryn collapsed in pain. Ani heard the attendant respond in sympathy.

Between gasps Taryn wheezed, "Cheater."

"Sorry, but I had to end this quickly, and you'll be fine in a few minutes." She knelt next to him. "Why are you so happy about our situation?"

He rolled onto his side facing away from her. "Do my parents know?" His words were tight with pain. Physical, emotional, or both?

"I don't think so. But Melli may suspect. Think about the times in recent years that Melli has commented and hinted that we should each find others to get involved with." She tipped her head and raised her eyebrows.

"You may be correct. Suspicions or knowledge would explain a lot." He groaned. "To be honest, Ani, I'm delighted you have Renloret." He failed to get to his feet. He sucked in a long breath and slowly let it out, hissing between his teeth. "When did you find out?"

"The eve you had your interview with Doctor Treyder."

"How?" He managed to get one foot flat on the floor and glared at her.

A shrug of her shoulders told him how she felt about his discomfort. She waited until he was on both feet but still crouched over before patting his back. "Your mother gave me our mother's journal."

"How'd she come by it?"

"Melli found it in Mother's dresser when she helped me

consolidate things after the funeral. She said I might find the answer about the twin in it."

"She didn't read it?"

Ani shook her head. "I don't think she would have even if it had been written in Northern."

"Lrakiran?" His breathing was settling and he was slowly easing upright.

At Ani's nod he asked, "Can you read Lrakiran?"

"No. Renloret read it to me. After all our research, we were prepared for almost anything—"

"Except the identity of the twin," Taryn said, finishing the sentence for her. "I hope you had enough alcohol on hand."

She chuckled. "We emptied the last bottle of Father's vaquin."

"Ouch, the whole bottle?"

She smiled her affirmation. "Yes. Renloret says it's the strongest he's had, which, I guess, is a rousing testament to Father's distilling technique and twenty years of aging." Ani patted the mattress.

He shuffled toward the bed. "I curse you for that move. I'll never give my parents grandchildren at this rate."

Chuckling again, Ani said, "I'm sure the doctors here can correct any damage I may have inflicted."

"Why'd you do it, anyway?"

"You didn't react as I imagined you would. You were so calm and smiling while I considered vomiting and cried like a child when I found out."

"Let's be honest, Ani. It clarifies your feelings and decision to break away from me." He gently placed a hand on her mouth to prevent her from interrupting. "It's all right. Really. Now I have an even better reason to keep an eye on you. We'll always be connected, and we can't deny our love for each other." He took her hand in his and brought it to his cheek. "I've always been faster to accept change than you. Perhaps we've both known all along. I'm all right, Ani. I'm not sad about this—perhaps a bit confused, but not sad."

They sat in silence for several minutes. Kela had stayed out of the way but now padded over and placed his paw on Taryn's thigh.

Tell him I welcome him into the family. He winked at Ani.

"Kela says, 'Welcome to the family.'"

"Thanks," Taryn replied as he ruffled the fur between Kela's ears.

There was a soft rumble from Kela in response. *Now that he knows who he is, shouldn't we be getting over to the Stone Chamber?*

Ani nudged Taryn's shoulder. "Are you capable of moving?"

"Probably. Why?"

"Kela points out that we should be introducing you to the alien whose life you are going to save."

"Really? Am I some kind of hero now?" He winked at her as he took her hand and eased toward the door. The attendant scrambled out of his corner and slapped his palm to the pad, opening the door. Ani gave him a short bow in thanks and pulled Taryn into the hallway.

"Don't let it go to your head, little brother."

"Little?"

"Yep, I was born first. That makes you my *little* brother."

CHAPTER THIRTY-TWO

A muttered, frustrated curse of the mildest sort left Singer Layson's lips as she added another book to the growing pile and grabbed the next one on the shelf. She was sitting on the floor, going through all of the books on the bottom shelf, reading the title of each aloud and occasionally pausing to open one and peruse the table of contents.

They had been scouring the shelves for almost half a bell. As another curse slipped through Layson's lips, Renloret stopped fingering through the bindings. None of the titles sparked even a bit of memory. He did not remember the exact title, only that the contents appeared to be very old, the printing or rather ancient hand scribing beginning to fade with age.

Why hadn't he noted the exact title? Why had he come to the library in the first place when he knew he should have gone directly to the meeting? He knew how distracted he got when he was around anything to do with the Stones or stars. A surge of urgency returned his attention to the bindings on the shelf.

"Come here, Renloret," Singer Diani said. Her voice was gentle.

He looked back at her, sitting at the table. "I'm not through with this row."

"You don't need to finish. Come here."

Heaving a sigh, Renloret left off his search and took a seat in the same chair he'd used at the beginning of this . . . assignment.

"What?" He didn't bother to keep the exasperation out of his voice. He'd thought this excursion to the library would be a mere formality. They would come, find the book, read the relevant songs, and get their answers. The Anyala Stone would be saved and life on Lrakira would return to normal.

Diani placed a hand on his arm in a motherly fashion. "I need you to relax, to remember what you were doing when the bells rang. Close your eyes, child. Breathe the air of your beloved books. Be calm. See the song on the page." Her voice was whispering, hypnotic.

He closed his eyes and breathed—slowly, steadily, and deeply. The words formed themselves on the inside of his lids. He smiled at the beautiful script, each letter patiently shaped by some scribe long ago, and whispered the words as they appeared in his memory. He remembered the aliveness of the paper between his fingers, and his heart ached to hear the tune that accompanied the song.

The bells in the bell tower rang, startling the singers and pilot. Renloret jumped out of the chair and walked directly to the nearest stack. Layson was still sitting on the floor at the end of the second row from the stairway. He nodded to her. "That's where

I pulled it from the shelf." He pointed to the shoulder-high shelf to his right. "And this is where I stuffed it when I left." He read the titles on the first two bindings before slowly extracting the third. Cradling the ancient tome, he headed for the stairs.

Diani hurried behind and pulled on his sleeve. "Let's be sure."

The three returned to the table and Renloret opened the cover.

"Why is such an old book not in the archives?" Layson whispered.

Renloret shrugged. "I've no idea. I was surprised to find it readily available to anyone. Similar to what Diani just had me do, my great-grandmother, Tivi, once told me I needed only to open my heart and I would find all the answers."

Memories flooded back, reminding him of a clandestine conversation with the ancient woman who sat in a rocker humming the most beautiful tune. "I remember her saying the Stones had plans for some of us and we had only to listen to the songs to discover what those plans were. She was very old then. I think I was twelve sun-cycles. She was the only one who said my interest in the Stones and their history made sense. She thought I would need it someday and told me to listen for the Stones' songs because they would show the way to the stars and the beginning of the Stones."

"What did she mean by 'the beginning of the Stones'?" Layson asked as she turned a page.

"I didn't think to ask her then. I wish she were around now. She passed a few moon-cycles after that conversation."

"The Kita Stone was bonded outside of the direct line, at Tivi's request, years before she passed," Diani advised soberly.

"Kita's choice of Singers has been wonderfully erratic, much to the consternation of Selabec. As the current Kita Stone Singer, Layson, do you know if there was a Ceremony of Passing for Tivi?"

Layson shook her head. "I have not researched how many Passings have officially occurred with Kita. I will ask when all the Stones are well. We may need that information to help us fully understand the songs."

Renloret placed a hand on the page to stop Layson from turning it. "Here it is."

The ancient script seemed to jump from the page to his heart. He was ready for it. The remembered tune his great-grandmother had sung seemed to fit the old syllables perfectly. He hummed as he silently read, his fingers tracing each line.

Gasps came from Diani and Layson.

"Our Stones are singing with you!" Layson announced in an astonished whisper.

Renloret stopped humming. "How do they know?"

"We were reading the words and the Stones heard us, and they just started singing. It's the same tune!" Diani replied. "How do you know the tune? It's not written here."

"It was the last song I heard Tivi sing," Renloret said. "It was the one that spurred my interest in ancient Lrakiran because I didn't understand the words. I liked the tune enough to research the language. It only took a sun-cycle or so before I was considered fluent at reading and speaking."

Diani shook her head. "Only one sun-cycle? It took me sun-cycles to become barely proficient. The Pericha Stone is constantly amused with my difficulties."

Renloret turned back to the book. "It was natural to my tongue and I was still young enough to learn quickly." Fingers on the lines of the second verse, he recited a few lines aloud in ancient Lrakiran and then he translated.

> *Plague and sickness spur Stones to send*
> *Singer and blade to chosen star unknown*
> *The Blood and Balance, in one birth two*
> *She, The Blood to be aged by Time-Song's end*
> *He, The Balance, in time to heal first a Stone*
> *Then home to awakened three to join anew.*

"Yes, we have the correct twin." He tapped the page for emphasis.

Diani frowned. "So it's true that The Balance is male?" Her shock was evident.

"Are you saying you didn't believe it possible even after studying the verse I wrote down?" He shook his head. Obviously, she was so steeped in one belief she could not function with a new blade even when it was held in her hand. "I'm not telling you anything new. This song has been telling every Singer for a thousand suncycles that The Blood and The Balance are opposite sex twins. You were not prepared because you Singers stopped reading the old songs and old prophecies eons ago. And you two did not believe us when we told you that the whole song—the whole prophecy—was important." He couldn't stop the accusatory tone. If they *had* been listening or at least reading, there wouldn't be any confusion or reluctance.

Layson touched Renloret's shoulder. "So it really is Taryn, Ani's brother?"

"Yes. And he should be fully awake and recovering from the effects of the anesthesia by now. Ani will tell him who he is. We are to meet them at the Stone Chamber with the book." He closed the book more gently than he did the last time, tucked it under his arm, and again started for the stairway.

Neither of the Singers moved. They just stood, staring at each other.

He paused on the second step. "Are you coming or not? You can talk to them on the way, can't you?"

Singer Diani appeared to come out of trance or, more likely, Renloret thought, a state of shock. "Of course we can." She tugged on Layson's robe.

The younger Singer blinked and followed. Unlike Diani, she still seemed to be in a daze. "Kita says The Blood and The Balance have just arrived and are waiting for us," she whispered.

"I know," Diani said as she towed the younger Singer down the flight of stairs.

CHAPTER THIRTY-THREE

The route they had taken to this cathedral-like building had been convoluted. Taryn was unsure he could retrace the path, especially since he had been trying to pay close attention to Ani's abbreviated story of his actual birth and how he became the son of Gelwood and Melli. Once inside the building, the smooth stone walls and floors cooled the air to a comfortable temperature. Ani stopped at a door she said opened to the Stone Chamber, and Taryn ran his fingers over the engravings. He raised his eyebrows in question. "Like the doors at the lake house?"

She dipped her chin. "Similar. Parts actually match my championship markings. Renloret says they're both in ancient Lrakiran and only a few people can actually read it. This one says I am Anyala, the Anyala Stone's Singer." She pointed at the identical patterns on the door. "See how they match?"

Taryn was impressed by the detail the carver was able to cut into the stone surface of the door. "Does it say anything about me?"

A shrug of her shoulders indicated she did not know. "He didn't translate the entire door carving." Ani pushed the door open. "Come meet the Stones of Lrakira."

Lush wall hangings surrounded a trio of pedestals, each cradling a large crystal. Two points of light, one amber and the other blue glowed softly, illuminating a stunning view of a blade buried hilt-deep in the dark green lump on the pedestal at the apex of the triangular configuration. Ani moved out of his way. Taryn patted his chest, where his notepad usually was. With a grunt of disappointment, he dropped the hand back to his side.

"Do they have notebooks here?"

She shook her head. "Sorry."

Well, he'd make do with strict observation. He moved to the center of the triangle to peruse the surrounding wall hangings. As he examined them, he tucked away in his mind the similarities between the banners in front of him and the ones so common on Northern that he'd forgotten what many of them represented.

A frayed and faded hanging depicting a rather gruesome sacrificial ceremony caught his attention. Bodies lay in piles while a group of robed people standing in a circle raised swords above their heads. Two rainbows arched away from the zenith of weapon points. The actual workmanship was exquisite, but he wondered why such a violent event had been chosen for the wall hanging. Other hangings showed people engaged in agricultural activities, magnificent aerial crafts floating above surreal landscapes, and what he thought might be general home life for residents of Lrakira. One even displayed naked warriors of both sexes receiving honor wreaths and arm tattoos from three gold-robed priestesses.

All the hangings were museum quality. He mentally figured the price certain individuals on Teramar would gladly have paid for a single hanging. They were priceless.

His penetrating gaze moved to the crystals, which Ani said were intelligent living beings. Living or not, they, too, were beyond price. He walked around the two crystals with brightly glowing centers. There was no change in the intensity or shade of color of the lights. Were these inanimate things aware of their surroundings?

At his internal question, the two lights began to flicker. Taryn glanced around the room, looking for wires or switches. Neither was apparent. He heard Ani chuckle as the blue and amber lights began to grow, filling each of the stones. The illumination gave the Stone Chamber a more cheerful feel than the supposedly injured green Stone elicited from Taryn. He studied the amber and blue Stones, which had begun to flick colored beams and waves of light from their bright interiors. Similar electrical displays created by artists for celebratory extravaganzas had decorated the buildings and streets of Northern's capital over the years. The fact that an object emitted light was not sufficient reason to believe it was alive. He had yet to hear any music, but he suspected people with instruments could hide in alcoves behind the rugs to provide mood music if needed. It could be an elaborate ruse.

Again, he wished for his notepad. How would he remember all of this when it came time to explain to his parents? His parents. A sigh escaped from his lips. He wished for a tumbler of vaquin. Straight up. Yes, that would be nice—not helpful, but nice. Gelwood and Melli were his parents, not Yenne and Shendahl

Chenak—or, rather, Yenne and S'Hendale Chenakainet. He decided he preferred the Teramaran pronunciation of his birth mother's name. He pushed those thoughts aside, arguing with himself that there was too much to discuss that couldn't be discussed until he had proven he was The Balance.

Standing before the green lump, he placed his hands on either side and leaned in to study the amber blade protruding from the supposedly solid object. It didn't make any sense. How could a crystal be stabbed without shattering? Was there a glimmer of life deep within the crystal? Not even a flicker. Were they too late? Had it died? He blinked. He had framed the question as if the crystal was alive. He still wasn't quite convinced of that. He was not yet convinced he was on another planet, either, though the buildings had quite a different feel from those on Northern. Ani said he would know for sure when the moons rose. Moons? She'd said three, hadn't she? Was this all a very poorly constructed dream? He decided it couldn't be because he knew he could not have come up with such an outlandish story line. This had to be real.

Taryn straightened and glanced over his shoulder as more people entered the chamber. Ani and Kela joined Taryn in front of the pedestals to greet Renloret and the two golden-robed women following him. He glanced back at the tapestry with its circle of gold-robed people holding blades aloft. Were they here to execute justice for the Stone if he failed?

Ani touched Taryn's arm and dipped her head at the women. "The one on the right is Diani. She's the amber Pericha Stone's Singer. And Layson is the blue Kita Stone's Singer."

The Singers looked uncomfortable, as if they were out of their usual surroundings. Taryn offered a smile and bowed.

"Do they understand Northern, because I don't know any Lrakiran?" Taryn asked.

Renloret answered as the trio halted. "They have translators."

The younger woman, the blue rock's Singer, rolled up a sleeve of her robe to show him a thin metallic bracelet on her wrist. "I give you greetings. Welcome to Lrakira. We wish it was under less stressful circumstances." The words were heavily accented but understandable.

"Me too, milady." Taryn looked at the pilot. "The accent is similar." The pilot grinned at him.

"I'm relieved that you will be able to understand what I say," Taryn admitted. "As you might imagine, this is all a bit surrealistic to me." He was trying hard to keep it all real enough that he could remember who he'd been before this rather outrageous turn of events: the sheriff of Star Valley. And whether or not he was The Balance, as Ani claimed, he was still the sheriff of Star Valley—a man of logic and common sense. "Shall we find out if this alien prophecy is true?"

"It's not an alien prophecy," the older Singer said.

"It is to me." Taryn cocked his head at Ani. "And you can't hit me unless I fail to save the rock." He leaned back a tad when he saw her clenching both fists. Perhaps he was being too flippant. Taryn brought himself to attention and held up both hands to quiet the protests that had started to issue from the Singers.

"I apologize if I sound disrespectful. This is all . . . foreign to me. I am trying to protect my sanity by going along with all this, but you must admit that I'm under a lot of personal stress. And as the sheriff of Star Valley, I wonder what will happen if I can't save the rock's life."

He paused to inhale deeply and pushed down the panic that really did threaten his sanity. Was he looking at the last moment of his life? "On my honor as a sheriff and a blade ring champion, I will do my best. I promise."

There was silence in the room. Taryn realized the colors had stopped bouncing around the chamber. He glanced at the amber and blue Stones. Fist-sized spots of light pulsed from the center of both rocks. The green crystal remained dark. He had not seen even a flicker of light since Ani, Kela, and he entered the chamber.

He suddenly remembered why Renloret and the Singers had arrived separately. "Did you find the book?"

Renloret nodded and placed it on the pedestal. "It's in ancient Lrakiran and should have been included in the Singers' training, but it has been ignored for several generations because it has been viewed as nothing more than a collection of fables. We haven't figured out everything yet, but here's the important part for now." He pointed to the page and began singing.

Taryn recognized a few of the words as being similar to those in the Song of Healing, which he and Renloret had sung in the cavern . . . how long ago? That song had saved Ani's life. The two Singers added their voices and moved closer to read the lines of the song over Renloret's shoulder. The amber and blue Stones seem to brighten as the trio concluded the two verses.

Ani spoke first. "So what does it mean?"

Renloret cocked his head toward Diani. The Singer cleared

her throat. "Basically, it verifies that The Blood and The Balance were to be twins born of a secret Stone Singer on a chosen planet other than Lrakira. The Stones were to have been notified of the birth so they could sing a time-song to age the twins to puberty. The Blood would have the needed hormones to save the people of Lrakira. She," she nodded at Ani, "would then be brought home. Once our people were safe, there would be a time of peace until one of the Stones would be endangered in some way, thus requiring *his* assistance." She looked self-consciously at Taryn. "We had presumed Ani was both The Blood and The Balance until we were told otherwise. We also assumed the twin would be female."

"In our defense, there is no record of a male Stone Singer, so we never expected that to change," Layson added apologetically.

Taryn waved it off. "There is nothing to defend, Singer. We were all looking for a girl." He glanced at Ani. "Even our mother was under the impression that Ani was both The Blood and The Balance, and she willingly gave her son to another woman to raise. That woman, the mother of my heart, had just lost her own in childbirth and Shendahl knew I would be loved and cared for. My parents do not know my true identity."

Ani's arm encircled his waist. Pulling her closer, he whispered, "Do we have to tell them?"

"I don't know," she replied.

Renloret seemed to have overheard the whispered question and added, "I think it is a blade yet in the making, Taryn."

"By your leave, Taryn, you are taking this change unexpectedly well," Diani said.

Taryn grinned. "I have often been accused of being too open, too accepting of the unusual or the impossible. It's a trait that has gotten me into trouble frequently, though it has also helped me remain calm in most emergencies, with the exception of this one. This has been . . . unimaginable."

He gave Ani a gentle squeeze and released her so he could turn to look at the book. "Are there instructions to guide me? Is there a special ceremony or song for this sort of thing?"

"This sort of thing has never happened before," the older Singer admitted. "I assume you just pull the blade out."

An expectant silence overcame them. All eyes watched as he wrapped a hand around the hilt. He pulled. It did not move. Taryn grinned at Ani. "If at first . . ."

Bracing the other hand against the Stone, fingers on either side of the buried blade, he inhaled deeply and began a long steady pull. As he exhaled, he felt the blade move. The surface of the Stone seemed warmer under his hand, and he saw a flick of light. Perhaps they weren't too late.

Another breath.

The muscles in his arms and hands strained. Heat. Definitely heat. Both hands seemed to be on fire. He did not release the blade. It was moving ever so slowly.

Another breath.

Green flames seemed to wrap themselves about his hands. The Stone was screaming in his head. His bones felt the pain and his whole being absorbed the anguish of the Stone. The Stone had feared that he, The Balance, would not come in time to save all the Stones, all the people.

The Balance

Was he on fire? He gripped harder, pulled harder. He pushed against the now radiant crystal. His mind filled with music as the amber blade slid out, and he was flung away from the pedestal. His back hit the cool tiled floor. Was he on fire, burning? He opened his eyes.

Colors.

Music.

Words echoed through his head.

Joy.

Life.

Balance.

CHAPTER THIRTY-FOUR

A cacophony of sounds and color flooded Taryn's senses. Voices sang in multiple languages. Shivers shook him as the harmonies tightened. Struggling to categorize, to identify, to understand what was happening, Taryn stretched out across the coolness of the chamber floor. Forcefully relaxing his grip on the hilt, he released the blade. The cramps in his joints eased. Ever so slowly, the colors in his vision calmed until he could see the minute stitching of the wall hangings in their delicate splendor. He'd never felt color before. He was positive it would be the last time he would. He cried as the sensation lessened to nearer normal though the music continued—dancing with the colors.

Moving only his eyes, Taryn took inventory. A Singer was draped over one of the pedestals, shoulders shaking. Was it Layson? Was she crying?

"Ani? Renloret?" His voice sounded harsh against the music. Was it inside or outside his head? Did it matter? He called again. Were they still in the chamber? Were they all right? Any injury the others might have incurred would be his fault. A groan directed his attention to the base of the Anyala Stone's pedestal where two forms were crouched, entwined—Ani and Kela.

"Ani?" the croaking question came from a form crawling across the floor. The pilot reached the huddled combination of girl and canine, drawing them into an embrace. Good. Renloret was alive. Taryn rolled to his knees and scanned the room for the second Singer.

A pile of gold fabric lay along the wall behind the trio of Stones. The air was suffused with shades of blue, amber, and green. Music reverberated within his body, a joyous intensity that made moving difficult. He wanted to remain still, to drown in the sensations, but duty propelled him toward the crumpled form. He crawled, not yet trusting his ability to stand.

Patting the form, he located a shoulder, then a head. He pulled the fabric away. Taryn fingered strands of gray-streaked hair off Diani's face.

"Singer?" he shouted, to be heard through the volume of music and color that blared through his head.

She placed a hand on his arm and squeezed. "My forever thanks. Help me up. We should attend to the others."

Together they stood, leaning on the wall, which shivered in time with the music pervading the chamber. Taryn shaded his eyes against the brilliance of the lights emanating from the three Stones. He wished for ear and sunguards, not that he really wanted either the colors or the music to cease. Their combined beauty blended with his being. Self-control ebbed back from wherever it had gone and his responsibilities as a sheriff began asserting themselves.

"Can you walk?" His voice rasped against his vocal chords. How had he injured his voice? A sudden desire for his mother's soothing citrus and honey tea brought tears to his eyes. He wiped them away. This was not the time.

Diani nodded and pointed. "I'll see to Layson." She pushed off the wall, and after a few staggering steps, she straightened and moved with more assurance to her compatriot.

As the two Singers embraced, Taryn made his way to the large green crystal. He ran his fingers over the spot where the blade had been. "No cracks. Not even a chip."

A tingling sensation rippled up from his hands. The music increased in volume, drawing him in. It was mesmerizing, painfully beautiful.

Jerking away from the resplendent Stone, he touched Renloret's back for balance as he eased down to the floor. Kela wedged his head between the men. A damp swipe of tongue seemed a request, and Taryn obliged by wrapping his arm around the canine's neck. He buried his face in the soft depths of black, silver, and white fur. A rumble of comfort accompanied another licking. Taryn did not feel the need to reprimand or push him away, instead experiencing the earthy animal smell of Kela's fur as grounding. And he needed that grounding at the moment.

He sighed as he turned his head to survey the chamber. The colors had diminished along with the volume of soul-binding music. He thought he could hear quiet words. The Singers shuffled towards him and his companions. Though smiling, they looked exhausted.

A fourth source of color came to his attention. It was the

blade he'd removed from the Anyala Stone. Taryn stood and gingerly moved to the glowing weapon. He gained strength with each step as the percussive explosion resulting from the blade's removal seeped away. It was the most impressive throw he'd ever encountered. He surmised that there had been a sudden release of energy when the blade slipped free from the crystal.

The light from the offending blade reminded him of the crystal blade Ani's mother had given to her at the championship crowning ceremony, though this one was amber rather than green. That glorious green blade had been buried a year later inside Shendahl's casket until it was dug up and subsequently stolen by Stubin Dalkey in his efforts to prove the presence of aliens on Teramar. It had been the catalyst for the Lrakiran Song of Healing Renloret and he had sung for Ani after her injury in the cavern. Along with the song, the then glowing green blade had accomplished everything needed to bring Ani back from the brink of death, yet it could not remove the coma device from her brain. With sudden insight, he understood the scars that traced ugly tracks across his own body. Ani and Renloret had probably healed his injuries by singing the same song and wielding the green blade.

Taryn picked up the amber blade. The glow brightened but did not burn. With a deep bow of respect, he offered the blade to Diani.

She caressed the crystal. It hummed in pleasure as she pressed it to her lips. "Again, you have my thanks for returning my blade to me and for saving the Anyala Stone. It will ever be a debt that cannot be repaid."

"The blade sings too?" He stepped forward so he could hear

the obviously happy tune issuing from the amber blade.

Diani frowned. "You can hear it? I hear it only in my head. I didn't think anyone else could hear it unless the Stones permitted it."

Ani unwrapped from Renloret's embrace and stood up. "I hear it too, but only in my head. It communicates telepathically, Taryn, similar to Kela. In fact, I hear all three Stones and blades. The blades are an octave higher than their Stones. Taryn, there is no real sound, only their colors."

"All the music is in my head?"

Ani nodded. "I think you're experiencing what I went through on my first introduction to Kela. It's overwhelming in the beginning, but you'll learn to separate the two, given time and exposure."

"Can Renloret hear it? Can Kela?"

Renloret stood beside Ani, clasping her hand. "I believe I am hearing it as well. I have had previous less dynamic experiences with different types of telepathy, not just with the Anyala Stone."

Kela barked. Taryn knew he had heard that through his ears.

Ani laughed. "He hears the Stones and the blades, but he only hears *my* thoughts. He's not sure he wants to hear everyone's thoughts. Evidently, mine are plenty."

"Did Kela hear the Stones when we were here before?" Renloret asked.

Shaking her head, she said, "Not like this. He says he was invited to participate because he was connected to me and I am the Anyala Stone's Singer." Her tone gave voice to a newfound confidence in the title.

"I can see he's excited to be included," Taryn said as Kela executed a tail to muzzle turn to show his pleasure in the shared communication.

"Will I hear all of them all the time? I'm not sure I could handle the distraction," Taryn said.

The two Singers stepped forward. Layson took hold of his hands. "Since I have been a Singer for only a short time myself, I can tell you. The rush of information will dissipate to conversational levels and then only when they need you or you them. They are getting acquainted with you. That is all."

Frowning, Diani added, "Which brings up a topic the book of songs did not mention."

"What was that?" Renloret asked.

"If, by removing my blade from the Anyala Stone, Taryn has become a Singer, which of us is he going to replace?"

Taryn heard the fear and confusion in the older Singer's voice. "Hey, I just got here and only did what I was asked to do. Personally, I have no intention of replacing anyone, nor do I want to remain on Lrakira and become some rock's singer." Both Singers gave quick smiles at his reluctance to take over their positions and his irreverent reference to the Stones. He glanced at Ani, who had a bemused look on her face. "What? Why are you looking at me like that?"

"I think I have this figured out," Ani said. "Let me talk this through, just as I let you talk through Treyder's goal."

"Talk, Sister." His grin and wiggled eyebrows brought a smile to her face as he hoped it would.

"The prophecy says The Blood and The Balance shall each

save one. I, The Blood, saved the people and you saved the Stone. But why name you The Balance? I think the Stones needed an unexpected event to occur so they could introduce the *possibility* of a male Singer to the people of Lrakira. Male balances female." She waved a hand to shush Diani and Layson, who appeared about to speak. "But as Diani has pointed out, there are three Stones and there are three Singers already. Why have an extra?"

"Like our mother thought I was?" Taryn couldn't help his comment. He flinched at the smack on his shoulder from Ani.

"No, Taryn. Don't ever grind that blade. Ever." Her remonstration silenced him and she continued. "This may be a slash in the dark, but what if there are more Stones, and what if more Singers, preferably male, are needed for full balance to be attained?"

"More?" The question came from Diani, Layson, and Renloret at the same time, the combined overlapping question carrying a tone of incredulity.

"Doesn't the first verse of the song say something like six will sing?" Diani asked. She turned to look at Renloret.

"Yes, it did," Renloret answered.

Taryn cocked his head toward Ani. "Okay, but from what I understand there are only three Stones on Lrakira. If there were more, wouldn't they have been found by now?"

"What if they aren't on Lrakira?" Ani whispered, causing the hair on the nape of Taryn's neck to rise.

"That's some slash in the dark, Ani," he replied. "If not here, then where else would they be? Why are they somewhere else?"

The Balance

A joyous three-note chord sounded in his head.
Teramar!
Reunion!

Circle of Seven sing safe passage
Divide by two and send in deep sleep
The Blood and Balance shall each save one
Awakening three to rejoice with time's message
Time will soon come for reunion's leap
Six will Sing joining three homes and suns

Plague and sickness spur Stones to send
Singer and blade to chosen star unknown
The Blood and Balance, in one birth two
She, The Blood, to be aged by Time-Song's end
He, The Balance, in time to heal first a Stone
Then home to awakened three to join anew.

CHARACTER/TERM LIST AND PRONUNCIATION GUIDE

Abren (ah-**bren**): Lrakiran word for open

Ani (**ah**-nee): Northern's 1st female blade ring champion, Renloret's rescuer, The Blood

Anyala Stone (ahn-**yall**-ah): largest of the Stones of Lrakira, green

Awarna (ah-**war**-nah): capital city of Lrakira

Bell: Lrakiran time equal to an hour

Brenlee (**brin**-lee): infant, Keci and Nonnash's sixth daughter

Chime: Lrakiran time equal to a minute

Cranite (**cray**-night): Lrakiran moon

Cushawk (**cuss**-hawk): a Teramaran medium-sized farm bird raised for eggs and meat

Cyralist (**sigh**-rah-list): bulbous hourglass shaped stringed instrument on Teramar

Daneeha (da-**nee**-ha): sheriff's secretary

Denert (**deh**-nert): smallest Lrakiran moon

Diani (dee-**ah**-nee): Pericha Stone's Singer

Digoson Mountains (**dee**-go-son): mountain range north of Awarna, home of Anyala Stone

Doven (**dough**-vin): village multiple hours north of Saedi City, Northern, Teramar

Ear/sunguards : protective insertables or coverings to prevent hearing loss or damage to eyes

Erid (**air**-id): largest Lrakiran moon

Appendix

Eteel (eh-**teel**): bass player and master composer of Star Valley Bashers, dance band on Teramar

Fairaden (**fair**-ah-den): medical assistant on original research team, marries Treyder

Flitter (**flit**-er): term used for multiple species of songbirds on Lrakira

Garrend (**gair**-end): fictitious name Ani gives to Renloret

Gednium (**ged**-nee-um): small purple fruit native to Northern, Teramar

Gelwood Avere (**gell**-wood ahv-**air**-eh): Taryn's father, grocery store owner

Highcraft (**hi**-craft): Northern term for master craftsman, the very best. Usually associated with sword blade creation or manufacture.

Hopper: small rodent native to Northern, Teramar

Isul Treyder (**eye**-sul **tray**-der): genius mechanical engineer, a bit crazy

Jinma (gin-**mah**): a type of stylized stretching exercise

Keci (**keh**-see): farmer in Star Valley, Northern, Teramar

Kela (**kay**-la): telepathic canine, Ani's companion

Kita Stone (**kit**-ah): blue Stone of Lrakira

Kiver (**keye**-ver): language specialist on rescue mission with Renloret, dies in crash

Kreline (**creh**-lean): large predator on Teramar's Northern continent

Kriswen (**chris**-win): gas giant, fifth planet in Teramaran solar system

Kursal Ceri (**curse**-all sir-**eye**): blade ring opponent known to Ani and Taryn

Layson (**lay**-son): Kita Stone's Singer

Leeshob (**lee**-shob): Mroz's herding canine

Lrakira (ulrrah-**keer**-ah) (L is barely pronounced and r is rolled): second of six planets in Lrakiran solar system

Luris seed (**lur**-iss): a citrusy seed used as a spice on Northern, Teramar

Appendix

Melli Avere (**mell**-ee ahv-**air**-eh): Taryn's mother, maker of fine teas

Milit/milits (**mill**-it/**mill**-its): Northern term for military personnel or soldiers

Moon-cycle: Lrakiran month

Moon-time: Lrakiran night

Mroz (mer-**rose**): bar owner, part-time coroner, Star Valley, Northern, Teramar

Nelham (**nell**-ham): senator, head of space protection committee, Northern Teramar government

Nonnash (**no**-nash): Keci's wife, mother of six daughters, Star Valley, Northern, Teramar

Ovline (**ahv**-line): a four-legged domesticated ungulate similar to cattle

Pericha Stone (pair-**ee**-cha): amber Stone of Lrakira

Renloret (wren-lore-**ay**) (t is not pronounced, think French): Lrakiran pilot of rescue mission

Reslo Chenak/R'Schlonick Chenakainet (**rehs**-low **chen**-ack / ruh-**schlawn**-ick chen-ah-kah-**nay**): Ani's uncle, Yenne Chenakainet's brother

Ryken (**rye**-kin): seven-year-old girl, Keci & Nonnash's third daughter

Saedi City (saw-**ee**-dee): capital of Northern continent on Teramar

Sancharos Peaks (san-**chair**-ose): mountain range on Lrakira, home of Kita Stone

Sarinne (**sah**-reen): Lrakiran communications officer in original research team to Teramar

Selabec (**sell**-ah-beck): Anyala Stone's Singer, mother of S'Hendale/Shendahl, Ani's grandmother

Sharnel (shar-**nell**): lead of Lrakiran rescue mission, 2nd pilot to Renloret, dies in crash

Appendix

S'Hendale/Shendahl (say-hen-**dal**e/shen-**doll**): Ani's mother, head medical researcher

Sheren leaf (**sheer**-en): a peppery leafed vegetable similar to arugula

Sheriff Driton (**dry**-ton): sheriff in neighboring valley on Teramar

Sholoret (show-low-**ray**): Lrakiran surgeon, finds and removes coma device

Silteene (sill-**teen**): a rare and expensive fabric woven on Lrakira

Slerdon/Slerdonians (**slur**-don/slur-**dough**-neons): planet of telepathic beings, have no voice box

S'Roadoss (sah-**row**-ah-dose): ceremony of Stone and blade bonding for Lrakiran Stone Singers

Star Valley: Ani's home village on Northern, Teramar

Stone Singer: liaison between Stones and their charges, the people of Lrakira

Stubin Dalkey (**stew**-bin **doll**-key): general in Northern continent's military, alienphobic

Sun-cycle: Lrakiran time designation equal to a year

Sun-time: Lrakiran time designation equal to a day

Tacara (ta-**car**-ah): starchy root native to Teramar

Taryn Avere (**tair**-in ahv-**air**-eh): sheriff of Star Valley, Ani's best friend

Tel-com (**tell**-com): communication devices, either audio and/or visual, Northern, Teramar

Teramar (**tair**-ah-mar): first of five planets in Teramaran solar system

Tezak Ganevek (**tay**-zack **gan**-eh-vehk): Star Valley doctor, coworker of Ani's mother

Tianet Mountains (tee-ah-**nay**): remote mountain range on Southern continent, Teramar

Appendix

Tivi (**tiv**-ee): Renloret's great grandmother, former Singer of the Kita Stone

Trimag (**tree**-mag): Lrakiran high commander of planetary safety

Tri-pronged sueders (**sway**-ders): four-legged ungulate similar to deer or elk

Udi root (**oo**-dee): a spice common to Northern, Teramar

Vaquin (vah-**quinn**): strong Teramaran liquor, blue in color

Viken (**vike**-in): Teramaran ringed moon

Vishon (vee-**shawn**): a fishlike creature native to Lrakira

Whirjerata (whir-jer-**ah**- tah): fruit on Southern Teramar, bears fruit every three years

Whis'jeras (whiss-**jer**-ass): fruit on Lrakira, bears fruit every three years

Whistlepot (**whis**-ill-pot): a small stove top kettle with a spout that sounds a tone when water is hot enough to produce steam.

Yantel (yan-**tell**): Star Valley sheriff deputy

Yenne Chenakainet (**yen**-nay chen-ah-kah-**nay**): Commander of Lrakiran research team, Ani's father

Zocanel Province (zo-**can**-ell): one of the provinces on the northern continent of Teramar

ABOUT THE AUTHOR

Allynn Riggs began telling stories before she could write them down, and after being nagged and cajoled by a determined collection of fictional characters for many years, she surrendered and shifted careers to tell their stories. The Stone's Blade series began innocently enough as a short story written when she was fourteen. The characters of Ani, Kela, Taryn, and Renloret have never left her imagination or dreams and waited patiently until she was ready to share their worlds with you. *The Balance* is the second installment of The Stone's Blade series.

When Allynn is not writing, she avidly participates in and teaches square dancing and hunts big game. The mother of three grown daughters, Allynn resides in Centennial, Colorado, with her husband, Bob.

To contact Allynn directly: email her at Allynn@timberdark.com
For more information check out her blog and Facebook page:
Blog: http://TimberdarkWriter.wordpress.com
Facebook: https://www.facebook.com/TimberdarkPublications

Thank you for reading *The Balance*. Gaining exposure as an independently published author relies mostly on word-of-mouth. So if you have the time and inclination, please consider leaving a short review wherever you can.